THE CONTRACTOR

F R A N K   O K O L O

Copyright © 2016 Frank Okolo
All rights reserved.

ISBN: 0692758747
ISBN 13: 9780692758748

CHAPTER 1

Novo-Ogaryovo dacha, 2010

SVR General Oleg Kalushkin, his deputy General Yuri Zamyatin, and Colonel (SVR) Grigory Artemyev sat inside a secure room in the split-level dacha. The fourth man, Colonel Pyotr Gulev waited, saying nothing. All were ex-KGB.

"I need not tell you, gentlemen," Kalushkin paused, his bald pate glistening in the subdued light of the room. "The president expects prompt action on this operation. Operation Infidel does not exist in our records, has never existed, and none of us know anything about it."

The three other men nodded. Kalushkin was short and bullish. His long, muscular arms hung at his sides, disproportionate to his build. His piercing blue eyes, inherited from his Georgian ancestors, protruded pig-like from his face. He bore an uncanny resemblance to Mussolini, although his files showed that he displayed none of *Il Duce*'s fondness for the flesh.

"Officially," he continued, glancing at each subordinate in turn, "President Grachev knows absolutely nothing about this plot. Unofficially, he does. As agreed, everyone on our side who is even remotely aware of Operation Infidel—including myself but excluding the president, of course—must take a monthly polygraph examination. Should any one of us fail the polygraph, he will be taken to our facilities, chemicals will be administered to learn the extent of the treachery, and the traitor will be summarily executed by firing squad. Our new Agent Monitoring Device will be implanted in all field agents involved in Infidel. I needn't bore you with the details, but in short the implant will enable us to track the movements of the agent and, if necessary, terminate that agent should we learn he has compromised the operation."

General Kalushkin paused, looking intently at each man. He spread out his hirsute cacti-like hands and said, "Let me recap the details spelled out at our last meeting two months ago. There used to be two superpowers. Now there is only one. Or so the Americans think. We still have over ten thousand nuclear weapons, and I assure you the concept of MAD—Mutual Assured Destruction—is still valid. You launch, we launch, and we both cease to exist. Think of it. We survived Napoleon, Hitler, and before them, numerous other invaders. Our biggest threat now is from America and her NATO alliance. The American threat concerns us most. That threat, as our Army and Air Force generals have pointed out, is from the Missile Defensive Shield—MDS, as they call it. President Reagan tried to build a similar missile shield in the eighties—they called it the Strategic Defense Initiative, the so-called 'Star Wars' program. It failed in Congress. Now the current American president claims he needs it to avert missile strikes by rogue states or Islamic terrorists getting hold of nuclear weapons. This is a son of the Star Wars program. Instead of space-based phased array weaponry, we have a missile intercept system that will be more or less ground based, with input from orbital satellites. Any intercontinental missile fired from our shores will be immediately detected either by highly sensitive heat sensors or other means and will be neutralized during trajectory. Our scientists are at least seven years behind in such technology, our economy is in shambles, the ruble is depreciating every day and only shored up by artificial means, and we simply haven't the money to research and develop a comparable defense system.

"During the Cold War, our SS-18s and SS-20s terrified the Americans. Those weapons carry more MIRV and MARV punch than anything known to man, then or now. They were forced to the negotiating table. SALT ONE and SALT TWO. Before that we had worked out an ABM treaty in 1972. MDS will change everything. The only assured destruction will be all of Russia. The Americans will be able to deploy this terrible counter-offensive weapon in less than five years, we estimate. We couldn't match it, even in ten years. I tell you this confidentially, gentlemen, for the reasons I gave earlier. We as a country spend almost 30 percent of our GNP on defense, military applications, and research. The Americans spend 4 percent of their GNP on similar applications, and even with increased appropriations for MDS by the war-minded President Deakin, they will spend less than 10 percent of their annual GNP. A lot can happen in ten years, but all our defense analysts concur on this point. We shall be at a great military disadvantage. Our missiles will be blown up during trajectory. Our bombers will not be able to penetrate coastal defenses. The only targets we might conceivably hit will be NATO-allied countries in Europe, and even those will be a danger to us due to radioactive fallout. We simply *cannot allow that!*" Kalushkin banged his hand down on the table with sudden force. The three men jumped. It was then that he realized he had been shouting.

Kalushkin reached for a water carafe on the side table and poured himself a glass. He drank thirstily, laid the tumbler down, and continued softly. "Comrades, we have been given the honor—we consider it the highest honor—of saving our country from catastrophe. The top Ground forces, Air Force, and Navy chiefs have each concluded in separate studies that the American Missile Defense Shield must never be allowed to come to fruition. If it does, we are finished as a superpower. If the MDS program continues and we cannot stop it, our government will be forced to negotiate—at grossly inequitable terms—a downward reduction in our nuclear arsenal, including targetable reentry vehicles, and the continued dismantling of our SS-18 and SS-20 missiles."

He paused and surveyed each man in turn. "Gentlemen, I informed you at the last meeting that Ramalan Sidi, that Al-Qassam madman, is trying to obtain four air-to-ground missiles from one of the breakaway Soviet states. Our intelligence is reliable. We know he is planning some sort of attack on America. I have suggested that he be given the missiles, on condition that I select one of the targets."

He paused, eyes glinting, and then went on, "A supercomputer is being built at a university in Illinois that will oversee the Missile Defensive Shield program. When this computer is finished, it will be the fastest supercomputer on earth. Although much of the hardware for MDS is being developed at Lawrence Livermore in White Sands, New Mexico, and also at some contract aerospace giants in California and New York, our scientists agree that if construction of this giant supercomputer were to be delayed even by two years, it could buy the Russian federation more time, and probably cause the MDS program to die a natural death at the hands of a fiscally minded US Congress appalled at the massive expenditures."

Kalushkin paused again, his eyes darting from one man to the next. "I proposed then, gentlemen, to allow Al-Qassam the honor of blowing up the supercomputer facility in Illinois."

This time Artemyev and Zamyatin nodded and reached for their own tumblers. Colonel Gulev said nothing. Kalushkin waited while they each poured water from the carafe, before spreading his hands out on the table.

"Of course, we had hoped that President Deakin would not be reelected for a second term. Since he has been and remains the major architect of this Missile Defense Shield, if he was not reelected, MDS would die when he left office—again primarily because the new man at the White House would be loath to spend so massively for an untested project when millions of Americans are out of work, welfare rolls are at unprecedented levels, and people are sleeping on sidewalks. However, that did not happen. Deakin got reelected by a record landslide margin. And he is pressing ahead with MDS. Since we have learned through our excellent intelligence that Al-Qassam plans to attack the White House and kill the president, it has become obvious that another solution to our problem now presents itself. To put it bluntly, our second option would be to engineer the death of this president by not sharing this information with our American friends as we had earlier planned.

"This is a crime they themselves have often accused us of, falsely, in their irresponsible media. In connection with John F. Kennedy. In connection with the deaths of other political opponents, world leaders whose ideologies are not in consonance with our own. Everyone knows we did Trotsky in Mexico, and I am proud that my own father played an important part in that successful operation. The Americans, too, have soiled their hands—Lumumba in the Congo, the failed attempts on our bearded friend in Havana. Well, for once, they will be correct. We shall try to remove their elected president, but it will be done in such a way that the action can never be traced back to us. The last thing we want is World War Three. Wars have been started for less. Look at Archduke Ferdinand in former Yugoslavia."

He smiled suddenly, the strain in his jaw pronounced. "And that my friends, was where we stopped at the last meeting. Now, I wish to hear how far you have gone in the arrangements for accomplishing our purpose."

Artemyev rifled through his papers and cleared his throat. "It has been arranged," he said. "Al Qassam's agent, one Barry Throck, will have to pick up his bank draft in Moscow. He will have a mild heart attack and be taken to the hospital. A Histayev-2 pacemaker will be fitted in his chest. He will be informed in the most humane manner of his terminal condition. After a suitable recovery period, he will be released to proceed with procuring the missiles for Al-Qassam."

"Why are they using an American?" asked General Zamyatin.

"They say he's the only one who can smuggle that kind of cargo into America." Artemyev shrugged. "That's what they say."

"Have we decided on the missile type he'll be allowed to have on the black market, Comrade General?" Colonel Gulev said.

Kalushkin nodded at Zamyatin. "Yuri, answer that."

Zamyatin glanced at his notes. The four men had considered three different missiles. Zvevda built two: the Kh-23 (AS-7 Kerry), which had a range of 5 kilometers and carried a 110 kilogram warhead, and the Kh-25 (AS-10 Karen), which had 10 kilometer range carrying a 90 kilogram warhead. The third missile was the AS-14 "Kedge" built by Spetztechnik Vympel NPO, which could lug a 250 kilogram warhead a distance of 12 kilometers. All three were air-to-ground missiles with radio guidance systems, though a semi-active laser could also control the "Kedge" and the "Karen."

"The AS-14 suits the mission well," Artemyev said. "I believe the airstrip from which they will make the attempt falls within the twelve-kilometer range."

"It does," Gulev said. "I worked on that with General Zamyatin."

Zamyatin went on, "We made some modifications to the Kedge. It will accept target coordinates, which can be changed by the operator. This was necessary since there will be no laser designator or TV guidance. The launch vehicle is rather crude, you understand."

Kalushkin nodded. "Good. I hope the purchase of the farm with the airstrip wasn't made with our funds or instruments traceable to us?"

"No, sir." Artemyev appeared shocked. "Al-Qassam paid through several blind fronts. They paid for the Air Tractor crop duster also."

"And the mercenaries? The two technicians Al-Qassam was looking for?"

"They recruited them, Comrade General. Ex-Soviet Air Force." Artemyev was on a roll and showed it. "As we agreed, none of our men should be involved in the actual operation. If they defect or are caught and interrogated, the risks are unthinkable. We allow the mercenaries to go and pretend we know nothing."

"Their names?"

"Gennady Beria and Anatoly Grimsky."

Pyotr Gulev spoke. "One thing bothers me, Comrade General. Al-Qassam has lots of young men willing to die. Why not put two of them who are pilots in rented airplanes and crash them into the targets? That is easier than all this elaborate planning."

"That, too, takes planning, Pyotr," Kalushkin said. "My understanding is that defenses at the White House have been beefed up, and Marines equipped with Stingers are part of the new security apparatus. More importantly, our intelligence reports that Ramalan Sidi wants to use only mercenaries for future Al-Qassam operations inside America. Three or four Arabs congregating anywhere arouse suspicion, and the security agencies are on full alert. So they're using mercenaries who don't look Arabic, for now."

"I see."

"And those mercenaries are not ready to make suicide bombings," Kalushkin said. "How else would they live to enjoy the huge sums of money they're being paid?"

The three men guffawed at his jest.

"One thing," Kalushkin continued. "Nabil will present himself as a representative from Boris. Sidi knows about Boris, our deep, deep asset in the capital. He has been tricked into thinking Boris's help is vital if both parts of the operation are to succeed, especially the second part."

CHAPTER 2

Dublin. Two Months later.

When Throck flew to Dublin, Ireland, on his way back to the States—ostensibly for a few days' vacation—and then tried to contact the American Embassy on Elgin Road 4, they knew exactly what he was trying to do. He had succeeded, in getting the missiles into America spoil through his hardware import business operating mostly from Eastern Europe. Except that Throck had stumbled on to the true nature of the merchandise he'd provided a false bill of laden for, and that meant trouble. Kalushkin's operatives knew this because they were watching him twenty-four seven without his knowledge.

He had to die.

They had intended to kill him anyway. Right after the missiles arrived on US soil. That was why they had dissolved some white powder in his drink at a Moscow restaurant. The drug had given him the mild heart attack that landed him in the hospital, where he had been equipped with the Histayev-2 pacemaker.

Barry Throck dialed the embassy number.

The recorded message said, "You have reached the American Embassy. For visa and consular services, dial 668-8085. For all other services 668-8777. If you require further assistance please wait on the line and someone will attend to you." Tchaikovsky's "Serenade No 13 for Strings" played fetchingly in the background.

"American Embassy." The young woman's voice floated into Throck's ear, crisp, feminine, loaded with all-American come-hither guile. Probably Wellesley or Vassar. Or Barnard. *God, they could transplant those types over here, too,* Throck marveled. He was suddenly glad to be American, glad he'd made the decision to rat out the Russians.

That was how it had begun. The embassy was skeptical at first, thought he was a madman. Then they took him seriously, and because it involved a threat to the President of the United States, they contacted the Department of Homeland Security in Washington, DC, who in turn sent over a Secret Service man on holiday in England to interview him. The agent's name was Angus Means.

That was when they struck.

Means met Barry Throck at the Garden of Remembrance on Parnell Street in downtown Dublin. The inscription on the plaque read, *Garden Of Remembrance: Dedicated to those who gave their lives in the cause of Irish freedom.* Right next to the bench where the two men sat, graffiti on the wall in bold, black letters was more explicit. Bloody Sunday: They Shall Not Be Forgotten.

They were still talking when there was movement by the gate of the Garden. Two men in dark blue suits and gray flannel slacks strode purposefully toward them.

———

Afghanistan.

Ramalan Sidi wore a light-blue toga-like garment that curled around his shoulder and midsection with the discreetness of a Tuscany mayor. A white turban crowned his full-bearded face, unlike the black ones worn by the Taliban. At six foot nine inches, he was tall enough for NBA basketball, this renegade scion of a wealthy Saudi Arabian family.

"My brother, look at me," he said to Nabil Hamdoon. "The infidels have gotten so arrogant; it is Allah's wish that they be punished by jihad. Their ships patrol the Mediterranean as if they own it. Meanwhile, they are thousands of kilometers from their own shores. They supply the Zionists F-15s, F-16s, and other weapons to massacre our people in

Palestine. Israel has refused to comply with the United Nations resolutions asking it to vacate illegally occupied land. America says nothing. Yet when Iraq does something one hundred times less serious, they are bombed. Nabil, this arrogance is too much!"

"I agree, my brother."

"They have bombed my training camps here and sent cruise missiles to a harmless building in Sudan, all in the name of punishing me. Anytime Hamas or Hezbollah sets off an explosion inside a discotheque or a bus stop, they blame me. If Abu Nidal farts inside his tent in Fallujah, their satellites pick it up, and it is blamed on me. For too long, Nabil, I have been America's scapegoat."

Ramalan Sidi paused, staring into the distance, into a past of harsh memories, into a future of harsh possibilities.

"No more. I am going to strike back in a way America will always remember. If someone is trying to kill you, you have an obligation to strike him down. I propose, Nabil, to kill President Donald Deakin and destroy the White House in Washington, DC."

Nabil stood still.

There certainly was logic in the leader's proposed act of revenge. The Americans had tried to kill him twice in the past. They had failed. They could succeed the next time.

"How is this to be done?" Nabil said.

"It needs a pilot, and you have been chosen among many willing martyrs."

Nabil stared at the man. "Many willing martyrs?"

"Of course. And when you fly that airplane for us—"

"My brother, I did not volunteer—"

"Yes, yes, I know that. Our sources said you alone could do what is required. You were handpicked."

"But—"

"This is big, Nabil. Very big. I can tell you that we have friends." He pointed northwest, in the general direction of Turkmenistan. "They are scared of Deakin, that useless cowboy, who now wants to build some kind of missile defense. It would tilt the superpower balance too much to the Americans. Our friends cannot allow it. I have arrived at a conclusion that although this operation looks like my revenge, in reality we are helping our friends and striking a blow at Big Satan."

"*Insha'Allah.*" God willing.

"This conversation never took place."

"We never spoke. I want to ask. Why me? You have Al-Qassam cells on the ground in infidel country. You have sleeper cells you can activate."

Sidi shook his head. "Anybody Arabic with pure Islam beliefs is under suspicion. Your mother is from Bosnia in the former Yugoslavia, and your father is Arabic. So permit me if I say you look less Middle Eastern than most. Most important, you are a pilot. This mission calls for a pilot."

"Al-Qassam has pilots."

"I am using outside contractors for this operation. Many of our operatives are under surveillance by intelligence agencies. They'll be watching the wrong people when the earth moves in Washington, DC."

"Okay, brother, I accept."

"I have also hired some Russians to help you. They are mercenary engineers. You will meet them in America."

"We have not discussed my fee for this mission, brother. I do not even know what I am supposed to do."

"Nabil, I am prepared to offer you the sum of 1.2 million United States dollars for the completion of this mission. That will be your retirement—how do the infidels say—nest-egg?"

"That is a lot of money, my brother." Nabil said. "Since I shall not live to enjoy it, my daughter will inherit all of it."

"Is that your wish for carrying out the jihad?"

"That is my wish. In the event of my martyrdom my lawyers will manage my estate accordingly."

"It will be done. The mission means a great deal to me. There's a man, one Major Sergei Brobov, we have hired. He has worked as a military attaché in Washington, DC, for years. You will spend one week with him, to learn everything there is to know about this mission."

"Okay."

"The money will be wired to your usual account in Switzerland. Through the usual shell accounts from Cyprus to the Cayman Islands, back to Switzerland. Unless you want it sent elsewhere?"

"This is fine. Half now, half after the mission is accomplished."

Ramalan Sidi smiled. "The entire amount will be wired into your account within three working days. I trust you, Nabil. And this mission is very important to me."

———

South Waziristan, lawless territory. Six weeks later
Nabil and Ramalan Sidi sat inside a cave deep in the mountains of southern Waziristan.

"The mission is almost ready, brother. But I need more things. I want backup. I want two seven-pod rocket launchers, airplane configured, and cache explosives, up to two thousand pounds. I want it in a secure location in New York so if I need it I can call for it."

"Why, my brother?"

"Missiles can fail. They can misfire or fail to explode when they hit the target. They may not fit the brackets on the hard points in the launch vehicle. I want to make sure the target is destroyed, and I want cache explosives and the rockets with universal mounts as backup."

"That will cost us a lot of money."

"It is necessary for the mission to proceed."

Ramalan Sidi was quiet for a long time. "Okay, my brother. You shall have it."

CHAPTER 3

Dublin.

The two men—one was blond, the other dark haired—held up badges bearing the Garda (Irish Police) crest. The blond man said, "Garda. Which one of you men is Angus Means?"

Means looked up quizzically. "I am. Why?"

"You are under arrest for impersonation."

"What!"

"Impersonating an officer of the Secret Service of America on the sovereign soil of Ireland."

Before Means could move, hands like steel vices pinioned him and handcuffs were clamped on his wrists. The notebook he had been writing on and the pen clattered to the ground.

"What in the hell do you think you're doing?" Means yelled. "I'm bona fide. Get your meat hooks off me!"

"I advise you not to resist arrest, Mr. Means."

"Goddamnit, this is a wrongful arrest!"

"That will be sorted out," said the blond suit. "We're taking you to Donnybrook Station."

"You've got to be kidding."

"Mr. Means, anything you say can and will be used against you in a court of law. You have the right to a lawyer—"

"Oh yeah? You have Miranda in Ireland too?"

"We do."

"Escobedo?"

"That too. You'd be surprised what we have. We're working on McDuff laws right now," Blondie sneered..

"Good. I want a lawyer. Call Jack Haines at the US Embassy and tell him you have arrested me. You and your sidekick will be pounding a midnight beat in Dublin's sleaze district before you finish hanging up the goddamn phone."

The dark one patted him down. No gun. But he removed Means's wallet and examined the Secret Service badge and the DHS seal. He didn't seem to be impressed.

"Came from London, did you?" the dark one said.

"This very morning."

The dark one returned the wallet to Means's pocket. "These things can be acquired in East Soho for the price of a plate of fish and chips. The IRA could produce them almost at will." He examined Means's cell phone. "Aha! Planning to detonate a bomb, are you?"

"Don't be ridiculous. That's an Apple phone."

The darker man pocketed the phone. "You will come with us."

Means was grabbed by each arm and led toward the gate.

"Tell them, Barry," Means yelled.

Throck found his voice. "Hey. He's legit. He's with the US Secret Service, you know."

"Perhaps," the blond one said. "But did you register with Irish authorities that you are a law enforcement agent on official business, Mr. Means?"

"Who says I'm on official business?"

"We've monitored your activities."

"Well, no, I—"

"If you were genuine, you should know that you cannot enter a foreign country and start using police powers on people without the knowledge or express permission of the host country."

"I didn't use police powers," Means protested.. "I was taking down a statement."

"It's a simple matter," the dark one said. "You will sort it out with our superintendent."

"He didn't impersonate anybody," Throck blurted out. "He's the real McCoy. I'm the one who called the authorities and asked to speak to an agent."

For the first time, the two men seemed to notice Throck. The dark one glared at him. "Are you also a Secret Service agent?"

"Hell no. I'm a private citizen. American. My name's Barry Throck."

Blondie appraised him. "Oh. You are Throck. Barry Throck?"

"How do you mean?" Out of the corner of his eye Barry saw the groundskeeper and his wife crossing the street on their way back from lunch break. He almost sighed with relief. He was safe with all these witnesses around.

"We are aware of your telephone call to the US Embassy. They briefed us. We know you are supposed to meet somebody here at a certain time. That is a matter of interest to the United States. It does not concern us." Darkie waved his arms offhandedly. "But this man here—" he nodded at Means, "is suspected of having ties to terrorism. He is wanted for questioning. We also want to know why he is impersonating an agent of the United States Secret Service."

The minute the darker man finished talking, Means *knew*. He just knew something was wrong. But they were already on the street, and he had been pushed inside a blue Nissan closed van that did look like a police van with gadgets and equipment lying around. He was shoved into one of the two seats in the back and manacled to a beam railing whileThrock watched helplessly.

Instinct.

Means couldn't put a finger on it. First, the accent. The two men spoke perfect English, but in a stilted way. This must be the Irish brogue he'd been hearing about for years. He hadn't known it to be so thick. He was damned if these two men didn't sound like native Corsicans speaking Dutch. And why weren't they arresting Throck? Throck was the real villain, the suspect, and if these two men were really cops, they should know that.

Nothing made sense.

Means had never been arrested in his life. Prior to this, in fact, he had done all the arresting—as many inmates at Joliet and Marion and Leavenworth would testify. In his mind, subconsciously, if anybody was going to be arrested, Throck was that person. He had been caught completely off guard.

Throck must have been thinking along the same lines. He grabbed the van door so the blond man could not close it. "Hey! Don't you believe any of it, Means. These guys are Ruskies. Russians!"

"You sure, Barry?"

"Sure I'm sure. I was there a couple months back." Barry straightened to his full height and faced the two men. "C'mon guys. It's me you really want. Say it."

The detectives exchanged glances.

"Russians?" said the blond man. "My friend, this is serious police work. We don't have time for jokes."

"Who's joking? I know that accent. You guys are Russians."

The dark man snorted. "We're both from Limerick. I've been told that our brogues are bad. Like real bad. I don't believe we've ever been told we sound Russian."

"That's right, Mr. Throck," said the blond man. "Perhaps you'd like to come along to the station to confirm which part of Russia we are from?"

"Damn right I would."

"Please step in. I'll have to handcuff you, of course."

"Not on your life!"

"Regulations. You are accompanying a detained person."

"No, thanks. I'll call a cab and follow you."

"You do that. And in the future, I don't recommend you interfere with police business. You could be arrested for obstruction. In Ireland that carries a stiff penalty."

Now Means was certain! *Regulations.* No police agency in Western Europe or America invited friends or relations to ride along with an arrested suspect to the station, handcuffed or not. He saw the gaunt frame of the Garden's groundskeeper and his petite wife standing outside the grounds little office watching the proceedings, an expression akin to pity in their eyes. A handcuffed suspect being herded into a Black Maria engenders pity and also a glad-it's-not-me smugness in onlookers. For one wild moment, Means thought, *if Throck is right and these thugs are really Russians, then I'm finished.* If he yelled and threw his body around (only his arms were manacled) and generally created a disturbance, perhaps more people would notice, and hopefully real cops would arrive on the scene. He was about creating a scene when something else happened that added to his total confusion. As the blond man made to close the van door, he thrust his head inside, looking around the van as though checking that all was in order. As he withdrew his head, the door already half closed on the sliding rail, he cocked his head so Throck couldn't see, and winked at Means. The door closed in Means's face.

In law enforcement circles, (and Means had been around long enough to have seen it a couple of times) it meant one thing: *We got you out. Something's happened, and we needed to get you out and leave the perp in the open.* Once they pulled out of there, his handcuffs would be unlocked, everything would be explained, and he would be debriefed. No doubt this must have been Ken Dwight's idea. Dwight was his immediate Secret Service boss back in Washington, DC. The fake arrest, pointedly ignoring the real suspect, putting him off guard. Something really had gone wrong, necessitating this whole charade. For the first time since the two men appeared, Angus Means, Special Agent Treasury, relaxed.

"Don't you believe any of it, Means," Throck shouted as the van drove off, the darker man driving. "I'll be right behind you in a cab."

But he hadn't gotten a cab by the time the van turned the corner and Means's last glimpse of Throck was of a Mike Ditka-type fellow on the sidewalk trying and failing to flag down a yellow taxi with a fare already inside.

In succeeding years at the FBI Training Academy in Quantico, Virginia, and at the Secret Service Agents Training School nearby, the case of Agent Angus "Flipper" Means would be textbook. Cadets would dissect the situation and proffer their own solutions, what they would have done confronted by the same events.

At that moment, however, handcuffed and helpless as the van drove away, Means felt terrible. If Barry was right and he had allowed himself to be immobilized by two thugs or foreign agents, then indeed his professional standards had lapsed. But dammit, what should he have done otherwise? He was a trained agent, with primary emphasis on detecting counterfeit money and apprehending forgers. In the past five years in Presidential Detail, emphasis had been on the protection of the President of the United States, if necessary by the surrendering of his own life. The investigation of all threats to the president's life, both oral and written, and the apprehension of the authors of such threats. He had been uniquely successful in the latter, earning a rapid promotion to Deputy Chief Investigator, Threats. If there was one thing being in law enforcement taught you, it was respect for the law. When those two jackasses Blondie and Colleague had identified themselves as garda, which was what the Irish police called themselves, he had automatically ceded authority to them since he was in their country and his powers of enforcement as an agent of the United States DHS did not extend to Ireland without prior official permission. In retrospect he hadn't really acted with unreasonable carelessness.

And that wink by Blondie—he had an idea that that made it alright. For some reason his superiors wanted him out of there; this being a foreign country and with no ready backup, they had enlisted the aid of the garda Perhaps sense could be made of the whole thing.

This last assumption was reinforced when, after three blocks, the van pulled over and stopped. Blondie unbuckled his seatbelt and entered the rear cabin where Means sat. Blondie had to stoop, because the cabin was not tall enough for him to stand up in. He grinned as he fished out a key ring, selected a blue key, and approached Means.

"Had you scared in there for a while, didn't we?" he said. "Orders from your people. Something came up. Here, you'll be free in just a second."

He was right! Damn, damn, and damn! Means exhaled a great breath of relief. "Well, I must hand it to you guys. You played it to the hilt. I was confused back there for a while."

Blondie inserted the blue key to unlock the handcuffs.

"Yeah. We've been told we're pretty good actors as a team," Blondie said, and twisted the key.

A faint click. Means jumped.

"Ouch!"

"So sorry. Did I hurt you?" Blondie's voice was a sneer.

The handcuff did not unlock.

Means tried to swing his hands free, couldn't, and knew with a sudden, depressing finality that he'd been tricked, that something terrible and fatal had been injected into his wrist. Blondie walked back to his seat without another look at Means. The van drove off again.

"You slimy bastards!" Means croaked.

There was no answer from up front.

"I'll see you thrown into the darkest pit of Hell," Means yelled at them. "Goddamn slimy pieces of shit, both of you. You and your piss-sorry goddamn watery asses!"

The dark-haired one looked back. "Don't get worked up, pal. The toxins will work faster and come at you all of a sudden that way. Just relax and be normal, and you go easy. Be like falling asleep."

"Sleep well," Blondie said.

Means was sweating profusely and had difficulty breathing. With great effort he twisted his body up to look at his wrist. There was a tiny puncture wound above the wrist bone. Strange handcuffs. He'd never seen ones like these before. The middle flange too big, like it had machinery inside. Two keyholes—one normal stainless steel, the other blue. Blondie had used a blue key, he thought dimly. Color-coded death. He shook his head to clear it, and ended up with his head drooping on his forearm.

The van stopped after some minutes. The sound of water. A tug-boat horn sounded in the distance. Quayside? Blondie came back, checked Means's pulse. He still spoke English. "He's almost gone. The pulse is weak. Come and help me."

"Sure." His partner left the wheel and opened the back door of the van. Blondie frisked him again, removing anything he thought might be a tape recorder and all the buttons on Means's coat in case one of them was a revolutionary new miniaturized recorder. He left the wallet untouched, with its silver DHS badge and photograph of Means's wife and two daughters. Blondie unlocked the handcuffs with a stainless steel key and threw them on the van floor. He caught Means to prevent him falling headlong. Suddenly Means lunged at Blondie, trying to rake his fingernails down his face, get on his nails vital DNA tissue—for if they ever found his body and tried to trace his killers. But Blondie was no slouch, or else he'd been expecting that, and he leaped back. Not that it strictly mattered; the two men didn't wear gloves and already had their fingerprints all over Means. Clearly they never expected to be tried for any crime in future. Means toppled to the floor.

"Nice try," Blondie said.

They bundled him out onto the sidewalk. The street was deserted.

"Have an everlasting sleep, Mr. Means," the dark-haired one said.

The van drove off.

Inside the van Vladimir said, "Were we right to leave him like that? He still had a weak pulse."

"He's dead," Andrei replied. "That's a walking dead man you saw, Vlad. That was enough toxin to kill ten racehorses."

His companion shrugged. "If you say so." He was silent as they drove north through city traffic. "We got the tape recorder. I think we got everything."

"We did. But . . ." Andrei and Vladimir were professionals, sleeper agents long domiciled in Ireland and reactivated when orders came about a new mission. Vladimir had an Irish wife and worked a white-collar job; his wife had no idea of her husband's dual nature. Andrei worked in the Russian Embassy in Dublin as a political officer, Grade Two. This was their fifth mission in four years, and all had been successful. They were both graduates of "The Farm," the Kormuschka—that training ground that was to the KGB (now SVR) what Quantico is to the FBI. Even now, mission accomplished, they spoke English, even though they itched to switch to their mother tongue to relieve the stress of the mission, or to just plain celebrate. A sleeper trained at the Farm wasn't even permitted to *think* in Russian once a foreign country had been chosen for him.

"Something bothers you, my friend." Vladimir glanced anxiously at his friend who was driving. "Confess to old Vlad."

"Moscow said Throck would be dead in ten minutes. Not to take him. We were to take only the Secret Service agent."

"That's what our orders were."

"Unless they have other operatives I'm not aware of, I don't see how they are going to take him out. And he's done a one-eighty for sure. He was giving away state secrets. Unless the hit team is going to fall out of the Dublin sky, Throck looked hale and hearty last time I saw him."

———

Means felt rather than saw the blue van's taillights fade. This was unreal. This was happening to him. He'd never believed he would die in the line of duty, yet he was sure he was dying now. He had been an agent when the Secret Service was under Treasury, and was still an agent when it was moved over to Department of Homeland Security in 2003. He couldn't believe what was happening to him. Blackness swept over him, a massive wave of weakness and nausea. Means fought the nausea and lost. He must have retched horribly and at length for he found his face only inches from the sour pool of his own vomit. It seemed to help. He struggled to a sitting position on the cobbled street. Incredibly he focused on a man walking in the opposite direction dressed in a black three-piece suit and narrow tie, bowler hat, and rolled umbrella under one arm. Was he dreaming? An eccentric Englishman walking down the middle of a Dublin quay? What more effrontery would the English inflict on the Irish? But the Englishman brought back a vision of Means's wife and his two daughters, now housed at the Heathrow Forte Crest waiting for him to finish the assignment and come home. It smote his heart that he might not.

"Help me!" he croaked at the Englishman. There was hope in that black, meticulous apparition, those black wingtip brogues, those dependable, perpetually arched eyelids and chiseled patrician nose. Here was order and predictability and sanity. Surely the man would do something, the right thing, save him.

"Help me, please!"

The apparition stopped. He stared at Means. At the vomit, at the well-dressed man sitting in the middle of the sparse traffic road. Means couldn't hear the words, but the tight lips formed the word, "My God!" The gentleman looked around desperately, and must have decided there was a pub around the corner somewhere and that Means was just an unfortunate inebriate, for he harrumphed once, set his bowler firmly on his crown, and hurried away.

Despair.

Means, baby, this is it. Blackness sweeping in. *Don't lose it. Mustn't lose it. The boys depend on you. The insurance would take care of the wife and kids.* He had a carrier policy somewhere, outside the government's own, that paid double the principal if he died on active duty. Gwen and the girls would be well taken care of.

Dammit, he wasn't giving up! Agency issue. It nagged at his brain. Yes, yes. Rolex chronometer. The wristwatch special issued to all agents on Presidential Detail. He wore it when he'd ridden sideboard on President Deakin's last visit to Denver. And kept it. Chief Strooker had insisted. Had a miniature microphone and tiny recorder built in, so they could monitor every agent's conversation—the last fifteen minutes, anyway. In case of another Dallas, events could be reconstructed around exclamations, agent's voices, and the president's voice, from the general chaos surrounding an actual or attempted assassination. He hadn't turned on the automatic recorder because he was on vacation, not on Presidential detail. Gratitude to those nerds at the lab who had dreamed this up.

His arm weighed several tons. He physically lifted his left hand with his right as leverage and brought it to his face. He examined the chronometer face. The second hand swam in his distorted vision. He pulled out the setting knob, until he heard the tiny beep. The second hand began moving. If it was moving it was recording. No need to do anything else. From the depths of he knew not where he forced himself to speak.

"Ken...Dwight...Meansca-callingin.I'vebeen...hit.Ithink...It's... true. Code . . ." He couldn't remember the code for a Presidential Assassination Threat, Top Priority. He was fading fast; he had to get the information out.

"Fox Detail. Agent Means . . . possible suspect Throck . . . JFK Continental . . . Saturday contact. Smurf One . . . not safe . . ."

Using his last ounce of strength, Means pulled out the setting knob that that would stop the watch and also save the recording so it wouldn't erase automatically after fifteen minutes. His unfocused eyes noted with satisfaction that the second hand had stopped. *I pledge allegiance to the flag . . .*

Agent Angus Means pitched down face forward and died for his country in a pool of his own vomit.

———

Moscow.
The two generals had entered the highly secret control room through the connecting door from Zamyatin's office. Both Generals Oleg Kalushkin

and Yuri Zamyatin had placed their hands palm-down on the photo-plate scanner that read their palm prints and authorized entry into the AMD program. The computer operator, Miroslav Danilov had sent the relevant codes via satellite to AMD 13.

At 35,786 kilometers above the earth's equator in geosynchronous orbit, the encrypted message was received. A powerful transponder in the belly of the satellite activated a pulsed signal, which shot out at light speed to Earth and interrogated eighteen agent-monitoring devices implanted in various humans and non-humans. Instantly it located the correct receiver in a busy Dublin street in the Republic of Ireland. The tiny receiver acknowledged the discrete interrogation and emitted a coded reply from its weak batteries. The mother lode in the satellite picked up the reply and ran through a series of self-tests, thirty-three in all, in the space of two seconds. All parameters were within limits, systems all green, and dutifully the satellite began a ten-second countdown. Ten seconds during which the life of Barry Throck could still be saved if either of the two watching generals or the lone adjutant hit the highlighted ABORT button pulsing on the screen. They did nothing of the sort: indeed they were there to make sure the specific signal was sent. Silence in the room as the numeric countdown continued. When the counter ran down to zero with no counter-instructions, the satellite transponder dutifully dispatched a powerful encoded signal to the Histayev-2 pacemaker buried in the chest cavity of Barry Throck.

The screen blinked. An oblong red wedge bearing the words TERMINATION IN PROGRESS illuminated.

It took about sixty seconds.

After one minute and ten seconds, the powerful transponder in the belly of the satellite sent another beam, querying the Histayev-2 buried beneath Throck's pericardium. The interrogation failed to detect a heartbeat. Inside the Histayev-2 itself, four tiny sensors measured five parameters in the adjoining heart tissue and relayed the results back to the mother receiver. In the tiny monitor housed in the mother receiver, five flat lines traced across the screen using a predetermined logic. No error messages were displayed. The cardiac arrest loop had been closed.

In front of the three men in the control room a single beep sounded. The screen blinked again, and the words SUBJECT TERMINATED appeared in a highlighted bold wedge, size twenty, Cyrillic Normal Font.

Out in the vast endless vacuum of space, the transponder reset itself. The huge solar panels of the satellite deployed automatically to recharge its batteries. A termination sequence always took a lot of juice from the power pack.

———

Dublin.

Barry was still trying to flag down a cab when the first pains of what he took to be angina seared through his left arm and chest. The blue Nissan carrying Means and the two Irish policemen—really, they weren't any more Irish than he was Mongolian—disappeared around the corner. In succession two city taxicabs sped by him, their drivers unimpressed by his outstretched hand and uplifted thumb.

Why should he follow them anyway? By now he couldn't possibly catch up with them unless they were held up at a traffic light. The "cops" had mentioned Donnybrook station, and that was where he was headed. Clearly the disclosure had been botched. If Zamyatin and his men knew he was a turncoat, why cart away the Secret Service agent and leave him, Barry?

Then it fell into place, crystal clear. The agent was being taken away to be killed. He, Barry, was being killed by the Histayev-2. He had suspected he was too young to have a pacemaker implant.

Oh God, no.

The pain bit hard on the left side of his shoulder, radiating all the way down to his fingers. A crushing tightness in the middle of his chest. Suddenly he couldn't breathe. He screamed involuntarily—or tried to. He sank to his knees, clutching his chest. He turned toward help, toward the groundskeeper and his wife who stood at the gate of their cubicle watching with concern. Inexplicably he suddenly yearned for the gate-keeper's uncomplicated existence.

The gatekeeper moved toward him. "Are you alright, sir?"

"He's not alright at all," his wife rebuked from the doorway of the cubicle. "I think he's having a heart attack. I'll call a doctor. Phil, you take care of him."

Phil caught Barry as he tumbled to the ground. He held Barry's head, uncertain what to do. "He's a-foaming at the mouth, Liz. Got any ideas?"

"Give him CPR, stupid! I'm on the phone," his wife yelled.

They were using an oxyacetylene torch inside his chest. Jesus, the fire! How could such pain be possible? He felt wet sloppy lips on his, full of garlic and cheap cigarette smoke. The stubble from a three-days' growth chafed with the wind being forced down his windpipe by an un-trained operator. Steady rhythmic pressure on his chest. The fire seared and seared, and at the point of screaming, which he couldn't do anyway, Barry floated in and out of consciousness.

"The ambulance is on its way," he heard the woman say from his semi-conscious state. "Here, Phil, let me. I'll do it better."

A change of lips. Softer, same garlic and cigarette after-breath, but the pleasant whiff of Elizabeth Arden cologne, less air being forced down his throat by a smaller windpipe. The kneading on his chest continued from the man. They were amateurs; their efforts were in opposition to each other.

Barry Throck thought it was bad timing when he heard the wail of ambulance sirens and decided then to stop breathing.

CHAPTER 3

Dublin.

Ken Dwight, Chief Investigator, Threats, (US Secret Service) had been assigned a car and driver from the embassy pool. He asked to be taken to Garda Headquarters in Phoenix Park. The driver, a medium-built Irishman in his early twenties, engaged the gears and swung the Toyota Camry into traffic.

Dwight thought back over the events of the last two days. The two sudden deaths had been less than fifteen minutes apart, according to medical estimates. Too much of a coincidence. Suddenly everything was a top priority. Faxes, e-mails, flying back and forth across the Atlantic. The shifting of flags from Threat Investigation 2403 to Top Priority Threat One. Hyram V. Strooker, US Secret Service chief, had immediately briefed FBI Director G. Everston Creed, and National Security Adviser Scott Bogan. The decision not to tell the president yet until further facts emerged. Admiral Hornsby, the CIA chief, had also been briefed. There had been the nasty business of informing Means's wife in London about her husband's death. Two agents had been assigned that task. She was now in a private home in London, under sedation. Means's daughters had been puzzled by the sudden burst of activity. Strooker immediately dispatched Dwight to Dublin to oversee the investigation, arrange for the transport of Means's body back to the United States (when the coroner was finished with it) and retrieve Means's agency wristwatch for wire data transcription. Larry Bodine in Devon had cut short his vacation and flown over to Dublin to assist Dwight.

Strooker had floated several contingency memos. The president's life was apparently in danger. Throck had been a participant or knew something pertaining to that threat. So vital was the information he had that he'd been monitored 'round the clock—had even said he was being followed during his telephone call. Throck had been cut down in the process of disclosing details to a Service agent who in turn died mysteriously minutes after several witnesses saw him being handcuffed by garda detectives. The gardai themselves denied any knowledge of the "arrest." The contact was dead, as was the investigator. Strooker put a hold on all unnecessary presidential movement outside Washington. There wasn't much in the upcoming weeks—two days at Camp David in Maryland, a speech to Rotarians at Reston, another to Kiwanis at Frederick, and a four-hour stopover in Champaign-Urbana, Illinois, to cut the ribbon on the new supercomputer built by the University of Illinois .

At Garda HQ, Bodine was already conferring with Chief Superintendent Ian McCloskey. The Interpol representative in Dublin was also there, as Dwight discovered when introduced to a dapper fellow with clipped brown mustache. Good sign. Strooker must be pulling out all the stops. Bodine shook hands with Dwight. He was an inch taller than Dwight and his eyes—usually hidden behind the Omnivision Bausch & Lombs when on presidential detail—looked bloodshot and the crow's-feet around his eyes more prominent.

Superintendent McCloskey clucked, "Sorry about all this, chaps. We have our own rules here, you know. We're chasing the same leads, I daresay. We'll get it all sorted out, and you can all get your exhibits."

The Interpol man said to Dwight, "I have told the superintendent that Interpol is keenly interested in this matter. It appears to be the work of a highly organized and technically savvy band. A terrorist cell backed by a government, a high-tech secret police, something of the sort. I have come across such before."

"Is that right?" Dwight said.

McCloskey said, "No trace of the blue van. Hundreds of them in Dublin. No one remembered to copy the plate number."

The Interpol man nodded gravely. "In London the CCTVs would have caught it."

"This is Dublin. The van's probably scuttled in a lake or something."

Dwight excused himself, pulling Bodine outside into the long marble corridor. A steady stream of gardai moved about on official business.

"Any leads?"

"I went over the room at the Doyle Skylon where Throck stayed. That was with official permission after the police—garda—went over it. Clean as a toothpick. He'd rented a Vauxhall Astra. The garda impounded it after Throck was found dead. Someone went in and sanitized the car. I got a waitress who works in the restaurant facing the car lot says she saw a man standing by the Vauxhall carrying a medium-size black bag. The man opens the trunk, puts bag inside, fiddles with it, then leaves minutes later with same bag. Hard to say if he took anything or not. Bag appeared full before and after."

"The waitress fix a time?"

"Couldn't be sure. About one thirty-ish or two o'clock."

"That jives with the time Throck left to keep his appointment with Agent Means."

"Fits alright. They figured he wasn't coming back and went in to remove incriminating evidence."

"Maybe. Maybe at that point they didn't know he was going to die. They figured he was going to rat, and they took his car apart to make sure he hadn't left any footprints."

"I'd buy that," Bodine said.

"Good work, Larry. I know its rough, cutting short your vacation and rushing over here. We sure appreciate it."

"Hey. Wouldn't want it otherwise." The big man shrugged. "It's personal. Flip was a friend. Mine as well as yours. Sally too. Our daughters attend the same school. Hell of a way for a Smurf One detail to go."

"Know what you mean. My wife's in dithers, too." Both men fell silent. Memories.

Dwight broke the silence. "You stay on a few more days, Larry. Maybe more. Tie up ends. We're making arrangements to ship back Means's body. The embassy's helping. Word is Means will be deep-sixed in Arlington. Taps and all."

"He deserves it."

"No less. Throck's ex-wife couldn't be bothered.. A half-brother has been located in Arkansas. He'll let the US Attaché know what they want done with the body. I'm going to see this man Corrigan, a heart doctor. Unless he tells me something earthshaking I'm off to Washington first thing tomorrow morning. Strooker wants me back in DC. The attempt, if it's going to take place, will probably be stateside. Smurf One has no overseas itinerary for the next five weeks. Until Brussels."

"Brussels?"

"Yeah. NATO summit."

———

New York. Central Park.
The contact was there. Blue sportsman's jersey and baseball cap with the magic words inscribed. He stared straight ahead, chewing gum audibly like any other American.

The rabbi took a seat next to the SVR man. He studied his Yiddish prayer book, nodding his head as if absorbed by the great liturgical wisdom therein. A jogger squatted half-a-football-field length away from them, flexing his leg muscles. Another jogger wearing a red headband did back presses then tied and retied his shoelaces. At this time of day not too many people were on this side of the park.

The jogger doing leg presses straightened and walked purposefully toward them. As he passed, he said clearly "You're clean." He broke into a trot and disappeared.

Yuri Zamyatin spat out his gum.

"Well, well, well," he said. "Now I know why they call you the Contractor."

The rabbi studied his beads. "Because I can pretend to be Jewish? If it justifies the end, why not?"

"Throck is dead."

He noted with satisfaction that the rabbi stiffened.

"How did the American die?"

"He sang. He opened his big mouth, as the Americans say, and sang like a popinjay. He had to be eliminated."

"I see." The rabbi considered this. "Is the mission compromised?"

"No."

"If he told details the mission is over."

"We were able to silence him as he talked. He was talking to a Secret Service agent, who, of course, taped the conversation. Just a simple pocket recorder. We seized it from the agent, killing him in the process."

"Did he supply the merchandise and my cache explosives?"

"We don't know yet. Throck is supposed to lodge at the JFK Continental on Friday. Saturday morning at ten o'clock, give or take five minutes, he is in his room. He gets a call from our contact in Washington, DC. Code-name Boris. He will verify that it is Throck he's talking to. If the missiles are in place—Boris has the means of verifying—he will then say, 'It's a go,' and hang up. It all has to be done in fifteen seconds to keep the call from being traced. Should the hotel switchboard take too much time transferring the call to the room, Boris will assume a trace is in progress and hang up immediately. He will contact you at a later time. If on the other hand he gets through to Throck—or whomever he thinks is Throck—and says, 'It's a negative. Repeat, a no-go,' then the missiles are not in place and for now, no mission."

"Where do I come in?"

"First, you confirm that the missiles are in place. Put a stooge—a drone—in Throck's room. Don't go yourself. We can't afford to sacrifice you. Find a hustler, an actor, someone you can pay money to stay in that room and receive the phone call. The room is already reserved in Throck's name. If FBI agents swoop in on your drone, you know the mission is compromised with or without Boris calling. You watch from a safe distance. See if the drone is followed." The general paused to look directly at the rabbi."Did you get your expense packet from Paris?"

"I did."

"Use it. You will need it in the weeks ahead."

"Would you like to be in my place for the same money?"

Zamyatin smiled. "No."

"One question."

"Yes?"

"Why not use untraceable cell phones? Why make calls through a hotel switchboard?"

"I give you one answer. NSA. They catch everything, any conversation they want. From thin air, cell towers."

The rabbi nodded.

The second jogger rose from his calisthenics and walked casually by. "Two uniformed NYPD. Foot patrol. Two hundred meters. One plainclothes man, northwest, five hundred meters." The jogger had a slight Russian accent, like the first. Probably attached to the UN mission.

"Thank you." Zamyatin passed over a padded envelope from his sports bag. "Inside you will find the map of a small town in Illinois. Read the instructions. Memorize and destroy them this night. The rendezvous only takes place after you confirm that Throck has not blown the mission. There's a gun for you also: 9mm Browning. Thirty-six bullets. Not counting the eight in the chamber. Teflon-coated, 205 grain. The president of the United States wears a flak vest beneath his double-breasted suit. His guard detail wears the same. These bullets will penetrate at medium or close range. No flank shots, Nabil. You shoot to kill if you use this weapon at all."

"Am I supposed to walk up to the target with this? I thought we had a plan."

Zamyatin shrugged. "You might come across him. That would save us most of the trouble, wouldn't it?"

"You were sent by Allah, I'm sure. I felt so naked without a gun. I was going to buy one at the store."

"Don't. Waiting period and background check. And the gun would be registered. This Browning is sanitized. No trace whatsoever."

"And if the police stop me, how do I explain the weapon?"

"Don't get stopped by the police." Zemyatin looked casually around. The foot patrols were almost abreast of the two men but were eyeing a couple of youths sharing a cigarette near a park bench.

They kept silent until the cops had receded.

Zamyatin spoke. "After today your only contact with us will be through Boris. Do you understand?"

"Yes."

"When Boris gives you any instructions, you take it as an order directly from Ramalan Sidi. Any questions?"

"None. But I would like you to open the envelope."

"What?"

"Open the envelope. If you're planning to kill me, we go up together."

The general's hard brown eyes glittered. He said nothing, but took the huge envelope and tore open the stapled end. Nabil could see the gleaming outline of the Browning, the packet of cartridges.

"You don't trust anyone, I can see."

"Only Allah. When my back is not turned."

Zamyatin rose. The meeting was over.

They shook hands quickly, looking each other in the eye, yet seeing only the tip of the other's nose. They turned and walked away in opposite directions, one the old pro, the other his contractor.

CHAPTER 4

Washington, DC.

The Oval Office desk was cluttered. The stack of black-bound National Security Agency daily briefings sat next to a framed picture of Doris Deakin, a white telephone on the left, the president's scratch sheet on the right Two long-stemmed writing instruments stood on marble pen-holders, a small brass plaque whose lengthy inscription Hyram V. Strooker, Chief of the Secret Service, never got to read properly because, then as now, he sat to the left of the president. In accord with tradition, no chair stood in front of the Oval Office desk, to avoid the visual of a direct threat to the president's power. A glass ashtray, a bronze sculpture of a horse, a Rubik's cube, and to the right, a stainless steel water jug.

Photographs of the First Family and an antique Chinese vase adorned the small, oblong oak table against the large glass windows that overlooked the Rose Garden. The Stars and Stripes on the right, and to the left the presidential flag, hung from two funicular North American eagles, gold-inlaid and wings outspread. The pale gold curtains beneath the heavy fuchsia overlay were parted, revealing a variety of white anemones and red roses in bloom. Even now, with autumn around the corner, the stunning colors of heliotropes, salvia, and chrysanthemums were already interspersed.

The sight never failed to enthrall Chief Strooker, despite his hundreds of visits to the Oval Office. Now, until the president found *le mot juste* and looked up from his crossword puzzle, there was nothing Strooker could do except to admire the view of the Rose Garden. He fingered the ornate desk, remembering that this marvelous piece of wood actually came from the superannuated timbers of *HMS Resolute*, a gift from Queen Victoria to Rutherford B. Hayes.

"Be with you in a moment, Hy," President Deakin said.

"Of course, Mr. President."

Strooker drummed his fingers some more on the timbers of old *HMS Resolute* and admired Doris Deakin's beautiful features. Fascinating how she grew more refined and mysterious with age. First Son Andy and First Daughter Beulah were in the picture also, both of them as independent and outspoken as their father. A photograph of the First Dog, a white pooch named Shakespeare, sat happily on a velvet cushion, pink tongue lolling, and a bronze-studded dog collar around his neck.

The president suddenly remembered why he'd been reelected. "Yes, Hy. What can I do for you?"

At last. "Mr. President, it concerns a matter of national security."

The president frowned. "I've been briefed this morning. Bogan just left here, and I talked to Stu Meyers on the telephone. What National Security matter? Bogan didn't say anything." Scott Bogan was the National Security Adviser.

"I'm talking about your personal security. We have reason to believe that your life is in danger. I've already briefed Director Creed and he's aware."

Deakin stared at Strooker.

"My life's been in danger ever since I won election to this office. You know that, Hy. Three thousand kooks write to me every year and threaten to blow me away. Some of them want to take me to Mars with them. Don't tell me there's a new dimension to this I haven't heard yet."

"We're taking this threat seriously. A number of events quite out of norm have occurred. We lost an agent—"

"Oh, yes. That poor fellow Means. I knew him personally. We decided he would get Arlington, didn't we?" He paused reflectively. "Gus was a good kid."

"He was." Strooker cleared his throat. "Mr. President, I'm going to cancel all your outside speaking engagements."

"Today? When? What's come up?"

"Indefinitely. Until we determine the extent of this threat. You'll plead ileitis. Everyone knows you've had that problem before. The doctors at Walter Reed will cooperate."

"You can cancel the meeting with the trade delegation from China," Deakin said. "The veep can handle that. Won't hurt bilateral talks. And cancel that press conference with the East Timorese delegation."

"I said outside engagements, Mr. President."

"The press conference will be held in the Rose Garden," Deakin continued as if he hadn't heard. "And Doris is hosting a reception for the British Prime Minister in the Jackie Kennedy Garden."

"Yes, yes," Strooker said abstractedly, peering at his notes. "The East side is out, I'm afraid, Mr. President. So is the Rose Garden. A sniper, a high muzzle velocity rifle with scope—who knows? I want to move everything indoors. I suggest the Roosevelt Room and the West Wing Reception Room in place of Rose Garden engagements. Mrs. Deakin will entertain the British Prime Minister's wife in the West Sitting Hall."

"Hyram, do what you want. That's what the taxpayers pay you for." *And you, Mr. President, just what do the taxpayers pay you for,* Strooker thought, but didn't say. *To sit on your butt fiddling with word games instead of studying bill manifestoes and signing legislation?* The steel-blue eyes fixed on him. "But for heaven's sake don't—don't you interfere with my trip to Illinois next week."

Strooker leaped to his feet, surprise blanching his face. "Mr. President! Your trip to Illinois?"

"Didn't you know?" Deakin's eyes were ice-cold blue slits. "When Air Force One touches down in Champagne-Urbana next week and the band starts playing 'Hail to the Chief,' you'd better make sure I'm the one stepping out of that airplane."

"Mr. P-President. I thought the Secretary of Defense was making the Illinois trip. It's not on your itinerary."

"It is now. You have any objection to my being there?"

"I've got the only reason in the world, Chief. I won't be able to guarantee your safety."

"I'll tell you this one more time, Hyram," Deakin said coldly. "I'm the father of the Missile Defensive Shield, in case you've forgotten. It's vital for our national defense and, more importantly, global security. When Ivan knows we have a system in place capable of destroying their missiles before they land on our soil, we'll get down to brass tacks. SALT ONE and SALT TWO will be swept under the carpet. They'll negotiate. Like global nuclear disarmament. When they know they can't win, they'll whine. Ever hear Ivan whine, Hyram?"

"Can't say I have, Chief."

"And that big whatchamacallum computer we've built at the University of Illinois. An ultra-supercomputer, I believe it's called. Capable of making so many zillion calculations in a fraction of a second. Just think of it, Hy. She's the brain behind MDS—my baby. And they're going to launch it next week Thursday. Overnight we'll be at least five years ahead of Ivan in the phased array intercept of intercontinental ballistic missiles. Guess who'll be there to cut the ribbon? Why should Meyers take the glory? It just isn't good PR, Hyram. This thing is my baby."

Strooker took out his little reporter's notebook and rapidly took notes.

"I owe it to the people of Illinois," the president went on dreamily. "I grew up in Illinois. Dixon. Heck, you know that. Before I went to California. Illinois gave me the biggest electoral margin for a president since Roosevelt. A Republican president at that. They repeated their mandate during my reelection. Go ask them. Illinois south of Chicago is solidly Republican, but even in the Windy City, the Democratic stronghold,

I took on the Daley machine and whipped their asses. Ask Adlai. You see, don't you, Hy, why I owe it to Illinoisans to be there on Thursday to launch their supercomputer?"

Strooker held up a hand. "Have you told anyone, or indicated to anyone, your intention to be in Champagne-Urbana next Thursday?"

"I just did. I decided it's too big an event for the Secretary of Defense only."

"Stu Meyers is among the best Defense Secretaries this country's ever had. So says *The New York Times*."

"I'll cut the ribbon. Stu Meyers can dance with the cheerleaders."

"Would you consider sending Vice President Walsh?"

"Never!"

"This could throw our security apparatus haywire, Mr. President. There's been no advance sweeping. We haven't locked up the nuts, sanitized the podium, handpicked local police detail. We haven't even screened the attendees. We've barely got one week."

"That's right. So you'd better get to work right away."

Strooker threw in his last card. "Would you consider, at the very least, using a double?"

"I beg your pardon?" The president pressed the intercom button on his desk. "Didi. Could I have my coffee now, please?"

"Right away, Mr. President."

"What does Creed think about all this?"

"He'll concur with any security arrangements I make. Right now he's busy with that wristwatch Means was wearing when he got iced. The FBI crime lab and the National Transportation Safety Board are taking it apart even as we speak."

Deakin frowned. "What have they got to do with it? I thought they only handled airplane crashes and train derailments."

"Well, yes, sir. They have the equipment for transcribing wire recorders from airliner black boxes. Agents on presidential detail carry a miniaturized version inside their wristwatches. It records last conversations, so to speak, in case of attempted assassinations, or in the event an agent sustains a fatal injury on the job."

"I see. That bad, huh?"

"We suspect foul play in the death of Barry Throck. His pacemaker appears to have been tampered with."

The door opened. Didi Watts entered carrying a silver tray and porcelain coffee pot and milk jug.

"Here you are, Mr. President."

"Thank you, my dear. I'll be ready to see Malcolm as soon as I finish with Mr. Strooker." Malcolm Levy was the Commerce Secretary.

"Just give me a buzz when you are ready, Mr. President."

Didi Watts left. Deakin helped himself to a generous cup and added two teaspoonfuls of sugar and milk. He stirred the coffee.

"Where were we? Oh, yes. You were suggesting we use my double. I think I've seen that fellow on late night TV. Jay Leno or Letterman, can't remember which. He's going all over the place making speeches, opening institutions, and doing stand-up gigs. Who the hell does he think he is, pretending to be me? We can't have him do that, can we, Hy? What will the American people think? They didn't elect the sonuvabitch, they elected me."

"I urge you to reconsider, Mr. President."

"It doesn't matter to hell what I do now. I'm a lame duck anyway." He paused, reflecting. You know, Roosevelt got a third term. It's not likely anyone else ever will. This here I'm doing is for the history books, Hy. It'll look good in my memoirs. I've got to leave enough material for historians to work with."

"The country needs you now, Mr. President. Not in memory."

Deakin shook his head. "Just couldn't do that to Edgar. He worked long and hard on my reelection. Jim and I are pals. We go back a long way. You're not sending any presidential double to Illinois. They deserve presidential material down there on Thursday."

"Vice President Walsh is presidential material. You handpicked him to succeed you. He'll be glad to go in your place."

"Have you discussed it with him?"

"No. He'll be glad to, though. I know so. And let me say this—I stay clear of partisan politics. A man in my position has to. But I daresay Vice

President Walsh will snap up the Illinois trip. He's going to run, won't he, when your incumbency ends? This will be a good start. Strengthen his grassroots campaign."

The president considered this, then nodded. "Okay, you win. We've got to have presidential stuff up there. Dick's as good as any. Isn't that Bob Simon's turf, by the way? Can't stand those Democrats, anyhow. Yeah, let Walsh and Secretary Meyers go to Illinois. The entire country will know the importance of MDS. It's taking up a good chunk of our GNP dollars, so the launch had better be top-heavy with key members of this administration." He took a sip of his coffee and suddenly roared like a wounded bull. He fumbled for the intercom.

"Didi, get in here!"

Didi Watts burst inside, nearly tripping over her high heels.

"This coffee tastes awful, Didi. The milk's curdled. I'm seeing bits of milk curd or something. Do you think I could have some real milk around here for a change?"

"I'll change it right away, Mr. President." Didi looked mortified as she carried the tray away.

"Thank you." The president thrust the *Post* aside, leaned back, and propped his long legs up on the desk. He sighed. "Now I know how Rodney Dangerfield feels."

He gazed up at the ceiling, at the seal of the president of the United States etched in low bas-relief.

"One other thing, Mr. President."

"Yes, Hy."

"I'm changing your bullet-proof vest. I've talked to ballistic experts, military authorities, and two police surgeons. They recommend unanimously the vest I'm going to give you. I tried giving it to you earlier, but your image-makers refused. Too bulky, and since when did Washington, DC, become Baghdad?"

"I already wear a flak vest. What's one with the other?"

"You're wearing a Kevlar five-millimeter lightweight combat armor. It's good basically for shrapnel and Saturday Night Specials fired from a distance. From a high-velocity rifle, protection is about 15 percent. From now on you'll wear a thirteen-millimeter ceramic plate. Weighs about twenty-two pounds versus six pounds for the Kevlar. So there's a big difference in weight, Mr. President. It's worth it, though. It'll withstand high velocity sniper bullets and you've got groin protection as well. It'll fit front and back, fastened with Velcro at the side. It's heavy, Mr. President."

The door opened and Didi Watts came back in bearing a fresh tray of coffee and milk. She laid it down on the side table.

"Here we are. I hope the milk's better this time, Mr. President."

President Deakin poured himself a cup and added milk from the small porcelain jug. He stirred in sugar and took a sip. He beamed.

"This is fine, Didi. Just fine."

"Thank you, Mr. President. Just ring if you want more."

"This should be enough. I imagine Doris will be having me over for lunch."

"The Commerce Secretary is still waiting."

"I know. Just give us a few minutes. Hyram here is concerned about my safety."

She smiled at Strooker. "Can I get you coffee too, Mr. Strooker?"

"No, nothing. Thanks."

Didi Watts left.

"How soon do I get to wear this new combat jacket of yours, Hyram?"

"As soon as the tailor can measure you for a new wardrobe. You'll need bigger suits and shirts to take in the size of the breast- and back-plate."

"I've seen those things on television. SWAT teams and ATF agents when they conduct raids. I'll look like a stuffed teddy bear. I'll be walking like goddamned Donald Duck."

"Better Donald Duck than a dead duck, sir."

The president sipped his coffee. "Damn right."

CHAPTER 5

Washington, DC.

Tammy Weasel hurried inside the ladies' room in the West Wing of the White House. She washed both hands thoroughly with soap and dried them under the noisy hand dryer. Then she chose an empty stall and locked herself inside. Normal people wash their hands after, not before! She deposited her handbag on a clothes peg, and still standing, unbuttoned her gray cotton blouse and unhooked the fasteners. Her full, round breasts were exposed. She shut her eyes for a few seconds while her fingers explored the areolas of both nipples, tracing circles around it. She felt the nipples erect. Her fingers crept to her crotch. Should she? It usually helped the milk expression. Naughty, naughty! She would do that at home, not here in the White House. She sighed as she retrieved the cellophane-wrapped infant's feeding bottle from her handbag. She unscrewed the plastic cap and, holding it and the bottle in one hand for control, she rammed the plastic mouth under her right nipple and began squeezing her breast. The milk spurted in long thin squirts. She alternated to the left nipple. After about five minutes she had collected a good quantity. She screwed back the cap and put the plastic bottle in her handbag. Mission accomplished! For good effect, she flushed the toilet.

She ran both hands down her long auburn hair from front to back. Imagine having to prepare Junior's lunch inside a toilet with all its floating unpleasantness! In this day and age? Perhaps she ought to sue. Way the cookie crumbles. Too bad about yesterday. Too bad about everything. There was no decent way to go about expressing milk in the environment she was in. She preferred doing it standing over the sink in front of the mirror, immediately after washing her hands thoroughly with soap. That was until Julie Berg, her colleague on the First Lady's staff, complained that she found it "disturbing." Besides, some weeks earlier, a male White House staffer had accidentally blundered into the ladies' instead of the gents' and seen the beautiful Tammy Weasel apparently fondling her breasts. She remembered the look on his face as he stuttered, "E-excuse me. Wrong stall," before he fled. Word must have gotten around because in the following weeks, in the hallway and elsewhere, several male staffers had given her long, hard looks and a Secret Service agent had winked knowingly at her. To avoid further speculation Tammy had retreated to doing her thing in the toilet with the door shut.

Damn them all. She would express milk for as long as she wished. Junior was eight months now. Her blond, blue-eyed darling. Two more months of milk expression left, three at the most. Tammy's own mother had believed in breastfeeding a baby the entire first year, and Tammy had followed her example, first with Sandy and now with Junior. Tammy's father was Irish, her mother German by extraction—she'd been Tamara Thompson until she married that jerk Brian. Her technique of milk expression hadn't changed since she had Sandy four years ago. She would breastfeed Junior in the morning using the left nipple. Once the baby was satisfied, Tammy would place him in the crib, put a fresh feeding bottle under her right nipple and express into that. She then made sure Sandy had been seen off to the neighbor's, Mrs. Fierstal, in the condo she had gotten from Brian as part of the separation deal. The expressed milk would be placed inside an ice-filled tiny ice chest like some crucial donor organ about to be rushed to a waiting transplant patient hundreds of miles away. On the way to work she would drop Junior off at the daycare center along with his feeding bottle. At noon the daycare providers warmed up and gave him the milk for his second feeding. If he felt hungry later they had her permission to use normal infant formula to bridge. Around lunchtime at the White House,

Tammy would feel full again and express into a fresh bottle that she kept inside the refrigerator in the cramped First Lady's staff office in the West Wing. After work she would pack the bottle inside the iced food flask again, pick up Junior from daycare and feed him right there at the center or inside the car from the bottle before driving home to Reston. Sensitive subject of breastfeeding in public avoided. Usually Junior would be bawling blazes from nipple deprivation by the time she picked him up. At home, before bedtime, he would get his regular nipple from her.

————

Yesterday. Just too bad about yesterday.

She had retreated to the West Wing staff toilet to express milk. Fumbling for the feeding bottle, it had fallen into the open toilet bowl. Although still sheathed in its cellophane seal, there was no way she was going to use it to feed her child. She'd rolled a thick wad of bathroom tissue around her palm and fished it out. She'd opened the door and pitched everything inside the trashcan. That had done it for the lunchtime expression. Now she knew how milk cows feel when the farm help are late in the morning. She had thought her breasts would explode. In a wooden cabinet beside the office coffee machine she'd found a porcelain milk jug and a small stainless steel one. She'd grabbed the stainless steel set, hurried to the toilet and expressed into it hygienically. Back at the coffee table she'd pulled two strips of plastic wrap and sealed the jug. Using a heavy marker, she'd written the initials T. W. on the wrap. The initials had been visible, the wrap had not been perforated, and she'd placed it inside the refrigerator for retrieval on her way home.

Two hours later Tammy had walked over to the coffee pot and filled a Styrofoam cup with steaming black coffee. She'd stirred in one packet of NutraSweet and stood there a moment savoring the thick coffee aroma, studying the artwork and kindergarten stickers on the refrigerator.

She had heard footsteps and turned to see Didi Watts hurrying toward her, balancing a tray with both hands.

"Oh, Tammy," Didi had cried, "I'm so sorry. I should have told you. I had to borrow your milk and there was no time to ask. He said the milk in his coffee had curdled, and he asked for another cup."

Didi had deposited the tray on the little table beside the coffee machine. With increasing horror Tammy had been able to see the presidential seal inlaid on the silver tray.

"You what?"

"I borrowed your milk," Didi had said, adjusting her steel frame eyeglasses. "It is yours, isn't it? It had the initials T. W. on it."

Tammy had opened the refrigerator door, peered inside, and closed it again. She'd suddenly found it difficult to breathe. "Didi, you *took* my milk."

"I know. I'm sorry. But I've called the kitchen to send over more milk cartons. You can take one of those to replace what I took. Tammy, the president was in such a dither about the milk in his coffee, he wanted another one. Like, fast. I just grabbed the first cup of milk I saw. I figured it belonged to one of the girls and sure enough it had your initials."

"Didi, you don't understand. That was my milk."

"And I took it. Won't do it again, sweetie. Promise, unless I have to. Consider it your bit for Old Glory." She'd given a short laugh, slapped Tammy playfully on the arm, and turned to leave.

"It was breast milk, Didi. For my baby."

Didi had spun around. "What!"

Tammy had nodded. The two women stared at each other, Tammy getting redder in the face.

"Breast milk?" Didi had repeated.

"For my baby. I was saving it for him."

"I thought you stored it in a feeding bottle!"

"I ran out."

"Christ, Tammy, this is icky."

"I know. Did he drink all of it?"

"The president? Yes, he did." She'd looked at the empty jug. "He must have liked it. He used all of it."

The president of the United States had swallowed a full cup of her breast milk.

Tammy had felt rising panic. "Should we call the Poison Control Center?"

"Tammy, don't be milky. What for? It's probably good for him. If it's good for your boy it's even better for him. All that protein and calcium."

"What if the Secret Service finds out? What I mean is, it's unpasteurized."

"So? Listen, kid. I saw him drink that coffee with your milk in it. He was beaming like a kid swiping a hot fudge sundae. He even popped some jellybeans into his mouth. When I came back to pick up the tray he says to me, 'That was good coffee, Didi. Did you put a little salt in the milk? Tastes good. I want the same every time you make my coffee, okay?' And I say, 'Yes, Mr. President,' and I zap on out of there. Now we both know the secret ingredient . . ." She'd leaned closer to Tammy and winked. "Maybe we'll feed it to him from now on. Nobody would be any wiser."

Tammy had pushed the hair out of her eyes. "Didi, we can't do that. I . . . it's obscene. Besides, my milk can only go on for a couple more months. Junior's almost nine months now."

"What'll I tell him when he asks why I couldn't make the same perfect cup of coffee like I did the other day?"

"Tell him maybe the jelly beans affected his taste buds. Tell him it's the same milk from the packet you're using."

"A thought anyway."

"Thanks, but no thanks."

Didi had studied the other woman carefully, her hazel eyes large and intelligent behind her thick lenses. She'd shrugged. "You know, he did ask for real milk. He sure got it."

As she'd driven home that evening Tammy kept glancing at the rearview mirror, expecting to see at any moment the blue flash of police lights. Or maybe the Secret Service would put an unmarked car on her tail. They might arrest her as she stepped into her apartment. Her ex-husband Brian was a lawyer, and she could almost see the docket.

That you, Tamara Ann Weasel, did expose the president of the United States to an untreated substance known as mother's milk, in that you exposed him to, and did cause him to ingest an untreated substance known as mother's milk in his coffee, thereby putting the president of the United States in danger of receiving a bodily harm.

But there had been no screaming sirens. No police cruisers pulling off the curb to cut her off. She'd picked up Junior at the daycare. He'd looked bubbly and healthy, clutching at her face, his pudgy baby hands flailing, his teething gums exposed in a smile of recognition. She'd kissed him on the forehead, thanked the daycare staff, and strapped Junior to the baby carriage in the backseat. She'd given him a pacifier and pulled a pink, woolen baby cap over his head. Then she'd headed for the Beltway evening traffic leaving the capital.

She had been home in thirty-five minutes. She'd parked the Cavalier among the rows of cars in the crowded parking lot of the Candletree Condominium complex. Carrying Junior in one hand and her handbag and flask in the other, she'd trudged up the outside staircase to the second floor and rang the bell at Mrs. Fierstal's door. The door had opened to reveal an arthritic dowager with wire-frame glasses and enough lines on her face to give Clint Eastwood a run for his money.

"I'm home," Tammy had announced.

"So I see," Mrs. Fierstal had said. "Had a nice day today?"

"Can't complain."

"I had a nice day too." She had a thin reedy voice. "The doctor's visit turned out okay. My cholesterol is fine and my rheumatism appears to have taken the week off. I got back about noon, and this afternoon some idiot salesman called me with a pitch about selling me insurance that would pick up the things that Medicare didn't. Guaranteed."

"You didn't buy?"

"I told him what he could do with his scam. I tell you, Tammy dear, it's getting harder and harder to keep a dollar to yourself. Everyone seems to want to take it from you."

"Hi, Mommy." Sandy Weasel had appeared at the door beside Mrs. Fierstal. She didn't have her mother's startling carrot hair; hers was brown and her face was a younger version of Tammy's. She'd been munching on cornbread.

"Hi, honey." Tammy had kissed her on the forehead. "Had a nice day at school?"

"Yes." She'd uncurled her fist to thwart the next question. "Mrs. Fierstal gave me corn cake."

"That's cornbread, honey," Mrs. Fierstal had said.

"Well, isn't that nice? And what do we say, Sandy?"

"Thank you, Mrs. Fierstal."

"You're welcome, sweetie." The dowager had beamed. The wrinkled face had seemed to break into hundreds of pieces, then rearranged itself again. "How's Junior, today? Behaving himself, is he?"

"He's an angel. Not a sound today."

"They catch on, you know. You bet they do."

"They certainly do." Tammy had taken Sandy by the hand. "Thanks a lot, Nelly. We'll be seeing you tomorrow."

"Sure thing, Tammy. Just ring."

———

In Strooker's office at the Executive Office Building next door to the White House, Dwight and his boss examined the two reports just in by e-mail. Strooker sat in the same chair Chief U. E. Baughman had used decades earlier. The two reports on his desk had been sent less than one hour apart. The first was from the NTSB lab, the other from Multimedics, Inc., makers of heart pacemakers. The NTSB, an independent agency, usually took its time unraveling the probable causes of airplane mishaps by painstakingly transcribing the cockpit voice recorder and analyzing the flight data recorder of downed aircraft; however, it had, with pressure from 1600 Penn., transcribed the last words of Special Agent Means in record time.

Beginning of transcript:

> *"Fox Detail, Agent Means . . . (undecipherable) Throck . . . (gurgle) JFK Continental . . . (undecipherable) next Monday contact. Smurf One . . . not safe . . ."*
> End of transcript.

Both men remained silent for a full minute. Agent Means had gasped out his last words in obvious pain, trying desperately to communicate something before the last waves of oblivion drowned him. Strooker thrust the paper at Dwight.

"Look at this, Ken. The transcribers couldn't possibly have known who Throck was. And we'd better tell them to work harder on those undecipherables—and the gurgle. We might learn something there."

"Right." Dwight was thoughtful. "The Smurf One, Priority Threat is a red flag." Smurf One was that month's code name for the president. It could be changed weekly, monthly, or even retained. In his agony Means had remembered, and clearly thought there was a real threat to the president's life. "I'm not aware of the president having any itinerary at the New York Continental."

"Neither am I. The other report—tell me what you make of it."

Dwight perused the report from Multimedics, Inc. The pacemaker from Throck's heart was a lithium-powered generator type, built to last about seven years before needing replacement. Multimedics could not say for sure who had made that particular pacemaker, but said that it appeared to have originated in Eastern Europe. It was a demand-type pacemaker, meaning that it did not have a fixed rate of beating and that the stimulating electrode could be made to beat at a low or high rate from a programmable source. The present setting of the beat rate, done by remote programming, could have resulted in a ventricular beat of fewer than six to ten beats per minute, which would be unable to sustain life. The patient would suffer a Stokes-Adams syncope (a sudden faint) and die from a cessation of the heartbeat. There were supposed to be impregnable safeguards to prevent pacemakers from ever allowing such a low heart rate. Multimedics incorporated such safeguards in all their pacemakers and had never recorded any malfunction in any of their products. In their opinion—and from independent tests—this particular pacemaker didn't have a high beat protection either. The patient could just as easily have been overwhelmed by a heart rate in excess of three hundred beats per minute, which they were able to reproduce in the pacemaker using their testing equipment. Limit loads on either side according to specifications set down by the Food and Drug Administration and the American College of Cardiologists, should never exceed bradycardia or tachycardia limits.

Strooker stated, "Throck was murdered."

"So was Means. He wore a body mike and they grabbed that, too. You could see where they tugged off the adhesive. Whatever Throck said to him is lost to us. Except the bit he managed to say into his wrist mike."

"Right. Now we've got to find out who murdered them. We think we know why."

"I'll get on to this Continental business right away. That would be a start."

"Good. How many Continentals in New York? Must be more than one."

Dwight shrugged. "Maybe five or more within the city. Much more than that if you include the entire state."

"Have our New York field office get on it. The president isn't going to be in New York the whole of this month or the next. If he's to address the UN General Assembly, we haven't been told yet. He won't be anywhere near a Continental Inn, so I can't quite figure out the connection yet." Strooker sighed. "Still, Means died getting that message to us. We've got to eat up every word in that tape."

"We'll check all New York Continental Inn bookings for the rest of the month. We'll start with the city. If we don't get any hits we'll work on next month's bookings."

"Yeah. That's standard. Please do."

"Chief, I take it you're vetoing further presidential travel until we know more about this threat?"

"I did. Can't make it too obvious, though. We'll play it close. Ken, I want you to put our best field agents on this. All the overtime they can handle. You too. I doubt you'll get much sleep for the next couple of weeks. You're used to it by now. Borrow agents from Counterfeiting if you have to. Let's crack this one."

"Yes, Chief."

"This is joint jurisdiction. The FBI is in. Creed gets briefed as we go along. We've worked joint before with Fibbies. This is no different."

———

The first lead came in from the 26 Federal Plaza (23rd Floor) of the FBI New York field office. One Barry Throck had a confirmed reservation at the JFK Continental for Friday and Saturday that week. It was made on an AmEx card issued to Barry Throck. The reservation had been made a week earlier. Dwight spoke personally to the field agent.

"Where did the reservation originate?"

"The hotel made a note on the reservation that the caller would be arriving by Aer Lingus and would like to be picked up by the hotel courtesy van. That would indicate that the person who made the reservation would be arriving from Ireland. Aer Lingus also confirms subject of the same name booked an Economy ticket to arrive in New York Friday evening. We checked all Continental Inns within the boroughs of New York City up to Staten Island and Long Island for coincidental bookings. All negative."

"Good. We'll concentrate on the JFK Continental. I want two agents there around the clock. Tomorrow's Thursday. This guy Throck is deceased, but he was a vital contact. We want to know if anyone uses the reservation or calls to cancel. If anyone checks in using the reservation, we want full room surveillance and wire tap. Warrants are on the way. If they call to cancel, find out where the call originated. And if anyone comes to the front desk to ask to see a Throck lodged there, we want that person or persons put under surveillance. No arrests yet. We want to see where he or she leads us. You'll need a Federal judge for the warrants, so get going. I'll fax the complaints and reasonable suspicion affidavits to you."

"Got you."

"Any questions?"

"You say this guy Throck is deceased. What if someone with that name boards the Aer Lingus flight in Dublin headed for New York?"

"I don't think so. That would be an interesting development though. That passenger becomes our man and the whole thing will make less sense than it already does."

"Thought I'd ask."

"I want to be informed of any developments. Call me here or at home. Anytime."

"Right, sir."

CHAPTER 6

New York.

Miskos Venovich hauled a battered duffel bag inside the lobby of the JFK Continental. The whole thing still sounded screwy. Some rich dude or whatever he was had paid him a lot of money to lodge in a hotel and take a telephone call. Weird, if you thought about it. But this was a public hotel; Miskos could choose any room he wanted within the budget provided, and if nothing else, he prided himself on being able to take care of himself. The money was good for one night's work.

He headed for the reception counter. He wore scuffed brown cowboy boots, a pair of Levi's, and a red-checkered shirt. He omitted the hat. It was as respectable as he could get to match his new persona. The desk clerk looked up with a smile.

"Welcome to Continental. May I be of service to you?"

"I booked a room. Throck."

It was hard, but the clerk kept on smiling. For just one nanosecond the smile had frozen in place. Venovich didn't notice. Desk clerks—at least the ones he'd known, mostly from seedy joints—didn't smile. He assumed that in a place such as the Continental, clerks smiled a lot. Professionally.

Behind Venovich, on one of the lobby divans adjacent to the main entrance, a man in a gray business suit lowered his newspaper a fraction. He had a clear view of the new guest. The man adjusted the volume of the plug-in hearing aid he wore inside his left ear. The mike was actually the second button on the desk clerk's coat, sewn on just hours earlier by

Secret Service agents. The conversation from the counter floated into his ear effortlessly.

A female clerk sorting letters into room pigeonholes, with her back to the counter, paused in her work. The batch she was sorting fell to the floor. She scooped them up, made a token gesture of filing an errant letter—just one letter—before returning to her desk with the remainder. She busied herself on a file. She was tall and thin and wore steel-rim eyeglasses, the studious secretary or sultry academician. She was careful not to look up at the counter. Too careful, Venovich noticed. He shrugged inwardly. He hadn't done anything wrong. And he didn't intend to.

His own clerk looked down at his computer screen.

"Let's see here." He tapped keys. "Throck. Throck . . . There you are. You reserved for two days, sir?"

"That's right. But I changed my mind. Ink me out for tomorrow."

The clerk stared at his computer screen. "You want to cancel tomorrow's booking—is that correct, sir?"

"That's what I said. I'm just staying one day now."

Cheapskate, thought all three Secret Service agents and the lone FBI agent listening in.

"Right." The clerk tapped more keys. "Here we are. And how do you intend to pay for the room, sir?"

"Cash."

The clerk looked up in surprise. "Your reservation was confirmed on an AmEx card. You now want me to issue a cash slip?"

"Uh, right."

"I am sorry, sir. I would need a credit card for you to check in."

Miskos had been told to expect it. He pulled out his Capital One card. Almost maxed out, but there should be enough to take care of two day's hotel rent.

It did.

"No problem," the clerk said when he'd finished with the card. "I just need some identification, please."

Miskos's blood pounded in his temples. But he hadn't been a New York cabby all these years for nothing.

"Uh, yes." Miskos coughed phlegmatically. "What you need?"

"Driver's license, passport, anything."

Miskos all but scratched his head. "Uh, well, you see, Barry's got it."

"Barry?"

"Yeah. Throck. That's my buddy. He'll show up later."

"I see. Then you're a party of two reserving the same room?"

"Yeah. We're . . . pals. We haven't had problems . . . this many questions before. We could go to another hotel if you guys don't like my kind of people here."

The desk clerk hesitated. It was on his lips to say, "I'll have to ask my supervisor."

Dammit, *he* was the supervisor. His ID card said so, and the man had seen it. When Federal agents approached him to help set up the surveillance, he'd decided he couldn't afford having any of the junior clerks screw up an obviously important operation. He'd pulled rank, given the guy on evening shift the day off, and manned the front desk himself. Now he was about to screw it up. What if the guy left? What if Throck showed up later and turned out to be real big fish—a United States senator, say? Or a congressman? Could even be a top White House aide. Damned faggots everywhere, right up to the apex. Why else would the Feds be interested? He, the manager, might learn something. Save it for the *Washington Post* or *The New York Times*. Perhaps a book deal with Simon & Schuster.

He walked to the partition between the key rack and the back office and pretended to search for an available key. The door to the manager's office—his office—was open and the Secret Service man posing as him gave him a nod. The manager relaxed. The book deal was still on. Might even throw in a few talk shows. Jay Leno or Oprah. He hurried back to the counter.

"No trouble at all, sir." The clerk's smile was plastic. "Pardon me if I sounded a bit . . . inquisitive."

"Damn right, you were." Miskos pulled out a scuffed driver's license, and handed it to the clerk. "Had it on me afterall. Sorry. No offense."

"That's all right, sir. We at Continental are always at your service and ready to help anyway we could.." *I would have fired a staffer for those clichéd words..* The clerk moved to the computer terminal again. "Let's see. That'll be—"

"Tell you what. Make it two days as before. Put it all on the card.. Barry might want to stay an extra day. Sorry if I'm sounding like an ass pickle." *What the hell's that? A new word spawned by the gay community?* Miskos smiled. He could always say, well, his pal never did show up.

"Not at all. You could always get the unused day refunded, less applicable fees, if you check out earlier." The manager cancelled the first invoice, balled up the printout, and flung it into a waste bin. He tapped more keys. A new invoice sheet rolled off the printer. "Here we are. That'll be three hundred sixty three dollars sixteen cents, including tax."

Miskos pressed a five dollar tip on the manager's palm.

The manager didn't blink. "Thank you, sir." He handed over the keys. "Room 4003. Enjoy your stay."

The manager watched the savvy youth lope over to the elevators, carrying his duffel. He would be the queen, the manager guessed. The man from Washington would be powerful, domineering, a power broker in a city where power is the major aphrodisiac. The manager sighed and ran thick fingers over his neatly groomed hair. He intended to man the counter all night—he didn't want to miss this Throck fellow when he showed up. He saw himself appearing before a congressional ethics committee, answering questions behind a bank of microphones while network cameras panned over him in the packed hearing room. His childhood love who had spurned him, leaving him to marry his current wife, might even see his face on the news and give him a belated call to set things right. He smiled.

Miskos Venovich was thinking: *Well, eleven hundred dollars left, after I deduct the plastic money. I'm earning every bit of it.*

———

At 11 p.m. Dwight was still at his desk. The White House was almost deserted. The floodlights were in place, illuminating in a dash of brilliance the front portico, the iridescent fountain, the yellow bloom of chrysanthemums. Dwight drank his second cup of coffee that evening—the sixth for the day—and pored over reports from Room 98, the notorious Threats room. At 11:10 p.m., the fax beeped and began feeding paper.

DISCREET SURVEILLANCE. AUDIO
ROOM 4003, JFK CONTINENTAL INN,
QUEENS, NY
Attention: Kenneth W. Dwight, Treasury
From: Sidney H. Feldstein, Special Agent

SUBJECT: Male white, 20ish, 6'1", brown hair, green eyes, sideburns. Attire: brown cowboy boots, red plaid shirt, blue jeans.

NAME: John Doe. Took room under booking of B. Throck. Credit card name: Miskos Venovich.

DATE: October 24, (Redacted)

Surveillance Report

5:46 p.m. Subject checks into Room 4003, a double room.

5:49 p.m. Subject turns on television set. Flips through channels. Settles on basketball game on ESPN. Lakers vs. Knicks.

6:01 p.m. Subject calls room service. Orders twelve pack of Schlitz Light, a bottle of Dewars Label Scotch.

6:12 p.m. Beer and Scotch delivered. Room service waiter departs.

6:16 p.m. Crumpling sound of empty beer can heard.

6:25 p.m. Second crumpling sound. Subject belches.

6:50 p.m. Third beer can demolished.
6:53 p.m. Subject farts. Says, "Damn good."

6:58 p.m. Subject calls Guliano's Pizza and orders Large Pizza (thin crust) with everything, no anchovies.

7:32 p.m. Pizza delivered. Delivery boy quotes price of $17.67. Subject hands over money and says, "Keep the change." Delivery boy says, "Thanks a lot." Sound of delivery boy's exit.

7:35 p.m. Subject works on pizza, slurps beer. Fourth beer can crumpled.

7"53 p.m. Subject belches. Switches TV channel to rerun of *Hogan's Heroes*.

7:56 p.m. Subject moves to bathroom and takes explosive craps. The words "Sh-it!" are heard after the first salvo.

8:11 p.m. Crumpling of beer can. At this time operatives estimate subject has consumed five cans of beer.

8:20 p.m. Snoring sounds heard. Indications are that subject is presently asleep with the *Mary Tyler Moore Show* (re-run) the featured program.

9:32 p.m. Subject awakens. Flips through TV channels. Settles on HBO film, *Visiting Hours*. Laughs loudly. Farts.

10:08 p.m. Subject places telephone call to a Manhattan number. Call answered by female who identifies herself as Sue, Sex Hotline, and did subject want a voice massage or a voice do-me (sic).

Subject queried what was available. Female listed menu, depicting things she would do or say over the telephone, such things being said in a manner calculated to cause subject's genitals to rise, inducing pleasure to himself and her. If subject was so inclined, the roles could be reversed and he could do things to himself and utter profanities or love-words that would make both of them come (sic) together. Conversation was terminated when female subject asked male subject for his credit credit card number for the billing. Subject mumbled, "Uh . . . um, I don't think I want to be doing that," and hung up.

The fax stopped briefly. Dwight was furious. Who did Feldstein think he was? A pulp novelist? The fax spewed out more paper.

At 10:49 p.m. subject left his room and took the elevator down to the lobby. He visited the magazine and gift shop and was observed by operatives to purchase one copy each of *Club* and *Hustler*. Subject bought a copy of *USA Today* and covered the girlie magazines he had bought with the newspaper. He also bought a jar of Jergens Moisturizing Hand Cream and a pack of Camel cigarettes. On passing the front desk on his way to elevator, night manager waved to subject and said, "Your pal show up yet?" Subject shook his head and said, "Naw. He'll be late."

Subject returned to room.

11:06 p.m. Room audio records sounds of magazine pages being turned.
11:16 p.m. A loud gasp, followed by heaving sounds. Agents Feldstein, VanDiver, and Getz, monitoring audio, rush to battle stations and turn up the volume thinking subject has been attacked by unknown assailants in room. Further audio sounds reveal however subject's gasp to be self-inflicted and of pleasure, not pain. Onanist sounds continue until 10:23 p.m.

11:34 p.m. Sound of beer can opening.

11:50 p.m. Sound of beer can opening. Slurping sounds.

00:12 a.m. Subject resumes snoring.

00:30 a.m. Subject assumed asleep. TV set turned off.

The report ended. Dwight looked at his watch. Almost 2 a.m. He searched the Rolodex for the New York field office in Queens and dialed. A sleepy agent answered.

"Queens field office. Duffy speaking."

"Ken Dwight from DC. I just got Feldstein's report. What the hell are you guys playing at—Candid Camera or factual reporting?"

Special Agent Duffy hesitated. "It's . . . Feldstein, sir. He gets carried away."

"He missed his true vocation. He should be writing pornography for a living."

"I agree, sir."

"I want to talk to him."

"He just left. He filed his report and went home, along with Getz and VanDiver."

"Who's monitoring the suspect?"

"Three special ops guys. Change of shift. Feldstein and co. will be back in the morning."

"Yeah, okay. Tell those jokers I don't want the hotel maids tampering with the suspect's room. Anything that leaves his room, I want analyzed. His garbage, beer cans, the lot. Nothing is thrown away. You got that, Duffy?"

"Count on it, sir."

"Good. I'm going home. Call me at home if something breaks overnight. I'll be with you guys in the morning. I'll be on the 7 o'clock Delta shuttle. Is that clear?"

"Yes, sir."

"Goodnight, Duffy."

"Goodnight, sir."

Dwight picked up his coat, turned off the lights, and went home.

CHAPTER 7

New York.

Miskos Venovich felt good. 9:55 a.m. He'd eaten a good breakfast. Eggs Benedict, two slices of toast, two bacon crusts, a pot of coffee, tall glass of orange juice. The orange juice had chased down the two tablets of Extra Strength Tylenol for the massive headache he'd nursed all morning. Despite the hangover, he felt good. He was expecting two calls. In a few minutes the phone would ring, first the one, then the other. He'd answer each one and then get the hell out of there, eleven hundred dollars richer. Fastest buck he'd ever made.

At precisely 10 a.m. plus twenty-three seconds, the telephone rang. Miskos picked it up.

"Throck speaking," he said briskly.

A gruff voice, like gravel churning in a cement mixer, came over. "It's a go, boy. A go. Go for it. Good luck."

The line went dead.

For a moment Miskos panicked, wondering if he had done his part correctly. He had followed "Throck's" instructions implicitly and he couldn't fault himself. He relaxed. Nothing to it. One down, one to go. Now for the call from the real Throck.

He didn't wait long. The phone rang again ten minutes later.

"Throck speaking," Miskos said.

"Did he call?"

"Who? Did who call?"

"Come off it, Miskos. This is your friend at the bar." This caller too was garbled. It seemed that every caller had a Midas muffler stuck up his nose. But the voice was definitely the stranger from the bar, the one paying for the hotel spree.

"Oh. Sorry, I got lost for a moment. Yeah, he did. He said it's a go. I repeat, a go."

"Thank you. Good work. You're a free man now. Enjoy your money."

"Thanks, buddy." But Miskos was talking to a dial tone.

In fifteen minutes Miskos had packed his duffel bag and appeared downstairs to ask for his refund.

"Checking out?" The manager's smile was wintry.

"That's right."

The manager was tired and beady-eyed. He had worked a marathon shift, having called the morning shift clerk on the telephone telling him to stay at home, that he was covered, that he the manager would punch him in and out of the time clock so he wouldn't lose any income. It had been a gamble and the manager had lost. It was happening right in front of him. This damned Throck fellow was leaving, no fireworks had gone off, his dreams of hiring a media publicist and putting his story rights on the auction block were going up in smoke right before his eyes.

The manager made a show of consulting his computer terminal. He then strode back to the side filing cabinet, obscuring the counter from his open office door. The two Secret Service agents in his office wearing headphones gave him a thumbs-up sign. So the bum would be allowed to leave. The manager had truly lost. He returned to the counter wrote up the refund.

"Your pal never did show up?" He didn't look up.

What is it to you? Screw you, asshole.

"No," Miskos said.

Miskos collected his duffel bag and walked through the huge automatic glass doors that hissed open as he approached and swung shut as he passed. He signaled for a taxi. The first yellow cab in the rank quickly pulled up. Miskos got in and gave an address on Tilden Avenue in Brooklyn. The taxi pulled out.

At least nine pairs of eyes watched the taxi as it left the Continental driveway into the adjoining access road and headed for the Van Wyck Expressway.

Ken Dwight sat in an unmarked car with a Secret Service driver and two FBI agents and watched the yellow cab drive away. They were covered. FBI agents posing as cab drivers manned the first three taxis in the queue. Dwight spoke into his portable transceiver.

"Alright, Feldstein. Move in. I want Room 4003 sealed. Everything in the trash hauled down to the field office for analysis."

"Right."

Dwight now palmed the Service mike in the car dash. "Central from Bulldog One."

"Go ahead, Bulldog."

"Did you get a trace on the calls?"

"The first call originated from Washington, DC. We can't be absolutely certain but it appears to have originated from the Capitol Hill area. We couldn't get an exact fix."

"The second call?"

"The party hung up too fast. I'd say the Jamaica Bay area is our best shot. Definitely New York area. I think—hang on a minute . . ."

There was static on the line, background noise. Central came back.

"Okay. A definite fix on the first call. Cell phone from the Capitol. Best we can do."

"Shit."

"Sorry, sir."

Dwight beckoned to the Service driver. "Let's move it. Keep a safe distance."

———

Nabil had called a taxi forty minutes earlier. The taxi came at eight minutes to ten and pulled in at the filling station mart where he was waiting. Nabil gave the driver the address of an Amoco filling station about five blocks away from the JFK Continental. The taxi arrived there at four minutes past ten. Nabil told the driver to park near the lube bay, adjacent to the toilet. The cabbie pulled the meter lanyard down to bill time instead of distance travelled. Nabil entered the gents' and stayed inside for nearly five minutes, doing absolutely nothing. He came out tugging at his trouser belt and headed for the pay phone on the other side of the pumps.

"Hey," the cabbie yelled. "What's with you? You gonna keep me here all day?"

Nabil retraced steps and handed the cabbie two twenties.

"I've got a phone call to make," he said. "This is your advance. I'll be keeping you quite a while. Just tell me when you need more money."

The forty dollars quieted the driver. "Be my guest, pal," he said.

The pay phone was one of those metallic boxes set at car height so you could park real close and dial without getting out. Three such phone banks were placed at two car-length intervals on the lot. Two banks were unoccupied. Nabil chose one and slotted in a quarter. He dialed the Continental Inn number.

"Continental Inn, may I help you?"

"Mr. Throck, please."

"Is he a guest at the hotel?" The switchboard operator snapped her fingers silently at the Service man next to her. He came alive, bending over his own hastily assembled switchboard, moving a rotary dial on a control panel.

"Yes," Nabil said.

"One moment." She paused, looking at the Service man. She already knew the room number. The agent gave her encouraging signals with his free left hand. The signals meant "Stall him, Stall him."

Eight seconds.

"He's in Room 4003," she said finally. "I'll connect you."

The caller had hung up.

"Hello? Hello?" She turned to the agent. "He hung up. Any good?"

"Maybe. Too quick to tell." The Service man kept his face deadpan. He wasn't about to tell her he had a positive fix near the hotel.

Nabil had hung up immediately when he sensed the operator was stalling him. He surreptitiously wiped his prints off the phone using the handkerchief he'd placed over the mouthpiece. The adjacent telephone port was now clear, the previous caller walking away. Nabil fumbled with the coin return to give the impression the phone was bad, then sidled over to the vacant port. He dialed the hotel again, handkerchief over mouthpiece.

"Continental, may I help you?"

"This is Special Agent Severino, Federal Bureau of Investigation. Give me Room 4003."

"One moment, please." The operator started to make the connection, then caught herself.

"Did you say 4003? I thought—"

"That's quite alright," Nabil said. "I'm the Special Agent-in-Charge. Put me through, lady. This is important."

"Excuse me, sir. I was told . . ."

The connection went through and Nabil heard the magic words, "Throck speaking."

"Did he call?"

"Who? Did who call?"

"Come off it, Miskos. This is your friend at the bar."

"Oh. Sorry, I got lost for a moment." Nabil could hear him catching his breath. "Yeah, he did. He said it's a go. I repeat, a go."

"Thank you. Good work. You're a free man now. Enjoy your money."

The line clicked dead.

Nabil wiped off his fingerprints, hoping the taxi driver was not looking at him. A dark blue Buick Skylark with a middle-aged couple inside had pulled into the next port. Nabil tried not to hurry as he walked back to the taxi, got in beside the driver and told him the JFK Continental. The driver started to object, then remembered the forty dollars the man had deposited. No problem, less than five blocks to the Continental. The meter lanyard went up to mileage billing and the cab pulled away. Nabil was glad to be out of there. The place would be crawling with agents in minutes. He respected American surveillance technology enough to know that.

"Surprised they still have them thingies," the cabbie said.

"What?"

"Payphones. Who needs them? Cells everywhere."

"Yeah. Got you," Nabil said. "Once in while you need to use a real phone with a real directory."

The cabbie nodded sagely. "Know what you mean."

There were six taxicabs in the Continental pick-up concourse. Nabil told the driver to pull in behind the last cab in the queue.

"Can't pick a fare from here," the cabbie said. "Ain't allowed to."

"I know." Nabil didn't. "Please cooperate with me. It's my wife. I think she's having an affair. She's holed up in there with someone. I just played a prank on them. I want to see him come dashing out." As he spoke Nabil pressed another twenty-dollar bill into the man's knuckle gripped around the steering wheel.

"Anything you say, boss."

The cab queue moved up only two spaces before Miskos appeared, carrying a worn duffel bag, and ducked into the first cab in the queue. The taxi with Miskos in it pulled out. The other cabs moved up in the queue. Nabil watched a dark green sedan ease out of the parking lot into the driveway and disappear behind the access road. Another sedan, a gray Plymouth Volare, crunched gravel as it swung in behind the first. The lead cab in the queue also pulled out—without a fare. Yet another gray sedan with three men in it went after the taxi in the macabre merry-go-round.

Two men each in the first two vehicles, three in the fourth, not counting the lone taxi driver. These men were specialists. Nabil had seen enough specialists—secret police, deep cover agents, homicide detectives, and subversive experts—he could almost always spot them without difficulty. The men in the sedans wore windbreakers over open-necked casuals and plain Western-style summer shirts. They all had crew-cut hair, the faces and profiles were clean, the jawlines set, the physiques athletic.

They were trying hard to look normal and failing badly. Everything about them screamed law enforcement and J. Edgar Hoover.

Nabil knew for sure.

Somehow or other the FBI and Secret Service knew about Throck's rendezvous at the Continental. He told the driver he'd seen all he wanted and asked to be taken to an address in downtown Manhattan. He was very thoughtful as the taxi pulled out. Did they know about Illinois? How come Boris had given a "Go" signal when government agents were sniffing at his (Nabil's) heels? Or was the FBI's knowledge of the plot very limited?

Questions, questions, questions.

He got off on the East Side, giving the cab driver a generous tip. He walked two blocks to an eatery and called another cab. This time to the busy Greyhound terminal where he collected his briefcase and overnight valise from the left-luggage locker. He surrendered his key, paid the tab, and entered yet another cab, giving an address in front of the United Nations building. He asked the cab to stop at the corner of East Forty-Sixth Street and the UN Plaza, paid the meter, and stood with his belongings on the curbside as if undecided. After a minute he started to walk away from the plaza. A black Oldsmobile Ciera pulled up beside him. The driver, a blond Cossack type whose two-piece suit couldn't quite hide his massive biceps, gave Nabil a thumbs-up sign. Nabil threw his valise into the backseat and got in beside the driver. The car moved swiftly into the stream of traffic toward La Guardia.

The Cossack held out his right palm. "Gun."

Nabil surrendered the Browning.

"Bullets."

Nabil retrieved the valise from the backseat and handed over the cartridge boxes. Driving with one hand the Cossack shoved the entire artillery under the seat. He said, "You'll get them back in Urbana, Illinois."

"Where is Yuri Zamyatin?"

The Cossack looked him over. "I not talk," he said coldly, and concentrated totally on his driving.

Nabil changed his appearance yet again as the car descended into the Queens Midtown Tunnel, up briefly through the Long Island Expressway, cutting north to the Brooklyn-Queens Expressway on up to Grand Central Parkway. By the time the car pulled into La Guardia he was once again a clean-shaven marketing executive on his way to a business convention in Chicago. The fake beard and mustache went in the glove compartment. The valise was sanitized—nothing incriminating inside. The airport screening devices would give him a clean bill. The Cossack dropped him off at the American Airlines terminal and sped off without a second glance. *What's his beef?* wondered Nabil.

After an hour-and-fifty-minute wait Nabil boarded an American flight to O'Hare. In Chicago he rented an Olds Cutlass from the O'Hare Avis, bought some road maps, and headed out the busy expressway to join Interstate 57 south to Champaign-Urbana. That evening he checked into the Howard Johnson's in Urbana.

CHAPTER 8

Washington, DC.

"There must be a hundred prints on that payphone," Dwight said to the man in the FBI Crime Lab in Washington, DC. ,

"Not really," said the Fibby. "The last caller obviously wiped the receiver with a handkerchief after use."

"Damn."

"Same thing I said. On the other phones, there's smudges, most of them overlapping. We call them clutter. Might be able to work on those. Wouldn't hold out much hope though."

"I want them quick," Dwight said. "How soon can I get the first matched prints from NCIC?"

"Long shot, like I said. Day or two."

"Yeah. Okay. Worth a try."

"Sure."

Dwight hung up, feeling frustrated. They had gotten a definite fix on the Amoco gas station and food mart just a few blocks from the Continental. Agents had rushed in to secure the place and fingerprints men had dusted and lifted. Only two oily smudges had been found. Expert hands had wiped the receiver clean. They had turned their attention to the gas station layout: two-thirds of the pumps were self-service, the others full-service. The telephone ports were closest to the self-service pumps, so any witnesses would be long gone. Three full-service attendants were present. No, they couldn't remember anything unusual. One attendant had seen a yellow cab parked over there—he pointed to the suspect port—and a totally nondescript man making a phone call. An FBI sketch artist spent some time with him, but he had only been able to make out the man's profile and back features; the attendant hadn't seen the man's face fully. There was a hidden security camera covering the cashier's station inside the mart and this had been impounded. However, it was unlikely that the suspect had been inside the mart.

The Secret Service grabbed Miskos Venovich when it became apparent he wasn't going to lead them to the head honcho. At first the burly Serbian growled that he wasn't talking, demanded a lawyer, and said that he knew his rights. He threatened to sue everyone to the Supreme Court if he wasn't released immediately. Agents were unimpressed and sat him down at the field office to confront him with the available evidence. They hinted that they could throw a few favors his way if he cooperated, perhaps talk to the judge when his day in court came up, perhaps lean on ICE regarding his immigration status—oh yes, they knew he had overstayed his visitor's visa by several years.

Miskos Venovich melted after that. He sang like a lark. He sounded incredulous when he said he knew nothing of any threats—it had only been a way to make a quick buck by lodging in a luxury hotel room and taking a phone call. His story had the ring of truth, though as per investigators' habit, they acted as though they didn't believe him. A hastily arranged polygraph confirmed the likelihood he was telling the truth. An Identi-Kit artist worked with him to produce a likeness of the person Miskos had met at the bar. The face was generic, male, white, bearded—could have been the face of former surgeon-general C. Everett Koop or the Ayatollah Khomeini depending on the angle one viewed it at.

Kent Murphy, the Service's legal adviser, recommended that Miskos be released for lack of sufficient evidence. He was asked not to leave town without consulting the FBI. Dwight put him under twenty-four-hour surveillance then called back Kent Murphy.

"Murph, what's with you guys over there? The man who called our perp also impersonated a Fed. Said he was Special Agent in Charge."

"Wrong. We don't have those in New York. Assistant Director-in-Charge."

"That's what I thought.' Dwight sighed. "And our bigfoot meatbeater—what are we going to charge him with? You guys come up with anything yet?"

"I'm sorry, Ken. We just don't have enough to hold him on. Not the money, not the audio." Miskos had $1688 and some loose change on him in genuine money when arrested—money he claimed the stranger paid him, plus his room refund and personal cash.

"You heard the audio—all of it?"

"All the seamy stuff."

"And you're telling me we can't hang him on that alone?"

"Not a bit. Sick, maybe. But nothing to make him a target for a crime of moral turpitude. Not even a misdemeanor."

"You got to be kidding. I know of at least one charge you can hang on him."

"What's that?"

"Excessive masturbation."

Dwight slammed down the telephone.

———

Champaign-Urbana.
Nabil walked across the quadrangle, past the two unmarked service cars at the side entrance, to the front doors of the Computer Sciences Building entrance. The unmarked cars probably belonged to the Secret Service advance party for the vice president's visit on Friday. Outside the building on the east side, workmen were putting the finishing touches on newly erected benches. A large podium stood before them, and the whole scene was marked and contained by yellow tape reminiscent of police crime scenes. Two uniformed campus security officers stood at the building entrance, one holding a portable metal detector. Nabil held up a battered university ID card. The guard scrutinized it. With more

than 45,000 full- and part-time students, the University of Illinois ID card was easy to come by in the Twin Cities. Although he wore an old Fighting Illini sweatshirt, a pair of old jeans, and had even hooked an iPod to his belt in an effort to appear as student-like as possible, the campus officer was not impressed.

"Been a while," he said, noting the expired ID.

"Yeah. Like to keep in touch."

The policeman handed back the ID, and his colleague scanned Nabil with the metal detector. The device beeped.

"What you got in there?"

"Keys. Loose change." Nabil extracted those and displayed them. The iPod also elicited a loud beep.

"Yours?" queried the guard.

"Right."

They waved him on, and Nabil breathed easier. The iPod was no ordinary multipurpose pocket computer. Inside was a fully miniaturized Glonass receiver (the Russian equivalent of the Global Positioning System) that could receive signals from Russian satellites in orbit and by triangulation provide real-time position updates and navigation data. It also held all the normal goodies expected of a modern pocket computer.

On either side of the hallway were the administrative offices and a few instructors' offices. He climbed the stairs to the first floor. Another security guard sat at the top of the landing but making no attempt to stop any of the students streaming to and from classes. Clearly he'd been trained to spot a certain profile. More glass offices, more instructors' cubicles down the hallway. Then the huge, sterile cold rooms housing the central processing units of the computers. He made several turns, climbed another half-flight of stairs and met yet another security guard at the entrance to the supercomputer building. After his ID was examined and the guard had muttered a desultory "Engineering?" that was both a question and a declaration demanding no answer, Nabil was waved through.

The supercomputer section looked even more sterile than the rest of the complex. Massive data storage banks sealed in transparent containers with double-walled glass partitions filled the entire room. Another room with the largest processor Nabil had ever seen sat adjacent to the one he was looking at, also glass fronted. Massive cooling fans and air ducts breathed invisible draughts of cold air through the rooms. Nabil had learned that the massive brain of the supercomputer was liquid cooled. On the opposite hallway, lit by non-glare fluorescent bulbs, were classrooms holding numerous terminals, a few printers, the occasional blackboard. Students in tattered Levi's and Mark Zuckerburg-type T- shirts, and professors not much more formally attired were busy at work. Two surveillance cameras hung menacingly opposite the heavy glass door to the CPU room.

In the middle lobby a department secretary sat at her desk, talking on the phone. Nabil stopped at a bulletin board on the wall beside her and perused the notices. The usual offerings: VISUAL BASIC, C+++, JAVA, HTML, AUTOCAD, ORACLE. He had taken three computer languages as part of his degree program in mechanical engineering years ago: FORTRAN, PLI, and PASCAL. They were now somewhat outdated, yet a familiar thrill coursed through his veins. He waited until the secretary dropped her phone and said, "I guess it's too late to register for any of these courses." He pointed to the bulletin board.

"Yes, it is. More than one month into classes. You couldn't possibly catch up."

"I guess not," Nabil said.

"There's a sandwich course in December. Runs two-and-half weeks."

"Sounds good. What do I have to do?"

"Early days yet." She gave him a dark look. "Come around again after Thanksgiving—tell you what, come after fall semester exams and we can sign you up. Professor Miller will be teaching the course."

"Is he around, by any chance?"

"Don't think so. I think he said he'll be running into Bloomington today for a conference. He'd be here tomorrow. Want to leave a message?"

"I'll just come tomorrow."

The woman ran her hand, adorned only with a wedding band, through frizzy hair. "Well, tomorrow's iffy. The vice president's visit on Friday has sort of put everything on hold. He's opening our new super-computer, you know. Fastest in the world."

"I heard," Nabil said casually. "Must be something."

"It is. Can I help you with anything else?"

"No. Thanks a lot."

To the right and down the hallway a little way from the middle lobby were the restrooms. He scooted inside the gents'. Five stalls, five wash-basins, three urinals. He chose the third stall—that would be right be-hind the brain of the supercomputer mainframe. Nabil hated American public toilets. The doors always ended a good twelve inches above the floor—enough ground clearance to leave anything below the knees visible. The toilet bowl held a cheap, clamp-type deodorizer. Perfect. He started to extricate the hand-held GPS unit from his iPod when he heard the outer door fly open and heavy footsteps march in. Nabil dropped his trousers swiftly and lowered himself onto the toilet seat. He held his breath. The footsteps crashed into the adjacent stall. A pair of white Nikes with scuffed insteps positioned themselves, and then faded blue jeans were lowered over them. The seat cover creaked under a con-siderable weight and a split second later, explosive dumps gurgled into the bowl. A second salvo, like tearing calico shattered the lull of the restroom and the stench bad-cheesed the enclosure, like a wind change on a French road passing a Limburger factory.

Goddamn. Nabil fielded the stink.

The man in the adjacent stall coughed self-consciously. No way the man could be FBI or Secret Service. If he was a Fibbie then he deserved the J. Edgar Hoover Merit Award for excellence in faking craps.

The can stank.

Nabil extended the aerial on the special iPod.. He pressed the ON button in the secret compartment. The tiny, liquid-crystal display screen flashed an INITIALIZING warning in Russian. Nabil made grunting noises to simulate a tough bowel movement and managed a tight fart while the receiver warmed up. Presently the flashing stopped, indicating that enough satellites in orbit had been acquired. A tiny green light on the side lit up, indicating the receiver was ready for input. Nabil pressed the AutoStore button twice—once for the receiver to calculate its present position and a second time to store it. A message appeared on the LCD screen: PRESENT POSITION STORED IN ALPHA. Good. He jotted down the coordinates on a piece of paper. He repeated the procedure a second time. This time around, the LCD screen told him the coordinates were stored in BRAVO file. He compared the two readings. The same. The GPS was uncannily accurate. He downloaded the contents of Alpha into the tiny homing device, which—either by accident or design—was shaped like a toilet deodorizer stick. He activated the battery in the homing device before removing the canister of the bowl deodorizer and inserting the homing beacon in its place. The seventy-two-hour battery life would be more than adequate to cover the period of the veep's visit. If the missile scored dead center on the homing device, it would more than adequately take out the supercomputer mainframe. Collateral damage would extend even to nearby buildings and artifacts. The missile could hit the target even without the homing beacon; the beacon only guaranteed it and was an extra precaution. So even if the janitorial staff changed the toilet bowl deodorizer, there wasn't too much harm done.

Satisfied, Nabil shut the lid of the iPod, returning it to its respectable and usual role. Minus the homing device, the unit was now a few pounds lighter. He heard clean-up sounds from the adjacent stall. Nabil flushed the toilet, coughed once for good measure, and left the toilet. As he washed his hands at the sink, the door of the adjacent stall opened and the Merit-Award crapper appeared. He was beefy and red-faced, with a full mustache and a checkered shirt with the two top buttons open. His face was flushed and he looked as though he had been exerting himself a great deal. He avoided Nabil's eyes as he ran water over his ham-sized fingers and then examined his thick neck and heavy features in the wall-length mirror over the sink. Probably one of those non-traditional students who worked full-time for the city of Urbana and took evening courses for self-improvement. As Nabil left the restroom the man was running a pocket comb through his gray-flecked, black hair.

———

Anatoly Grimsky and Gennady Beria, the two mercenaries, had removed the hopper and the spray boom attachments on the Air Tractor and were grinding new bolt brackets for the missile attachment points when Nabil returned from the U. of I. computer center. The third man Schmidt, a deep cover from New Mexico, stood watch on the top ledge of an old grain silo that commanded a 360-degree view of the surrounding area. Beria and Grimsky gathered around Nabil . The introductions had taken place earlier..

Nabil activated the Glonass receiver inside the Walkman and accessed File Bravo to retrieve the coordinates of the toilet where he'd planted the homing device. They compared the coordinates with those of the supercomputer's massive CPU obtained by sensors from orbiting Soviet satellites. The toilet stall was only two meters away from a crucial part of the supercomputer. A bomb blast of any significance within the toilet confines was as good as a direct hit for their purposes. The special explosives being used for the mission was pound for pound more powerful than any non-nuclear material known to man.

Nabil made calculations. The two missiles with the warhead and solid propellant would weigh close to three thousand pounds. He would have to drain some fuel from the Tractor, leave just enough for takeoff, a loiter capability of, say, ten minutes, and a-return-to-launch-site endurance of another ten minutes. In all, thirty minutes of fuel endurance would be more than sufficient for the mission. Takeoffs on grass required a greater distance than conventional surfaces, and Nabil wanted to be doubly sure that the Tractor would lift the payload. The Air Tractor was as yet an untested launch vehicle.

At 3:40 p.m. Beria gingerly lifted the "brain" of the first missile— comprising the guidance system and an advanced micro-processing center—into the nose cone. This particular phase of the operation was supposed to be carried out under sterile conditions. The best Grimsky and Beria could do under the circumstances was to retain the polythene wrap over the instrument, install *in situ*, and just before the final screws were driven in, draw out the polyethylene wrap and immediately mate the nose cone to the fuselage flange. Through a plug-in socket into the guidance system, Beria loaded the target coordinates into the computer. He performed a comparator check, which was satisfactory. He gave way to Grimsky, who checked and crosschecked the coordinates. He also performed a Random Autonomous Integrity Monitoring (RAIM) check on the missiles' tracking system. Grimsky invited Nabil and Beria to do the same. Neither of them thought these precautions unusual. They were professionals from the Cold War era. When a wrong input into the target designator could mean a date with the firing squad on a cold morning in Siberia, these precautions were routine. A ground check demonstrated that the missile was able to lock onto Nabil's device in the toilet, as GPS is not line-of-sight limited. Grimsky repeated everything with the second missile. Satisfactory. Everyone breathed easier. The device in the toilet was only a backup. Just prior to release the missile sensors would lock onto the homing beacon in the supercomputer building, but it would still rely on its own preprogrammed coordinates for primary target acquisition. On the remote chance that the two onboard sensors in the guidance system failed, a third system would take over and guide the missiles unerringly to the homing beacon. Target devastation was a foregone conclusion. If the homing beacon were discovered by the FBI or even moved more than twenty-five feet radially from the precomputed nexus of the supercomputer CPU, the missile sensors would automatically assume a rogue transmission, reject all guidance signals from the beacon, and fly to the last generated impulse from the primary sensor acquired before the onset of failure.

At last the missile-housing bolts were in place, the release pins hooked up. A pulley arrangement from the lanyard in the cockpit that normally controlled the spray boom now activated the release fasteners for the missiles. Three drop tests (minus the warhead) were accomplished. Each time the release pins worked as planned, and the missiles dropped onto an old mattress placed beneath the Air Tractor. Everyone was satisfied. The warhead was gingerly inserted into place, all switches in the unarmed position. Tomorrow, prior to launch, the warhead would be manually armed.

CHAPTER 9

New York.

A lead came in at 5:30 p.m. Monday. A taxi driver for a Queens Yellow Cab remembered a fare he'd carried on the night in question. An agent—Albert Spraldoni from the FBI Brooklyn-Queens, NY, field office—showed the cabbie the photograph composites. The cabbie rejected the bearded visage but paused long enough at the beardless composite for the interrogating agent to say, "Take your time, buddy. We got all the time."

"I think it's him."

"Who?"

"The guy I picked up."

The agent pretended to be bored. "You're sure?"

"Well . . ."

"Then you're not sure."

"A bit more lean in the face—like a hawk, you know? And a mean hook to the nose. I'm positive."

The agent pulled out a crumpled pack of Kools, offered one to the cabbie, lit one himself and exhaled expansively. "Tell me about this guy."

"Well, I picked up this fare by the corner Amoco a couple of blocks from the Continental. JFK Continental, by the way. Cold and neat and efficient, if you know what I mean. I thought he was a cop. Same look, same gestures. In my line of work you get to know who's what. Maybe an undercover narc, something like that. He had a slight accent. Had me pull over by the air hose, then gets out and walks back down to the drive-in phone port. I guess maybe so I can't hear what he's saying. Dude looks up a number on a piece of paper and dials it himself. I thought he looked—"

"Dialed the numbers himself?" the agent asked.

"That's what I said. Yeah, he did."

"The telephones at that location," Spraldoni interrupted, "are Touch Tones."

The cabbie blinked. "Yeah. That's what I mean. He punches in the numbers, talks into it. Maybe he didn't get the party he was looking for. Hangs up. Then he coughs, sort of a harsh coughing spell. Pretends he's got spit and shit on the telephone receiver. Takes out his handkerchief and carefully wipes everything off. Neat."

"You saw him do that? Wipe the telephone receiver?"

"Sure did."

The agent wrote everything down. "There are four telephone ports on that side of the gas station. Did you see which one he used?"

The cabbie answered without hesitation. "Second on the left coming in from the west entrance."

They were getting somewhere. Spraldoni nodded. "Talk to me."

"Yeah. Well, he gets back in. Says he's sorry he's putting me to all this trouble. Says he's got wife trouble, thinks some dude is screwing his wife. He's got incontrovertible proof. She's holed up with the guy at the Continental. Wants to catch them in the act. Grounds for divorce. You know, lawyer stuff. He flashes a lot of dough. Gives me some, promises more. I don't buy any of what he's telling me—about his wife and shit—but heck, I ain't paid to ask questions and like the guy ain't committing no crime and neither am I . . ."

"So what did you do?"

"He has me drive over to the Continental and park at a spot where we can see anyone and everyone leaving and entering by the front door. We sort of just sit there and wait. I ask the guy if I can smoke, and he says sure. I smoke a cigarette, and just for the hell of it, I've left the meter running, which don't make any difference here 'cause the guy obviously is paying more than the meter'll ever read for the waiting time. That first forty he gave me, why the meter ain't got up to nine dollars yet. And he promised me more, he—"

"So what happened?"

"Well, pretty soon this guy with a battered duffel bag comes out. Mind you, other people been coming and going into the Continental all this time, but this guy . . . something's different. He hails a cab and gets into it. The cab moves off. Apparently he's a guy a lot of people are waiting for. 'Cause all of a sudden all hell breaks loose. What I mean is, people are jumping into cars and squealin' tires and peeling off behind this guy. Like some kind of merry-go-round. Shit, you ought to think that with four or five carloads of cop—and these were no ordinary cops take it from me; Fed cops more like—taking after this guy, it ought to be like in those crazy TV shows with car chases and stunts. Nothing like it, it was all quiet and organized. What I mean is, they were obviously following this guy but they kept their distance and tried not to make it too apparent. But I seen it. And so's my fare. I know he seen it 'cause he sits there after all the cars have gone off chasing the guy with the battered duffel. He sits there quiet and thoughtful, staring at nothing in particular, and after a while he has me drive off and drop him at a busy intersection on Guy Brewer Avenue, if I remember correctly. 'Course I remember cause he gave me another twenty-five bucks. To buy my silence, I suppose. Then he sort of disappears into the crowd. Real professional, that guy. I wouldn't want to be on the wrong side of him."

"And this guy with the duffel bag, did your fare mention that that was the man he suspected was sleeping with his wife?"

"Nope. Never said a word. Didn't need to. I'm no kid, see? Plain as the hair on your head he was interested in the dude with the duffel bag just as much as the Feds were."

Spraldoni's pen raced across his notepad. "You got the money he paid you with?"

"Nope. Spent it. Or turned it in. Can't remember which. Don't keep money that long. Got to pay my cab lease." He paused. "Got another drag on you?" The cabby's face resembled that of a family dog begging for scraps from the dinner table.

Spraldoni shook out another cigarette from the crumpled pack. Once the cabbie got it going, he asked, "Do you know if the guy you picked up was armed?"

"Must have been."

"Be more specific."

"I didn't see any piece, you understand. I just knew it. He was packing heat alright. He's the type. Definitely."

"You make the heat?"

"No. But he was carrying. Somewhere. I just know it."

"You didn't see anything? No bulges?"

"No, nothing."

"And you said this guy had an accent?"

"That's right."

"What kind of accent?"

"I would say . . . Middle Eastern. Yeah. That kind of accent."

"What made you think he was a narc?"

The cabbie shrugged. "I can't quite put a finger on it. He just looked . . . a bit like you. He had this look of secret police or an agent. No matter how hard he tried to look normal, everything about him said cop or cop hitman."

The agent laughed. He shut his notebook. "That's all you can tell me?"

"That's about it."

"And we can always get in touch with you at this address?"

"Sure thing. If I'm out working, the dispatcher can always give me a buzz on the radio. What do I get for this? The Good Citizen citation for keeping my eyes open?"

"More than that," the agent said seriously. "Consider yourself lucky to be alive."

Tuesday morning. 9:05 a.m.

The second cabbie, the one who had carried Nabil to the street opposite the UN Mission, had been located. His description of the fare tallied with that of the first cabbie. He had dropped off the stranger, if he remembered correctly, at the corner of East Forty-Sixth Street and the United Nations Plaza. As the cabbie had pulled away, the man had started walking toward the UN building. Almost immediately an ash-colored sedan had pulled up beside the sidewalk, the man got in, and the car sped off.

Special Agents VanDiver and Spraldoni interviewed this second cab driver. "Anything special about the man?" VanDiver asked.

"Not really. Well, now that you mention it, he did have a, well, like a . . . military bearing."

"Would you explain?"

"You know what I mean. Stiff, precise movements, honor code, that sort of thing. He paid me, tipped me exactly 10 percent, said, 'Thank you, sir,' and walked away. He wouldn't rob you, if you know what I mean, but then again he'd slit your throat without blinking if cutting your throat fell within the normal range of his duties."

VanDiver regarded the cabbie thoughtfully. "Is that right?"

"You betcha. And what's more I can tell you his name."

Spraldoni's shock was profound. He managed to keep on scribbling. Probably a fake name. VanDiver actually dropped his pen. "I'm sorry," he said, retrieving his ballpoint. "I'm not sure I heard you correctly."

"I can tell you his name," the cabbie repeated.

"I'm listening."

"Just before the guy paid me, he opened his wallet. This was just as we're pulling up short of the No Parking area before the UN. Stacked full of bills. Credit cards, too. He tried to peel off a couple of twenties to pay me. One of the cards fell off and he quickly picked it up. American Express card. But not before I seen the name on it. Samir Muvdi. Yeah, Muvdi. I'm pretty sure. My own mother is from Lebanon originally, so I reckon I'd find it easier than most to remember a name like that."

Spraldoni asked, "Did he know you saw the name?"

"Don't think so. What's it matter anyways? Those plastics are pretty easy to get these days and with a bunch of aliases, too."

"Right you are," VanDiver said.

But now they had a name.

Someone at the Queens field office of the Secret Service remembered that surveillance cameras were mounted on several locations at the UN Boulevard. Since the FBI considered the UN building a high priority target for possible terrorist attacks, hidden cameras unobtrusively panned the street twenty-four seven for cars that loitered, double-parked, or were left abandoned near the Mission building.

The FBI and the UN's own security agency, cooperated speedily in all aspects and that same evening the tapes scrolled. The black-and-white pictures were fuzzy. Cars in the two lanes moving down the stretch. A taxi pulling out from the curb after apparently dropping off a fare. That fare entering the camera's view. A man about six feet tall walking purposefully away from the UN Plaza. A car that looked like an Oldsmobile Ciera veering abruptly and pulling up beside the man. The man getting in, the car speeding off. FBI lab enhancement of the photos could not produce a distinct license plate number—the car had not been near enough to the UN to be considered a terrorist threat. They'd only been able to tell they were New Jersey plates. Where had the car gone? Who were the men inside the Ciera?

At 1:42 p.m. that same Tuesday, Ken Dwight sat at his desk reading Spraldoni's report just faxed in. Certain aspects bothered him. Why had the first cabbie thought the man was a narc? The second cabbie thought the stranger was military. Cabbies, by necessity, learn to read people, occupations. Maybe the thread was beginning to unravel. A cop. A military man. Perhaps a trained agent. Could one of his own men be involved in a threat against the president of the United States and in the murder of Agent Means? The official assumption now was that Means had been murdered. Was there a narcotics connection? Unlikely. Means had never so much as inhaled marijuana or ingested any hard drug. Those questions were asked on the pre-employment and annual polygraphs required of every Secret Service agent. Means's dossier confirmed it. He had also passed every random blood and urine test—required for agents on presidential detail. What was the connection? Middle Eastern accent. Drugs? Colombia. Peru. The president had signed legislation and sent DEA helicopters to Bogotá to assist the government in diminishing the capability of the fragmented remnants of the Cali and Medellin cartels. Those folks obviously were not happy about that. Some Latinos did racially resemble people from the Middle East.

Muvdi. Samir Muvdi.

The name went out on all FBI crime network wires. Three Muvdis appeared on the FBI computer, those ever arrested or convicted of one crime or another. All checked out. None knew the stranger or had relatives connected to the man in question. Clearly this man Samir Muvdi was the "Middle Easterner" Miskos Venovich had met in the bar. The one who had given him money to take the phone call in the hotel. That action alone reeked of cartel easy money. Maybe the case belonged to DEA or ATF. Except that there existed a threat to the president of the United States.

Dwight placed a call to an assistant in the Executive Office Building. "Call DEA and ATF. See if they have anything on a Muvdi, Samir. Male, white. Distinguishing characteristics: Arabic, possible Roman nose. Priority, please."

"Right away, sir."

Next Dwight placed a call to Special Agent Spraldoni of the Queens, New York, field office. "Good work on both reports."

"Thanks, chief."

"I want you to check all the airlines in New York City and the surrounding area. Check all departures and arrivals from last week Thursday. LaGuardia. JFK. Newark, Teterboro. Name to look for: Samir Muvdi. Muvdi." Dwight started to spell out the name, but remembered it was Agent Spraldoni who'd faxed over the report in the first place. "We want to know if he traveled and where to. Pay special attention to flights outbound to Lima or Bogotá or Mexico City. Got it?"

"I'll get right on it, sir."

"Al, I know it's tedious work checking passenger manifests, given the thousands of people entering and leaving New York daily. It's a long shot."

"No problem, sir."

Spraldoni, Dwight knew, was a good legwork man. His confidence in the man was not misplaced, but even he was surprised at the speed with which the next communiqué arrived.

At 4:09 p.m. Dwight's telephone rang. Spraldoni again.

"Got something for you."

"How'd you do it?"

"Since 9/11, airlines flying into the United States are mandated to send the passenger manifest to DHS and TSA for pre-clearance. Just entered the name in the computer and sent it searching airline manifests from last Thursday. Nothing on Samir Muvdi. So I reversed it, with Samir as last name. I got six hits on Samir, none with other name as Muvdi. On a hunch I tried substituting the middle letter 'v' with 'l' and 'h' and 'z,' as in Muldi, Muhdi, or Muzdi. It took with a Samir Muhdi. Turned out to be a sixty-year-old Syrian national accompanied by his wife traveling by British Airways to London on his way to Damascus. I ran the program again with 'd' this time in the middle 'cause I noticed that most times I mentioned the name to airline ticketing clerks or even some of our field agents, they ended up pronouncing it Mudvi instead of Muvdi. Figured that the ticketing agent probably made the same mistake. I ran it on the original as Samir Mudvi and guess what—it came right back with three tickets sold under that name. One from New York to LA. One from New York to Madison, Wisconsin, via Chicago. Third one from New York to Reno, via Houston. Tickets bought three different locations; two downtown, one at the airport. Paid cash, therefore all three tickets fully refundable, minus service charges. Three different cities, and all three flights leaving at the same time. Classic ploy to confuse investigators. Hopped on the Chicago flight. American."

"Goddamn!" was all Dwight could say.

"Yep. Subject left LaGuardia Thursday afternoon for O'Hare on an American flight. Seat 32B. Looks a good bet. From the time subject was picked up by vehicle near the UN building, allowing for the drive to LaGuardia, and a conservative seventy-five minute wait for the flight—time of departure would seem reasonable and consistent with our man. Seat 32B is in coach."

"I would say that's a good lead."

"Could be."

Dwight took a deep breath. "Good work, Spraldoni."

"Thank you, sir. I'm afraid from Chicago the subject seems to have vanished. He missed his Madison connection."

Dwight pondered this. "Maybe he doesn't like commuter aircraft."

"Could be."

"Get hold of the passenger manifest for that flight. Let's locate the passengers on the seats right next to him. 32A and 32C. Got that?"

"I already did that. Seat 32C is an aisle seat. Nobody occupied it for that portion of the flight. 32A was a window seat occupied by one Harvey Michelson of Schaumburg, Illinois. Seats 33A, B, and C, and 31A, B, and C, were all occupied. We're working right now on locating those passengers and the flight attendants who served them. Any one of them may have noticed something unusual."

"Fine work, Spraldoni. I'll get our boys in Chicago to go see Michelson right away."

Dwight hung up. *Sonuvabitch is good. He'll have my job one of these days.* Dwight dialed the Chicago field office on the direct line and ordered that two agents be sent to interview Harvey Michelson. All available agents from Chicago's field offices should fan out and locate those passengers on adjacent seats and the flight attendants for that sector.

Westbound at Flight Level 360 aboard Air Force Two, a Boeing 747-300, Vice President Richard Walsh went over the speech he was to deliver at the launch of the University of Illinois supercomputer. Damn those speechwriters! There would be no teleprompters, no cue cards. This would be raw, cold speech with no props, and he had never looked good without prompters. Probably why he was only vice president. He sipped the watered-down martini topped with a lemon wedge that had been thoughtfully provided by one of the flight stewards. He needed it for his nerves.

Damn Don Deakin and his missile defense toys. That was the main reason why he, Dick Walsh, was flying halfway across the country in a humongous crate to give a useless speech to a bunch of college kids and scientists and Service Chiefs. The damn MDS concept was too expensive. And unproven. The Federal deficit had ballooned like a goddamned dirigible and was now out of control. The fiscal surplus of the Clinton years all frittered away. Sometimes he wished the old geezer would just drop dead from a heart attack so he could become president in Deakin's stead. His first official act—after the swearing in and the late geezer's burial at Arlington, of course, or his California ranch—would be to freeze funding on MDS. Veto the damn boondoggle. Divert the money to needy programs. The hell with the conservatives. Columnist George F. Will had once written that Walsh was considered a moderate despite his long conservative voting record first in the House and later in the Senate. Maybe the sumbitch was right. Maybe that was why he'd been made veep—balance the ticket against what many considered the president's far-right intractability. Walsh drained the tumbler dry as the steward appeared with another martini and a cookie tray.

"Thanks, Steve."

"You're welcome, Mr. Vice President."

Evelyn Walsh stirred from the light sleep induced by the lullabying whine of the four Pratts whizzing the big Boeing at Mach .84 through the skies. The steward seized the opening to ask, "More espresso for you, Mrs. Walsh?"

"Thank you, no, Steven." Evelyn yawned. The espresso clearly hadn't done its work. The demitasse holding the earlier joe, her second, was just short of empty. Too bitter. She eyed her husband sipping his martini.

"Dear," she said, when the steward had left, "why not save your stomach for the reception? And our dinner with Norma and her husband."

"No harm is done, dear. Relax."

She still retained just a little of her native Cockney accent. Five decades had turned the once pretty, Dorset-complexioned English lass into a heavyset granny type with white bouffant hairdo, frill-neck dress skirt and blouse, and ancient wire-rim glasses sitting on her nose. Yet America loved Evelyn Walsh. She was Motherhood and American Values and Pumpkin Pie. *Redbook* readers had twice voted her America's most admired woman. She'd beaten Jackie O. in one reader survey of America's most influential women.

They had two children, Dick Jr. and Norma. Dick Jr. lived out West in California with his wife Sue. Norma was an assistant professor of psychology at Bradley University in Peoria, an hour-and-a-half's drive from Champaign-Urbana. Norma and husband Jim Delbecki and their three children would be driving down to join them at the dinner reception along with Illinois governor Jim Edgar, the Service chiefs, the university president, and two senators. Evelyn had been looking forward to this trip. A photo album of Norma's family lay in front of her on the bolted mahogany table. Evelyn had gone through it twice since they'd lifted off from Andrews one hour ago. She had presents for her grandchildren.

Walsh leaned back in his seat, loosened his tie, and tried to snooze. Behind him in separate compartments of the airplane were members of the press corps and Secret Service personnel. Up front were a group of his aides, two senators, more Secret Service men, and the Service chiefs.

Thirty minutes later he was still snoozing when pressure changes in his eardrum and a drop in decibel level told him Air Force Two had begun its initial descent into Willard, Champaign-Urbana, Illinois.

CHAPTER 10

Schaumburg.

Harvey Michelson owned an FTD-accredited florist shop on Main Street, Schaumburg. He greeted the three men—two agents and a police sketch artist—from his cluttered workbench. He wore a large green apron over white paisley shirt and knit tie.

"Come into my office, gentlemen." He dropped the flower stems and led the three men into an outer office that held files and bookcases instead of flowerpots and cymbidiums.

Yes, he had sat next to a man perhaps of Middle Eastern origin in the airplane. No, nothing unusual. Kept to himself, didn't look as though he wanted to talk to anybody. At one time the man had looked at his watch and brought out what looked like rosary beads—you know, those things Catholics use when reciting Hail Marys.

Harvey continued, "Anyway, he holds the beads between his thumb and forefinger and moves from one bead to the next ever so slowly. All this time his eyes are locked forward in this distant look and his lips are moving slowly. I figured he was praying. It struck me he probably wasn't Catholic. Maybe Muslim. I thought Muslims pray facing Mecca—east, you know? We were heading west, toward Chicago. But I didn't dare ask him, wasn't my business. And, oh yes, I did confirm he was Muslim. Didn't eat pork. I remember reading somewhere that Islam forbids the eating of pork."

"Could you explain further?" one of the agents asked.

"Well, when they brought the lunch tray—the usual sandwich with a layer of cheese, lettuce, tomato, and pickle, plus the other stuff, I noticed our friend carefully removed the ham before eating the sandwich. It was then I said, 'Airline food's mediocre, huh?'

"He nodded.

"'You must be a Muslim,' I says to him.

"He looked at me for the first time. His eyes were cold—liquid cold—like his face. Intense. Not sinister, just . . . someone who held rigidly to his beliefs.

"'Could be,' he said. He went back to eating.

"I wasn't about to be put off. I'm Harvey Michelson. I'm an FTD florist. You don't get to be that if you can't make friends. So I say, 'Let me see, you must be from Kuwait? Qatar?'

"He shook his head again.

"'Oman? Saudi Arabia?'

"'I'm from Turkey,' he says finally.

"'Turkey!' I say. 'I've been to Turkey. Istanbul is a pretty interesting city, isn't it?'

"'I wouldn't know,' he says. 'I'm a Mediterranean Turkey.'"

The agents laughed despite themselves. Harvey Michelson chuckled.

"Obviously that put an end to the conversation," Michelson went on. "The guy just didn't feel like talking to anybody. He must have had something pretty important on his mind. Earlier, before the in-flight service and our brief conversation, he'd unfolded a small map. One of those RAND Corporation maps. A couple of times I saw him trace his finger down from Chicago southward."

"Did you notice which area southward?" an agent asked.

"Matter of fact, I did. Champaign-Urbana or Danville, Illinois. Thereabouts. He placed his thumb firmly on it and seemed to be inspecting the surrounding area. I'm sure of it. Didn't know I was looking, cracked my eyelid a wee bit. Thought I was sleeping."

"You're quite sure it was Champaign-Urbana?"

"Positive."

The agents exchanged glances.

"Anything more you could tell us, Mr. Michelson?" the lead agent asked.

"Nothing more I can remember. After we landed he went on his way and I went mine."

The sketch artist moved in. He worked for the Cook County Sheriff's office and was on loan to the Secret Service. He was a little martinet with handlebar mustache. He set up his easel and sketchpad beside Mr. Michelson, looked him in the eye and said, "Describe him in detail, as much as you remember. Let's start with the face."

As Michelson talked, the artist sketched. Within minutes, the outline of a figure began to emerge. One agent took notes. His partner went outside and called Ken Dwight on his cell phone. The time was just after 11 a.m.

"Urbana!" Dwight exploded, after the agent had briefed him. "Yeah, okay. Good work. Get on with the sketch. When you finish, take a photo—several photos—and e-mail them to my office. Include your report."

By the time the agent reentered Mr. Michelson's office, the artist was packing up his easel. They thanked Michelson for his cooperation.

"Anytime," Michelson said. "Hey, if you guys run into that gentleman, tell him I really don't care he's from up the Mediterranean. Tell him I'm a Bosphorus Turkey."

Michelson guffawed.

———

After the agent called from Schaumburg, Dwight made three telephone calls. In ten minutes, he had determined that a certain Samir Muvdi had rented an Avis car from O'Hare. Vehicle type: Olds Cutlass.

With shaking hands, Dwight immediately called Hy Strooker. "We think we've found our man, sir. He's headed for the Champaign-Urbana area."

Within minutes, Dwight had a hook-up with Air Force Two, now on the tarmac at Willard. He issued the security alert. Vice President Richard Walsh was already at the U. of I. campus, giving his speech to an SRO crowd.

An artist's impression of the man known as Samir Muvdi rolled out of Dwight's office printer as he spoke. This picture went out with a BOLO (Be On the Lookout) alert to every police station and law enforcement agency in Illinois. The make and number of the car rented by the suspect was also released.

It was 11:26 a.m., Friday.

———

Champaign-Urbana.
The supercomputer launch was being telecast live on two local television networks. Grimsky watched. The moment Vice President and Mrs. Walsh took their seats on the dais, waiting for University of Illinois President Bergstrom to introduce them, Grimsky emerged from the kitchen doorway and gave Nabil a thumbs up.

Inside the cockpit, Nabil flipped on the master switch, the fuel pump, and energized the starter. The turbine whined, the propeller spun, overcame her inertia, and soon became an invisible disc. Beria tugged away the chocks, careful not to nudge the gleaming metallic gray nose cone of each 1500-pound missile slung beneath the wing of the Air Tractor. On receiving the chocks-clear signal from Beria, Nabil advanced the throttle from beta mode to positive thrust. Nabil swung the Tractor around, kicking dust and loose grass on Beria and Grimsky as they ducked for cover. As he taxied toward the runway at a good clip, Nabil selected takeoff flaps and verified deployment.

Nabil put away the radio. He swung the Air Tractor around at the strip's end. The eight-foot windsock to his left indicated an easterly wind. He was taking off to the east. In the distance, by the farmhouse garage, Beria squatted over a portable control panel. When Nabil began his bombing run from the east, he would pass over the field again as his Initial Point, at which time Beria would remotely arm the missile warhead. A second arming device was provided by a fine wire that would snap, closing a circuit, once the missile release pins were pulled. The release pins via the same circuit also activated two engine start igniters for the hydrazine propellant. Within three seconds of release, full ignition of the rocket motor would send each missile hurtling on its deadly trajectory. Nabil hoped the jostling and bumpiness of take-off from the grass strip would not dislodge the release pins or snap the arming wire. If all else failed, yet a third device would arm the warhead once missile velocity exceeded two hundred knots. Impact velocity of the missile would be in excess of Mach 1.3. Limited telemetry would be available from the missile during its brief pre-impact burn so Beria could monitor its progress downrange. Beria was also the range safety officer. In the event of a serious malfunction, Beria could remotely detonate the missile. The primary targets were the supercomputer mainframe, the vice president of the United States, the service chiefs, and MDS scientists and engineers from Los Alamos and Sandia National Laboratories in New Mexico, who were on hand to witness the launch of the supercomputer that would operate their brainchild. Wiping out scientific talent connected with MDS was part of the mission—but arbitrary civilian casualties were not.

Lined up, Nabil pushed the throttle forward, waited for the internal turbine temperature to stabilize, and slammed the throttle forward to the stops. Of course he would over-torque the engine, but the limiters would take care of that. This would be a military-style operation as much as possible. The Tractor leaped forward. Nabil steered with the rudder and the tail came up quickly. The ag plane trundled down the grass strip, fighting more parasite drag than usual. Finally the required numbers came up on the airspeed indicator, and Nabil eased the Tractor into the balmy October sky. He leveled off at two hundred feet AGL, still on runway heading, to avoid being picked up by Champaign approach radar. He bled up the flaps slowly. The speed crept past 140 knots, increasing. He reduced power to maintain present airspeed. He swept out three miles, keeping an eye out for unmarked towers or radio masts. He started his course reversal; first a left 80-degree turn followed by a right 260 degree. Somehow, in the turn, he had edged up to 320 feet AGL. Probably still undetected by Champaign radar. Completing the course reversal, he was now inbound, three hundred feet above the ground, positioned for the bomb run. He slammed the throttle to full torque, trimming slightly nose down to pick up more speed in the shallow dive. He was flat out for the field now, westerly heading. He left the condition lever on full max for the run and the noise was considerable.

One hundred sixty knots on the ASI, increasing. Grass strip coming up. Beria squatting by his instrument, Grimsky standing nearby watching, two tiny figures becoming larger. He had picked his Initial Point, the squat farmhouse on the left near the middle of the field. He was redlining and the buffeting increased as he bore down on the IP. He would time from there, and he needed the speed for the leapfrog trajectory prior to missile detachment. He pickled the bomb, checked once more that the aircraft transponder was turned off—including the altitude-reporting feature. In less than a minute, he would appear on the Champaign controller's scope, and he wanted only a fuzzy primary. One hundred sixty knots. He screamed past the two figures on the ground, saw Beria rising as he sent the signal from his control panel arming the warhead.

Now!

Nabil pulled up on the control stick steadily, at the same time nudging the throttles to full torque. Up, up. Not the brutal stick-to-crotch jockeying of the jet fighter pilot—Beria had warned him not to pull more than 2G on the leapfrog or the missiles might separate prematurely. He was through 1000 feet and climbing within seconds, the airspeed bleeding off alarmingly. He leveled off as the altimeter wound past 1500 feet, the pre-determined release altitude, but his momentum carried him to 1800 feet. He shoved the stick down to prevent a stall, then pulled the spray boom handle of the ag plane. He felt the airplane lighten considerably as the missiles detached. He yanked the stick hard right and down in an escape maneuver that would also place him downwind for landing on the grass strip. He would be landing with some tailwind. No time for niceties now.

He was still in the bank when he saw a sight that would always thrill him every time he remembered it. A white plume of smoke that grew impossibly fast in the direction of the target. Another plume of white smoke just seconds behind—the second missile with a two-second design delay. It took less than a minute. Even in the daylight, the flash was spectacular. He heard several explosions. The missiles crossing the sound barrier, and those from the detonating warheads.

He was on the ground three minutes later and taxiing rapidly toward Grimsky and Beria. He pulled out the 9mm Browning and held it by his side as he cut the engine—just in case the two Russians had orders to eliminate him after the mission. But Grimsky and Beria were thumping one another on the back, grinning like fools. Nabil sheathed the gun, climbed down from the ag plane, and they jumped at him to exchange high fives and low fives.

"We need champagne for this," Beria punned.

"What for?" Grimsky asked. "You just got the whole Champaign city. Vodka would be far better."

Both men laughed. Nabil kept an eye on the barn loft and tried to keep one of the two men between him and it, where Schmidt was on watch duty. If Schmidt had a scope rifle, he could take all three men out. Nabil didn't trust the Soviets.

"What you guys doing?" Schmidt's voice startled all of them. He emerged from behind the garage, carrying the demolition gear. "We have two minutes to get out of here, fellows. Let's go. Good work," he added.

The three men stacked all the vital equipment to be destroyed inside the Tractor. They also placed three separate soapdish bombs in different areas inside the ag plane.

"It was a beautiful thing," Beria crowed as they worked. "That beacon Nabil left in the toilet, we picked it up right before launch. You should have heard the boom as the rocket motor ignited. The bombs went right to the target. Magnificent. Bye-bye Star Wars."

They were ready in three minutes. Grimsky emptied two gallons of gasoline into the Tractor cockpit and fuselage. They retreated to the driveway, drove the three remaining cars some distance, and stopped. They all got out to watch. Schmidt brought out a remote detonator, keyed in the right numbers, and asked everyone to duck. A moment later, the Tractor blew up horribly, gouging the sky with the third explosion of the day. The Tractor burned fiercely. Only a few charred pieces would be left. Nabil was sorry to see the beautiful ag plane destroyed. She had been a fine bird.

Nabil got out his belongings from the rented car and threw them into Grimsky's Toyota Sienna. The same reason he had insisted that Grimsky take his car. A bomb under the bonnet was not unlikely from any of these men.

Grimsky protested, "You again?"

"Me again." Grimsky caught his briefcase as Nabil threw it to him. "I know you will understand."

"What the heck?" Grimsky said.

All the cars were rented anyway and could be dropped off at any Hertz, Avis, or National depot nationwide. All charges billable to sanitized credit cards. Schmidt and Nabil would go alone as usual. Grimsky and Beria together in one car. Disperse. Reunite in Washington, DC, for the second operation—excluding Schmidt, who was returning to his deep-cover base somewhere in the continental United States and would not be involved in the second operation. The four men shook hands solemnly, congratulating one another on the successful mission.

And went their separate ways.

———

Air traffic controller Jose Aguilar was on duty that Friday morning at the Willard Airport tower. To be assigned to handle Air Force Two was the high point of his career. It was just another blip on the tower scope, another curl of thin black smoke on the horizon. The pilot's impersonal voice announced outer marker inbound. Aguilar just as impersonally cleared it to land. The gleaming deep blue Boeing 747-300 with a gray stripe floated over the threshold and laid rubber in a brief puff of white smoke on the east–west runway. The ground spoilers deployed, the reversers thundered. The big Boeing slowed.

"Air Force Two contact Ground 121.7."

"121.7."

"And you're welcome, sir."

"Good morning to you."

Mel Sprague, a supervisor who was a controller Grade One and could work any position from Approach to Tower or Ground, was handling Ground. It wasn't actually voiced, but each one knew that Sprague was there in case anything went wrong. In his career, he'd had occasion to handle Air Force One twice, right from the days of George Bush, Sr. Aguilar didn't mind his work being monitored. The Secret Service had demanded it, said it was routine. Sprague delivered taxi instructions in his reassuring monotone, delivered in staccato fashion, not a word wasted, bred from long years in the Aurora (Chicago) Tracon and Dallas-Forth Worth axis, both high stress environments for controllers. Aguilar watched as Air Force Two taxied to the red carpet.

Still, Aguilar was disappointed. Up until last week, it was supposed to be the president of the United States opening that computer whatchamacallit. When he'd seen the roster two weeks earlier and seen that he had drawn duty for the presidential visit, Aguilar's chest had expanded two inches. A naturalized American from Oaxaca, Mexico, he knew he'd finally arrived as a mainstream American if he could be trusted to handle Air Force One. One ambitious and envious controller had tried to swap shifts to get in on the presidential action, and Aguilar had told him to go jump in a mesquite bush. Then the NOTAM that downgraded it to a vice presidential visit. *Shit*, Aguilar thought; the medicine men back in his village were still working overtime to retard his progress, their unvarnished evil leaping continents.

The intercom tinkled. Approach downstairs.

"Jose, I got two more airplanes for you headed for Buble. You gonna accommodate them?" Buble Intersection was a fix some twelve miles from Willard.

"Sure. Like everyone else. They'll hold."

"You got any idea how much longer?"

"Stan, couple of minutes more. The veep's party has disembarked. They'll be out of here soon. Five minutes probably, then I'll cut them loose."

"Yeah. Okay," came Stan's doubtful voice.

Aguilar picked up his binoculars and surveyed the eastern sector where three airplanes were now holding. He couldn't see any of them. He lowered the binoculars. On the Flightstar ramp were two medevac helicopters—a Sikorsky S-76 and an Aerospatiale Dauphin—with crew on standby alert. Aguilar knew that a trauma center, Humana Hospital in Urbana, had also been put on standby alert with two teams of trauma surgeons and nurses and two ORs and one ER on open alert. Blood banks in the area were also on alert, and Humana Hospital even stocked up with extra packets of the president's blood type, B-negative. When the visit became a vice presidential affair, some of the logistics remained in place, due to the short time frame.

Five minutes later, Aguilar reopened the airport to normal traffic. Traffic holding at Buble and elsewhere was stack-descended and cleared for the approach as appropriate. After everything was back to normal, Aguilar relaxed. He brought out a packet of pretzels he'd bought from the vending machine downstairs and broke into it. He held out the packet to Sprague.

"Want some?"

"Thanks, no."

Aguilar shrugged and returned to his monitor. The veep's party must now be approaching the supercomputer center. If he was lucky, Air

Force Two would still be leaving on his shift, but he didn't count on that. VIP flights were notorious for delays.

Sprague turned to Aguilar. "What's the latest on that ELT signal?"

"Nothing, far as I know."

With one hand, he increased the volume on the emergency frequency of 121.5, which is monitored by every airport control tower in the United States. Sure enough, a faint *bleep-bleep, bleep-bleep.* An emergency locator transmitter, designed to be triggered in the event of a crash to help search-and-rescue teams locate the crash site, had been going off since yesterday, somewhere in the Champaign-Urbana area. A routine check of all overdue flight plans, IFR and VFR, and a check with the national coordinator for search-and rescue-operations accounted for all overdue aircraft. No reports of any aircraft missing in the area. A student pilot who had gotten lost on a cross-country flight from Ottumwa, Iowa, and was now somewhere in Galesburg, had called her instructor by telephone to let him know she was just fine one hour after the ELT went off. Her aircraft ELT was in perfect order.

A SARSAT satellite, curiously owned by the Russians, had also picked up the signal and narrowed the source of the transmission to a half-square-mile area—right inside the University of Illinois campus. Within forty minutes of the first interrogation of the ELT source by satellite, a second briefing by Russian officials to the National Coordinator Search and Rescue downplayed the earlier assessment and suggested the signal came "probably from a dysfunctional transmitter of an old ELT, perhaps one with weak batteries, in the area downtown of the Illinois city."

A tall order!

That seemed to lay the matter to rest, especially as there were no reports of a small airplane crashing into the center of the U. of I. campus. Still, Sprague had notified the Civil Air Patrol, and they had promised to send out a team to the campus to check out the source. Sprague thought he knew the answer to that one. It had happened before, and it was probably the case now. An absentminded UI professor taking home or to his office the detachable ELT from his airplane and somehow accidentally activating the thing. ELTs had been found bleating away inside moldy socks, inside filing cabinets, and more than one boudoir. The red-faced owners of those errant ELTs when confronted had apologized profusely, said that ELT thefts at the airport were rampant (which was true—they fetched a thousand bucks on the fenced avionics market), and promised to be more careful in the future.

"They're sending someone out there sometime this morning," Sprague said. "Ought to have taken care of it by now, you'd think."

"I guess."

"False alarm. Disturbs everybody." Sprague left the volume on low as a reminder for him to tell someone to act on it by noon.

"Know what you mean. I betcha—" He broke off to clear a Beech Musketeer to land.

They were still talking ten minutes later when the intercom tinkled again. Approach again. The speaker was on, and without breaking stride, Aguilar said, "Yes, Stan."

"Jose, you got any traffic by St Joseph?"

Aguilar rechecked his scope. "Not that I know of."

"I got a primary. Not much. Slow traffic. A prop job, altitude unknown."

"Nothing, Stan."

"Probably some farmer fooling around in a J-3 Cub," Sprague snorted.

Aguilar lifted his binoculars once more in the direction of St. Joseph. He choked on his own breath. "Hey!"

Sprague grabbed his own binoculars and was beside Aguilar the next moment. "What is it, Jose?"

Stan's voice from Approach came in urgently on the open line. "I got unreported traffic, altitude, destination unknown, two—goddamn it, now one, had two briefly there, closing fast. Real motherfucking fast. What's the clown think he's doing? This is controlled airspace, for Chrissakes. Got it, two fighter jets. Hey, Mel, they got F-16s out there? Gotta be, gotta be. . . . They should have told me," Stan muttered.

"Goddamn!" Sprague's binoculars had found the objects.

"Goddamn sonuvabitch," Aguilar repeated, staring at the fast-moving objects.

It was mostly contrail: a white cottonseed puffball that was like no contrail Aguilar had ever seen, because it was low and moving fast—impossibly fast—and it couldn't have been an F-15 or F-16 because they didn't have that much smoke signature. A sudden, blinding white flash downtown. Then another. Seconds later the deep rumble of the explosions reached them. Aguilar felt it shake even the control cab's reinforced walls.

At the same time Aguilar noticed it, the bleep-bleep of the rogue "ELT" stopped. Aguilar's first desperate thought was, *It had to happen on my shift! The shamans back in Mexico have really done it.*

"Oh my God, two Tomahawk missiles!" Sprague shouted, and hit the emergency button.

———

Evelyn Walsh heard it first. Her husband Vice President Walsh had been on the podium just six minutes, long enough to make his traditional opening joke to relax the service chiefs and the audience. He then launched into MDS, detailing the history of the revolutionary concept that would alter the balance of global tensions. MDS would one day be reality, he enthused. This supercomputer that could make so many trillions of calculations in nanoseconds was the reason he, the service chiefs, and everyone else were here. To celebrate man's technological ingenuity. That supercomputer was inside the building right behind him, all systems were "go" and the machine was roaring to be cut loose.

Applause.

After it died down, Walsh started to say something. Instead he saw a bright flash and felt roaring in his ears, a bell that seemed to be tolling from nowhere and everywhere at once. His lungs were scorched, and he was fighting for air. He heard dimly the screaming of the crowd as he sank into a black bottomless void. Whatever was happening, it couldn't be good at all. Not good at all.

Evelyn Walsh heard a ticking sound at the same time something brutal and evil smote her in the chest, amidst a whorl of whirling fragments, bits of masonry and glass. Darkness. She couldn't breathe. She knew vaguely that she must breathe if she was to live. She tried to scream and didn't have the energy even for that. Debris continued to pelt her, yet she felt distanced from it all. Even from the confusion, the cries of the wounded, the screams of the terrified, and the mad scramble by those alive to get as far away from the scene as possible. She heard a low moan and thought it came from her. If only she could breathe; the dust seemed to be layered inches thick in her lungs. She struggled, and it seemed her lungs would burst through the roof of her mouth if she didn't draw in just one lungful of clean air, blessed clean air. Oh God, no. If she didn't . . .

The white light burst upon her suddenly.

It was brilliant, a revelation disclosing a leaf-clad brook splashed in golden autumn colors. It was morning, the air clear and crisp above the tree line, but a thin mist hung over the silent brook that curved through meadows where the grass never rose more than ankle height. The imprint of God lay across the meadows; an Unseen Footfall that trod the realm. She knew then it would be alright. She saw her uncle Alistair and her niece Joanne, he in his quaint Scottish kilt and oxford pumps, she in a frilly summer frock. They had died eight years apart. Back in the 1970's.. They waved at her, beckoning from the brilliance of the incredible white light. There was a tranquility on their faces that Evelyn herself yearned for. They seemed happy to see her. Evelyn felt such peace descend upon her as she had never before known. The Good did exist, and she sought it. She smiled back at her uncle and his daughter and glided over—how effortless!—to join them.

CHAPTER 11

Champaign-Urbana.

Evelyn Walsh floated. She floated near the roof of the ambulance that tore through city streets, lights flashing, sirens wailing. Below her on a gurney, two paramedics were attending to a bleeding old woman. Shocked, she recognized the frail woman on the gurney as herself. Was she really that old? Stringy white hair, brown age spots on the face—or were those bruises? Wires and tubes ran from her body into IV tubes and monitoring devices. Why were the two men applying what looked like two ironing paddles to her chest and watching her jump? She felt removed from it all, only a slight tug on her chest whenever those dreadful things were applied. She didn't want the paddles. They disturbed her, brought her back from the peace and the Good that uncle Alistair and niece Joanne were enjoying. Peace that she, too, wanted to enjoy.

She was back in the old woman's body, and she wondered why that was so. The technician peered at the oscilloscope. A squiggle had appeared, the machine beeped. Another squiggle.

"I've got a heartbeat," yelled the technician.

The third paramedic who was hooked up by headphones to a surgeon at Humana Hospital said into her microphone, "We've got a pulse."

"Good," said the trauma surgeon at the other end. "Continue massaging the pericardial sac."

"Got it."

The ambulance slowed, then sped through a red light. The technician bent over Evelyn Walsh's chest and noticed for the first time that her right breast was completely missing. Adjoining tissue was disfigured by keloids; even the lymph nodes under her armpit had been removed. News that had been judiciously kept from the press. After taxes, the technician cleared $48,876 annually. He wondered if he could sell the story of Mrs. Walsh's radical unilateral mastectomy to the *National Enquirer* for $100,000. If he could take cell phone pictures of her missing right breast, maybe he could go to *Hustler* magazine. He would demand half a million from Larry Flynt and get it.

The other technician laid aside the cardiac defibrillator and wondered if he'd be invited to a White House reception when this was all over. They were both jolted out of their thoughts when the ambulance pulled into the emergency entrance of Humana Hospital. The trauma team was waiting to receive Evelyn Walsh.

———

Washington, DC.
ABC News interrupted regular programming to announce the bomb blast at the University of Illinois campus. Scores of people were reported killed, many more injured, including possibly Vice President and Mrs. Walsh. NBC and CBS followed in a similar vein. On CNN, it was a breaking news story. Since all major networks already had anchors or senior correspondents on scene to cover the supercomputer launch, it was a matter of cutting live to Champaign-Urbana. Indeed, two network correspondents had been injured in the bomb blast, one critically. Local anchors quickly filled in the gap. It would take up a major portion of the evening news. One network anchor was already on his way from New York by chartered Learjet to cover the disaster.

Secret Service Chief Hy Strooker and FBI Chief G. Everston Creed were on different telephones briefing President Deakin, who was at

Camp David. The president was preparing to leave immediately for Washington, DC. A statement for the entire nation was being prepared by close advisers and speechwriters to be read by the president that afternoon.

At a cafeteria inside the Capitol, a man named Boris was eating lunch when the newsflash came. He listened attentively. He was eating spaghetti with white clam sauce and pairing it with two glasses of port. He chuckled after the newsbreak. When he had finished, he made a phone call on his untraceable cell phone.

———

Nabil drove east on Interstate 74. It was difficult, but he drove exactly at sixty-five miles per hour, plus or minus three. Through Danville, Veedersburg, Crawfordsville. His heart leaped every time he passed a squad car. Indiana state troopers seemed to be everywhere. One hid in a ditch, aiming his radar gun at oncoming traffic. Nabil was almost on top of him when he saw the squad car inclined up the ditch slope. He caught a glimpse of a mustachioed face, determined and cagey behind dark Ray-Bans, balancing the radar gun on the window ledge like it was an extension of his dick. Then Nabil was past, the speedometer hanging on the sixty-seven miles per hour he had been doing. He stepped lightly on the brakes, scanning the rearview, expecting to see flashing lights and hear the urgent wail of a siren. The Toyota Sienna slowed, sixty-five . . . sixty. . . . Nothing. He breathed again. Must watch it. Couldn't afford to be pulled over now. By 3:30 p.m. he had left Indianapolis behind. He cruised now on I-70 eastbound.

The van's AM/FM kept him briefed on events as he ate up the miles. Half-hourly updates followed by twenty-five minutes of music and commercials. From Illinois through Indiana, and now as he crossed into Ohio at Richmond, the news was that a terrorist bomb had exploded at the University of Illinois Computer Center, destroying the much-ballyhooed supercomputer that was a key part of the Strategic Defense

Initiative building block. Vice President Walsh and Mrs. Walsh were among the casualties; the vice president had suffered a major concussion, a broken left arm, and serious internal injuries, but was expected to live. Mrs. Walsh was currently undergoing major surgery from unspecified injuries, and the prognosis was grim. Air Force General A. E. Avramson, head of the SDI program was confirmed dead, as was General Jimmy Tuttle III, chief of army staff. Twenty-three people had been killed by the blast—most military brass, scientists, and a few civilians. At least 116 people were injured, many seriously. And these were only preliminary numbers.

Police and the FBI were looking for the suspect. There followed a brief description of Nabil—quite accurate, too. The man went under the name Samir Muvdi, was thought to be of Middle Eastern extraction, and should be considered armed and extremely dangerous. Anyone sighting him should report to the nearest police station, police officer, or other law enforcement agency. President Deakin had cut short his Camp David stay to rush back to the White House. He would address the nation any minute now, and they would carry the broadcast live.

Nabil drove with one hand and opened his valise with the other. He brought out his beard disguise. He waited until there was no other vehicle within half a mile and then turned the rearview mirror until he could see his face. He kept the speedometer glued at sixty-five, thanks to the cruise control feature, and tried not to weave as he attached the theatrical beard to his face using one hand. It was difficult but manageable. The Sienna stayed true to its lane, and finally Nabil had the beard firmly and acceptably in place. His mustache was genuine, but the beard added an unusually thick upper fluff. Nothing he could do about that. He would have to adjust it once he reached a restroom. He straightened the rear view mirror.

He dared not stop! He had passed up rest area after rest area, fearing that someone might spot him, note the make of the car, and make a swift phone call. The thought of stopping to relieve his bladder actually made the problem worse, and his bladder pulled at him urgently. He tore his mind away, praying for darkness to envelop the land so he could do the deed. He was glad he had switched cars with Schmidt back in St. Joseph. How had they traced him so fast? He had passed Springfield, Ohio—he looked at his watch—thirty minutes ago. It was getting dark now and Columbus was only ten minutes away. In Columbus, he would do what had to be done. Columbus was a large city.

It was just after 7:00 p.m. when he entered Columbus and negotiated his way through city traffic. Part of the interstate wound through the heart of the city, and he fought to stay on the correct lane and correct route.

President Deakin's speech on the radio had been concise and tough. He asked the nation to remain calm. The ugly foot of terrorism had once again landed on American soil, and there should be no doubt that it was terrorism. Whether domestic or international remained to be determined by investigators. But make no mistake, those responsible for this heinous act of cowardice would be sought and brought to book. Law enforcement officials were working around the clock. He thanked everyone involved in the rescue effort: the triage teams set up in the wake of the blast, the fire fighters, policemen, nurses, doctors, and even ordinary citizens who had opened their homes up to emergency personnel or donated blood and blankets. He was in contact with the families of Vice President and Mrs. Richard Walsh; it was too early yet to comment on their condition, but together with the nation he prayed for their complete recovery. He reminded the nation that America was not under siege—the agents of terror were. Their capture and subsequent trial was a foregone conclusion. He ended his speech by intoning emotionally, "God bless you all. God bless America."

———

On the outskirts of Columbus, the traffic thinned considerably, although the lights of the great city cast a luminescent glow on the clouds that hung low over the city. Nabil could wait no longer. His bladder ached.

Moreover, the fuel needle was edging toward empty. He pulled into a large Mobil gas station. He avoided the self-service pumps, because then he would have to go inside to pay and the klieg lights would expose him too much. He used full-service and stayed inside the car. Through the window he told the attendant curtly, "Fill her up."

He watched as his windshield was cleaned with squeegee and mop. He tipped the attendant fifty cents, and then pulled over to the far side near a sign advertising free air. He walked back to the men's room, which was attached to the building facing the lot and could be accessed without having to go inside the mart. He was inside for about four minutes, emptying his bladder thoroughly, washing his hands, and adjusting the beard disguise so it wasn't askew. He would have loved a hot meal, but that was out of the question for now. Later, he would find a small, out-of-the-way motel and lodge for the night. He would think out the plan during the night. He would have to ditch the car somehow and use another alias—he still had two others in his briefcase. As he emerged from the men's room, he had a direct view of another gas station across the road. A dark red sedan was just pulling up alongside the full-service pumps. Nabil did not give it another glance, just noted it in his subconscious, as per his training. He fumbled for coins and bought two cans of soda, two Twinkies, and one energy bar from the vending machines next to the ice chest on the side of the building. He carried the snacks in one hand and the soda in the other, although ready to drop everything and lunge for his gun if it became necessary. He turned the corner to cross the lot to his car and froze.

A police car was parked two cars down from him. Nabil fought to remain calm. He walked carefully, steadily, toward the Sienna. He wanted to run away, the other way, any way. The cruiser was a big Ford Crown Victoria sedan bristling with aerials. It bore the emblem of the Ohio State Police on the side and a female officer in an oversized Stetson and Texas Ranger-style uniform sat behind the wheel, reading a Barbara Cartland novel while simultaneously eating from a Kentucky Fried Chicken takeout pack. The big cruiser's engine ticked over in low idle, the crackle and static of police talk rent the early night air. The cop must have pulled in while Nabil was in the can.

The trooper looked up as he passed. For one long, infinitesimal moment, she locked eyes with him. She was young, about twenty-six or twenty-eight, with blond, close-cropped hair and an alert, intelligent face. The shock of eye contact caused Nabil to fumble, and a can of Coke fell from his grasp. It hit the pavement and rolled back several yards. Cursing, he went after it, bent down to pick it up, inadvertently kicked it a few more yards, finally retrieved it and walked back to his car. The policewoman had lost interest in him; she was immersed in her book.

Maybe I'm getting too old for this sort of thing. Nabil furiously ground the starter and gently eased the Sienna out of the gas station. He found the access ramp to I-70 East and followed it. He glanced furtively in the rearview mirror. No sign of the state trooper. He relaxed. The beard disguise had saved him. How would the woman—the trooper—have felt if she'd known she had just looked into the eyes of the most wanted man in America and hadn't even known it? At the very least, a one-rank promotion would have awaited her just for his apprehension. He smiled as he accelerated into the flow of eastbound traffic out of Etna toward Buckeye Lake.

His smile vanished when he glanced in the rearview mirror again and saw the big police cruiser easing into traffic a half-mile behind—and gaining.

CHAPTER 12

Columbus.

Ohio State Trooper Jane Tipsword had pulled into the gas station after she bought two pieces of original recipe chicken, with biscuit, coleslaw, and a medium Diet Pepsi from the nearby KFC. This was her favorite spot when patrol duty brought her to the vicinity. The exit ramps from I-70 merged into the same road leading back to the access ramps, the two conjoined by a four-lane viaduct beneath which expressway traffic sped by. If she got a call, she could be on the interstate, eastbound or westbound, in forty-five seconds flat. She finished the coleslaw and took one bite out of the chicken leg before opening the Danielle Steele novel to the page she'd marked earlier when she had to stop to respond to a multiple pileup on the westbound highway ninety minutes earlier. This was the part she loved most. The elusive heroine had pulled out all the stops, the dark handsome hero had battled through all the obstacles placed in his path, and it was time to claim his bride's hymen. Corporal Tipsword blushed. Still!

That was when the Geiger pinged.

Startled, she looked up to see a bearded neatly dressed gentleman walking past. He held two cans of soda and some snacks from the vending machine in both hands. She looked around for the offending truck or eighteen-wheeler that usually triggered the alarm. Instead she made eye contact with the gentleman. He dropped a Coke can and went after it. She almost laughed. She sometimes had that effect on men, right from her teenage years. She dreaded the day the magic would no longer work. The man retrieved the soda, and as he walked past the cruiser a second time, the Geiger squawked again.

No doubt about it.

Like all state police cruisers in most states, Corporal Tipsword's cruiser was equipped with a small Geiger counter, used to monitor interstate transportation of radioactive material. The device was mounted near the rear window. An audible chime and a discreet red light on the dashboard were activated by a "hit." In the last ten months, Corporal Tipsword had only lodged two hits. She had pulled over both vehicles. Both had been eighteen-wheelers; the drivers had the correct paperwork and everything checked out. The Geiger was fine-tuned to eliminate nuisance squawks from microwave towers and TV stations. Still, there were false alarms and this was probably one. True, you could get a hit sometimes from cars under surveillance by a different police agency, if an RF magnetic beacon or other type of monitoring device had been affixed to the car. But she'd be damned if the darn thing hadn't gone off each time the bearded gentleman walked past her cruiser. Was he carrying a miniaturized radioactive device on his person? An ankle bracket for keeping tabs on parolees or serious sex offenders? Was he under surveillance by some agency? Feds possibly. They loved those radioactive isotope monitors for high-tech surveillance. She looked at the black and white blow-up of the terrorist named Samir Muvdi clipped to her dashboard. It had been circulated to all troopers at the state police barracks. This man was bearded, no resemblance at all. But the nose did have a Roman hook. She watched the Sienna pull out of the lot—he was clearly hugging the curb to avoid her reading his license plates. Illinois plates, she noted.

Illinois!

She put the novel and the half-eaten chicken leg away. She nudged the gear from park to drive and followed the Sienna at a good clip.

He stayed in the right lane, so she did the same. She swung to the left to overtake two cars and then tucked in right behind him. Now he could make no mistake that he was the object of her curiosity. She picked up her mike and called in the license plate numbers. She could see the small tab on the license plate that indicated a rental car. The red halo from the Geiger monitor light gave the passenger side of the car a strange sheen. The meter showed only a small deflection. Whatever he was carrying, it was only a small amount. They stayed this way, the pursued and the pursuer, for half a mile, glued like tag-team partners. The Sienna stayed within the speed limit.

The plate numbers came in from the dispatcher: Hertz rental, origin Chicago. Officer Tipsword flicked on her flashers and the high wattage side lamp and hit the siren briefly. The Sienna pulled over without a fuss. He had to have been expecting it. She flicked on another switch to activate the dash-mounted video camera. A cop's best ally in court. Or during internal investigations if a suspect's lawyer alleges faulty procedure or use of excessive force. She got out of the cruiser, holding the long black flashlight in her left hand, her nightstick swinging from her hip belt, slapping her thigh. The state police-issue Smith & Wesson .38 swung from the same ammo belt that did nothing to hide her feminine curves. The ten-gallon Stetson gave her a frontier-woman look.

Nabil had known he was in trouble when the police car latched onto his tail and stayed there. He eased the heavy Browning out of his waistband and laid it on the seat beside him. He threw his jacket over it. This might be a routine traffic stop, but he didn't think so. As far as he knew, he had not violated any traffic codes or exhibited DUI behavior. When the siren wailed, he slowed and pulled over like any respectable citizen.

His right hand stole under the jacket, gripped the Browning, and nudged the safety to off. He saw the trooper emerge from the cruiser, noted the swing of her hips as she walked toward his window. Traffic was light streaming out of Columbus. Headlights raced by at intervals, accompanied by the scream of high-rev engines. He lowered the car window. A pity she had to die. What a waste of good fox!

She stood a hand's length away from the window, aiming the flashlight into the car's interior. She was younger than he had first gauged, her nose arched slightly and a spot of color highlighted one cheek. Her face was all-American, and she met the statutory height requirement for a state trooper: five foot ten in her police oxfords.

"See your driver's license, sir?"

Out of his peripheral vision, Nabil noticed a car slowing down behind them. Motorists instinctively slow down on sighting a police car—even one with a pulled-over suspect. This car, however, almost drew to a stop alongside the cruiser. There was a sudden spurt of acceleration, and a dark red vehicle pulled up alongside the Sienna. Something stung Nabil on the left cheek at the same time a car backfired twice. The state trooper had started to turn around. Two exit wounds appeared at the front of her uniform. Those were shots, not backfires. She made a strangled sound that came out a sigh and started to topple. In a flash Nabil grabbed her arm, pinning her to the window, intending to use her body as shield from whoever was doing the shooting. The trooper's flashlight fell, rolled to the side, the beam still on. Nabil brought up the Browning, straining to see around the officer's body.

"Get in! Quick! Leave the car."

The voice came from the red car. It was still abreast of Nabil's car, constituting a road hazard. Even though the hazard lights were on, there was no doubt it would be rammed from behind any moment now. Already one irate motorist, leaning on his horn, had sped past, raining verbal abuse. Something in the voice from the red saloon sounded familiar. Nabil absorbed all this in one split second.

In another he took everything else in.

"Move forward! Get off the road," he ordered the occupants of the red car, who—looking around the trooper's body—he could now see were two men.

Still holding the slain officer's left hand and literally pulling up her entire weight to prevent her from falling to the ground, he jerked the body toward him, her head coming in through the open window. He thrust her hand between the steering wheel, wound the seat belt loop twice around the arm, killed the engine, then swung the steering wheel to the right until it locked. Now the trooper was anchored in place, looking as though she was leaning inside the minivan to inspect something suspicious. Her cleavage rested on his face, her neck was smooth and pale white and trace sweat reached his nostrils. Cordite also. A St. Christopher medal hung from a pendant around her collar, and she was very dead.

Nabil grabbed his gun, coat, and valise and pushed himself out the front passenger door in a hurry. He glanced back at the cruiser, its headlights blazing, red lights revolving on the roof lantern. The red saloon had pulled over in front of the Sienna. The right rear window rolled down, and he thrust his coat and valise inside, opened the door, and jumped in as the car, tires squealing, jerked forward. The powered windows rolled silently up, and the car accelerated.

Nabil lay back in the crushed velour rear seat, breathing hard. He studied the two men in front. Late twenties or early thirties, rugged, looked like they spent a lot of time at the gym. Same ilk as the Cossack who had driven him from the front of the UN building to LaGuardia. A device that resembled a small TV set lay on the pedestal, its cord plugged into the lighter socket. It emitted a green glow and had a grid-like picture on the screen. A tracking device.

"Who are you?" Nabil asked the men. "I'm sure this was no coincidence. You were following me."

The men exchanged glances. "We got you out. That is what matters," said the android that wasn't driving.

"What happens from here?"

"As before. You continue to the destined place. The plans will continue for the other."

"That is the instruction from Boris," added the driver.

Now things were beginning to make sense.

"So Boris told you to follow me?"

"Not correct. We rescued you, that is all. Our orders were to make sure you got to the Pennsylvania border. Then we turn back."

"Then another surveillance team takes over?

"We don't know."

"Why Pennsylvania?"

The man shrugged. "Perhaps it is the destined place."

Two police cars raced by in the opposite direction, sirens screaming, lights flashing. Officer Tipsword's body had been discovered. Nabil examined his face in the rearview mirror. A slight furrow on the cheek that could pass for a shaving nick—and bits of gore from Tipsword's body. The Cossack had used a heavy-caliber weapon. He wiped off the blood with his handkerchief. The second bullet must have impacted bone, diverted, and fallen off.

"Now we cannot take you to the Pennsylvania border," the driver said. "Some motorists saw this car next to the police car when we shot the state trooper. The description will soon go out. We have to drop you soon, and get out ourselves."

As he spoke, the other man disconnected the tracker, wrapped the cord around it, and stuffed it into a briefcase. The driver braked, swinging right to take a truck-stop exit. Both men watched the rear-view mirror. A motorist could have witnessed the shooting of the state trooper and trailed the car, perhaps calling the police on a cell phone.

Nothing but normal traffic. The Cossack accelerated again, heading toward the industrial complex off the exit, only to brake hard at an intersection, swing a one-eighty and head back the way he had come. A Union 76 truck stop filled an entire acreage near the expressway entrance. More than a dozen eighteen-wheelers, various pickups, and vans were parked in orderly lines all over the lot. A large rectangular bungalow housed the restaurant, cash office, mini-mart, petroleum products, and spare parts shop. The restrooms, as usual, were outside at the side of the building. The soda machines stood in front near the door entrance. The fuel pumps were scattered over the ramp, which included on the far side a lube center with two or three semis in various stages of repair. The lot opposite the restrooms held the greatest number of eighteen-wheelers.

The Cossack drove behind the long trailers, keeping the car between the rigs and the waste-oil outhouse and garbage disposal. Several trucks had their engines running. Nabil wondered why. It was still fall and diesels cold-started as easily as they did in summer.

The car stopped. The Cossack said, "Jump on the rig. They won't find you."

Nabil hesitated. "What about you two?"

"We'll ditch the car. Don't worry, we can take care of ourselves."

Nabil got out of the car. He glanced around furtively. Nobody. The manner in which the Cossack had parked gave anyone looking the impression that the occupants were throwing their trash into the garbage disposal. Why had they stopped at that particular trailer? Perhaps the wire lock on the rig looked easy to tackle. Did they really expect him to hitch a ride cross-country inside a dark, dirty truck container? What if they put a bullet into his back? Not likely.

"Hey, Joe!" a voice hollered across the ramp, quite near. "Get a move on those damn dusters. We're outta here, and you ain't doing shit."

Nabil had seen a half-open door on a Kenworth three trucks behind as they drove past. He ran that way, the valise knocking against his leg, and he dodged between two rigs. The huge diesel of the Kenny rumbled reassuringly. Thank Allah it had a cabover. He vaulted in, keeping his head low. A brown curtain on string rollers covered the cabover; he parted it and peeked in. Nobody. He vaulted again into the recesses of the cabover, landing on a foldaway steel bed in a jumble of blankets, pillows, old denim clothing, and a discarded fast food sack. Two cowboy boots were wedged between the folding mechanism and the floor. The compartment smelled of engine oil and sweat. The chatter from the CB radio was ceaseless. And a radar detector on the dash also beeped annoyingly. He peered over the empty front seats. He supposed the truckers were inside the restaurant, filling up on coffee and donuts, bantering with other truckers, unwinding. He could see the dark red saloon car driving away in the direction of the town.

The brown curtain ensured privacy. Unless the truck driver wanted to use it himself, of course. Nabil arranged the curtain so he could see into the driver's cabin through a crack near the parting rod. He removed from his valise a custom noise suppressor and affixed it to the Browning. He placed the pillow on top of the gun, making sure the safety was on to prevent accidental discharge.

"But, honey, they could have figured it out by their selves! I thought they was into dogs-owning." A woman's voice floated in the night air, clear, homespun, gravy in her Midwestern twang.

Nabil ducked. A husband and wife team? He raised the cot, settling himself among the clutter on the floor—clothing, shoes, fast-food take-out wrappers. He kept his gun hand free and pulled the foldaway cot down. The cot and the blanket covered him nicely. It was tight and it was uncomfortable, but he felt secure from any but the most inquisitive search.

Without warning, the passenger door flung open. A deep male voice said, "Git in there!" Somebody did. A woman. The cheap fragrance was unmistakable. The driver's door opened, and a man climbed into the driver's seat of the rig.

"Oh-hhh, a Kenny!" the woman cooed. "I love it. I think Kennys are the best."

"They're okay," the man growled. "A Mack's okay, too. MAN diesel, now that's a rig for you."

With a blast of the horn, the semi jerked forward.

CHAPTER 13

Columbus.

It was hard, even painful at certain times, but Nabil bore the discomfort as the truck quivered, shook, and bounced its way onto the Interstate. It was smoother on the highway. He had no idea where they were headed, but he knew he could always get back to the rendezvous point. His immediate problem was to evade capture.

The driver swore.

"What is it, hon?" the woman asked.

"Damn fuzzbuster. Gone bonkers again. It's been bleating since we left the stop, and I ain't seen no Smokey around. Have you?"

That explained the beeping from the dashboard! Nabil listened as the driver got on the CB radio, yelling jargon about his handle, his position, and had anyone seen Smokey twenty miles east of Columbus? *Good*, Nabil thought; they were headed east. Not satisfied with the responses he got, the driver replaced the mike, grumbling.

"Goddamned sonuvabitch. Thought I fixed the sumbitch couple of months back. Can't be that many TV and radio stations around." He switched off the radar detector in anger.

"I aim to make Wheeling 'fore I turn in for the night," the rig driver told his companion. "Get a head start tomorrow. Be in Boston late afternoon. That suit your schedule, baby?" He shook with laughter.

"Stuff you, Bill. Wheeling's as far as I go."

Bill lit a cigarette. "Want one?"

"Gave it up. You know that."

"Shucks, that's right. Been a while since I gave you a ride, huh, Becky?"

"I been there all this while."

"Never did see you."

"I know you didn't. Men are all the same—different piece of pie every other day. Sure you were giving rides, but not to me."

After a silence, Bill said, "We'll catch up, baby. You mark my words, we'll catch up."

"Can't wait, Bill." Her voice was loaded with scorn.

Silence. The acrid cigarette smoke had started to seep inside the compartment where Nabil lay. He hoped he wouldn't feel the need to cough or sneeze. That would be disastrous.

Becky must have been feeling the smoke, too. She said, "Open that window a bit, please. I can't breathe."

"Sure."

The ventilation helped. After a while, Bill said, "Hey, seen that movie some years back? *Turkish Express*, something like that?"

"I don't think so."

"Come on. You seen it. Everyone has. American boy on vacation in Istanbul gets caught with drugs. The prison warden's fucking gay—"

"*Midnight Express*? Yes, I have. Why?"

"Yeah. You remind me of Turkey. Don't know why I said that. Something here reminds me of Turkey."

"What in God's name are you talking about? You completely lost me."

"You know. Turkey. Iran, Iraq, Kuwait, all those goddamn countries."

"So?"

"You been with another man today, Becky? An Iranian man?"

A long pause. Becky said, "I left my house not quite two hours ago, Bill. I've not been with another man. No one."

"Sure?"

"Positive. Look, if you'd rather I got down—"

"Cut the crap. I swear I smell an Iranian man in this cab. Hard to explain, but I sure knows what I mean. You been eating Middle Eastern food, Becky? Indian, perhaps?"

"Quit it!" Becky shouted. "You were the one bought me the big meal cheeseburger and grits and those greasy onion rings in that goddamned truck stop. Now quit it. Just quit! But now you mention it, I was gonna say I thought your new hair varnish kind of smells like Beirut."

Bill ran a self-conscious hand through his hair.

"I was right," he grumbled. "Must be that sumbitch who wiped my windscreen at the stop while I was topping up the tanks. Sumbitch had to climb inside the cab to do that, and his smell ain't washed off yet. Didn't look none too clean to me. Real dark, too. Gotta be him. Else he's from parts of coalmine Kentucky I never heard of."

The truck slowed and left the Interstate. It moved at walking pace and then stopped. Harsh fluorescent lights permeated even Nabil's hiding place. Nabil, in his prone position, gripped the gun tighter and waited.

Bill gathered up some papers and hopped down from the cab.

"Be right back, baby," he said.

Four minutes passed. Becky farted, long and heartily, like rapid gunfire. "Bless me," she said. Then voices outside.

"Hell of a way to get on a weigh bridge, partner."

"Son of a gun. No one does it better, I can tell you."

"What you haulin', Bill?"

"Merchandise. Stuff."

"Two sixty over."

"No shit. I got a broad in there."

"I can see that. Knocks the pants right off me. Look, I'll take off one fifty on account of her. You still got one hundred ten unaccounted for. I know the tare weight of your rig, Bill."

"I topped up in Columbus," Bill grumbled. "Plus I'm haulin' from Indy. Maybe they got an extra box or something back in there. Those people count wrong sometimes."

"Yeah. I guess."

There was tearing of paper, more grunts. Someone spat on the ground. "You hear of the killing of the vice president?"

"What!"

"Well, he ain't dead, just injured. But his wife is. I reckon she is. She's in a coma and not expected to recover."

Bill sounded genuinely shocked. "That's bad. They catch the person done it?"

"Persons, more likely. Terrorists and whatnot. Makes you wonder where we're headed."

"Sure does."

"You haulin' all the way to New York, Bill?"

"Boston. You got the bill of lading right in front of you, Carlyle."

The man named Carlyle chuckled. More paper was torn, exchanged hands. "You have a nice one now."

"I'll try. So long, buddy."

"Yeah. See you."

In minutes, they were back on the Interstate. "Damn weigh stations," Bill grumbled. He fumbled with the radar detector. Again the beep-beep of active capture confirmed by the green light on the device. He turned off the gadget in disgust. "Goddamn fuzzbuster ain't worth a motherfucking piece of shit."

"Bill," Becky said indignantly, "you are talking in the presence of a born and bred Southern belle."

Bill stared at her. "Southern belle? Southern belle?" He roared with laughter.

"Shut up."

"Southern belle. I like that. Run that by me again."

"I told you to shut up."

Bill lit another cigarette. "Did I ever get to tell you 'bout a friend of mine who went out with a good ol' Southern belle down in the South?"

"Don't believe you ever did."

"Yeah, well I guess Florida's in the South."

"Well, tell me."

"Sumbitch friend of mine goes down to Florida for his annual vacation and winds up on the beach. My friend walks down the beach, admiring all the beautiful folks sitting on the sand and lying on their recliners, all come out for a swim and tan and shit. And he looks up and sees right in the middle of the beach the most gorgeous blond woman he's ever seen. She's sittin' there all cute in a beach chair, and he's never seen anyone so lovely. He can't help himself and so he walks over to her and he's tongue-tied 'cause he ain't seen so much beauty in one package before. He can't believe it—thinks he's hallucinating—when the blond looks up at him, smiles, and says, 'Hi, hon. Looking for some fun?' My friend just about shits in his pants. Can't believe his luck and all that. Long and short of it is, he buys her a drink and one for himself—several really, he needed it—and takes her to a restaurant, and they have a nice dinner where she tells him she's a Southern belle from Georgia, and he shouldn't expect anything more after dinner. Only that's all bullshit 'cause she turns out to want it more than he does and afterward they end up in his hotel room and spend the rest of the night fucking each other's brains out. My friend's never had it so good."

"Is that right?" Becky's voice was noncommittal.

"Damn right. Except he wakes up in the morning and finds he's got the worst dose of clap this side of the Texas panhandle. The girl's gone and ain't nothing he can do about it now, 'cept go to a doctor and get his clap all cleared up. Which he does. Well, the next year my friend gets another vacation same month as the previous year and winds up in Florida again. He walks down the beach again 'bout the same time, and he looks up and there's the same gorgeous blond, same beach, same spot, sitting on her beach chair. She looks up, smiles at him, and says, 'Hi, hon. Want to have fun?' My friend looks at her and says, 'What are you selling this year—cancer?'"

Nabil's involuntary laugh was drowned by Bill and Becky's guffaw. By the providence of Allah, they didn't hear him. When they had finished laughing, Becky said, "And I'll tell you what, Billy Joe. That was no friend of yours. That was you."

Bill looked at her with something close to respect. "Okay. If you say so."

After a prolonged silence, he said, "Why don't you hold me some, baby?"

"No can do. It isn't safe."

"Safe?"

"You're driving."

"Don't hurt none."

"Says you."

"Come on, Becky."

"Alright. But if you start to lose control of the rig, I'm hands off."

"Get on with it."

Nabil could hear Becky move closer to Bill. The sound of a zipper opening. The rig swayed uncertainly.

"Watch it," Becky warned.

"Just hold on to it."

Silence. Rubbing sounds. Becky's shrill voice, in awe. Or faking it. "Look how big it's become."

"What are you going to do about it?"

"Plenty of time at the hotel. Wheeling's just ahead."

"Play with it, hon," Bill pleaded. "Just play with it."

Nabil could hear her working furiously on him.

"Don't stop!" Bill gasped.

"Are you going to come like this?"

"Watch me."

"It's taking so long. You won't have any left for me when we get to the motel."

"Who cares? Just takes longer is all."

Seven minutes later, Becky said, "You still ain't come, honey."

"I'm not young anymore, Becky. Takes a goddamn while."

Becky stretched and yawned. "Well, I'm tired. My hand's tired."

"I was about to come. Why did you stop?"

"Oh really."

"Come on, hon."

"Try and come in the next five minutes. I don't want to have tennis elbow."

"Very funny."

She pumped some more. After about four minutes, she said, "No good, Bill."

"Don't stop!"

"It's not—"

"Don't stop, goddamn you!"

"Honey, I can't—"

"Don't stop!"

Five minutes later, she said, "It's gone down again. Bill, I'm sorry. My hand's aching. Both hands."

Bill sounded dejected. "Maybe if you kissed it for me, it would stay up."

"In the motel. I promise." She leaned over and zipped him up as far as she could. She lay back in her seat, wiping her hands on a tissue, then spent some minutes straightening her hair.

They reached Wheeling a few minutes before 11 p.m. The Kenworth pulled into a Days Motel parking lot. "You go get us a room, hon," Bill said, "while I park the rig." He gave her sixty dollars.

Becky left. Bill backed the rig into a parking spot. The parking brake hissed as it took hold, and Bill jumped down from the cab to secure the rig.

It was a bad spot for Nabil. Light fell squarely on the cab's interior. Nabil gripped the Browning tighter. He knew what would happen next. Bill would come in, reach over and grab his battered overnight bag containing a clean shirt and boxer shorts for tomorrow. The foldaway cot hid Nabil. But if Bill switched on the inside light, if he rummaged inside the bundle of used clothes and junk, if he even looked closely at the positioning of the hammock . . . Nabil would have to shoot him. Through the pillow. With the silencer in place, Billy Joe would never know what killed him. He covered his body completely, knowing Bill must surely look inside the cabover.

Bill climbed back into the cab and killed the engine. He was singing Julio Iglesias's *Moonlight Lady*, hopelessly off-key and with poor rhythm. He coughed phlegmatically, reached inside the sleeping berth and lifted out his brown overnight bag. He jumped down again and resumed his song while shutting and locking the cab door. The tap-tap of his cowboy boots echoed on the tarmac, moving toward the motel lobby.

Nabil emerged from his hiding place. His muscles were cramped, his body stiff. Pain shot through his joints. He waited a couple of minutes for his circulation to return, surveying the parking lot. Too much light from the high-arch lampposts. The lot was full, indicating near-full occupancy. But he knew that Bill and Becky would get a room, because the neon *Vacancies* sign was still lit. Even as he watched, the neon blinked once and changed to *No Vacancies*. Bill and Becky had taken the last available room.

A steak joint cum cocktail lounge was right next to the motel. Cars from its lot spilled into the motel's. Noise, laughter, boisterous piano clanging reached him. Each time the lounge door flew open, the noise cascaded briefly on the lot. It must be rowdy in there.

He would have to steal a car.

Why not steal the Kenny? Bill wouldn't miss it until morning. But Nabil had a fear of driving rigs. Of course he could move it forward, but the two or three times he had tried in the past to reverse an eighteen-wheeler, the cab had gone one way and the trailer the other. He had given up after many attempts to reposition and accepted that he'd need to attend a course to learn.

Besides, he wanted something more nondescript. Several late-model cars could be seen in the lot. The car next to the rig was just fine. A Buick LeSabre four-door, three or four years old. Bill had parked the rig behind the motel; the glass-fronted lobby with the night clerk was on the other side. Most of the glass-paned rooms facing him at ground- and first-floor levels had their floor-length drapes pulled. One was partially open with no interior lights; two were partially open and had lights. No movement in any of them.

He vaulted into the passenger seat formerly occupied by Becky. He fingered the set of three master keys attached to his key ring. He opened the Kenworth's door from inside and jumped down, holding his valise, and closed the door softly. Stretching up both hands, he drew himself up in a long, bored yawn for the benefit of anyone who might be watching: he could have just left the cocktail lounge early. He inserted the first master key into the Buick's door. The second one opened it. He was inside in seconds, the tarmac lights providing more than adequate light to break open the plastic cover of the steering bracket, pull out the wires. He had no wish to use the master keys; one needed practice with the other method. He severed the relevant wires using his teeth, rubbed them together, and the Buick purred into life. He rolled down the front windows, thrust the Buick's gear into drive, and glided out of the lot. Nobody paid him any attention. The Buick had a half-full tank, and he had no idea how to proceed to Washington, DC. He stopped at a busy all-night gas station, topped up the tanks, and bought road maps covering the Midwest from Ohio to the entire East Coast. He discovered the car he had stolen had Pennsylvania license plates. In a few minutes, he was out on the Interstate, headed east.

CHAPTER 14

Pennsylvania.

Nabil left West Virginia eastbound to Pennsylvania, joining the Pennsylvania Turnpike on I-70/76 south of Pittsburgh. Well past midnight now. Twelve hours had passed since the missiles demolished the supercomputer center. Nabil clicked on the cruise control, and the big Buick surged forward under automatic throttle. He lapped up the miles, the markers receding at regular intervals. His headlights cut a ready swath through the night. Sixty-five miles per hour, the legal speed limit. How sad for Americans: to have such good roads and be unable to floor the throttle and watch the car take off. He missed the freedom of Germany's autobahns. Huge eighteen-wheelers passed him like he was stationary, their wind displacement pushing the Buick sideways.

He was alone for intervals, enveloped in the surreal world of bright halogens, the music of the tires on black tarmac, the landscape limited to the occasional light from farm hamlets, ghost towns, Podunkvilles.

He fought the urge to tuck in behind one of the giant rigs and nudge the speedometer up to seventy-five. Most rigs had radar detectors or CB radios and generally knew where Smokey was. But the stakes were too high for Nabil, and he didn't want to risk being stopped on any pretext. He heard a new sound, the rattle of loose gravel, the grinding of uneven traction. Allahu Akbar! He wrenched the wheel sharply to the left. The tires squealed, and the car swerved on the blacktop. He had hit the brakes coming out of the swerve, and this action disconnected the cruise control. Nabil had fallen asleep for God knows how many seconds. Cruise control and a sleepy driver were a lethal combination.

He drove on manual pedal, forcing himself to stay awake, and plugged on. At Breezewood, I-70 south would take him to Hagerstown, Maryland, and down to Frederick. Join I-270 south to the vicinity of Washington, DC. It looked good on his map. The trouble was staying awake.

The micro-sleeps occurred frequently. On three occasions, one or two wheels left the blacktop, sang on gravel, before he wrenched the Buick back into its lane. He must have yawned a hundred times, talked to himself, then sang, first in French, then in English, and in his native Arabic. He told himself that he had enough willpower to resist sleep. And road hypnosis. And . .

He couldn't remember anything momentarily—who he was, what he was doing driving through this starry night to the hiss of tires on asphalt, around curves, through hills, tunnels, long stretches of turnpike. He shook himself awake, forced himself to regain what must have been his fifth or sixth wind, and plodded on.

A tiny voice in his head told Nabil that the prolonged effects of sleep deprivation were insidious; running off the road during a micro-sleep could happen at any moment. It was a voice Nabil had learned to listen to over the years. The dashboard clock read 2:42 a.m.

Nabil drove slower now, fifty-five miles per hour, and pulled into the next rest area. Only three cars in the lot. He killed the engine. The wind rustled the leaves in hushed silence; the occasional harsh sound of a racing engine reached him from the interstate. He emerged from the car and stretched. He walked inside the building with its giant wall map covering the state and the country and the big red arrow with the words *You Are Here*. He was still in Pennsylvania.

He used the urinal, tidied his hair and beard disguise, and stole a full roll of tissue paper from the dispenser, before heading back to the car. He cracked the front windows a bit to let in the chill morning air, locked all the doors, reclined the driver's seat, and was asleep in an instant.

When he awoke, the clock read 4:36 a.m. He looked around. Only two other cars in the lot. A cream-colored Mazda 626 and a red Ford Mustang. The man and woman inside the Mustang slept in their seats, heads tilted toward their respective windows. Probably couldn't afford a motel. The Mazda occupants were nowhere in sight. He went back inside the rest area lobby and bought two Twinkies and a can of Fanta from the vending machine.

He had abandoned his earlier snacks in the Sienna after the incident with the state trooper. By now he was ravenously hungry. Back in the car, he ate slowly and studied his maps again. Still no sign of the Mazda occupants. He cranked the Buick's engine, reversed, and then drove out the winding access road to join the interstate.

He felt refreshed, in control of the car and his destiny. The yawns came less frequently now. Glancing now and then in the rearview mirror, he felt certain he was not being followed.

He pulled into Hagerstown, Maryland at ten minutes past seven o'clock in the morning. He stopped at a Texaco Mart and topped up on gas once more. The pumps were all self-service, so he hopped out and pumped the gas himself and went inside to pay. He helped himself to some courtesy donuts and coffee beside the cashier, but he was still hungry. He drove around the corner to a McDonald's and bought an Egg McMuffin sandwich and two orange juices through the drive-thru window. He parked in an unobtrusive corner of the lot, removed the ham from the McMuffin, and ate slowly, drinking the gas-station coffee. The car radio was on, tuned to a local station. News of yesterday's bombing was still the top headline. Department of Homeland Security was working on leads. Suspects would be announced soon.

The Mazda 626 crept slowly into the lot. It had four-rib concentric alloy wheels that splash a silver sheen as the car moved. It was a beautiful car, cream colored, and the driver appeared intent on something straight ahead. Nabil caught a glimpse of a woman's white face as the Mazda maneuvered between cars, through the McDonald's lot, and into the Texaco gas station. It headed for the free air section. The driver got out and fiddled with the air delivery hose and squatted beside the left rear tire.

Nabil stopped eating when the Mazda pulled in. He did not believe its arrival was a coincidence.

Our instructions are to follow you as far as the Pennsylvania border.

The two Cossacks who'd rescued him in Ohio had been useful. He had stolen a car in Wheeling, totally unknown to whoever was following him, yet they had been able to keep up. Was the valise tagged? Boris's people—it must be them—were good.

A large neon sign advertised a nearby mall. Nabil finished eating and drove to the mall. A Kmart Superstore advertised twenty-four-hour service. There were few cars at this time of morning. He parked, went inside, and headed straight for the men's section. He purchased three new shirts, two pairs of pants, a packet of Hanes T-shirts and underwear, and one light winter coat. He went to shoes and bought two pairs, plus socks. He also got two dress ties and handkerchiefs. Even toothpaste, a comb, shaving cream, and a razor. Total change of wardrobe.

Twenty-five minutes later, he was heading southeast as though leaving town, the sack containing his old clothes thrown on the backseat. After ten minutes of driving, he came upon a bowling alley next to a row of one-story office buildings. He swung the wheel sharply, raced to the rear of the bowling alley, and pulled up beside two large garbage dumpsters. He got out, pulled out the sack containing his old wardrobe, and flung it into a dumpster. Same for the valise. Apart from the new wardrobe, all he had on him now were the gun, money, and the small, coded address book. He got back in the Buick and drove quickly to the adjoining office block, now filling with cars as people arrived for work. He parked in the space between two cars facing the road so he could see the dumpsters behind the bowling lanes. He killed the engine and waited.

It took another five minutes.

She came around the corner at a good clip and drove past the bowling alley and the office blocks before she realized she had overshot the coyote. She slowed, exited off an adjacent block of apartments, and came back up the access road hesitantly. She made the turn-off to the bowling alley, and slowed to a crawl. After two bracketing maneuvers, the Mazda 626 drove unerringly to the dumpsters at the rear of the bowling alley. Nabil shifted position slightly to be able to see her.

She stepped out, clutching an empty Mister Donut paper box. She was in her middle to late thirties, wore glasses, and her hair was pulled back into a severe knot at the nape of her neck. She lifted the dumpster lid—the one containing Nabil's old clothes—and threw the donut box inside. She looked around furtively, then propped the dumpster lid fully open with both hands and wedged it. She poked around. She dragged the valise and the sack containing his old wardrobe to the edge of the dumpster. She popped the lid, scrutinized the contents, and lifted Nabil's clothes from the sack. She put everything back, shut the dumpster lid, and returned to her car.

Didn't find my body, did you, sweetheart?

Nabil could almost feel her frustration. He saw her wipe her hands on a tissue. Then the Mazda jerked forward, did a one-eighty, and drove swiftly to the access road. She sped off in the direction of Hagerstown.

Radioactive isotope spray, thought Nabil. Your basic aerosol spray incorporating a radioactive tag. Invisible when sprayed on clothes or objects, it gave off a unique signature easily picked up by surveillance equipment. Beria or Grimsky had probably sprayed it on his clothes back in St. Joseph when he wasn't around. Orders from Boris. They couldn't have known that state troopers carry radiation detectors in their cruisers. The radioactive dust embedded in his clothes would be active for weeks and would survive several laundry trips. He might as well be carrying a signboard proclaiming "Nabil."

He waited five minutes and consulted his maps. He would join Highway 40 instead of the interstate and continue on to Frederick. Why make it easy for them? He started the Buick and headed for the exit of the lot.

———

Champaign-Urbana.

Vice President Walsh's room was in a heavily cordoned area of the ICU. He had been moved there following eight hours of surgery and another five in the recovery room. Hordes of Secret Service agents and police officers loitered outside the door. Two doctors and a nurse were in attendance. The senior surgeon came to the door.

Strooker led him out of earshot from the rest of the group. Dwight tagged along.

"How is he, doc?"

"Stable." He looked quizzically at the two men.

"Don't worry. I'm Chief Strooker of the Secret Service. Mr. Dwight here is my assistant. Talk freely."

The doctor relaxed. "He's suffered quite a bit. Both lungs ruptured. A major blood vessel torn. We've repaired that. Blast wave concussion, both eardrums ruptured. Flying projectile injuries, extensive lacerations—we've put in a lot of stitches. We reattached most of the arm, what we could find. He won't lose the arm. Nasty gash on the thigh from flying debris. We did a thorough wound debridement on that, and we're delaying primary suture. Came out of the recovery room last night. Still in shock, but he'll come around."

———

A crisis center had been set up at the FBI field office in Champaign-Urbana. Hy Strooker and Special Agent Vernon Tiddy of the FBI's counterterrorism unit went from one conference to another. Dwight and two agents drove out in a Secret Service car to the St. Joseph farm airstrip, now identified as the launching point of the operation. The area had been cordoned off. FBI fingerprint technicians swarmed the place. The charred remains of what had obviously been an aircraft were visible. Possibly some form of accelerant fused to an ordinary soapdish bomb. The experts sifted through the remains. Several witnesses had seen a yellow airplane performing low level maneuvers the day before at about the time of the blast. Two had seen a "long arm of flame" streaking out of the airplane a few seconds before the explosion at the University of Illinois campus.

Also coming in were reports that an Ohio State Trooper had been shot and killed outside Columbus after pulling over a suspicious Toyota Sienna. The Sienna had Illinois plates and had been rented in Chicago. The renter's name was a generic Jamie Pugh, probably not the renter's real name. The dashboard cam on Trooper Tipsword's cruiser had captured every gruesome detail. The man seen emerging from the Sienna had turned to the camera just once, and his face matched the computer-generated mug shots of a bearded Samir Muvdi. The man for whom an all points bulletin had been issued. The man who sat next to Harvey Michelson on the American Airlines flight to O'Hare. Moreover, tire prints from the Sienna had been taken and were being faxed to Urbana, where technicians were waiting to compare tread patterns with those found on the ground at the airstrip. Prints from the Sienna would be run through the NCIC computer. A new and worrying dimension was the discovery that the Geiger counter on Tipsword's cruiser had recorded a hit before she'd intercepted the vehicle. Whatever it was that triggered the Geiger was no longer there when the vehicle was impounded.

But Strooker and Giddings and FBI chief Creed could now link a face to the growing evidence of terror.

———

A nationwide toll-free hotline had been set up by the Department of Homeland Security, so any citizen could report sightings of the man known as Samir Muvdi. Another toll-free number had been set up in the Champaign county area—this one manned by mental health experts. Counselors were available for callers needing help to deal with the effects of the explosions, those suffering post-traumatic stress disorder, or those just looking for a sympathetic ear. The phone jacks lit up night and day.

FBI Director Creed ordered checks of all storage warehouses and hazmat depots in and around Washington, DC. Sniffer dogs, Geiger-equipped state police cars, teams of personnel swept across the District of Columbia and into parts of Virginia and Maryland.

President and Mrs. Deakin wanted to visit Vice President and Mrs. Walsh in the hospital and tour the devastated computer building. Strooker and FBI Chief Creed vetoed the idea. For now.

CHAPTER 15

Washington, DC.

That Friday morning, the day after the University of Illinois bombing, a top-level meeting had been held in the White House involving President Deakin, Secretary of State Dick Thornburgh, House Speaker Stepzinski, and Secretary of Defense Stuart Meyers. It was a historic event for a Democratic Speaker to attend a closed-door meeting with a Republican president. The word was that Speaker Stepzinski had taken over the responsibilities, ad hoc, of the vice president, since he was next in line by the Constitution, and the doctors were not yet sure if the wounded Vice President Walsh would ever again be able to fully perform his duties. The president was loath to appoint a new vice president until the doctors delivered their final verdict, and so Speaker Stepzinski was included in the daily NSA briefings. Tammy hadn't known about the meetings until the House Speaker bounded in, accompanied by Didi Watts.

"Hello, girls," Didi said. "Speaker Stepzinski has been meeting with the president. Since this is the first time in the history of the United States that the first lady's staff is occupying an office in the White House and not in the Executive Office Building, the Speaker has insisted on meeting members of her staff. He met with Mrs. Deakin upstairs for about ten minutes."

The Speaker had a florid, beefy face crowned by a full head of startlingly white hair. Black, horn-rimmed spectacles balanced precariously above a gigantic, ski-slope nose. The Speaker was immaculately attired in a gray pinstripe suit, white Van Arpels executive shirt, and red polka-dot tie. Glossy black wingtips adorned his feet. He had a direct gaze.

"Mrs. Deakin is quite upset about yesterday's tragic bombing. So she's confining herself upstairs. I guess you know that already." His voice couldn't be said to contain a Midwestern drawl, but it couldn't be said to be clipped, either. "She was quite close to Dick and Evelyn, you know. She was godmother to their granddaughter. The girl was named after her, too." He sighed. "Anyhow, Ms. Watts here has graciously consented to show me around. I don't quite know what I was expecting—certainly not this many beautiful women."

Peggy Swisher giggled.

Mrs. Neal said, "Thank you, Mr. Speaker. I think I speak for all of us when I say that we are very distressed at what happened to Vice President and Mrs. Walsh. Having said that, we welcome you aboard our ship of state, so to speak. A bipartisan executive branch is a refreshing state of affairs."

The girls murmured at this unexpected speech from Mrs. Neal. Julie Berg added, "Refreshing, that's the word. Can we get you some coffee, Mr. Speaker?"

The Speaker smiled. "Thanks, but no. Won't be here long." He turned to Mrs. Neal. "You are quite right, young lady." This time, Peggy and Tammy giggled. Mrs. Neal wasn't a day under fifty. "I believe at a time such as this, we should bury bipartisanship and forge a common bond. If we put up a united front, we can strike fear into our enemies. By the way, which direction is the First Lady's mail running in the aftermath?"

"Nine to one in favor," Peggy Swisher said. "The phone calls, that is. Ringing off the hook. We've had to reroute calls to the interns. Otherwise we won't be able to do anything else. The e-mails coming in, same percentages, only so many. Same for Twitter. Servers have crashed. IT's been busy getting them back online. It's too early—just happened yesterday— for the regular mail, but I think it'll run along the same lines."

"Everyone is disgusted at what happened," Tammy added. "This thing has really united America."

"It sure has," Julie said. "Nobody likes those kooks out there. Killing innocent people."

"Glad to hear the country's putting up a united front," the Speaker said. He looked from one girl to another. "I'm afraid I didn't quite get your names."

Didi Watts stepped in. "How silly of me. Julie Berg, Mrs. Neal, Peggy Swisher, Tammy Weasel."

The Speaker shook hands with each, as Didi Watts rattled off their names. When he got to Tammy, the Speaker paused. His handshake, firm to begin with, became a vise. He looked Tammy straight in the eye and said, "Tammy Weasel. You wouldn't know a Brian Weasel, would you?"

"He's my husband. Ex-husband," she added hastily.

"He's big on the gun lobby circuit. National Rifle Association. How's Brian doing?"

"He was doing just fine when I saw him last month. He visits the kids twice a month."

"Brian shouldn't have done that. A fine lady like you." The Speaker still had Tammy's hand crushed in his.

"It was mutual. We grew apart."

"And I understand that during one of the, ah, situations before your separation, he actually threatened you with a gun?"

Tammy didn't like having her private life made public. And how had the Speaker gotten that information? "Yes."

The Speaker seemed to read her thoughts. "I was Chairman House Subcommittee on Domestic Violence before I became Speaker of the House pro tem. Tell you what, your testimony before the select committee would be most . . . insightful. How about that, Tammy?"

She wanted to say, "Mr. Speaker, you are amputating my wrist." Instead she smiled and said, "That would be nice, Mr. Speaker."

———

The next day a teenage congressional page presented a letter to Tammy. It bore the seal of the House of Representatives. There must be a mistake, Tammy thought, as she tore open the letter. It was a handwritten invitation asking Tammy to dine with Speaker of the House Mario Stepzinski (D. Illinois) and his wife Sophia at their Silver Springs, Maryland, home on Sunday night.

So quick!

"He was a cute-looking page," Peggy observed after the uniformed page left.

"Are you into pages, too, Tammy?" Julie asked brightly.

"Certainly not. I'm not a congressman."

They all laughed.

"Hey," Peggy Swisher said coquettishly, "do you know why Congressman Cranfield could never be a novelist?"

"No, why?"

"He couldn't get past the first page! Haha!" Peggy took off before they could bash her.

Congressional page scandals had rocked Capitol Hill recently, with Congressman Dean Cranfield (R. Iowa) accused of sleeping with a seventeen-year-old page. Cranfield chose to resign rather than face the ethics committee hearings, returning to his former private life as a podiatrist in Des Moines.

"What am I gonna do?" Tammy wailed, waving the Speaker's handwritten invitation. "I'm getting in deeper by the minute."

"Perhaps you should call Mrs. Deakin," Mrs. Neal observed. "You are on her staff, after all."

"Good idea," Tammy said. "Do you think she'll object?"

"There's the phone. Ask her."

Tammy dialed the First Lady's chambers upstairs.

Mrs. Deakin answered herself. "Yes?"

"Mrs. Deakin. I . . . this is Tammy downstairs."

"Oh, Tammy. How are you, dear?" Mrs. Deakin's voice sounded muffled and constricted, like someone with a bad cold.

"I'm fine, Mrs. Deakin. I'm just calling to check with you on something. The House Speaker was passing through and he met with us. He . . . he's invited me to his house for dinner Sunday night. His wife will be there."

"Oh, he did, did he? Well, I—*a-a-choo! A-choo!*" The explosions rocked the phone. "Sorry," the First Lady said, "my cold has gotten worse."

Tammy tried to sound concerned. "It sounds really bad, Mrs. Deakin. Have you seen Dr. Mallard?" Mallard was the White House physician.

"Yes I have. But it has to run its course, Tammy. He invited you, did he? That old lecher. And so soon after what happened to Dick and Evelyn."

Tammy said timidly, "That's why I wanted to check with you. I mean, it's not proper. I'm a Republican, and he's the bulwark of the Democrats, if you know what I mean. But if you object—"

"Nonsense, Tammy. Of course I don't object. Sophia and I go back a long way. His wife. She was a bit actress once. B-movies. Hush! Don't mention you heard it from me."

"Of course I won't."

"You go and have a good time. My regards to Sophia and Mario. I wasn't able to meet him in the Lincoln Room just now because of my cold. Wouldn't do to have these germs flying around. I was able to talk to him briefly on intercom. I'm awfully upset about Dick and Evelyn. This sort of thing just doesn't happen in America. I guess when I'm upset my immune system becomes depressed, and I pick up bugs easily. You go and have a good time, dearie, and don't worry about politics."

"Thanks, Mrs. Deakin. You want us to hold all your calls until you get better?"

"Not really. Only the negative ones. I don't want any depressing news right now. How's the mail running?"

"Just tweets and e-mail coming in. Snail mail will probably start in on Monday. The e-mails just in—most of them—are addressed to the

White House and start off with 'dear Emily.' I guess they're not quite sure where the vice president lives."

"Do I look that old to them? Alright. Just forward them to her mailbox and keep mine. Render unto Caesar's wife her mail." Mrs. Deakin's voice dropped to a whisper. "Any calls from him?"

"But I thought the president—"

"Not that one. Him."

"Ole Blue Cataracts? No, nothing, ma'am."

"When he does call, pass it on the usual way. You understand. Otherwise, no calls. I'm indisposed."

"I understand, Mrs. Deakin."

"*A-choo!*" exploded the First Lady.

CHAPTER 16

Silver Springs.

It was an ordinary Georgian two-level house in a tree-lined suburban street—neat lawns, beveled brick walkways. Most senators and congressmen, Tammy knew, lived in unpretentious homes—excluding scions of old money. She was aware that Speaker Stepzinski also rented a fully furnished three-bedroom apartment at the Watergate complex. He worked long hours and slept at Watergate during the week, retreating to Silver Springs on weekends.

She parked the Chevy Cavalier curbside and walked up a concrete walkway to the huge oak door with the circular brass knocker. Tammy wore a low, sequined gown with black halter-top, and black, high-heeled shoes. A black handbag hung from her left shoulder. Her makeup was minimal: eyebrow liner for a pronounced arch, two spots of rouge on a neutral foundation for the cheeks, and one-shade lip gloss. She thought she looked slutty, but Mrs. Fierstal, her neighbor, had given her approval, as had her daughter Sandy.

The door opened on the second knock and the Speaker himself stood framed in the doorway. He wore brown tweeds over a black turtleneck and had a sturdy cigar clamped between his teeth.

"Come in, Tammy. Do come in." The Speaker was all affability. He held open the door with one hand; the other clasped a martini on the rocks. "Meet my wife Sophia. Sophia—Tammy Weasel."

"How do you do?" Tammy extended a hand. Instead Sophia Stepzinski pulled her into a loose embrace and kissed her cheek. She wore a simple evening gown by Maxine.

"You are most welcome, Tammy. Mario's told me all about you. Thank you for coming." She was a tall woman—almost as tall as her husband—with round Slavic features and a certain accompanying skin effluvia that is Eastern European.

"Thanks for inviting me."

Dinner consisted of caviar canapés and a bowl of minestrone, followed by a cheesy, scalding-hot lasagna straight from Sophia's oven. Sophia and Tammy quietly demolished two bottles of Pinot Noir. The Speaker contented himself with more martinis. When the dishes from the entrée had been cleared away, Sophia trundled off to the kitchen to appear yet again with a delicious mousse made from fresh New England strawberries. After the meal, Tammy— postprandial lethargy notwithstanding—rose to help Sophia with the washing up.

Sophia grudgingly allowed it, muttering, "But you are our guest, sweetheart. You just relax."

"I want to help."

"If you insist."

"Do you have children?" Tammy asked.

"Only two. All grown up and skipped the nest to seek fame and fortune. Two boys."

"Gracious me. Aren't you lucky?"

"Depends which way you look at it. I don't have to worry about her getting breast or cervical cancer."

Tammy laughed.

Later, they sat on wicker chairs on the back patio under a white awning surrounded by steel netting. The Speaker sat between Tammy and Sophia. The muted lights of the city glowed in the distance. In the sky, they could see the moving red beacons and flashing strobes of the occasional airliner maneuvering to land at Dulles. Sophia had placed a space heater on the wooden floorboard, as the chill of the October night mandated. The Speaker lit another fat cigar and belched smoke luxuriously.

"You don't mind the smoke, my dear?" asked the Speaker

"Oh, no. I'm quite used to it. My father smoked those fat Cuban cigars all the time."

"Can't get genuine Havanas anymore," the Speaker mused. "Not without violating the trade embargo. This'll have to do, I guess."

"They aren't Cuban?"

"No. These are from the Dominican Republic. Quite good."

They talked for about an hour. Mostly about everything. Afterward, the Speaker drained the last of the martini and rose. Clearly, the dinner was over. He held out his hand. "I must get back to work in my private office upstairs," he told Tammy. "Sophia and I consider it a real pleasure to have had you over for the evening."

"Thank you, Mr. Speaker."

"Mario. I told you."

"Thank you, Mario."

"It has been a real pleasure, Tammy," Sophia repeated. "Do come again, and soon."

"I am overwhelmed, Mrs. Stepzinski. I can't believe the hospitality you've lavished upon me this evening."

"Oh, you. We thoroughly enjoyed having you as well."

The Speaker and his wife saw Tammy off to the door. As they passed the living room with its elegant colonial motif and high-backed Lincoln chairs, Tammy spotted the telephone on a card table attached to an answering machine. All the lights were lit up. No wonder she hadn't heard the telephone ring even once throughout her stay. Of course, the Speaker was a very busy man and all of Washington sought his ear. He evidently hadn't wanted to be interrupted during his dinner with Tammy. Later, she supposed, he would sort through the calls and return those worth answering. They watched her get into her car.

"Come back and see us sometime, dear," Sophia called again.

"I certainly shall. Thanks for a great evening."

The Speaker waved. "You drive carefully, hear?"

———

Washington, DC.

President Deakin perused the FBI report sent in by G. Everston Creed. National Security Adviser Scott Bogan, who had gone over the briefing earlier with the president, sat on a chair alongside the desk and watched as the president's face turned redder and redder and finally a deep, tight purple.

"I don't believe it!" Deakin thundered. "The lying SOBs. Whatever put that into their heads in the first place? This is a direct attack on the people of the United States. On our soil!"

Bogan sought a measure of damage control. "Mr. President, the evidence is circumstantial at this stage."

"When the Japs sneaked in and bombed Pearl Harbor, we went to war that same evening. I think what I ought to do is declare a national emergency, hit every goddamn red button and put our boys on DEFCON 4!"

Bogan rose from his chair in alarm. "Mr. President! I implore you. Let's take it easy. There's protocol. We could summon the Russian ambassador."

"I'm going straight to Grachev to find out what's going on." President Deakin picked up the red telephone that was a direct line to Russian President Mikhail Grachev in Moscow. "You're welcome to listen in, Scott," Deakin said. "It's on speaker."

Bogan knew this would be tricky. Only three days earlier, the Russian president, like other European leaders, had called President Deakin to condemn the missile attack in Illinois and offer condolences to the American people and the victims of the attack. Even the Russian ambassador had visited the White House, bearing a sympathy message from the Russian people. He had also sent large bouquets of flowers to Vice President and Mrs. Walsh in their respective hospital beds in Urbana. Now Deakin was going to lay blame for the attack on the Russians.

It was a little after ten o'clock in the morning in Washington, DC, and early evening in Moscow. Mikhail Grachev's voice boomed over the speaker. "My good friend Donald, I presume. How are you today?"

"I would be fine, Mikhail, if I didn't have reason to believe you've been throwing bombs into my backyard. The evidence is piling up, and it's all pointing east."

"Wait, wait, my friend. I cannot understand you. Oh ho! You make the joke, of course. I see."

"Would I joke on the hotline, Mikhail? Tell me it's not true, all the evidence I'm getting."

A pause. "Wait. I get the translator."

Deakin wasn't fooled. President Grachev's English was passable; he was buying time to gather himself. Besides, a quick, digitized translator activated by voice-prompt was built into the hotline and could be activated by the flick of a button. However, Deakin knew that Grachev disliked the disembodied metallic voice squeaking and hissing through the speakers as much as he himself did.

Indeed, at that moment, Grachev was pressing the button on his intercom and asking his secretary to send in the interpreter at once. In less than one minute, the man—a certain Major Ratkovic—was in the room.

Deakin now spoke to Major Ratkovic, who in turn spoke to President Grachev. Grachev growled back in Russian and his words were passed on to Deakin in English. The exchange went thusly:

"You say I throw a Molotov cocktail in your backyard, Donald? Ho ho! What joke."

"I am being very serious, Mikhail. A lot of circumstantial evidence has turned up and it is all pointing east. I am quite disappointed to think that Russia could be implicated in this major incident."

"Do you have a suspect or suspects for the bombing?"

"We could have."

"Did the suspect say we were responsible for the missile? Nonsense. He lied to save his own skin. We have extended our condolences to the American people and the victims of the blast and continue to do so. We hope Vice President Walsh and Mrs. Walsh survive. Poor Mrs. Walsh. I hear she's in an irreversible coma."

"I didn't believe it at first," Deakin went on as though he had not heard. "Not even a hiccup from our early warning satellites—nothing. I got to hand it to you, buddy. You were able to explode two crude but effective missiles right in our backyard. Not even from Cuba. How on earth did you dream this one up?"

A painful pause. "Are you making a formal accusation, my friend?" The Russian translator's voice had hardened, presumably mimicking Grachev's.

"I could be."

"Well," snapped Grachev, through translator. "Go and file a formal complaint with the UN Security Council."

"We will, when we've got all the proof. Count on it. This wasn't part of the Reykjavik agreement. This could jeopardize the entire structure of the Accord."

"Good. I am happy you realize that. Our countries made SALT TWO possible. Do you think I want to destroy everything we have worked for? Even as I speak, your inspectors are watching our engineers and scientists dismantle those multiple-warhead weapons of mass destruction you and I spoke of. And our engineers are also monitoring on your side a similar dismantling of MIRV and MARV weapons to meet the agreed quota. What is this you accuse me of, Donald? Russia denies any involvement in wanton murder!"

"Mikhail, when Congress and the American people learn that your people were behind this attack, there will be chaos. There'll be calls for a retaliation. Already the Armed Services Subcommittee and the Foreign Intelligence Subcommittee are awash in rumors of a possible Russian connection. Soon, very soon, I'll have to come clean to the American people and explain how Russian-designed missiles tried to scuttle our MDS program."

The Russian president whistled through Major Ratkovic. "So, that's it. The missile defense shield. I should have known. Your baby. The one we complained threatens the ABM Treaty of 1972. And you think we are responsible? Let—"

"I know so."

"You're wrong. One hundred percent wrong. But . . . because of our friendship, Donald, I promise you I shall look into it. Russia is a big country. I shall ask what is going on from my generals. If somebody used technology from our missiles to bomb that campus, I shall find out. You give me what—two days? One week, perhaps, and I get back to you?"

"Forty-eight hours, Mikhail. Forty-eight. The Armed Services Subcommittee hearings start this afternoon, and you're the only topic in town. Got it?"

"I get back to you, my friend. Thank you for calling the president of Russia. Goodbye, Donald."

———

"Chief?"

"Yes, Ken?"

"Here's the list you wanted. The three Smurf One look-alikes. The photos and files."

Strooker took the photographs and the files. He had ordered Dwight to prepare and bring one of the three presidential doubles they had on file to Washington, DC. Someone or some organization was after the president, and it seemed prudent to let his double handle some of the upcoming engagements. At taxpayer expense, of course. There was even talk of finding a Doris Deakin double so the "First Couple" would be complete. Strooker studied the files, sighed, and laid them down. "Alright. Brief me."

Dwight consulted his notes as he briefed. The first man, Rex Martin, lived in Jerome, Idaho. From the video files, he had the closest resemblance to President Deakin, but Dwight knew him to be moody and taciturn, the opposite of Deakin in disposition. He loved the outdoors, backpacked, and went whitewater kayaking on the Snake River Falls and might not be a good candidate.

The second man, Kevin Keik, lived in New Jersey and had capitalized on his remarkable resemblance to the president to earn a full-time living.

He had retired from his career as a high school biology teacher and now earned several hundred thousand dollars annually on the nightclub circuit around the country as a Deakin look-alike.

The third man, Dave Shipwrek, was not at home in his Moon Township, Pennsylvania, suburban house. A call to the Pittsburgh-area office of the Secret Service sent two agents to his house. They confirmed that he and his wife had gone on group tour to Israel.

Dwight called Kevin Keik.

"I don't know, son," drawled Kevin Keik, and Dwight had to refrain from instinctively prefacing his own statements with "Mr. President" or "Sir," so close was the voice pattern to that of President Deakin. "You'll have to talk to my agent. I don't know if you guys can afford me. I suppose it's my bit for God and country. Still, he's got to okay any deal I get into. Here's his number."

Marvin Flatsch, the agent, was even blunter.

"My client requires twenty-five thousand dollars a day plus expenses. If this is a matter of national security, as you say, then that ought to be no problem. Kevin Keik is as patriotic as they come. He was wounded at An Loc, as I'm sure you know. But Kevin's also an elderly American facing the same problems elderly Americans face—violent crime, cuts in Medicare, skyrocketing hospital bills, and Social Security payments that face collapse in the near future. If Kevin ends up living his last years in a south-side tenement hole, he is likely to become the victim of a violent crime, all because he didn't have the money to live in a good retirement home or better. What I'm saying is, Kevin Keik is booked solid for the next two months. If he cancels all those bookings to accommodate you guys for how long— two, three weeks?—then he's going to get compensated for lost income and some kind of guarantee that he won't get sued by the promoters."

Dwight took a deep breath. "Mr. Flatsch, the funds at my disposal are limited. I would have to talk to my superiors and the General Accounting Office."

"Then talk to your superiors," Flatsch snapped irritably. "If you guys can afford hundred-dollar toilet seat covers, like I'm reading in the

Washington Post, Kevin Keik's paltry fee ought to be no problem. Call me when you're ready to talk money."

"Wait! Mr. Flatsch, I am authorized to negotiate for Mr. Keik's services on behalf of the US government. We do need your client now, for matters of the highest security reasons—"

"Cut the bullshit. When are you going to talk money?"

"Well, you know how government works. The voucher is drawn up; it goes to the GAO, before the auditors, then back here for more signatures and approvals before disbursement. This all takes time. What I'm saying is, we will pay whatever reasonable fee we arrive at to your client. But we need him now. Our lawyers will negotiate with you. You will get paid eventually. It's backed by the full faith and credit of the United States government."

"The full faith and credit of the United States government," Flatsch echoed. "Tell me something, are you guys for real?"

CHAPTER 17

Halethorpe.

The lobby of the nursing home resembled a scene from an otherworldly movie. The fetidness hit you like a warm blast wave once the automatic doors swung open. The musky, indefinable odor of human decay, the whiff of age, of terminal infirmity. The fleeting (and welcome) clinical scent of astringent or antiseptic. Nurses moving about like automatons. Repeated calls to residents, many in wheelchairs, some shuffling back and forth in the grip of senile dementia. Orders given, orders not received. Or even, who cared? Colostomy bags were in more abundance than normal body plumbing. The musk given off by prolapsed uteruses from not a few female residents overpowered even the kitchen smells from the adjacent dining room and its medley of clanging, clattering cutlery, plates, as the afternoon meal wound down.

Just coming in the door brought utter despair to Tammy's heart. The phrase "lost souls" always leaped to her mind on seeing this section of humanity: people's mothers and fathers, aunts, uncles, grandfathers, and grandmothers, in the sunset of their lives.

The nurse at Reception remembered her. "Mrs. Weasel. How are we today?"

"Just fine," Tammy said. "And how is she?"

The nurse managed to keep smiling. "Mrs. Thompson had a touch of flu about a week ago. She's feeling a lot better now. Temperature's okay. She'll be mighty glad to see you."

She'll be mighty glad to see you. Great speech. Mom hasn't made one emotive gesture in two years. She doesn't even remember I'm her daughter. Yet the nurses confirmed that after each of Tammy's visits, Mrs. Thompson's blood pressure dropped a few points and a peaceful expression came over her face that lasted several days. But Alzheimer's had wreaked terrible havoc on the seventy-three-year-old mind and even Tammy's visits could not allay the progressive disease.

Her mother sat in a wheelchair in the recreation area, staring in rapt vacancy at nothing. She moved her head to and fro in tune to a melody only she could hear. *She's hearing a choir at the Sistine Chapel sing "Nearer my God to Thee."*

"Hi, Mom."

The bobbing did not stop.

"It's me, Tammy. Your little girl."

The nurse straightened the apron on Mrs. Thompson's chest. A trail of saliva reached from Mrs. Thompson's drooling lip to the apron. Tammy wiped it off with a tissue from her handbag.

"Look who's here to see you today," the nurse said cheerily. "She brought you the goodies again." The nurse knew that Tammy always brought strawberry cheesecake and strawberry yogurt—her Mom's favorite in the days before Alzheimer's made her indifferent to food. She whispered to Tammy, "She was fed not quite half an hour ago. You can try, though. Here, I'll help you wheel her to her room." She reached for the wheelchair handles, but Tammy grasped them instead.

"Mind if I do that myself?"

"Sure." The nurse straightened Mrs. Thompson's frock. "You be nice to Tammy now, hear?" She left.

Tammy released the footbrake and pushed the wheelchair and its uncaring passenger into the elevator. She pressed the button for the second floor, and when the elevator stopped, she wheeled her mom to Room 231. Once inside, she threw her handbag down, took off her coat, and unwrapped the paper sack containing the cheesecake and yogurt.

"Strawberry cheesecake time! Doesn't it look good, Mom? Oooh!" Always, at this crucial time, Tammy felt the levity in her voice to be false and insincere; she despaired of her Mom's reaction, or non-reaction, yet there was no other way. Using the plastic spoon she had bought from the supermarket, she scooped a small dollop from the yogurt cup and nudged it into her mother's mouth. The first two attempts fell onto the drip apron. The third portion entered but was not chewed at all, just swallowed.

"Good girl!" cooed Tammy. "Here's more." The nurses had said that more often than not she had to be spoon-fed. "Isn't that lovely. You've always loved strawberry, haven't you, Mom? Don't worry. You'll always have strawberry. And anything else you want." The fourth portion went down.

Mrs. Thompson stopped eating.

"Come on, Mom. Eat up. You've lost a lot of weight. Was it the flu you just had? But we're back to normal, aren't we? Eat up, Mom, good girl."

"You . . . Tammy," Mrs. Thompson said.

"That's right, Mom. Tammy's right here. Your little girl. Remember me? I got my red hair and freckles from Dad, and everything else from you, including my green eyes and nasty disposition. Haha. Remember Dad? Your husband. He's passed on now, let's see . . . about eleven years ago. Richard, to you. Dick Thompson."

"Tammy . . ." The old woman frowned.

"That's me. Your little girl. Here, Mom, see that photograph on the card table? That's me and Sandy and little Tom, your grandkids."

Tammy brought over the framed color photograph and held it up close. The woman did not see it. Sighing, Tammy put it back on the table beside the other pictures—one of Christie, Tammy's younger sister in California, and her husband. The daughter who never called or wrote. There was also a picture of Tammy's father taken in his fifties, another of her mother in her early forties.

"What do you want with me?" Mrs. Thompson asked suddenly.

"Oh, Mom. I want everything with you. Because I'm your daughter and I love you, wherever you are. I'll always love you."

"I don't know any Tammy."

"Yes, you do, Mom. Yes, you do." Tears flowed freely down Tammy's cheeks now.

It wasn't just the hopelessness of it all. They'd sold the house in Halethorpe during Dad's long battle with cancer to help pay for the experimental treatment where Medicare left off and insurance refused to pay. There wasn't much left after estate taxes and then having to put Mom in a nursing home. Mom's illness and the incessant expenditures had contributed to the breakup of Tammy's marriage. Another payment was due at month's end on the nursing home charges. *How much longer can I keep this up?*

Tammy pulled herself together. She rose and tidied up the room, putting aside the bric-a-brac of her mom's life—the things she couldn't part with, on the mantelpiece, inside the wardrobe, on the faded snakeskin handbag she hadn't used in years. Painful memories. She straightened Mom's hair using a brush and comb. She used a wet towel to wipe the pale face and changed the chest-guard apron. She applied deodorant under Mom's armpit from her own handbag. "You've got to look good and smell clean, Mom. Lots of gentlemen out there."

She spent the next hour reading to and talking to her Mom. Tammy read from *Grimm's Fairy Tales* and later from Sylvia Plath; her mom had enjoyed reading these books in the years before Alzheimer's. None of these efforts drew a response. Afterward, Tammy wheeled her mom back down to the rec room and kissed her on the forehead. "I'll see you again soon, Mom. Soon. You be good, hear. We'll beat this thing together, you'll see." Even though the doctors had said there was currently no cure.

On the way out, she stopped by the cashier's desk and deposited two hundred dollars for incidentals into her mom's account. Toothpaste and toothbrush, visits to the resident hair salon, an extra pair of bedroom slippers, soda, anything. She had better keep an eye on those incidentals though. It emptied out fast. Four months ago, she had scrutinized the itemized deductions for incidentals and queried an $8.95 charge for female sanitary napkins. At Mom's age! Her last period must have been, what, eighteen years ago? The matron investigated. It turned out that the purchases had been made for a certain Mrs. Sarasota Thompson, a mentally challenged lady, who, at forty-eight, was the nursing home's youngest resident. She was on estrogen therapy for, among other ailments, osteoporosis, and was having a delayed menopause. The matron apologized and credited the same amount to Tammy's mom's account. Yet the mistrust remained.

The drive from Halethorpe back to Reston fatigued her even before it began. Visiting her mother always gave Tammy a genuine emotional lift, perhaps from filial obligation, but it left her tired and full of despair at the end. *How much longer can I afford to keep her there? Then what? Does she move in with me? Dear God, how do I cope?*

———

Foxhall.

The storage depot was off the highway just south of Foxhall. A K-9 team had swooped down on the depot when their dogs detected explosives residue. The sales clerk thought he remembered two men renting a unit a couple of weeks earlier. There was no reason not to rent them storage. He couldn't remember any more details about the two men; they'd looked normal and one wore glasses. No, no foreign accent. Wait a minute—a security camera mounted at the gate would have all the details they needed.

The camera was confiscated, the tapes wound back to the day in question. The tape was grainy, but it picked up the U-Haul pulling into the depot. Two men left the truck and entered the sales area. Fifteen minutes later, it showed them leaving the premises. The faces of the two men were not visible, only generic, and not enough to muster a Wanted poster. The license plates of the truck were not readable, and even the efforts of the FBI National Crime Laboratory, which had the latest en-hancement techniques, only produced two readable letters of the license plate number. The sales clerk agreed to undergo hypnosis to see if he could remember more details of the two men. Racked by the conviction that time was running out, Dwight actually set up an appointment with a DC-licensed hypnotherapist for later that afternoon when a call came in that the FBI had located the U-Haul truck by a process of elimination.

What was amazing was that the rental truck had been returned only the day before. It sat in the lot among other rentals, in orange and ash colors, merging with other similarly painted trucks and vans.

The sniffer dogs went crazy around it. It had recently carried explo-sive material. The truck was impounded.

"Oh, I remember the man who rented it," said the U-Haul agent, a woman with the disconcerted look of a Miss Miniver. "He was alone, I think. He had an accent. He was a bit dark. Sort of Middle Eastern, you know."

"Did he indicate what he was going to use the truck for?" asked an FBI agent.

"I didn't ask, but he volunteered that he wanted to take his boat down to the Potomac, and his wife had taken the estate wagon that could pull the boat trolley. He paid cash, but we still require a major credit card before we give out our trucks." She sorted through the recent vouchers until she found what she wanted. "Here we are. He used a Visa card. The name on it is Said Kokubani, MD."

CHAPTER 18

Frederick.

Nabil dumped the car in a mall parking lot in Frederick after purchasing two disposable cell phones from a local 7-Eleven. He had two encrypted telephone numbers on a piece of paper in his pocket, one for Dr. Kokubani, the other for Boris. Boris could only be called between the hours of ten and eleven at night, and then only in an emergency.

Nabil called the number listed for Dr. Kokubani. A man answered on the second ring and identified himself as Nasser. Nabil identified himself as Mr. Muvdi.

A pause. Then Nasser said, "I suppose you are the foreman for the project?"

"I am," Nabil replied. "How is the project?"

"It's still there. The other workers are on it right now. The demolition will soon take place, and they are waiting for you."

"Good. It is an evil monument, this project we speak of, and it needs to be brought down. Can you come and pick me up?"

"Where are you?"

Nabil told him. Less than an hour from the suburban Colesville residence of Dr. Kokubani. Nabil hung up and walked across the street to a Jack in the Box. He bought a cheeseburger meal with fries and chased it down with two tall glasses of iced tea. The big glass windows offered a good view of the plaza lot. Fifty-five minutes from the time he placed the call, and well into his third iced tea, a bright yellow Chevy Corvette pulled into the lot in front of the Laundromat.

Nabil watched a young man of about five foot eleven in blue jeans and checkered shirt sporting bushy black hair and a full mustache head for the Laundromat and its single unoccupied payphone on the outside wall. Nabil waited, watching the lot while the youth made apparently futile attempts to call somebody. He was not followed. Nabil chucked the remains of his iced tea into the garbage and walked outside and across the street to the Laundromat. He whistled, and the youth turned. He replaced the receiver and sauntered over in long, jerky strides.

"I am the project manager."

"Nasser Kokubani."

They shook hands and got into the Corvette. It was the Stingray version, probably '09 or '11 model. Nabil hated low-slung sports cars. If they were being tailed, the yellow two-seater with its long sleek bonnet might as well be a homing beacon. The youth, however, edged carefully into traffic and merged into the four-lane highway. It was difficult for a Stingray, but the speedometer needle hovered at sixty-five. The car didn't complain. Nabil relaxed.

"Beria and Grimsky arrived yesterday," Nasser said. "They are already working on the second and third projectiles."

Nabil nodded. The Beech T-34 owned by Dr. Kokubani had been purchased two years earlier as surplus equipment from the US Navy. It came equipped with two hardpoints, one on each wing.

"I'll give you a checkout on the T-34 tomorrow," Nasser said.

"You fly?"

"Quite well, thank you. I'm a reservist in the Air National Guard. Two weekends a month. Avionics technician. I do have my Commercial and Instrument tickets and I'm also a CFI. I work full-time at a Radio Shack outlet."

"Good for you. I presume you are Dr. Kokubani's son?"

Nasser grinned. "A bit late to ask that. First son. I fly better than my dad. I'm still hoping for a chance at Air Force UPT."

Forget that, Nabil thought. *Not after you've helped us with this project. No branch of the services will touch you with a ten-foot drill sergeant's stick.*

"Have you collected the missile components?"

"Yep. I went with Jim Freidman. He's the one who rented the storage where we kept them."

"This Freidman—I've never heard of him."

"He's American. Ex-CIA. Boris said he can be trusted completely."

"A Muslim?"

"No, no. I don't think he belongs to any religion. Except of course any religion that pays the most money."

"I don't like the direction this mission is going. Too many unsecured assets."

Nasser shrugged, keeping his eyes on the road.

After a while, Nabil said, "Tell me, why are you doing this? Why get involved?"

Nasser took a long time to answer. "Family," he said.

———

The house was in the heart of rural Montgomery County, a two-story Georgian mansion with an old-fashioned rectangular hedge surrounding it. It was adjacent to another reclusive hobnob of the affluent, Indian Spring golf course. The house had a three-car garage, and about two football-field lengths away stood two normal-size white trailers. A barn converted to an aircraft hangar stood half-a-football-field length away, and an orange windsock on a twelve-foot pole fluttered in the cool October breeze. The airstrip was a faded green scar that ended about one thousand feet from a rural road; two red flag markers about one-foot high on each end marked the usable length of the grass runway. From the boundary looking west, the putting greens of the ninth tee could be seen, as well as the occasional golf cart.

Nabil's reunion with Grimsky and Beria was professional and courteous, though affectionate. They congratulated one another on the success of the Illinois bombing and for having made it this far. Then back to business. Beria started to brief Nabil on the progress of the second mission. However, Nabil raised a hand, pleading sleep, and was shown to Nasser's house trailer, where he swung himself onto a quilt-covered bed in the guest bedroom and promptly slept for five hours. When he awoke, Dr. Kokubani had come home from the clinic and dinner was ready.

Dinner consisted of pita bread and spaghetti with tomato sauce, meatballs, and a liberal sprinkling of mozzarella cheese. Two bottles of cheap red wine were passed around the table. The Russians had chosen to eat theirs in the house trailer they were occupying, the one next to Nasser's.

The doctor apologized for the dinner. "My son cooked this." He was about five foot seven and had a full black beard heavily tinged with gray, as well as intense dark eyes and a hooked nose that looked as though you could grasp it like a door handle. Remnants of an English accent lingered in his speech, as did his native Farsi. Nabil knew the man was a millionaire, an ophthalmologist who had made his fortune in cataracts and Lasik surgery and owned a chain of optical stores across the northeast. "My wife and our youngest daughter have gone to Florida. I asked them to. I'll be joining them in a few days. I'll be in Florida when the fireworks go off."

"I'll give him a checkout on the T-34 tomorrow," Nasser said, sprinkling mozzarella into his spaghetti.

"Do that," his father said. "Stay clear of the TCA. Dulles and Washington National." He turned to Nabil. "I've asked Nasser to take over the cooking and housekeeping arrangements for now. My wife employs a housekeeper who comes four times a week. She eats lunch when she's here. I conveniently put a little extra ingredient in her soup two days before your Russian friends showed up. She will be ill for the next ten days or so. Long enough to conclude the mission. Her daughter called me, offering to come in her mother's place, but I assured her the matter had been taken care of."

"This is a big house," Nabil said. "Surely you must employ a groundskeeper."

"We employ the services of three teenage boys who do the work part-time. In summer, we turn away a lot of schoolboy help. Nasser checks them out himself on the tractor mower and I insist, for insurance reasons, that they be at least seventeen years old. I've called each one of the regular boys to let them know we shan't be needing their services for the next three weeks."

He went on, "Nasser lives here with me in one of the house trailers near the hangar. You will share quarters with him. Separate bedrooms, of course. The Russians are sharing the other. Do you have any questions?"

"Your other daughter?"

"She's away at college. Barnard. We shan't be seeing her until December."

"College? What's her major?"

"Men."

"What?"

"She's majoring in Men," the doctor said.

Nabil laughed.

"I kid you not. What else do they do nowadays on those campuses?"

Nabil thought he understood the setup. After the operation, when Beria and Grimsky and Nabil were safely out of the country, Kokubani's wife and daughter would be "released." The good doctor would tell the authorities his wife and daughter had been kidnapped by terrorists; he'd been ordered to cooperate, or else. Essentially correct, except that the real hostages were in faraway Iran. He had been indoctrinated enough on what to say regarding the terrorists, such that neither polygraph nor sodium pentothal would trip him. Of course, the two men accompanying the doctor's wife and daughter to their Boca Raton vacation home were to ensure that neighbors saw them. Keeping wife and daughter inside the bungalow home and not allowing them to wander off the premises would reinforce the impression of a hostage situation.

Nabil said, "You know, the authorities found the grass strip in St. Joseph, Illinois. They know we used a crop duster launch platform.

They'll be looking closely at all private grass airstrips or even paved ones near major airports in key cities around the country.'"

Dr. Kokubani smiled. "My dear friend, there are over 11,600 privately owned airstrips in this country, and 10,800 of them are strictly private use. Those are figures from a pilot's association to which I belong. No way the Feds could mount surveillance on that many airstrips. Many have no discernible boundaries, even. Just a length of road or grass behind a farmhouse."

"I'll take your word for it. How's security here?"

Nasser answered, "Our friends really went overboard on that one. Motion sensors, invisible radio fence around the airfield perimeter. They were prepared."

"Let's hope none of your friends will choose this time to pay you a visit," Kokubani told his son.

"No one. I made sure of that."

———

Overnight, Nabil studied the T-34 airplane manual. He crammed the aircraft limitations, V-speeds, operating specs. Promptly at ten o'clock the next morning, he met Nasser at the hangar. Dr. Kokubani, it turned out, had two airplanes: a Rockwell Commander 114, and the Beechcraft T-34. The Commander had been pushed to the hangar's northeast corner to give Beria and Grimsky working room.

The security was superb. A ten-inch video console monitored the status of the all the motion sensors and the radio fence. Four strips of high explosives were placed at strategic positions in the hangar. Beria and Grimsky each wore on their belts a device that resembled a black cellphone. Nabil knew what it was. By pressing a few coded buttons on the remote detonator, either man could, from anywhere within a hundred yards, blast the hangar and its contents sky-high, leaving a twenty-foot crater and nothing bigger than a matchbox for ATF and the FBI to sift through. None of the missile components must ever be traced to Moscow.

Grimsky pulled Nabil aside. "We'll be ready to launch day after tomorrow. One thing. The missiles are fire-and-forget, not radar- or wire-guided, as you know. The guidance system could be jammed by deliberate radio interference. What I'm saying is, like in Illinois, we need a backup homing signal at the target. If the guidance system malfunctions, a standby receiver would pick up the emitter signal and guide the missiles to the target. We have two missiles, doubling our chances of one malfunctioning, although I do not think it will. Still, we get peace of mind, no?"

"Have you talked to Boris?"

"No. I have three transmitters left. We only need to plant one inside the White House."

"Boris will take care of that," Nabil said. "That was my briefing."

They pulled the T-34 outside and Nasser preflighted. He drained fuel into a glass sump and found water globules at the bottom. He discarded the sample on the ground. He collected two more samples until he was sure no water remained in the tanks.

"She's a beauty, isn't she?" Nasser observed, explaining that the T-34 was decommissioned from nearby Patuxent years ago and repainted blue and white.

"Your father loves to fly obviously," Nabil observed, "keeping two airplanes."

Nasser laughed. "The doctor syndrome. Doesn't know what to do with his money. The Commander is for personal transport; the T-bird is for personal fun. Hey, this is nothing. There's a doc over at Manassas owns a Tucano. Now that's as close as you can get to a jet and still fly behind props. Fast, agile, fully aerobatic. I don't know how much the doc paid for it—I hear a little over a million, though he's never come out and said so. And that's the used airplane price. Doesn't want folks to know how rich he is. And believe me, that thing came complete with zero-zero ejection seats. Dr. Polk's the sonuvabitch's name, a plastic surgeon. He must be doing a lot of face lifts and tummy tucks to be able to afford that airplane."

"You don't say."

"You should see him at the airport, getting ready for a flight. His wife actually climbs the little ladder as he goes through the whole charade: harness secure; brakes on; chocks off; seat parachute secure; seat ejection armed. He pulls out the red-flagged safety pin, hands it to the wife, who dutifully takes it, climbs down the ladder, removes ladder and places it along with the ejection safety pin in one corner of the hangar. Then the doc shouts, 'Clear!' and she shouts back, 'Clear!' and the sonuvabitch fires up. At least he has the sense to run through the razzmatazz outside on the ramp, not inside, or one day he'll punch himself out the hangar roof."

Nabil nodded. "I know the type."

Nasser put on his gray Ray Bans. "Ready?"

"Yes."

"Hop in the back then. You'll be flying, I'll sit up front." They climbed in. "We'll call DCA Approach once when we're airborne and get vectors to the practice area. We'll be doing steep turns, approach and departure stalls, a few chandelles and lazy-eights and a couple of landings. We'll need about an hour for all that. This thing has some sort of Gosport tube. I don't like it, so I suggest we use the David Clarks for inter-cockpit talk. Got all that?"

"Roger."

"Good. I'll read the checklist and you crank her up when we get to the 'Start' items."

———

"Doc, I need some of that stuff you gave your housekeeper," said the deep rasping voice. "You still got some?"

The caller could have been using voice-altering technology, or even placed a hanky over the mouthpiece, so bad was the distortion. Kokubani, however, was unfazed and apparently knew the caller.

"I sure don't," Kokubani said. "I rinsed all the vials and threw everything away. What do you need it for?"

"Something important. Can you get me some more?"

"Well, it's not easily obtainable. It's a culture, you see. I have to grow it. Takes about forty-eight hours. Virtually untraceable after you administer it."

"Day after tomorrow okay?"

"In the evening. Thereabouts."

"I'll send Jim Freidman over to pick it up."

"In the evening, like I said. I'll leave the vial with Nasser."

———

Washington, DC.

"Tammy Weasel?"

"Speaking."

"I'm Stan Doherty. I represent a law firm in Baltimore. I need to see you this afternoon. It's about your mother, and it's rather urgent."

Tammy's heart convulsed. She found herself starting to hyperventilate.

"Mrs. Weasel, are you there?"

"*My mother?*" Her voice was a whisper.

"Yes. It's alright. Nothing's happened to her. I happen to be in DC, and I think we can get this sorted out right away. It seems your mother may have come into some money, and I need to talk to you first."

Tammy found her voice at last. "Some money. Has . . . someone died?"

"I'm not at liberty to discuss details over the telephone. I'll be having lunch this afternoon at the Senate cafeteria at one o'clock. I'll leave the Senate building at precisely twelve forty-five, and you can meet me at the Capitol end of the mini-subway—"

"I don't have a pass. I can't lunch there at that hour."

A chuckle. "I thought you White House staffers had access everywhere. I'll have a pass for you waiting with the maitre d'. I suggest you come alone. Please be prompt."

The phone clicked dead.

Julie Berg looked at Tammy with concern. "You okay, honey?"

"I'm fine, Julie. Thanks."

Was it a scam? One of those telemarketing ploys. . . . *Yes, ma'am, you've indeed won fifty thousand dollars' worth of tax-free gifts in our bonanza raffle draw. Congratulations! You may collect the gifts or the cash equivalent at your convenience. However, for our services, you will need to pay only three hundred dollars in order to collect this money . . .*

She was Tammy Weasel. She knew better than to sign any check or hand over cash.

The bit about her mother.

She dialed the nursing home number in Halethorpe. "Could I speak to Mrs. Thompson?"

"Which one—Sarasota or Gwen?"

"Gwen."

"One moment. Who is speaking, please?"

"Tammy Weasel. I'm her daughter."

A pause. "Mrs. Weasel, you ought to know your mother doesn't answer phones. She isn't . . ."

"Coherent? Is that what you're trying to say? I know that. What I mean is, is she alright?"

"Of course she's alright. She was this morning when I saw her."

"Oh. How long ago was that?"

"Just over an hour ago. Do you wish to speak with the nurses on her floor?"

"No. That's alright. Just checking. Thank you very much."

CHAPTER 19

Washington, DC.

Stan Doherty, clad in a dark gray business suit and ash-colored silk tie, was one of the thousands of lawyers, lobbyists, and politicians who clogged the nation's capital. In his late thirties, his brown hair started some distance up his temple, and he brushed it back fiercely. His physique was trim, though not lean; the thin, pencil-line moustache and a three-inch scar from the earlobe down to the middle jawline gave him the look of a shyster. He had been waiting for her even though she had arrived at one o'clock sharp. She had introduced herself to the maitre d', who led her to a partitioned corner table for privacy. The restaurant buzzed with hectic lunchtime activity. Virtually everyone wore dark gray business suits or skirts.

"I'm Stan Doherty."

They shook hands.

"Tammy Weasel." She sat down. *If he's a lawyer, maybe he works only for the mob.*

The waiter came, and they ordered bean soup and ravioli. Stan Doherty had hazel gray eyes, and they probed Tammy's with frank curiosity.

"Tammy, I think it's fair to say that you're very close to your mother?"

"Yes." She held her breath.

"And to your daughter Sandy and son Thomas. A fair assessment?"

"Yes."

"About your mother—believe me, I empathize with you deeply. The true cost of looking after an Alzheimer's patient on a skeletal budget is known only to those who have to bear such a burden."

"Thank you. You said something about some money."

"I am coming to that. This makes what I have to say easier to swallow."

Tammy stared at him

"Let me clarify a bit," Doherty said cagily. "I represent the highest interests of the Republican Party." He held up an embossed card with the inscription *Permanent Delegate, Republican National Convention*. The official seal of the GOP was engraved in the card's center with the name Stan Doherty beneath. Doherty sighed and replaced the card in his coat pocket. "Tell me, what did you make of Watergate?"

"Nixon's Watergate?"

"Yes."

She shrugged. "Dirty politics. I don't know much about it except what I read in school. And that book *All the President's Men*. That was a long time ago."

"What impression do you have generally of what took place?"

"What do you want me to say? I mean, it was . . . unethical. The burglary, breaking into the office of Daniel Ellsberg's psychiatrist, the lies afterward, the erased portions of tapes. Okay, so it was criminal. What else do you want me to say?"

The bean soup arrived with warm bread rolls and butter. They each reached for their plates.

"You are very close to the First Lady, are you not?"

"Look," Tammy snapped irritably, "what does this have to do with my mother?"

"Please, Tammy."

"Yes, I am."

"How close is Mrs. Neal?"

"The First Lady's private secretary? Quite close. She's been with the family right from California, and they won't let her go. She's getting old, though. Can't take dictation quite as fast, and the computer is a strange toy to her. But Mrs. Deakin's quite fond of her. But either Julie Berg or I get called in to take dictation. We transcribe the Dictaphone and read the mail as well." She stopped. A thought had occurred to her. "Why am I telling you this?"

"Because you trust me," Doherty said simply.

"I'm meeting you for the first time, and I signed a nondisclosure agreement when I took the White House job, promising not to talk to reporters. I'm not to publish or tell for a period of ten years after I leave my job."

Doherty grinned evilly. "You're telling me because I'm legit. I'm not a journalist. No hidden microphones."

Another thought had occurred to her. Was this a security check—one of those crazy schemes hatched up by White House Chief of Staff Don Panella to plug potential leak sources? Periodic false memos sometimes swept through the White House and if a newspaper published the harmless, leaked information, Panella kicked ass in the department in which the memo had been floated. If this was a test, she'd already failed.

Their ravioli arrived. The restaurant wanted quick turnaround. The waiter hovered. "Can I get you anything else?"

"Another Diet Pepsi for me," Tammy said.

Doherty glanced at his watch. "Another beer."

Tammy frowned. "I thought delegates are appointed for party conventions. I don't quite understand your being a permanent delegate. Is it like the United Nations, or something?"

"Think of me as a representative of the highest quarters of the party. That's precisely why I'm here. What do you make of a Deakin third term?"

She considered. "He's a lame duck. There's no way he'll be nominated for a third term. I've heard some of the talk. FDR got away with it, a record four terms even, but I mean, I don't think it's constitutional any more . Are you sure Deakin will agree to a third term even if it becomes possible?"

"He will. No doubt about that. He may even have floated the idea himself. The truth remains that he is one of the best presidents America has ever had. He's dealing with the Middle East in the proper way. His policies and actions have earned America the respect she deserves in the world. No doubt about it—he's as popular as FDR or JFK, and the American people want him to continue. Our private polls show that. It would require an almighty act of Congress, passage by both Houses, and ratification and all that. The Supreme Court may have a say. And all this has to be in record time for next year's race. You see what I'm getting at? It's not impossible, yet it's unlikely to happen."

"So why are you mentioning it to me?"

Their drinks arrived. The waiter left.

"What I'm about to tell you is highly secret. You must never, under any circumstances, mention it to anyone. I happen to know you have a Section Q clearance." He paused for effect. His eyes never left her face. "There is a move within the party and with the president's knowledge and approval to have him up for a third-term nomination. We believe he will win again with a landslide. But before we announce him for a third-term candidacy, we must prepare ourselves against the barrage of attacks certain to come from the opposition. Deakin already is the oldest serving president in US history. If he goes for a third term, he may *die* the oldest serving president. The Democrats have raised questions regarding his health—specifically his ileitis, his prostate, and an old football back injury. We intend to refute all that. Here's where you come in. We have learned that the Democrats—who you know at the moment control a majority of Congress—are prepared to use as an argument against any proposed third-term constitutional amendment, the allegation, indeed belief in many circles, that the president has a persistent intestinal problem—some say benign colon polyps that could, in time, mutate into cancer—that necessitates his going to the gents' room several times in a short period of time. The Secret Service agents guarding him see nothing unusual in his toilet trips—nothing unusual in a seventy-year-old man. The White House physician is keeping mum, in line with the Hippocratic oath. Before we seek a constitutional amendment for a third term, the GOP intends to verify the accuracy or falsehood of these claims. There's no point in electing a president who will be dead of cancer or diabetes one year into his term."

"He could do a colonoscopy and have the polyps removd in the process," Tammy said. "My Mom underwent hers some years ago."

Doherty nodded. "He may have other things going on in there we don't know about. His prostate, his pancreas. We don't know. We just want to verify a few things."

Here Doherty removed what looked like a medium-sized pocket calculator from his pocket. He pressed a button and the display window lit up briefly. He glanced around the crowded restaurant furtively. "This is a device that monitors the number of movements in, say, a sensitive-documents room. It has been adapted for other uses. This particular one has a Velcro patch and attaches to the water cistern of a normal toilet. Its sole purpose is to monitor the number of flushes in a given day from that toilet. Any doctor will tell you that the number of bathroom visits in a given time can give you clues as to the health of the individual. Are you with me so far?"

She began to understand. "You want me to put this thing in the toilet to monitor how often the president visits the can?"

"Correct. You have access to the First Family living quarters on the second and third floors. We just need to know how much time the president of the United States spends in the can. It's for the good of America."

"You're mad."

"All we need is a three- or four-day reading. Then you retrieve the device."

She picked up her handbag. "I'm leaving. I came because I thought you had something worthwhile to say. All that talk about money was baloney."

"Tammy—"

"Even if you paid me a million dollars, I still wouldn't do what you want. Did you think I would betray the president and the First Lady? I'm on her private staff, for Chrissakes. And I consider myself a patriotic American—"

"Tammy—Mrs. Weasel, I implore you—" He put out a hand to stop her.

"Don't touch me! I'll pay my part of the lunch bill—"

"Take a look. To your left. Four tables away."

She did. She started to speak and stopped.

"Please sit down." Doherty watched her closely. "Who do you see?"

She didn't answer.

"Representative Warren Foote, Republican Whip, talking to Mario Stepzinski, Speaker of the House," Doherty went on. "Oh, yes, we do have bipartisan lunches here at the Capitol. Look around you, Tammy. What do you see? Power brokers everywhere. God, we're eating with the most powerful men in America. You think it's by accident? Half the people in this room know why you and I are here."

She looked around. At that moment, Speaker Stepzinski half-turned toward her. His gray-tinted spectacles glinted briefly in the light thrown by the recessed white fluorescents. He seemed to look right at her and through her. He appeared not to recognize her at all. He resumed his earnest talk with Warren Foote.

It was true. She had sensed more than usual eyeballing from the men in the restaurant and had shrugged it off—what else was new? Men were puppets responding to pheromones. Or so she'd thought. And she just happened to be ovulating. She chided herself now for her conceit.

Doherty said gently, "I understand how you feel, Tammy. Believe me, this thing is big. Bigger than all of us in this room. Think about it. Is it really a crime to want to know a few things about the man who would rule us—and the free world—for the next six years counting from today?"

She didn't answer. Her mind was in turmoil.

"And here's the kicker. The committee has approved the sum of forty-two thousand dollars to be made available immediately to your mother. We know how much you love her. How pressed you are for funds toward her upkeep, since your separation from your husband. We also thought you might be leery of accepting cash gifts because of White House ethics policies. Your mother will be moved to a private facility, all expenses paid, for two years. She will be much better looked after. She could be transferred as early as tomorrow if you wish." He smiled. "The committee thinks of everything. Of course if you prefer the cash payment . . ."

"The dirty tricks committee," Tammy said.

"Sorry?"

"Nothing."

"One more thing. This device I just showed you comes in several shapes to help avoid detection. Naturally, you want to be discreet when taking polling samples of this sort." Doherty chuckled. "This one looks like a pocket calculator. We also have ones that look like an electric razor and a cordless phone. Which type would you prefer?"

"You're assuming that I've agreed to plant your device."

"You will, Tammy. There's no immediate hurry, though we would like the experiment concluded within a fortnight. We do want the device inside the White House tomorrow. Any time tomorrow. Even if you don't get the chance to put it in the First Couple's bathroom."

"And if someone finds it?"

"They'll assume it's a cordless razor or pocket calculator. You can't tell the difference unless we show you how. Just leave it on your desk, or inside a drawer until you're able to use it. But it must be inside the White House tomorrow. The reason is we have a receiver in the DHS building, and we want to test whether the equipment is functioning properly."

"It's a bug."

"It's not a bug. You have to believe me, Tammy. Remember, inside your desk drawer tomorrow at the latest. I'll come by your apartment this evening to show you how to set it up and to bring the cash payment if you wish—"

"How do you know where I live?"

"The committee knows everything."

"You're still assuming that I've agreed to go through with this thing."

"You will do it."

"Why?"

"Because you love your mother. And your children, Sandy and Tom." Doherty's smile was sad. "I have friends who would do things you wouldn't believe. And what's more, you will not be so rash as to mention this conversation to anyone."

————

Trenton.

Kevin Keik sat in the cabin of the C-21A (military designation for the Lear 35) as it thundered down the Trenton, New Jersey, runway and vaulted into the sky. He heard the solid clunk as the gear buried itself in the airplane's belly. Across from him on the club seating arrangement sat an FBI agent. Two Secret Service agents were also in the airplane as it sped toward Washington, DC. The C-21A belonged to the VIP wing of the Military Airlift Command at Andrews.

A Secret Service agent served him orange juice in a glass tumbler. Kevin Keik smiled. His agent, Marvin Flatsch, had handled the negotiations well. Keik was getting double his standard fee plus expenses for being a presidential double. He'd had to cut short a gig at a VFW Legion hall to accommodate the Secret Service. Flatsch had let it be known that Keik was down with the intestinal flu and would be out of commission for at least the month. A Doris Deakin look-alike had also been located in Portland, Oregon, and she was being rushed to Washington, DC, as well.

Kevin Keik leaned back in the leather swivel seat, loosened his tie, and sipped his orange juice. *It doesn't get better than this.*

————

"We have an asset," Freidman explained. "She will take the device into the White House tomorrow. Once the transmitter is anywhere inside the White House, it will be okay. We would prefer it to be in the vicinity of the First Bedroom—inside the loo, in fact. Architecturally, experts say it will cause maximum damage to the White House if a bomb were placed there."

Grimsky and Beria listened intently. Nabil sat on a hangar chair, watching all three. He didn't quite know why, but he didn't trust the American. It wasn't just the scar on his jawline, or the vain buccaneer-thin mustache. A vague unease.

"So what you ask?" Grimsky said.

"You program the transmitters—three of them—so they start emitting the signal from ten o'clock tomorrow morning. She should be inside the White House by then."

"She lives there?"

"She works there."

"Three? Why three? That's all we have left."

"I want her to choose the shape she thinks will be easiest to smuggle inside the White House. After she picks one, I'll return the other two and you can deactivate them."

Beria's eyes met Nabil's. Nabil nodded almost imperceptibly. Grimsky saw it and brought out all three transmitters.

"The calculator and the razor varieties will look most natural in a woman's handbag. She is a woman, no? We shall keep the cell phone type because if you take those two, this will be the only one left with us."

Freidman shrugged. "Fine. Just program the other two for ten o'clock tomorrow. It will transmit for what, forty-eight hours?"

"Correct." Grimsky did not tell him that tests had shown the device could transmit for seventy-two hours before the batteries died. He also didn't mention that a passive tracker imbedded into the device always worked, whether the batteries were on or off. Grimsky quickly programmed the timers and gave them to Freidman.

Beria said, "After she makes her choice, please return the other one immediately."

Freidman smiled. "Edgy, aren't you? I'll return it tonight, how's that?"

"Fine with me," Grimsky said.

Freidman hesitated. "Boris asked me to pick up some stuff for him. Some kind of vial, from Dr. Kokubani. Is it ready?"

"Not yet," Beria said. "He said to tell you it would be ready tomorrow evening."

"Shit. In that case, why don't I just come back tomorrow evening— five, thereabouts—return the transmitter and pick up the stuff? Just to save me making two trips out here."

"Suit yourself."

Freidman hesitated again. "Where's Nasser?"

"He isn't back from work yet."

As soon as Freidman's Mitsubishi Diamante crunched its way down the gravel path onto the main road, Nabil jumped up and grabbed the keys to the Nissan Pathfinder from the worktable. "I want to follow Freidman," he said to both men.

Beria smiled. "I don't trust him either. He almost got his hands on all three transmitters."

"Exactly. Never trust an American who has worked for the CIA."

Grimsky picked up the GPS tracking device from the junk on the floor. An arrow cursor overlaid a Google street map on the portable screen of the device, and its extension cord plugged into the cigarette lighter socket. He handed it to Nabil. "Don't let the police catch you with this."

Following the Diamante was easy, as the street map of Washington unfurled on the device screen . Nabil kept his distance. Freidman was a trained agent and would know when he was being followed. Just in case he was stopped by police for any reason, Nabil had a fresh set of identity papers, including a State of Maryland driver's license under the name Yani Youssef, a businessman of Lebanese origin.

He followed Freidman south from Colesville until they reached Interstate 495 West. The Pathfinder hummed right along. More than once, Nabil had to slow to keep from crowding Freidman's Diamante on the multi-lane traffic. I-495 branched south again over the Potomac, and he joined the Beltway going west, past the Wolf Trap Farm for the Performing Arts. The Dulles Airport access road and tollgates loomed ahead, and for a moment, Nabil thought Freidman was leaving the country. However, the Diamante swung right, toward Reston.

It was dusk now, and rapidly getting darker. The Diamante weaved through an upper-middle-class area of Reston and drove into the Seven Oaks condominium complex. Rows and rows of several-tiered apartments. Freidman drove slowly until he came to a crescent-shaped parking area. . Nabil had to backtrack once—and quickly—when it appeared that Freidman was going to drive twice around the oval of hedge brush separating one part of the complex from the next. He did. Apparently he was checking out an address. He stopped in front of the U-block quadrant and backed into a parking space.

Nabil parked by the T-block quadrant, which gave him a view of the Diamante and the U-block building entrance. He could make out Freidman's blur in the growing darkness. The man was smoking a cigarette.

An hour passed. No change. Freidman was ex-CIA. Surveillance was his middle name. More cigarette butts flew out the car window. Nabil was getting restless.

A Chevy Cavalier drove into the U-block quadrant an hour and ten minutes after the wait began. By Nabil's rough count, it must have been the twenty-sixth car to enter or leave the U-quadrant. The parking lot lights made the Chevy and its occupants quite visible. A woman and a child emerged, bundled against the October chill. The woman reached in and pulled another child from the car seat in the back. The three headed for the U-block entrance—the woman fumbling for her keys while balancing the parka-clad kid on her right hip. She stopped at a mailbox to collect her mail. Nabil noted the particular mailbox.Three minutes later, a light went on in an upstairs apartment. Other lights came on, visible only through small gaps in the drapes.

The woman and her two children had not been followed.

Ten minutes later, Freidman casually sauntered into the lobby. From Nabil's viewing position, it looked as though he bent over to speak into a wall intercom. A buzzer must have sounded, for Freidman jerked open the door and walked inside. In less than a minute, the drapes on the second floor condo where the lights had come on were pulled aside. The woman who had gone up with the children stood framed in the low light. Even from that angle, Nabil could tell she was an extraordinarily beautiful woman, with her tumble of red hair and statuesque proportions. Bot hands reached up, swept her hair once, twice, her back to the window—Nabil assumed facing Freidman. Then she moved inside the room and was lost to view.

Twenty-five minutes after he went in, Freidman emerged purposefully, got into his car, and drove off, looking neither left nor right. For some reason, Freidman's cocky departure troubled Nabil. *We have an asset . . . she will take the device into the White House.* Was he also fucking the beautiful asset? Nabil felt a pang.

He left the car, walked casually to the mailbox the woman had checked earlier. A simple name written in black marker: *T.Weasel, Apt B3.*

Back to the car, he wrote the name down on a piece of paper and checked his watch. 7:23 p.m. He started the engine, nudged the gear into drive and headed back for the Kokubani house out in the Maryland countryside.

CHAPTER 20

Washington, DC.

Hy Strooker and G. Everston Creed sat around the table with members of the Special Task Force.

"We've established that Dr. Kokubani did rent the U-Haul truck," Creed said.

"No question about it," said Stu Daniels, an FBI Tasker. "His prints came up on the driver's side. No PARs, but I was able to pull his INS file to get his prints—he's a landed immigrant. He asked for a truck with a boat hook. We've confirmed that he does have a boat and goes out for a spin once in a while on the Chesapeake Bay. On this occasion, he didn't use the truck to pull his boat. He didn't need to rent the truck at all. Two of his three cars are equipped with boat-towing gear."

"It wasn't Dr. Kokubani who pulled the van out of the warehouse?"

"No. Two younger men did that. One of the men matches the description of the doctor's son, Nasser Kokubani. He's an engineer and a weekend warrior. National Guard. US citizen, born here and whatnot."

Strooker said, "What's the story on Dr. Kokubani?"

Daniels consulted his file. "Medical school and internship in Tehran. Came over here to do a residency course. Mount Sinai in New York, Mayo Clinic in Rochester, Minnesota. Board certified eye surgeon. Been practicing in the US for the past twenty-six years. Settled in the Maryland area about seventeen years ago. He's fluent in Farsi, English, and French. Owns a chain of optical stores. Has a practice in Aspen Hills and is affiliated with four area hospitals. Last year, he paid the IRS

$181,403.19 on an aggregate income of 1.2 million dollars. Substantial line item deductions. Three audits in the last fifteen years. Clean-living male adult, non-smoker, social drinker. Married, three kids, all grown. His family back in Tehran was real big once—close to the Shah, special privileges. The Khomeini Revolution wiped out most of his near and extended family. His only surviving brother lives in Tehran. Dr. Kokubani himself has no history of political thought or action. He became a naturalized US citizen nine years ago."

The men around the table digested the information.

Creed said, "Why would he be doing this, then?"

"Who knows? A closet Islamic fundamentalist? Some family coercion back home?"

"Anything on his ICE file we can nail him with, for starters? Inconsistencies in his application, perjury—something we can use to persuade the ICE commissioner to seek adverse action on his citizenship? Right now, we have enough for a search warrant and arrest, but what we don't want is a smart-aleck lawyer showing up in court the next day and talking out of both sides of his mouth to spring our prize catch. We want multiple lines of indictment, ironclad charges."

"I'll talk to Immigration, see if there's anything."

"We'll mount an all-points surveillance on that there farm," Creed crowed. "I want to know everything that goes in or comes out of there. If a gnat farts in the underbrush, goddamn it Daniels, I want to know about it. And it's all got to be discreet and very high tech. They mustn't know we're onto them. We want to know who's behind these people and why."

"Consider it done."

"The wiretaps, electronic surveillance—have the papers ready before noon. I'll get a federal judge to sign them. We can get going early this afternoon."

"Right, sir."

Strooker smiled at Creed. "You haven't heard the kicker yet, Gary. The good doctor also owns two airplanes parked in a small hangar on his own private airstrip. Sound familiar?"

"The hell it does." Creed paused. "Hey, Ken, let's call Langley. See if they can position that KH-11 spy satellite for us. We need live pictures of that establishment. Quick time. Hy and myself will get the reports, but you coordinate. Got that?"

Dwight nodded. "Got it."

"Surveillance should be in place one o'clock this afternoon at the latest."

"Understood," Daniels said.

Creed looked around the table. "Throw me some ideas, gentlemen. Otherwise the meeting is over."

"I got one," Strooker said. All eyes turned to him. He spread out the detailed map of the Maryland suburb and his forefinger traced an imaginary circle. "I notice that this Kokubani estate is adjacent to the Indian Springs golf course. Makes our work real easy."

————

Andrews Air Force Base, Maryland

Kevin Keik walked down the air stair of the C-21A onto the red carpet. A small group of men were there to meet him, among them Ken Dwight.

"You're the Secret Service guys," Keik drawled. "I can smell you guys a mile away. How's y'all doing?" He saluted perfunctorily. "President Deakin at your service."

A man approached Keik and shook hands. "Ken Dwight. White House Detail Chief. This way, Mr. President."

"Well, y'all's sure efficient, I tell you that." They started toward the line of three black limousines. "You guys sure don't waste time getting me in on the act, do you? I haven't been briefed properly, by the way. What's more, I need to get me a couple of beers under my belt—they didn't serve none in the airplane—take a shower, and go see my barber."

Ken Dwight looked straight at Kevin Keik. "Mr. President, you'll do all that after your golf game this afternoon."

————

Montgomery County.

The clatter of helicopter blades had Nabil tumbling out of bed from his afternoon nap. He ran outside to see Grimsky and Beria also catapulting out of the hangar. The three men peered at the sky. Beria ran back inside the hangar and emerged with a pair of Zeiss binoculars, which he trained at the sky.

Two choppers. One, a Sikorsky CH-53E Super Stallion bearing the seal of the president of the United States, settled down by the office and refreshment shack of the golf course. The other, in dark-gray marine colors, remained aloft, circling the golf course perimeter.

"Bell 206," Beria said.

"Impossible." Nabil took the Zeiss from him. "That doesn't sound like a piston helicopter." He trained the binoculars. "It's a turbine, alright. I can't be too sure, but it's either a Bell 212 or a Sikorsky S-76. I think it's an S-76. Fast, maneuverable—" He stopped. An ominous-looking pod beneath the chopper's nose caught his attention. Two pods in fact. The first, a routine, police, multi-million candlepower searchlight. The second, a round, faceless alpha shape on gimbals, just behind the NightSun—as the searchlight was called.

"What is it?" Grimsky's voice quavered with fear. The motion sensors around the Kokubani estate had been silent all afternoon. Now they watched the remote console display for signs of an imminent raid by law-enforcement officials.

Nabil knew. A FLIR pod. Forward-looking infrared radar. The fact that the device was on gimbals gave it 360-degree vision.

The beep of the motion sensor tripping sent all three men scrambling again. A yellow, low-slung car knifed through the driveway and sliced toward the hangar and house trailers. Nasser Kokubani returning from work.

He was alone and looked flustered.

"What's going on?" Grimsky demanded.

Nasser ran a hand through his rough hair. "The president is playing golf at Indian Circle this afternoon. I just got stopped on the road leading to the house. Local cop. He said they were helping out the Secret Service and keeping people away from the course. I told him I lived here and had to show him some ID before he'd let me in."

"It sounds too pat," Nabil snapped. "Has he played golf here before?"

"Well, yes. Once or twice in the last couple of years. Usually with a visiting head of state or a movie star. Clinton played every other week, and others, too, but then they'd use the congressional golf course closer to Bethesda." Nasser paused, clearly uneasy. "Heck, maybe he's here for security reasons." He smiled at the irony.

Nabil trained his binoculars again. The chopper was on the far side, her noise barely audible. He panned the near greens. Two men dressed like caddies casually patrolled the seventh green—the one nearest the grass runway. They held walkie-talkies and spoke into them, although none looked in the direction of the farm.

The *whup-whup* of the airborne chopper grew loud as it approached for another pass at the near green.

"What's with the chopper?" Nabil asked Nasser.

"That's easy. Most times the president is at a function, one chopper is usually airborne, patrolling. It stands by for emergency evacuation—medical or otherwise. It's also an excellent security platform."

An excellent security platform. The FLIR pod. The contents of the hangar. You didn't have to put two and two together.

"I don't like this," Nabil said. "The chopper must be distracting his game. I say we've been compromised. We get out. Now."

"Maybe not," Beria said. "Boris hasn't called, has he? The plan for a self-destruct with fast egress is for him to call us first. He's right up there at the top of American governance and would know if they were planning a raid. I say we continue as before."

"I agree," Grimsky said.

They didn't hear the second beep of the motion sensor monitors. They were outside, and the noise from the chopper drowned it out. But they saw the white Mitsubishi Diamante coming down the driveway.

"Freidman," Nasser said.

Freidman pulled up in a small cloud of gravel dust. He got out. "Seen anything unusual?"

"We were wondering."

"Seems the president is teeing off on the fifth hole or something. You would think he would want it a bit more peaceful when playing. Wonder what his handicap is."

"Go and ask the Secret Service," Beria said dryly.

"I'll ask Boris instead. He ought to know. That's why I came anyhow. Got something for me? A vial? For Boris."

"You said you were coming in the evening."

"I'm early."

"I think it's ready anyway," Grimsky said. "Come inside."

Freidman followed him to the trailer.

Something was askew. Nabil couldn't pin it down, just a nagging suspicion. He stared at Freidman's Mitsubishi sedan. Something about Mitsubishis in general tugged at his subconscious, specifically the Lancer, Sapporo, and Galant models: the trunk was accessible from the backseat. He thought he had read somewhere that this was true of all Mitsubishi four-door sedans. He glanced after Freidman and Grimsky. They had entered the house trailer and the curtains were drawn. Unless he was specifically looking, Freidman couldn't possibly see him from inside. He made up his mind.

"Time to go and see Boris myself," he said to Nasser and Beria, putting a finger to his lips.

They watched Nabil open the rear door of the Diamante and get in. The rear seat was upholstered into two separate units. He leaned the left one forward and, sure enough, could see right into the trunk. He burrowed into the dark enclosure and pulled the seat back behind him. He hoped the looks on Nasser's and Beria's faces would not give him away.

Freidman and Grimsky emerged from the caravan, the former clutching a small vial containing a brackish liquid.

"Tell Boris this is compliments of Dr. Kokubani," Grimsky said.

In order to distract Freidman, Beria added: "And while you're talking to him, find out what's happening with the helicopter and the president's sudden interest in golf. We need to know if it's time to get out of here."

"I'll do just that." Freidman got into the car and cranked the engine. He didn't notice Nabil's absence.

"We got a positive signal from the test," Beria said. "The transmitter is in place. We could launch this evening. Why does he want us to wait until tomorrow morning?"

"Because tomorrow there will be a top cabinet meeting at the White House," Freidman said. "The entire cabinet of this administration will be present, and they will be wiped out."

———

Inside the cabin of the S-76 Sikorsky, two men hunched behind two consoles. One manned the FLIR imager, the other the video monitors. The FLIR operator was ex-Army and now worked for the metropolitan police. Working the thermal imager, he had no difficulty picking up the three men who trooped out on hearing the noise of the chopper. Presently a sports car screeched in, and there were now four men looking up at the helicopter. But the FLIR operator's greatest triumph was the image he was seeing inside the hangar. The fantastic tale of the two airplanes—one of them with two hardpoints holding missiles.

His colleague, the video man, was streaming live images to FBI headquarters from the FLIR. He supposed these pictures were giving the brass a Pentagon-sized apoplexy down there.

A second car pulled in and the men were now five. Damn. The heat from the cars' engines—that of the sports car and now the new arrival—made a large red blotch on the imager pictures that blotted out some other details. The operator spun his dials to desensitize the gain. There.

"Okay, Vince," he spoke to the helicopter pilot over the headset. "Bit more to the left. Left. Right there."

The pilot complied.

Then, "Let's move on over to the other quadrant of the grid. No sense in making them suspicious."

"Right, dude."

The chopper moved off to the far green, over a crest—apparently interested in the second tee. While it looked to those on the ground like the chopper was investigating a totally different area, the thermal imager was still tracking the suspects on its 360-degree gimbaled pod. But the picture was lost for a few seconds when the chopper disappeared behind the slope and rose again. In those few seconds, Nabil entered the trunk of Freidman's Mitsubishi Diamante.

"Previous heading, Vince. I just lost them."

"Which heading?" The FLIR man had confused the pilot. "Gimme a heading, partner."

"Steer right. Ten, fifteen degrees. Okay."

"You got ten. Now fifteen."

"They're coming up again. Shit. Let's do an orbit, please. Right around that fir tree or whatever. I want to paint 'em real good."

He had them now. Good thermal signatures from the cars just come in due to the heat. Then the—holy shit! There was a stiff in one of the cars, and it was moving off.

"See what I see down there, Alex?"

"Yeah," the video man said. "Somebody's been iced and put in the trunk."

"Must be. Real recent, too. The imager's painting residual body heat." He paused. "I wouldn't swear to it, but I thought the stiff just moved. Something's going on, Al."

His colleague grunted. "Yeah, well, the Fibbies are out there to pick him up. We can't break radio silence. The brass are seeing everything we're seeing, too. Leave it to them."

"I guess you're right." The FLIR operator wondered if the FBI and ATF would raid the place immediately. The pictures he was beaming down were just too hot.

Beneath him, the "president" and his golfing partners and caddies—all Secret Service or FBI—putted on the fourth. A caddy handed the "president" a different driver, and he took his Tiger Woods stance, measured the fairway, flexed, flexed yet again, and then whacked a two hundred yarder (it looked like it!) down the green.

But the chopper was not interested at all in what the fake president was doing.

CHAPTER 21

Washington, DC.

At the corner of Tenth Street and Pennsylvania, across from the Justice Department, was the J. Edgar Hoover FBI Building. Inside the operations room, a few doors down from the director's office, G. Everston Creed, Hy Strooker, and Bruce Kohlbus, the ATF chairman, watched live pictures from the S-76 Sikorsky orbiting the Indian Springs golf course. The task force ops room was manned twenty-four hours a day, collating information, and this was the most significant piece yet.

"Damn," Creed swore. "Damn sons of bitches. Right in our backyard."

Creed shook his head. "I don't believe what I'm seeing."

A separate computer-generated picture on another monitor froze the two airplanes inside the hangar. The Commander 114 was clearly visible, as was the tandem seat T-34, her wings and lethal cargo on two pylons.

"We ought to go in there right now and put them out of business," Kohlbus said.

"Those look like Tomahawks under the wings," said Creed.

"More like Hellfires," Kohlbus said.

"How in the hell could a prop-job T-34 carry hardware that big?"

Strooker said thoughtfully, "Those missiles are meant for just one target. I think they're meant for my charge and his place of residence. They couldn't get him at Champaign-Urbana, so the mountain comes to Mohammed."

"You're damn right," Kohlbus said.

Strooker turned to Creed. "Brief me on the surveillance."

"Dr. Kokubani is at his clinic in Aspen Hills right now. He did two corneal transplants this morning—cataract operations—at Montgomery General Hospital, saw patients, had lunch, and is back in his clinic seeing post-operative patients. His son Nasser is on his way home from work here in DC." Creed stopped, staring at the live pictures from the Kokubani estate. "We're looking at a car pulling into the compound now," he continued. "We'll soon be able to read the license plates and tell who it is. Those three men standing there beside the hangar—I'd give my hangnail to know who they are. I bet—"

The phone rang. Kohlbus picked it up. He listened for a moment before handing it to Strooker. "It's for you."

Strooker hesitated, then pressed the speakerphone button.

"Strooker speaking."

"Ken Dwight, sir."

"Yes, Ken."

"The control tower at Washington National just called. They've called twice now. Apparently they're picking up some sort of transmission on the emergency frequency 121.5. They want to confirm if an aircraft has crashed into or in the vicinity of the White House before they alert Search and Rescue."

Oh, baby. It's happening.

Strooker's head reeled with the new information. His vision swam. Something, some memory, tugged at the corner of his brain.

"Apparently," Dwight continued, "the signal has been on for some hours now. They thought it was a nuisance transmission except that a SARSAT satellite—that's a search-and-rescue satellite—has picked up the signal, plotted the grid, and it appears to emanate from inside the White House. They figure maybe some of our equipment is malfunctioning."

Strooker found his voice. "Ken, this is a serious development."

"I agree, sir. If you remember the deposition from Jose Aguilar, the controller at Willard in Champaign-Urbana, they were also investigating a similar emergency locator transmitter signal just before the U. of I. explosion." Dwight paused. "I'd like your permission to evacuate the White House immediately."

"Where's Smurf One?"

"In the Oval."

Strooker paused. Creed and Kohlbus watched him intently. The modus operandi was unmistakable. Yet he was looking at live images of the terrorists and apparently the weapons platform. If he evacuated and disrupted a visiting Head of State's important meeting with the president . . .

Now, if they had rolled out the T-34 from the hangar or other indications the operation was under way. . . . Was this a decoy? Even as they spoke on the telephone, the real airplane or missile could, this minute, be on its way to the White House while attention was focused on the wrong farm. After Illinois, he would never underestimate those people again. If a missile struck the White House, killing the president . . . posterity, the nation, the Joint Chiefs of Staff, and the *Washington Post* and *The New York Times* would never forgive him.

"Do it, Ken. Move Smurf One at once to Blair House—no, on second thought, strike that. Not enough time. Move him downstairs to the nuclear-proof bunker. Smurf One, Two, all Smurfettes. Other White House staffers . . . hell, give 'em rest of the day off. They have five minutes to leave the premises. Tell them a roach nest was spotted in the Lincoln Room or something, and the whole building has to be fumigated. Understood?"

"Yes, sir."

"Then call the control tower at DCA. Tell them to send somebody who can locate where this bleeping noise is coming from—immediately. I'll be right there myself." He looked at the video monitor again. "Ken, I want all staffers to leave the place. That includes you. There could be danger. There won't be enough time to warn you if the missiles launch."

"I'll stay," Dwight said.

"Goddamn it, Ken, that's an order!" Strooker banged the receiver down.

Creed was the first to break the silence. "Hy, if they pull out that T-34 and get ready to fly it, we'll take out the goddamn farm. You have my word."

"Goddamn right," Kohlbus growled.

Strooker reached for his coat. "Thanks, fellas. I got to get out there and take care of Number One. Do me a favor and get the FBI and ATF SWAT teams ready to take out the place if they so much as hiccup. Take no prisoners, is what I say."

"There won't be any," Kohlbus assured him.

"Do we call in F-16s?" someone asked.

"Let them be on standby. They can scramble in minutes if we need them, if these jokers try starting the airplanes."

"No prisoners," Strooker repeated.

" 'Cept those for the coroner," Creed added.

Three minutes later, Strooker was in his car and giving orders on a guarded radio frequency. "This is Chief Strooker. We have indications of a possible strike attempt, target assumed to be La Casa Blanca." His agents would understand. "Cannibal Five defensive positions in effect. Shoot first, don't ask questions at all. Am I understood? Over and out."

————

The exact number of times the White House has been evacuated or put under the highest alert is classified. It is certain to have been more than once. On aeronautical charts, the airspace above the White House and a bit of the surrounding area is restricted airspace—no aircraft may fly inside the boundaries, except for Marine One, the CH-53 helicopter used to fly the president and the First Lady from the White House to Andrews. Some say the defenses around the White House are many and secret and quite capable of rendering good accounts of themselves. Others say there is not as much as a single Stinger shoulder-fired missile guarding the White House. For obvious reasons, the White House will neither confirm nor deny either observation.

Inside the office of the first lady, Tammy, Julie Berg, Peggy Swisher, and Mrs. Neal took the news matter-of-factly. Fire drills and nuclear-attack drills were bad enough. But this leave-everything-get-out-now order was something else. There was talk of Orkin coming in to fumigate the place, but Tammy didn't believe it for one moment. The alarm must have something to do with the toilet-flush recorder that Stan Doherty had given her. It was now inside her bureau drawer. No opportunity yet to place it where it was meant to go. It resembled a big pocket calculator—not big enough to cause significant damage if it was a bomb. Yet if they found it inside her desk drawer . . .

It hadn't been easy to smuggle it inside the White House. When she'd walked through the metal detector turnstile, a loud beep had sounded. The uniformed Secret Service agent stopped her immediately.

"Mrs. Weasel, please empty everything in your handbag into the container." He indicated an open plastic container on a table beside the turnstile.

She'd complied. Then he had her walk through the turnstile again, and she came away without setting off the alarm. He studied the contents of her handbag: keys, nail varnish set, comb, brush, two safety pins, a tiny package of Ultra-Thin tampons, powder set with round mirror, and a pocket calculator. He nodded.

"Have a nice day, Mrs. Weasel."

"I'll try."

"Don't do anything I wouldn't do. Haha."

What did he mean by that?

Now they were evacuating the White House the same day she had brought in the device. Tammy was the last to leave the office. She took the device from the drawer, wiped her prints off it with a tissue and placed it inside a filing cabinet beside Mrs. Neal's desk. She picked up her handbag and hurried from the room.

———

At the time that Strooker was on Speakerphone with Ken Dwight and giving orders for the White House evacuation, both G. Everston Creed and Bruce Kohlbus and the third Tasker were listening intently and so barely paid attention to the live FLIR images. They missed Nabil's entry into Freidman's trunk (though they would catch it later when rewatching, when it was too late). They did catch the picture of the Mitsubishi leaving Dr. Kokubani's farm. Creed keyed his walkie-talkie after Strooker had left and told his men: "A suspect vehicle just left the premises. I want it followed to destination. Don't apprehend yet. Keep out of sight. Understood?"

"Yes, sir."

———

The ride was hot, uncomfortable, and seemed interminable. Nabil hadn't known that the streets of the US capital rivaled those of Beirut for potholes. When the car finally stopped, it seemed to Nabil that of the 206 bones in his body, not one had escaped the jouncing ride.

The car engine died. Freidman was whistling a tune off-key. It sounded like *I Wanna Hold Your Hand*, an old Beatles melody. The door opened, the springs creaked, and the car was relieved of Freidman's weight. Through a crack of daylight in the trunk, Nabil saw Freidman feeding quarters into a parking meter. Finding a parking space was easy. The rest of Washington, DC, was leaving for home in the suburbs.

Nabil pushed the backseat forward and cautiously looked out. Freidman was walking toward a large, ugly building across the street.

He could see immediately that Freidman was being followed. Two men emerged casually from a parked car and sauntered toward the marble entrance. Another off-white Dodge Aspen cruised slowly past the Mitsubishi, the two men inside peering at Freidman's disappearing back. Nabil knew that scenario only too well. He ducked beneath the window line until the Aspen had passed a safe distance.

Something had gone wrong.

He clambered into the backseat from the trunk, trying to act like another bored passenger waiting for the other members of his carpool to arrive. No one cared really: Washingtonians were on their way home, walking with steely determination toward the subway or to high-rise parking garages. From the familiarization exercises in Kandahar with the FSB's Major Brobov, Nabil recognized immediately that he was on Independence Street across from the Sam Rayburn building, one of three White House office buildings. He could see the Botanic Garden and farther up from it would be the Reflecting Pool.

Freidman had gone inside the Rayburn building. Nabil couldn't follow. There was sure to be a metal detector doorway, and Nabil didn't really want to be without his gun. Assuming he could even enter the building.

The homing transmitter—the one shaped like a Remington electric razor—lay on the seat beside two plastic tags. Freidman had forgotten to drop off the transmitter after his asset had made her choice; perhaps the noisy chopper over the Indian Springs golf course had distracted him as it had everyone else. Nabil picked up the plastic tags and knew at once he was back in business. One was a visitor's pass to the House Gallery, current for that day. The other, also a visitor's card, was to the Senate restaurant and had expired the previous day.

Who the hell was Freidman?

Nabil brought out his Browning 9mm and wiped off his fingerprints. He deposited it, along with the extra clip of bullets, on the floor beneath the backseat carpet. He clipped the Gallery visitor's pass to the outside of his coat pocket. He opened the sidewalk-side door and stepped onto the pavement. Nobody gave him a second glance. The off-white Aspen had vanished, but Nabil had no doubt it was nearby. He really needed that gun. Then again, he needed to warn Freidman. He needed to find out who the hell Boris was.

The mission was somehow compromised. That much he was sure of.

If they were tailing Freidman, then they knew something. The "presidential" golf game, the helicopter with the FLIR pod—what a laugh. An excellent observation platform. He didn't have to maintain visual contact with Freidman; he simply followed the men following him. He was right. They were FBI. They tripped off the metal detectors, both the walk-through and the hand-held that the security man waved like a magic wand as he asked them to step aside and empty everything inside their pockets. The two men didn't even look at him, merely flashed their badges in his face and walked on.

Nabil followed. As expected, his keys tripped the detector. The operator briskly frisked him and waved him through.

It was a maze of hallways, offices, hurrying aides, those going home, those working late, the clatter of office printers, copiers, the muted glow of laptops, busy thumbs working iPhones—this was the world of power. He looked around twice to make sure he himself was not being followed. Freidman stopped to use the elevators. Nabil busied himself reading a notice on the bulletin board. From the corner of his eye, he noticed Freidman enter the elevator. One of the FBI men went in with him. The second Fibby lounged around, watching unobtrusively which floors the elevator stopped at. Another elevator arrived, disgorging hordes of administrators and staffers going home. The Fibby entered that one alone, and the doors closed behind him.

Nabil edged closer, as if waiting for a free elevator. Both had stopped on the third floor. He glanced at his wristwatch. As if on impulse, he walked toward the lighted doorway marked Stairs. He pushed the door open and bounded up the stairs. He was on the third floor in no time.

The hallway was almost deserted. Freidman sat on a leather chair in the mini lounge, leafing through a periodical. No sign of either Fibby. Nabil started down the hallway casually.

Freidman got up and walked over to the bank of numbered mailboxes. He took an envelope from his pocket and thrust it into a mail slot. It was obviously some kind of a drop. Nabil was not fooled. In the world of subversion and counter-subversion, the real drop had taken place where Freidman had been sitting, perhaps on the leather couch or somehow with the periodical. Or it had yet to take place. To anyone watching—and by now Freidman must have known he was under surveillance—an important document had just been deposited in the mail slot. Freidman started down the hallway.

And saw Nabil.

It was the barest of flinches, but Freidman didn't check his stride. A shadow flicked across his face and was gone. He was an old hand at the game. Two stainless-steel water fountains stood between him and Nabil at a small alcove in the wall, and Nabil walked toward them. He depressed the hand lever and was drinking from one while Freidman came to the adjacent fountain.

"What is the meaning of this?" Freidman hissed. His head was bent down as if waiting for the water to spout correctly.

"You were followed. I came to warn you."

"I know." Freidman drank. "I'll enter the restroom. They'll follow. We'll take care of them."

"Okay."

"You got a piece?"

"No. I don't need one." *If I'm wrong about Freidman and he's a mole, I've just killed myself.*

"Good."

But it happened the other way around. As Freidman rose from the fountain and started down the hallway, the first FBI man was already halfway down it, trying hard to look like a congressional aide finishing last minute tasks. His hands were conveniently inside his pockets. As if on an afterthought, he pushed open a restroom door.

Freidman followed.

Nabil flicked lint off his trousers, stamping both feet on the hallway floor as though ridding them of water droplets. No sign of the other Fibby. Nabil sauntered to the restroom, pushed open the door.

Freidman occupied a toilet stall. His brown shoes were visible through the aperture. The FBI man had made a mistake, a mortal one. He straddled a urinal, actually passing a stream, both hands down by his pelvis. His back was not presented to the stall where Freidman was;

indeed, he was eyeing Freidman's feet while engaged in his own activity. Nabil approached the adjacent urinal, unbuttoning his trousers as though his own bladder were bursting.

The FBI man sensed danger. He turned as Nabil bore down on him. He squealed, a low inhuman squeal of abject terror and threw up his hands in self-defense, abandoning his micturition. Nabil pinioned him from behind in a full Nelson. His thumb locked on the C2 vertebra. He snapped back and up, up, twisted savagely and heard the man's neck snap like a dry twig, a horrible pitiful sound coming from his throat. He dropped to the ground, a human rag doll. His legs kicked once, and he was beyond help.

The stall opened, and Freidman eyed the dead man without expression. "Well done."

Nabil quickly relieved the dead Fibby of his Glock 9mm and extra ammunition clip. Nabil removed the FBI badge from the dead man's wallet. He was pulling the dead man into an empty stall, assisted by Freidman, when the door flew open and the second FBI man burst in. He was tall, wore dark-framed glasses, and the bureau issue Glock 17 in his palm was a natural extension of his hand.

Freidman threw himself at the agent, and the two men went down. A shot rang out. At first, it was not clear who had been shot. Both men were grappling for the gun. They tumbled end over end, grunting, straining, and gasping. Then it became clear who had absorbed the lead as Freidman's strength ebbed. With great ceremony, he collapsed on top of the FBI man. A dark, round stain grew at the back of his coat. The Fibby retrieved his gun and tried to free himself from under Freidman.

His glasses had fallen off, and he was breathing in spurts. His myopic eyes held Nabil's. "You—you're . . . under . . . arrest," he muttered.

He was raising his gun when Nabil fired twice at close range into the agent's head. The agent had been raising his left hand protectively across his forehead when the first bullet shattered the wrist and entered his skull at an angle. The second bullet went unimpeded into the frontal lobe, causing irreversible damage.

Nabil turned Freidman over. The glazed eyes said it all. Nabil ran to the door, looked both ways down the corridor. No one in sight. That would change in about four seconds as the security guards responded to the gunshots. Nabil ran to the door stairwell and pushed the door open. Feet pounded up the stairs. He shut the door again and ran toward an emergency exit door at the end of the hallway. A lighted red sign proclaimed that it would sound the alarm when opened. Nabil didn't hesitate. He pushed through. All sorts of flashing red bulbs and a klaxon erupted.

Outside he breathed the cool dusk air. The streetlights were on; the Capitol at dusk bustled with activity. He didn't care. Pandemonium had broken out in the Sam Rayburn building. The workaholics and last-minute procrastinators spilled from the building's guts. He straightened, pocketed the gun, and took the corner facing First Street. He cannoned straight into a uniformed Capitol cop.

Thinking quickly, Nabil flashed the dead FBI agent's badge and pointed to the second-floor fire exit. "Quick. In there! I'm going after him. Accomplices went that way."

The cop drew his gun and ran toward the fire escape. Nabil walked purposefully to the main gate, merging with the crowd throwing themselves out of the entrance. Squad cars screeched up and officers piled out, running toward the building, guns drawn. Nabil laughed involuntarily; it was just like in the movies.

But it was very real, and he was the main actor. He found Freidman's car in the same spot as before. Parked several meters away he identified the Dodge Aspen that had been tailing it. He dearly wanted to get in the Diamante and retrieve his Browning and its special steel-jacketed bullets. But he knew better; cops would surround him in seconds.

Instead it took him less than twenty seconds to get into the Dodge Aspen. Nothing special about breaking into unmarked cop cars. All that training in the jihadi camps was paying off now: when he would be timed breaking into and starting a "stolen" vehicle and had only forty seconds to drive away the veshicle.. From three minutes fifty-one seconds, he had finally whittled it down to thirty-five seconds under the constant belittling of a tough, ex-thief instructor from Cairo who had left his lucrative trade to join the *fedayeen*. A skilled thief in Harlem, New York or Southside Chicago would consider himself rusty if he accomplished the same task in anything more than twenty seconds. Nabil had no knife, so he tore open the plastic cover using his bare hands, isolated the relevant wires and dug his teeth into the insulation. He rubbed the exposed wires together, and the Aspen rumbled to life.

After he had mistakenly squirted washer fluid and sent the wipers nodding vigorously across the windshield, he found the headlights, slipped the gear into drive, and edged out into traffic. The portable red beacon of the cop car lay on the pedestal between the front seats. He would use it if he had to. The radio volume was turned down low; he could hear the incessant chatter in the background. He raised the volume; the voice of the Metro dispatcher filled the car interior.

He turned on C Street over Capitol Street and back into D Street. Then right on to New Jersey Avenue. He followed New Jersey to Interstate 395, driving out of the city.

He knew that many police departments buried GPS tracking devices on all their squad cars so they could be located at a glance on their city map. Nabil wondered if, at this very moment, he was not a blip moving across someone's electronic street map. But he had to warn Grimsky and Beria and the Kokubanis. The phones surely would be tapped. Boris might get to warn them before he got there. Nonetheless, it was his duty to warn them, to make sure the T-34 and the two missiles went up in smoke so that nothing could be traced back, ever, to Russia or to Ramalan Sidi.

CHAPTER 22

Montgomery County.

The telephone inside the hangar rang. The cordless phone extension from the house trailer number. With the scrambling device made from a secretive lab in Europe. Grimsky answered.

A voice said, "This is Boris. Who am I speaking to?"

Grimsky paused. The circumstances, what with the helicopter buzzing around and nobody briefing them, called for expletives undeleted. He said instead, "Grimsky."

"Get out of there. Now. Destroy everything. The FBI is about to raid the place. Do you understand?"

Grimsky's face turned white. Beria hurried over from where he'd been reading a Pasternak novel.

"The devices are ready," Grimsky was saying. "We can launch within five minutes. Nasser could take up the airplane—"

"Negative. The president has been moved from the White House—"

"He's right here playing golf. We know where he is," Grimsky blustered.

"That is not the president," Boris said patiently. "Take it from me. Blow up the place and get out. Rendezvous as planned. Is that understood?"

Grimsky took several seconds to answer. "I understand."

The phone clicked dead.

Beria had been watching his colleague's face and didn't wait for the conversation to finish before starting evacuation drills. He already had his remote detonator out and was punching in the relevant codes. Then they were running to the trailers to grab their essentials and to alert Nasser, who was enjoying a bong pipe on the back porch.

In five minutes, they were ready.

Nasser jumped into his yellow Corvette. He was clad in a light autumn coat, jeans, brown work shoes, and lugged a rucksack. "I know another way to the road," he said. "Follow me."

Beria and Grimsky climbed into the Pathfinder with their meager belongings. The four-wheeler bounced across the uneven grass field parallel to the landing strip, but fell behind the Corvette. The cops had been stationed at the south entrance, so the escape route—if it could be called that—paralleled the golf course on a track abutting the highway. Beria stopped the vehicle after barely a hundred yards. Grimsky took out the remote detonator and extended the aerial. He aimed the device in the direction of the hangar behind them, waited for the flashing red lights to synchronize, and punched the detonate button.

———

A sudden red glow filled the infrared imager inside the S-76, overwhelming the heat sensors. The FLIR operator knew immediately what had happened: an explosion of substantial magnitude. He fiddled with the sensitivity switch and yelled out new vectors to the pilot. He picked up again the two automobiles heading toward the highway. Two people inside the larger vehicle, a sole occupant in the other.

"Alex, take a look. See what I see?"

The video man grunted. "Yeah, I'm with you. They're making a break for it. Time to break radio silence."

The pilot agreed. Those on the ground would appreciate why. He keyed the mike. "Copperhead Two to base."

"Go, Copper Two," came Creed's steely voice.

"Sir, suspects are in egress. I had to break audio."

"Yes, Sergeant. I'm seeing it on the live feed. I just ordered the boys to move in. Hang around awhile, will you?"

"Roger, that. Ah, I'm a bit low on fuel. Loiter endurance down to five minutes. We'll come in after that."

"Uh, got you."

"They blew up the barn, and they're running for it," the pilot said in case the people down there didn't know how to read imager pictures and were misinterpreting the red glow that filled half the screen.

"They won't get far," Creed said.

"Like I said, sir, ah, the fuel situation. Five minutes is all I can, uh, give you."

"No problem, Sergeant. Did your best. Over and out." Creed's voice now had an exasperated edge to it.

Creed was frustrated. Bruce Kohlbus threw up his hands in fury. Their baby had leaked, and the terrorists were doing their own demolition. Both men had looked forward to holding a national press conference after the raid and displaying the weapons cache and the two live missiles they had captured at the doorstep of the Capitol.

Damn, damn, and damn.

The SWAT, ATF, and FBI raiding teams were still being assembled when the hangar and its incriminating contents blew. They were being discreetly smuggled into the area and digging in for what they assumed would be a long wait when the explosion occurred and thick black smoke rose from the hangar location. Creed's coded order to commence the raid immediately crackled over the radio, and the few units already assembled charged into the Kokubani estate.

The second explosion occurred just then, sending the first wave of SWAT men back to cover.

Grimsky's timing had been slightly off. The timer on the second batch of explosives had been set for thirty minutes after the first to finish off any remaining evidence and also to take out anyone sifting through the wreckage. Either by sympathetic detonation with the first or an incomplete turn of the timing screw, the second explosion rocked the Maryland countryside only four minutes after the first. No human fatalities were recorded.

———

Washington, DC.

Heavy concrete barricades were placed on Pennsylvania Avenue around the White House. Two buffer zones were erected to foil would-be truck bombers and snipers. Security patrols swarmed the White House carrying short-stemmed Uzis and MP5s. It was aesthetically revolting to see armed guards wading through the magnificent profusion of chrysanthemums, heliotropes, and salvia of the Rose Garden in autumn. In the Jacqueline Kennedy Garden and the Lyndon B. Johnson Children's Garden adjacent to the White House tennis courts, agents knee-deep in flowers scoured the place with metal detectors. Aerial countermeasures were just as thorough: two Stinger-equipped Marines on the White House roof scanned the skies constantly, their shoulder-launched missiles ready.

The nuclear-proof bunker beneath the White House had an independent air system, worldwide telecommunications, medical services, and enough food and living arrangements for a three-month confinement.

Inside, President Deakin chafed at the order that had sent him down there. He frowned at his wife.

"I'd rather be up there with the troops facing those terrorists. If the American people hear that I was bundled into a bunker at the moment of truth, my credibility will suffer."

"Relax, honey." The First Lady patted his hand. "You are more valuable to the American people alive than dead."

Deakin stroked his chin pensively. "You know, when those Puerto Rican nationalists attacked Blair House back in the fifties, I heard a rumor that Truman ran under a table."

"I don't think he did anything of the sort, dear. I once talked to Margaret, Harry's grand-daughter. She says her mom told her it never happened. She was a kid then but she remembers. Anyway, I'm sure they'll soon determine the nature of the threat and we'll be out of here."

"Oh, we know where the threat's coming from, my dear. Creed, Kohlbus, Bogan—they've all briefed me. Bunch of half-baked terrorists. We'll soon find out who's bankrolling them. I'll send in F-22 Raptors to incinerate them." He paused thoughtfully. "I may send in Rambo."

The First Lady said nothing. After a while, Deakin said, "I bet ol' Give-'Em-Hell Harry never blinked when those Puerto Ricans blasted their way into Blair. Probably just walked out to the balcony stiff as a ramrod and shouted down at them, 'Here I am. Come get me, you cheapskates!'"

———

Montgomery County.
The Pathfinder bounced across the field toward the flat blacktop where the rural highway bisected the field. Because Beria had stopped the Pathfinder so Grimsky could detonate the wired hangar, Nasser in the Corvette had shot ahead and made the blacktop ahead of the police cordon. As Grimsky watched the Corvette's rear lights fade into the distance and Beria floored the Pathfinder's throttle, the disheartening sign of a blue-and-white Montgomery County Police squad car, lights flashing, startled both men. The cop car raced the blacktop aiming to cut off the Pathfinder.

Beria swung the wheel desperately, the four-wheeler hit a rut, jumped crazily, landed on one wheel, and then all four. Beria went all out for the small rise leading to the blacktop that Nasser in the Corvette had avoided. Beria knew if the police cruiser tried to follow, the rise would cause the cruiser to overturn. But the cruiser hung on every step of the way.

Grimsky glanced sideways and saw two uniformed cops in the car. The driver swung his arms on the wheel in a yo-yo fashion and had a determined, tough, street-cop look. His partner, looking like Clint

Eastwood in a *Dirty Harry* movie, cradled a pump-action shotgun in both hands, the muzzle jutting through the open window as both cars jockeyed for position.

Grimsky produced a revolver from his pocket and the Pathfinder jerked as Beria released one hand from the steering wheel to push Grimsky's hand out of sight. "No! We don't have a chance! Not yet, anyway."

Grimsky swore in Russian and hunched his body forward, as if willing the 4WD to reach the rise—now four hundred yards away—in the next second.

A dark shape rose suddenly in front of the Pathfinder, and the clatter of the helicopter burst in upon them. Suddenly a light brighter than any either man had ever seen, or would ever see, blinded them. Beria screamed "Shit!" and ground the brakes. He had no choice. Every millimeter of ground, every blade of grass was illumined with startling clarity, and his eyeballs were seared by the unbelievable energy of the white light thrown at him. Known as the NightSun, the searchlight from the chopper generated thirty-two million candlepower, and it was all aimed at the Pathfinder that now slalomed crazily. The police cruiser pulled alongside, and a voice boomed over the loudspeaker, audible even above the noise of the chopper, "This is the police! Pull over *now*, and stop. Police! Pull over, now!"

Beria slammed his foot on the brakes and swung the wheel. The Pathfinder spun a full circle and skidded to a stop in a cloud of dust. Even as the cruiser was still stopping, the policemen bundled out of the car, one holding his service revolver and the other the shotgun.

"Get your hands up!" barked the cop wielding the shotgun. "Now! Get them up, c'mon, let's see them."

Grimsky dropped his weapon and raised both hands, as did Beria. Neither man could see properly, and even though they avoided looking directly at the horrendous searchlight, it was like being in the center of the sun. Both men felt naked, as though the light was both an X-ray and an immobilizer.

"Get out of the car. Slowly."

Again the silent pantomime.

"Turn around. Spread your legs and lean against the vehicle."

The chopper sound deepened. The radio in the cops' portable transceivers crackled, but the transmission was lost in the noise of the chopper. Mercifully, the monster backed off, banked to starboard, and the NightSun was switched off. The radio crackled again.

"Copperhead Two to base. Suspects in custody of ground unit. I see backup pulling up now. More backup on the way. I'm low on fuel. Coming home to Mother, over."

"Roger that, Copper Two. Andrews is reporting one thousand overcast and two miles if you can't make Mother on your, ah, present fuel. How much endurance you got left?"

"Twenty minutes."

"Ah, Roger. Mother's been told you're coming in for more milk. Good job, son."

The chopper noise faded.

While the shotgun-wielding cop provided cover, the other cop frisked both men for hidden weapons.

It's all over, Grimsky thought. *What fools we were*. How could the president still be playing golf at night? The cyanide pill in his capped molar required a specific procedure to activate it. He wondered if Beria would do the same. Out of the corner of his eye, he could see reinforcements arriving, a white police vehicle with a single revolving red light on its roof. The car pulled up, and the cop came running over with his gun drawn.

"FBI." The man flashed a badge. "Good work, you two. Hate to take all the glory, but we have jurisdiction on this one."

Something in the FBI man's voice made Grimsky and Beria almost turn around.

"Figures," said the shotgun-wielder. "Fibbies own the goddamn jurisdiction. Where the hell are the others?"

"They won't be coming."

The cop frisking the two men paused. The one holding the shotgun froze. Maybe it had occurred to him that FBI agents shouldn't have accents, however faint. He started to turn around. A sound like two handclaps came from the direction of the "Fibby" and the cop's head exploded into pulp. The other went for his gun, and Nabil plugged him with two quick shots. He collapsed like a deck of cards.

Nabil said, "Quick. Into my vehicle. Let's get out of here."

"You can say that again," Beria said.

They took the guns from the dead cops and jumped into Nabil's vehicle. The Aspen threw gravel and sped away.

———

Nabil did not go to the safe house whose address he had memorized. For them, no safe house in Washington, DC, would be secure now that the mission had been blown. Nasser and his father were fools. They were not professionals. They would be caught and would sing under interrogation. He drove to a nearby hotel with a large cabstand and parked a block away.

Beria went first. He walked down the hotel esplanade and entered the first taxi in the file. Cab drivers could usually remember when and where they picked up a recent cold fare from the streets. But if a fare walked up from the hotel entrance or sidewalk and gave an address downtown, as Beria did, the cabbie likely wouldn't give it a second thought.

Grimsky followed five minutes later, repeating the same procedure. Their exfiltration plan was different from Nabil's; he couldn't fault Yuri Zamyatin for that.

Nabil looked for a suitable location to dump the unmarked Fed car. He'd removed the red light from the roof; on the outside, the car looked like any other. The radio chatter was unabated, and he could generally make out that the dispatcher was coordinating with Metro police and had just about every available squad car rushing to the Kokubani farm. Nabil parked the car on a busy street and walked five blocks away to another big hotel. He entered a cab and said, "Take me to Reston."

The driver swung his meter lanyard and growled, "Out of city limits. Cost you a dollar above the meter."

Nabil settled deep into the seat so that the driver could not catch a direct look at his face. "No problem."

———

Reston.

Tammy had just finished feeding Tom and was checking in on Sandy, who was doing her homework, when she heard the urgent tones of CNN's *Breaking News* coming from the TV set in the living room. Tammy picked up the remote and increased the volume.

The FBI and ATF, in conjunction with local police SWAT teams, had raided a farmhouse in rural Maryland. Terrorists were believed to be harboring there, and apparently some sort of attack had been planned against vital structures and/or high-ranking members of the Deakin administration. Reports were still sketchy, since print and television reporters were being kept away from the scene, but it was thought that the terrorists had blown up the farmhouse as the SWAT team moved in. CNN had learned that the farmhouse, which also had a private grass airstrip, had been under surveillance before the order to raid the place came in.

On the screen, she could make out what looked like a burning barn loft, thick black smoke rising into the starry night sky. The reporter, her hair streaming in the wind, stood against the backdrop of police cars and fire trucks and flashing red-and-blue lights; she said that the resemblance of this current activity to the events in Illinois a little more than a week ago was starkly evident. A terrorist using the alias Samir Muvdi and suspected to have participated in the Illinois bombings, had recently been sighted in the Washington, DC, area. FBI sketches of Mr. Muvdi had shown a close resemblance to a notorious Middle Eastern assassin known simply as Nabil. More details would be available when the press corps was briefed.

Tammy watched all this, transfixed. Could these be the same people from Illinois? It had been rumored that their target had been the president then. Were they now going for him right here in the capital? And who was this Nabil fellow?

The doorbell rang, jarring her from her thoughts. She hadn't been expecting anyone. She went to answer it. Peeking through the telescopic eye-viewer, she saw an official-looking man in a dark-gray suit and regulation black tie waiting patiently. She cracked open the door until it held against the chain.

"Yes?"

The man displayed a law enforcement shield. "FBI. We would like to talk to you."

Dear God. It's happening. That man Doherty. She had never trusted him. She took two deep breaths then opened the door fully. The man stepped in. Apparently he was alone.

"Mrs. Weasel?"

Tammy ran her fingers through her hair and hoped the man didn't notice how nervous she was. "It's not pronounced that way. It rhymes with 'vessel'."

"Mrs. Vessel, I need to speak with you."

She took another deep breath. "If it's about the . . . the device for measuring toilet flushes, I've decided to come clean in the morning and tell everything."

The man gave her a strange look. "What are you talking about?"

He was tall and lean and had a gaunt, predatory face with prominent incisors. He went on, folding his coat neatly and placing it on the sofa. "I thought it time we got acquainted."

CHAPTER 23

Washington, DC.

It was the next day, and the press conferences were still going on. The White House lockdown had been lifted, although stringent measures remained in place.Mike McGory, the White House Press Secretary, was giving his second news briefing of the morning. No, the terrorists had not all been caught; authorities were working toward that goal. Yes, Dr. Kokubani had been picked up on his way home from his private clinic. His son Nasser had also been picked up—posthumously. A police car had spotted the yellow Corvette and given chase. Other squad cars joined. The Corvette was clocked going at speeds around 110 mph. The inevitable happened. Nasser took a corner too fast; the car had fishtailed, spun, and wrapped itself around a utility pole. It took Montgomery County firemen more than two hours to extricate his remains from the wreckage. Nasser's death was a pity, McGory said. The FBI had been anxious to question him.

He took questions warily from the press.

Was it true, asked the NBC correspondent, that a famous terrorist named Samir Mudvi, who reportedly had been in Urbana, Illinois, at the time of the U. of I. bombing, had also been spotted at the Kokubani farm?

McGory sighed. He didn't know about famous terrorists; notorious ones, yes. At this time there was no definite proof. Of course the suspected involvement of certain world-class terrorists had not been ruled out. And the possibility of one or more foreign powers being involved had also not been ruled out. The president was reviewing the situation. He had been briefed, he was in constant touch with all heads of relevant departments, including the Department of Homeland Security, Secret Service, FBI, ATF, and the CIA. McGory went on and on, the practiced bureaucrat and hired mouthpiece, saying everything but giving away nothing. He had been born for the role. The newsmen scribbled furiously and live feeds from the South Lawn were almost obligatory.

Chief Strooker sat in his office with Ken Dwight and Larry Bodine, plotting strategy. A transmitter had been removed from a filing cabinet in the office of the First Lady's personal staff. Four women worked in that room: Mrs. Neal, Peggy Swisher, Julie Berg, and Tammy Weasel. Dwight had already questioned each one of them and all had denied any knowledge of the device. Mrs. Neal had a nervous tic that manifested itself several times during the interview. He wondered about that. Probably her age and too much coffee. Tammy had looked disconcerted, overly anxious. Larry Bodine would conduct a second interview for each of the four women; Dwight wanted to hear his opinion of those two.

Strooker did not believe in management meetings and further meetings during crises. He ordered polygraphs for every White House employee or staffer. They couldn't refuse; it was part of their employment contract. He intended to start with the four women in that office and, if that yielded a positive result, would probably go no further.

All the uniformed Secret Service agents working the White House metal detectors had been suspended for dereliction of duty. They would take polygraphs immediately. One uniformed agent remembered seeing something like a pocket calculator in a woman's handbag after the detector was tripped. That area's surveillance camera had been down for maintenance. He couldn't for the life of him recall who it was. Since more than 1,700 people were employed in the Executive Office of the President, and presumably a good portion of that number were women—though many were crammed into the Executive Office Building next door—it would be a tall order to give polygraphs to all of them.

Strooker had no doubt what would happen to the uniformed agent who had seen what he thought was a pocket calculator in a woman's handbag. He would be reassigned to chasing counterfeiters for a branch of the treasury. Word from the FBI lab was that no prints had been able to be lifted from the calculator-like device. The device had been taken apart by techies, but some critical yet unknown piece had melted inside the device, leaving only the calculator chip still functioning. The device was bagged and placed in storage in the Evidence Room.

Strooker had sent an agent to Radio Shack to purchase five identical pocket calculators by Hewlett-Packard. He placed each one inside a transparent polythene bag to give the impression it was the original, then dispatched one each to the five different polygraph examiners who would be conducting the interviews. The five polygraph teams, contracted from private firms downtown, would interview staffers from dawn to midnight if necessary. High on the priority list were the four secretaries in the First Lady's staff office, all members of the cleaning crew with after-hours access to the offices, and all security agents.

———

Tammy was not upbeat at all that morning. For one, Special Agent Larry Bodine had interviewed the women in the First Lady's staff individually, repeating the questions Dwight had asked earlier.

Agent Bodine: "Have you ever seen this calculator before, Tammy?" Holding up the device.

Tammy: "No."

Agent Bodine: "Does this calculator belong to you?"

Tammy: "No, it does not."

Agent Bodine: "Prior to today, did you see this device or a device like it, on the desk or drawer of any of your colleagues?"

Tammy: "No, I did not." She shook her head emphatically. Didn't blink. "Can't say I did."

Agent Bodine was watching her closely. He paused to write something down in his notebook.

Agent Bodine: "Well, then, do you own a pocket calculator?"

Tammy: "Of course. Everyone does."

Agent Bodine: "Identical to this one?" Holding up the device again.

Tammy: "Not really. No."

Agent Bodine: "Do you mind if I see it?

Tammy: (blustery) "I don't have it with me. Probably at home somewhere, I hardly ever use it. I use the one on my cell phone if I need to, like everyone else."

Agent Bodine nodded. His gaze dropped, and again he wrote something in his notepad. Without looking up he said, "Tammy, would you be willing to take a polygraph test?"

Tammy hesitated. "Sure."

"Sure about that?"

Tammy coughed. "Positive."

Bodine wrote on a piece of paper, which he tore out and handed to her. "Fine. We'll schedule you for tomorrow morning at 9:30 a.m. Downtown. Kline, Gadau Associates. It's here on the paper."

She examined the paper, folded it, and put inside a folder in her purse. Smoothed her hair.

Bodine watched her closely. "Meanwhile, if you have a change of heart, or remember anything about the pocket calculator—no matter how trivial—call me. Any time, day or night. Can't reach me? Call Ken Dwight. Clear?"

"No questions."

Bodine nodded as she rose. "Please send in Miss Berg next."

As Tammy left, she surmised that the reason she felt beat that morning was because she had opened the *Washington Post* to find the glaring headline: *TWO FBI AGENTS KILLED IN CAPITOL DRAMA.* On a sidebar, a lesser caption: *EX-CIA MAN DIES IN SAME SHOOT-OUT.* And underneath the caption a photograph of the man she knew as Stan Doherty. Only Doherty was not his real name. He was called Jim

Freidman, and he had been killed in a shoot-out inside a restroom in the Rayburn Building that had also left two experienced FBI agents dead.

And television news networks were awash with rumors of a purported terrorist named "Samir Muvdi", whose picture FBI agents positively identified as one Nabil Hamdoon, a.k.a. The Contractor, a terrorist for hire as deadly and notorious as the onetime Carlos. Nabil had been seen in Illinois and was now thought to be in Washington, DC.

The events of the previous night still seemed an ongoing nightmare.

A terrorist in her apartment.

———

Incredible. But there he was in her apartment. And they were talking like housemates. She'd brought him decaf coffee and butter chestnut cookies. He drank two cups of decaf and polished off the cookies before admitting that he hadn't eaten. She heated up a can of Campbell's cream of mushroom soup and microwaved a huge leftover spinach soufflé. He devoured it.

At one point, Sandy wandered into the sitting room in her pajamas and stockinged feet. She stopped when she saw the stranger. "Mommy, who is this man?"

"Oh, honey. He's a . . . friend."

The girl walked up to Nabil and extended her hand. "I'm Sandy. What's your name?"

The stranger took her hand. His lips parted; a glint of stained teeth showed beneath the garish moustache.

"Call me Uncle Ted."

"Uncle Ted," Sandy repeated. She flicked a nonexistent cowlick from her forehead. "Are you a policeman, Uncle Ted?"

"No. Just Uncle Ted."

Tammy lifted Sandy onto her lap and fiddled with the girl's hairpins. "Have you finished your homework, love?"

"Yes. I'd like some milk."

"In a minute." She replaced the last pin and set Sandy on her feet. The little girl padded to the refrigerator and helped herself. *"Mister Roger's Neighborhood* is on," Tammy called. "I won't object if you watch. Thirty minutes only."

"It's over already," Sandy said.

They watched her drain the last drop of milk and set down the glass before wiping her mouth.

"Uncle Ted, take care of my mommy."

"Off to bed!" Tammy snapped.

After Sandy had left, Tammy went to check on little Tom. Nabil followed her and was alarmed to see wires running from the crib to a small alarm in the sitting room.

"The SIDS monitor," Tammy explained. "There's another one in my bedroom."

The only SIDS Nabil knew of were the SIDS and STARS on Jeppesen approach plates in airplanes. "What's that?"

"Most parents have one these days. Sudden infant death syndrome. A number of babies each year die in their sleep from turning over the wrong way. They suffocate. The monitor lets out a shriek if the baby stops breathing for even a few seconds."

"Wonderful." Nabil peered inside the crib. The tot was asleep. "How old is he?"

"Ten months."

"Same father as Sandy?"

She nodded.

"But you're divorced?"

"Separated."

Silence. So she went on. "Brian and I separated soon after Sandy was born. On and off. In between, we bumped into each other a few times. It's hard sometimes . . . we couldn't resist. We were better friends separated than married." She shrugged. "I got pregnant with Tommy. We have a legal separation, pending divorce proceedings. I knew I'd keep him, even though Brian offered to pay for the D and C. The divorce notwithstanding, Brian and I now agree Tom is the best thing that ever happened to us. It hasn't changed our minds about the separation. I've made it clear though—no more sex while the divorce is pending."

"Why did you separate?"

"I wanted it. The usual. Irreconcilable differences. And he beat me."

"Beat you?"

"Yes. As in battery. Battered wife."

"Did you press charges?"

"No. Hurts the children."

The man looked sympathetic. "Perhaps you should move to another city. Seeing him . . . the old passions resurface."

She smiled wistfully. "Not anymore. I saw him a few months back at the Capitol. I felt nothing whatsoever. Just another lawyer with a briefcase hurrying to a meeting." She shook her head emphatically. "It's over and done with."

They talked about other things. She drank hot chocolate; he took more decaf. It was unreal, as though talking to the Most Wanted Man in America was entirely natural, not the semi-hostage situation it was.

She asked how he'd been able to locate her address. He explained how he had followed Freidman to her house as he delivered the transmitting device. After the White House lockdown and the burning down of the Kokubani estate with the two airplanes, he'd fled the estate like everyone else. And with the police and media alert for the Contractor out there, he had figured the only safe place for him in Washington, DC, was her apartment.

She knit her brows in confusion. "Wait a minute. A lawyer named Stan Doherty delivered the device. And the . . . thing he gave me was not actually a device for measuring the number of times a toilet is flushed. It was a transmitter?"

"That's right."

What exactly had Freidman told her?

"That's right."

She said softly, "The terrorist attack planned to take place . . . I . . . so I was conned into being a participant?"

"The less you know, the better."

How dare you? I'm very patriotic, don't you know that? She was silent for a long time. Nabil drank more decaf and waited.

Finally she looked at the wall clock and faked a yawn. "Almost ten o'clock," she said.

"Is it?"

"Yes. And time for me to go to bed. Now if you'll excuse me, Mr. . . . .?"

"Call me Muvdi. Samir Muvdi."

"Mr. Mudvi, I have to go to bed now if I'm to get up in the morning."

"Muvdi."

"Alright, Mr. Mudvi—did I get that right?"

"No, you didn't. Why does every American insist on turning my name around?"

"Take it easy. It's not personal. You just called me a weasel at the door."

They glared at each other.

Tammy took a long shot. "And I happen to know from watching the news that your real name is Nabil. Why don't I just call you Nabil?"

He studied her for a long moment. "You may."

"Nabil," she said, "now that it's late and it doesn't look as though you are going to kill me—or are you?"

"I haven't decided."

"Well, please remain undecided. I very much want to live. Hadn't you better be going . . . and perhaps come back when you've decided?"

"Nice try. I thought you knew." He sighed deeply. "I'm going to be your guest for the next three or four days."

———

It made sense. Unless she was a suspect—and he didn't think she would be until she failed a polygraph—her apartment was the safest place in the capital for him. The authorities would scour the hotels, motels, airports, and bus stations—even the docks. All hotel registration cards would be scrutinized and checked in that most ancient and effective of police methods—dogged legwork. But he wouldn't be there.

They had talked much longer, even after her mention of bed. Nabil had no fear whatsoever that she would rat him out. That alone unnerved her. Like Doherty—Freidman, rather—he hinted at the dark things that would happen to her, to her mother, her children, even her sister in California, if she breathed a word to the authorities. His associates were so much more than ruthless.

He had been contemptuous of the Witness Protection Program, how she could be taken into protective custody and enrolled in it if she sold him out. She would be spirited to a new city, with new identities for herself and the children, and supposedly a new life. He'd assured her she would be dead in four months. There were files somewhere on computer discs and no matter how few people had access to those files, somewhere, sometime, with money and the right person, those files could be read and hit men dispatched to their location.

Ask ex-mobsters who had broken *omerta* and been swallowed up in the Witness Program. Only you couldn't ask many of them because the dead don't speak. He had friends more ruthless than any mob boss.

All he needed was a few days, he assured her, and he would be out of her hair. Then she could go to the FBI and confess, plead Stockholm syndrome. His friends wouldn't come after her for that, he promised. What was more, for her cooperation, he would make available to her the sum of eleven thousand dollars as a token of gratitude.

No, no, no, no! She was adamant. She would never take money from him or from any other organization bent on destabilizing the political structure of the United States of America. She would rather die instead. It was bad enough to harbor him under coercion. To take money for betraying her country—never! And if he ever sent money to her anonymously, she would absolutely turn it over to the FBI. When he did leave, he had better hide and hide well. Because the minute he set her free, she would call the FBI. She knew if the FBI raided the apartment while he was there, he would fight to the end. He had vowed never to be taken alive.

He insisted that everything should go on normally. She would go to work as usual, take Sandy to school, Tom to his daycare.

Of course if Sandy's teacher—prodded by FBI agents—asked Sandy if a man was staying in her mom's apartment, she was intelligent enough to say yes, Mom's boyfriend lived there. Did Mom's boyfriend look foreign, like perhaps he was from Turkey? In a place like DC, the power seat of the nation and possibly of the world—with thousands of foreign diplomats and embassy staff—Sandy would be quite used to cultural diversity and to her young mind one executive type was the same as another. Tammy was to impress upon Sandy that she had actually been seeing Uncle Ted for some time and now he was to live with them. She would even hint that she was considering marrying Uncle Ted as soon as the divorce from Dad became final. She was not to discuss any of this with Mrs. Fierstal next door. The old crone was prudish and would be upset—possibly enough to gossip—if she learned Tammy was living with a man who was not her husband.

He did not seem to fear that she could make outside contact from the bedroom while he slept on the living room couch. Still he disconnected the house phones as routine precaution and seized her cell phone, saying he would give it back in the morning.

He slept on the living-room couch, she in the bedroom.

———

He decided he could use Tammy's telephone. By the time they found out her involvement and got around to checking her phone records, he would long be gone.

Boris answered at the third ring. "Yes?"

"The project manager speaking."

A pause. "Are you calling from a secure line?"

"Yes," Nabil lied.

"Where are you now?"

"I can't tell you that, sir. I'm sure you know by now what happened. Your two salesmen got your warning and threw away the goods. Two policemen apprehended them but I was able to spring them. They've both made it to branch offices, I'm sure."

"They're safe," Boris said without enthusiasm. He sounded tired, defeated. "You guys screwed up the mission. There was a leak somewhere."

"Freidman's dead," Nabil said instead.

"I know."

"He was making the drop when he . . . ah . . . fell. Did he—were you able to receive the goods he was supposed to deliver?"

"I got it alright," Boris said. There was pride in his voice; his boy had come through. "Freidman made the drop before he died. He was a professional. The same cannot be said for you guys right now."

"We came through in Illinois."

"This is DC. This is the one that really matters."

"I'm still in charge of the mission. It isn't over yet."

"What the hell are you talking about?"

"This is the time to strike, to really hit them. They think they've wrecked the hardware and the organization. They think we're on the run, and they'll relax some of the security they've built up in the past few days. We'll take them by complete surprise."

"You and who? Will you please tell me what the hell you are talking about?"

"I have a plan. Remember the cached explosives and the rocket launchers I ordered as backup? I have friends in New York. A blind Imam. He heads a cell. I'll give him a call."

———

Before Tammy left for work that morning, she had kissed Nabil fully on the lips with Sandy watching. He had insisted on it. His mustache felt bristly and razor-like, like the rest of him. It took effort, but she had done it. Nabil had her pull all the drapes across the windows and doors, leaving the apartment bathed only in the soft, artificial light of the ceiling lamps.

After she left with the children, Nabil examined the door closely. Standard Yale lock, a deadbolt, and steel chain. If he used the chain, whoever unlocked the door would know that someone was inside. The deadbolt had a stop-lock feature that locked the door from the inside so that it could not be opened from the outside with the key.

The FBI wouldn't have search warrants on her yet. They could ask the apartment manager to let them in—he would have a set of duplicates. Either way, the door had to be able to open from the outside; they would know Tammy was at work. He knew they wouldn't do that. Their case woule be thrown out in court for illegal entry.

He went back to the front door and strapped the deadbolt. He left the chain alone. If the condo manager tried to open the door with his duplicate and it didn't open, the conclusion would be that someone was inside the apartment or she had changed the lock. The latter would not be unusual for a single woman living in the suburbs of a high-crime metropolis. The deadbolt would resist for a while any attempts to crash down the door. It would give him plenty of time.

None of this would happen. Not yet. His instinct told him she wouldn't rat on him, considering the safety risk to herself and her children. He rather liked her, come to think of it.

Tammy.

Even the name sounded cohesive, suggesting a vague binding receptacle. She reminded him of what was beautiful and desirable in American women. She reminded him of something else. He thought about it. Ah, yes. Kim Basinger in that James Bond film he had seen in Athens. Everything was there, down to the full, sensuous mouth. Except for the hair. Tammy was a redhead.

These thoughts were pleasant, and he found himself walking to the door of her bedroom, the one that had been denied him the previous night. He opened the door gingerly. It was like opening a delicate secret. New vistas would be thrown open to him, old ones deciphered. The bedroom would hold her effusive female attachments, and he was almost afraid of what he might discover.

A queen-sized bed much too large for one woman dominated the room, with two heavy, light-blue patterned quilts draped over it. The airy color matched the intricate pattern of the blue wallpaper lining the entire room and ceiling. You couldn't tell where one ended and the other began.

Tammy's fragrance lingered, like an invisible trace of her. Chloè? Givenchy or Guerlain? Nina Ricci? Smelled like L'air de Temps. He couldn't tell. The wardrobe was full: dresses, skirts, halter-tops, jeans, shirts, neatly folded or on plastic hangers. Clothes by Yves St. Laurent, Armani, Christian Dior, Nina Fredericks. Her favorite color was green. Easy to tell. More clothes in that color than any other.

He walked over to the chest of drawers and pulled out the top two. Fresh underwear of all sorts—bikini, shorts, pantyhose—all neatly folded and tucked. He closed the drawer and looked around furtively. A gilt-framed photograph of Tammy and little Sandy sat on the beige mantelpiece. He examined it a while, pausing over the full, pouting lips, the green eyes gazing directly at the camera, mystery, mischief, and impishness compacted into the eyes in a rare blend of natural sexual candor that she probably was unaware of.

Apart from the occasional whore in Paris, or Amsterdam, or Hamburg, or Beirut, Nabil's interest in women had been greatly reduced since the death of his beloved wife Noor from an Israeli air raid. The stirrings of repressed passion over this . . . this Tammy, embarrassed him.

On impulse. he walked over to the Kelvinator washing machine next to the clothes dryer and freezer. He lifted the lid. The hamper was half full. Clothes, mostly Sandy's and Tom's, and, judging from the sizes, several which unquestionably belonged to Tammy. Two black nylon panties, one white cotton panty, and a white bra carelessly thrown in. Nabil picked up the white panty and examined it. There was a barely perceptible stain in the front oval, the part that aligned perfectly with where her . . .

His thoughts collided in a jumble of high excitement. He felt the blood rushing to his loins. She had worn that particular one only yesterday, and his hands shook holding onto Tammy's underwear.

He sniffed at the discolored area and his senses reeled with the pungent, base effluvium of Tammy. He buried his face in it, drinking in the tangy, pudendal musk, feeding on it. The room spun around and he was aware that he was not himself.

"Tammy. . ." he whispered. "Tammy, Tammy . . ."

His erection stiff as a cannon barrel, he walked around the room, whispering hoarsely, Tammy's white cotton underwear perched on his nose.

CHAPTER 24

Washington, DC.

"Fragments recovered from the scene of the burn-out hangar match missile components that we've seen in Afghanistan," ATF chairman Bruce Kohlbus said.

He was in a conference with Chief Strooker and FBI Director Creed. "We intercepted a telephone call to the Kokubani estate. The caller told them to get the hell out of there, that a raid was imminent. A man with a Russian accent answered the phone at the Kokubani estate. Gentlemen, let me remind you that two white males, apparently of Russian origin, were seen in the St. Joseph, Illinois area along with this Nabil fellow. These same white males and Nabil—we have excellent shots from the helicopter videos and imager—show up in a Maryland suburb, and once again we have mayhem. Every time these guys surface, general aviation airplanes configured to carry munitions are seen, buildings blow up, and so do the airplanes. When we sift through the wreckage, what do we find? Russian-made hard casings. I say this, gentlemen, without equivocation: Ivan, for whatever reason, is involved in this plot. Regardless of the presence of the Contractor. Do you agree with me on this, Hy, Gary?"

Creed nodded. "I should think so, Bruce."

Strooker said, "What I find troubling is the inside connection. A call was made to the JFK Continental from the Capitol, if you remember. Now we have another call to the Kokubani house from the Capitol, warning them of the raid. Then we have the placing of the transmitter inside the White House. This suggests high-level involvement, by a person or persons known to us."

Creed squirmed uncomfortably. "That, too. The fact that Freidman, ex-CIA, dies in a shootout with my boys inside the Rayburn building after leaving the Kokubani farm, tells us a lot. Did we find out who he went to see and why?"

"Not yet. The Contractor showed up there, too. God knows how he got there, but he was."

"Right." Creed's face tightened. "Now he's carrying an FBI badge from one of my men. I lost two yesterday. I knew both men, and their wives . . ." His voice changed. He was silent for a while, then muttered, "Bless their souls."

The three men observed a pensive silence. After a while, Strooker said, "We should find and question everybody who was in or visited the Kokubani house during the last two weeks. For starters."

Creed seemed glad of this reprieve. "We found Mrs. Kokubani and her daughter in a bungalow in Boca Raton, Florida. Apparently some sort of hostage situation. The two hoods that were guarding them left hurriedly after receiving a telephone call. Our pal from the Capitol again, I bet. Mrs. Kokubani and her daughter called the local police after the hoods left. I'd wager they had no knowledge of the goings-on back in Maryland."

"Possibly," Kohlbus said. "Surely an estate as large as the Kokubanis ought to have housekeepers, groundskeepers, some sort of help. They would have seen something."

Again Creed nodded. "One of the two house trailers near the hangar was actually occupied by permanent help up to about eighteen months ago. The help was terminated and asked to vacate the trailer. Since then, Dr. Kokubani has employed part-time help—mostly schoolboys, college freshmen on summer vacation—to look after the grounds. His son Nasser moved into one of the trailers. I believe that preparations for the attack we just foiled probably began shortly after the groundskeeper was asked to leave. Dr. Kokubani retained only one part-time housekeeper.

She took ill about ten days ago and is presently hospitalized. Some kind of colon bacteria or food poisoning. The doctors are still running tests. She's so sick we haven't been allowed to talk to her yet."

Kohlbus's hollow laughter doubled as a cough. "You think the doctor engineered the housekeeper's illness?"

"Possibly. The doctors are not sure exactly what's going on. She's running a constant high fever. They've sent samples to the Center for Disease Control in Atlanta. Hell of a coincidence."

"What's the angle on Kokubani?" asked Strooker.

"He's not talking," Kohlbus said. "He's had conferences with his lawyer, plotting strategy. Charges haven't been filed yet, but I'm willing to bet he'll be charged with at least three counts of domestic terrorism and attempted domestic terrorism and a host of federal charges."

Creed said thoughtfully, "We'll have to keep hammering the president about Russian involvement in this thing. The evidence at this stage is incontrovertible."

"If we could catch those other three men, that'd be a clincher. We're scouring all of DC and the Maryland and Virginia suburbs. Those sonuvabitches just disappeared."

"This guy, Nabil," Strooker said. "The Contractor. I'm worried, from what I hear of his exploits. This is one loose cannon I don't want in Washington."

———

Moskva.

General Yuri Zamyatin stepped out of his bathtub onto a brown rubber mat. His *dacha* was one of the best along the Moskva, and he was proud of it. He draped a towel around his waist and started for the terrace where, as was his custom, he would lie beneath the artificial light of the ultraviolet lamps. He stopped when he realized the lamps had not been turned on.

"Igor!" His voice thundered across the room. His aide must be the most incompetent oaf this side of the Gulags.

Feet pounded up the stairs. The door opened.

"Igor, you fool—"

Zamyatin froze. Two uniformed men from the military police and a civilian in a black mackintosh, obviously SVR, strode in.

The civilian spoke first. "Comrade General Zamyatin?"

"Yes."

"I'm Colonel Blasov, SVR. I have orders for your arrest. From the Praesidium of the Supreme Soviet."

"What are you talking about? This must be a terrible mistake."

The Supreme Soviet no longer exists. It has been replaced by the office of the President of Russia. There must be a mistake.

"There is no mistake," the SVR man said quietly. "Please dry yourself and come with us."

Ten minutes later, General Zamyatin was hustled into a waiting limousine and the car sped off.

On another *dacha*, this one on a hill overlooking the Volga, General Grigory Artemyev was also being escorted into a waiting Chaika automobile.

In Moscow, deep within the walls of the Kremlin, Mikhail Grachev's telephone rang. He had been expecting the call. He picked up the receiver, listened intently, and then gave further instructions. He replaced the receiver and pressed the bell under his table. A trusted aide rushed in.

"Get me General Lebdev."

"At once, Mr. President."

When General Lebdev was ushered in fifteen minutes later and the two men were alone, Grachev handed him a file folder containing three photographs each of five men, taken full face, side profile, and full portrait. Two of those five men were Generals Artemyev and Zamyatin. The other three were two army colonels and one major.

"I am delegating this to you," Grachev said. "Go to the Gulags in Siberia. Pick five men who are the exact replicas of the men in these photographs. Five prisoners whose cases are hopeless—those facing life sentences with hard labor and without parole, those facing capital punishment for sedition. Look especially for those with terminal illnesses who resemble in look and build these five men in the photographs. Do you understand?"

"I understand, Comrade Premier."

"Good. When these prisoners have been located, have them released from the Gulag into your custody. Have them brought to Moscow at once. I shall put a Tupolev 134 at your disposal. I want you back in Moscow with these prisoners in three days. Absolute top secret. No one must hear or know why. Is that clear?"

"Yes, Comrade Premier."

"President, Igor. Times have changed."

"Yes, Mr. President."

"You may go."

General Lebdev saluted briskly and departed, carrying the file folder.

CHAPTER 25

Moscow.

The arrest of five Russian top-echelon military officers flashed across news wires. They were wanted in connection with aiding an unnamed Middle-Eastern faction in bombing selected targets in America and attempting to assassinate the president of the United States.

TASS, the Russian news agency, was the first to break the news, followed by CNN and Reuters. The plot, according to TASS, was illegal and unauthorized. The plotters' real aim had been to destabilize Russia by making it look as if the Politburo was behind the attack. The Russian president would be discredited, paving the way for a military coup. The men, according to sources, would be swiftly court-martialed and dealt with according to Russian law.

US National Security Adviser Scott Bogan was in the Oval Office briefing President Deakin when the telephone hotline from Moscow pinged and the red light atop it glowed.

"What do you know?" Deakin mused. "Ivan is calling." He picked up the receiver. "Good morning, Mikhail."

"It is afternoon here, my good friend Donald. Good morning to you."

"Good morning and afternoon to you. What can I do for you, Mikhail?"

"My good Donald, I am afraid I have not too good news for you."

Scott Bogan smiled, rustled papers, and made to leave. Deakin motioned him to stay.

"Mikhail, I am truly disappointed at what I hear. The American people are disappointed at the antics of the Russian Federation and her leadership."

"Donald, my good friend," Grachev's voice was somber, "I am also disappointed at what my generals have done. I had no knowledge whatsoever of their actions. The entire incident is a shock to my administration. I trusted them. They had access to funds. They worked with terrorists and a top assassin from the Middle East and even disassembled Russian missiles and shipped them to America to do their evil deed. They were caught just in time. I assure you they will all be court-martialed and shot."

"The United States," Deakin said calmly, "has never—even at the height of the Cold War—plotted to kill the Soviet Premier or bomb the walls of the Kremlin."

"I know, I know," Grachev blurted. "Russia regrets the incident, believe me. Many people will be shot for this. Many more will be sent to Siberia after our inquiry is complete. Let me assure you that we shall cooperate with your administration in getting to the bottom of this. I have asked the SVR and FSB to hand over to me personally the pertinent files on this . . . attempted coup by these five people. The parts I think you will find useful I shall hand over to you."

"You'll have to do better than that, Mikhail. Both Houses of Congress demand an explanation. The American people demand an explanation. You've got to do more."

Premier Grachev smiled. He had already discussed this with the SVR chief. Word had gone out to agents in Washington, DC. Find and kill Beria and Grimsky and Nabil (a.k.a. Contractor). It was sad but necessary to get rid of Beria and Grimsky. If they were caught and interrogated under scopolamine, their testimony would be highly damaging and embarrassing to Russia. Premier Grachev and the SVR chief had also chuckled over the notion that it wouldn't hurt to employ the services of US law enforcement agents in killing Nabil. They knew he would never be taken alive.

Grachev and the SVR chief knew where he was. The cost to the SVR would be an already compromised safe house whose proprietor the SVR had known for some time was a double agent. There were other safe houses in the District of Columbia. Grachev's smile widened as he opened the file before him to the relevant page.

"Got a pen, Donald?"

"I can get one. What is it you have to tell me?"

"Take down this address." He read the address to President Deakin. "There you will find the Contractor. I am informed by the highest intelligence source that he is there."

Deakin scribbled the address on Oval Office stationary. He pushed the paper over to Scott Bogan.

"Get on this immediately, Scott. Tell Creed and his people to find that man and take him into custody. We'll make a present of him to the American people."

———

Reston.

At 6:14 p.m., Nabil heard voices in the hallway outside. In a flash, he darted inside Tammy's bedroom, gun drawn, and waited. The voices continued for about three minutes. Then the click of keys in the lock, and the door opened. Sandy entered, followed by Tammy, carrying little Tom. Through a crack in the bedroom door, Nabil watched as Tammy locked the door again. He pocketed the Glock and walked into the living room.

"Uncle Ted!" Sandy flew into Nabil's arms.

"My lovely child!" A bewildered Nabil lifted the little girl up, spun twice, and deposited her on the rug. Tom, from his perch on his mother's arms, gave Nabil a gummy smile.

Tammy pulled away, hugging Tom tightly to keep Nabil from trying the same thing with her son.

"Had a nice day?" Her tone was neutral.

"Average. I heard voices at the door."

"Oh, Mrs. Fierstal. She's in the next apartment. The one I told you about. Sandy usually waits in her apartment after school until I'm back. It'll be different next week though. She was just telling me she'd be driving to Raleigh in North Carolina tomorrow to stay with her son and his family for a week."

A red flag waved in Nabil's mind. Was the FBI already onto her? And him? Were they clearing the apartment next door to set up monitoring equipment and a raiding team? Nabil looked intently at Tammy, searching for signs of deception. He found none. Then again, she might be a gifted actress.

"What happens to Sandy?"

"She'll stay at the pre-school until I pick her up in the evening. They have afternoon facilities." As she spoke, she placed Tom in his tip-proof high chair while Sandy ran to her room to change. On the table were the wrappings of the tuna sandwich and two yogurt containers that he'd devoured for lunch.

Tammy tried not to wince, and announced instead, "Dinner will be ready in forty-five minutes."

———

She narrated to Nabil about being questioned by Agent Larry Bodine and being scheduled for a polygraph at 9:30 a.m. the following morning, Saturday. How just about an hour before closing, Larry Bodine had dropped in to reschedule hers again for Monday at 10 a.m., saying that Klinefeld, Gadau had prior commitments they couldn't shake.

Nabil heaved a silent sigh of relief. He knew what would happen once she took the polygraph. She would flunk; they would be onto her and then him. He had two days at the most. They might already be tapping the telephones of all the women working in the first lady's office. Even the throwaway cell he was using—he suspected the NSA would be involved to "capture" all cell calls emanating from

Tammy's apartment complex. The NSA uniquely had the equipment and wherewithal to do so. If Mrs. Fierstal next door was indeed leaving for Raleigh, why not use her landline phone? Assuming that, too, wasn't an FBI setup.

Tammy had brought home copies of the *Post* and the *Times-Herald*. The happenings at the Kokubani estate were still headlines. The two dead cops shot by Nabil when he rescued Grimsky and Beria were deified on the front pages, their service records eulogized, their lives detailed.

President Deakin had issued a statement mourning the loss of these two officers along with that of the two FBI agents killed at the Capitol, also in the line of duty. It was a sad day for law enforcement in America, his message read, and his and Doris's hearts—and the hearts of every American—went out to the families.

The same front page displayed an old picture of Nabil taken more than eleven years ago in Beirut. He was number one on the FBI's Most Wanted List. He considered it an honor.

A photograph of the late Nasser Kokubani also appeared on an insert, showing the Corvette wrapped around a utility pole. The accident had severed power to a residential district, and the Chesapeake Light Company had just restored power to the affected area.

A third photograph featured the dead Jim Freidman, aka Stan Doherty. Most of what he read now he'd already seen on television. The print version elaborated on the known facts and speculated even further on the unknown. "White House sources," and "insiders," and "Pentagon sources"—the usual signs of lazy reporting.

Nabil had risked it and made the call to the blind Imam in New York. The Imam promptly acknowledged in coded words and said Plan C would be activated. Nabil wondered if the chain of events had been activated, and if the man known as the Engineer was at this moment boarding a flight in Cairo, Istanbul, Athens, or Islamabad bound for New York.

Sandy refused to sleep until Tammy spent some time with her, reading nursery rhymes to her.

Nabil had hoped Tammy would invite him to share her queen-sized bed; the couch became uncomfortable after only an hour of sleep. No such luck. He could hear sounds from the bathroom as she washed her hair and later the angry growl of the blow dryer. She appeared briefly in a transparent pink nightgown, tossed her hair, and with a curt, "Goodnight," shut the bedroom door in his face, leaving behind the poignant, sensuous whiff of L'Air du Temps.

Nabil sighed. Some troubled thirty-five minutes later, he slept in his boxer shorts and tank top, and later in the night when it got cold, covered himself with a blue blanket.

———

Saturday morning, the doorbell rang as Tammy cleared the breakfast things. Nabil grabbed his jacket and darted inside her bedroom. He drew his gun and nudged the door to within a fraction of closing while motioning to Tammy to answer the doorbell.

Sandy was staring at him from the parlor, and Tammy physically grabbed the girl's head and turned it to face the doorway, putting a finger to her lips. She walked over and tugged open the door.

It was Mrs. Fierstal announcing she was on her way to Raleigh and asking Tammy to look out for her apartment.

"Well, it's getting on in the morning," said the dowager. "I reckon I better get going if I'm to make Raleigh sometime this evening. The interstate is rather crowded these days."

"Have a nice trip, Netty. Don't drive too fast."

"Oh, I couldn't," she confided. "Don't have the nerve. Don't have the pedal-to-the-metal feet either." She giggled like a schoolgirl. "Don't even have the eyesight." She readjusted her spectacles as if to reaffirm their presence. "But I'll get there."

"Are you sure you ought to be driving?" Tammy asked with concern. "Isn't it easier to fly? Or take Amtrak?"

"Oh, I do it every year, and I've managed so far. My arthritis bothers me now and then is all."

"If you insist," Tammy said doubtfully. "Need help with your suitcase?"

"It's already in the car. I asked Mr. Woodenberg in number twenty-three to take it down for me. Thanks. I'm going now. Don't do something I wouldn't do." She waved a childish goodbye by opening and closing her fingers.

Tammy waved back. "Drive carefully now, Netty."

After the dowager had gone and the door was shut and locked, Sandy said in plaintive tones, "Mom, why does Uncle Ted run into the bedroom when the doorbell rings?"

Tammy stopped in her tracks. She said carefully, "Well, honey, you wouldn't understand. You see, Uncle Ted had a wife and baby boy before. His wife was a shrew and nagged him a lot—"

"What's a shrew, Mom?"

"I'll explain someday. The point is they argued a lot, and so just to get away from her, Uncle Ted left everything, including his job, and ran away from her and the child. Every time the doorbell rings, Uncle Ted has a fit and thinks it's the law coming to arrest him. You do understand, don't you, dear?"

"You mean like you and Dad divorced, except Daddy's making his payments and doesn't have to run away?"

"Shush, kid. I'm a working mother. I don't need a cent of your Dad's money. Your father was an assistant state's attorney when I married him, and I was making more than he was back then."

"When is Daddy's next visit? I can't wait to see my Daddy again."

"Next weekend, hon."

"What will Daddy say about Uncle Ted?"

"It's none of his beeswax. And Daddy won't know unless you tell him. I've got my life to live and so has he. His visiting rights are only part of the deal. Now, shall we change the subject, please?"

"I want to talk to Missy," Sandy huffed. "She's the only one who understands me."

"Then go talk to Missy."

Sandy left. Nabil pocketed the gun and advanced into the room. "Who's Missy?"

"Her talking doll. A Barbie. Look, Nabil, I've got to go to the supermarket today. I've got a ton of laundry to do, and I've got to return some overdue rental movies. I'll take the kids with me to the supermarket. That okay with you?"

He stared at her.

"Okay or not okay?" she repeated.

He took a deep breath. "I'll have to trust you. You only need to break that trust once, my dear, just once—and your beautiful head will be shish for my kebob."

She frowned. "What was that?"

He smiled at her.

———

After Tammy had left for the supermarket with the kids, Nabil wandered into her bedroom again. He searched diligently for any of her soiled panties. No jackpot this time! She'd hauled everything inside the Kelvinator, the timer had been set, the appliance was already gyrating to the wash cycle, warm water setting. He lifted the lid. The washer stopped, resumed when he dropped the lid. He stood there pensive. Should he go into Sandy's?

Perv. Shit, Nabil, what's with you?

He tore his mind away. In the living room, he flicked on the television.

The Kokubani affair was still hot news. G. Everston Creed was speaking to reporters from a podium bearing the Department of Justice seal. Creed said the FBI had a number of leads on the terrorists and it was only a matter of time before they were brought in. There was no way they could leave the country. They could save themselves and their families a lot of trouble by giving themselves up now. They would receive a swift and fair trial under the American justice system.

Nabil forced his mind to more important things.

He needed to find out if there was another way into Mrs. Fierstal's apartment short of opening the front door; no way would he risk being seen by someone in the hallway. He scouted the apartment. The rear balcony of Tammy's apartment was separated from its neighbor's by a high wall divider. It might be possible to splay one's legs and swing from one to the other, thwarting the divider. One could even look down while doing so and not get vertigo; the American second floor was not very high off the ground. That option, too, left open the possibility of being seen.

Another door beside the kitchen cabinet on the far side would open onto what he assumed would be a storage area. The keys were on top of the refrigerator and it turned out to be an enclosed area with a garbage chute and a door at the opposite end, which he guessed would lead to Fierstal's kitchen.

He sidestepped the chute, got out his master keys, and in less than one minute was inside Mrs. Fierstal's kitchen. It was clearly a dowager's kitchen. Rows of homemade pickle jars and sauces lined the storage cabinet.

The sink looked crusty and disused, even though it was a stylish, stainless-steel basin like Tammy's. Plates were piled on the sideboard, cracked enamel ones mingled with old spotless crystal.

He moved into the living room and it was like stepping back in time to the Roaring Twenties. Three generations of Fierstals in framed color photographs and black-and-white ones, lined the beveled mantelpiece.

On top of the 32-inch Zenith television and on window ledges were autographed photos of Glenn Miller and his band, another of Woodrow Wilson, yet another of FDR, and Senator Everett Dirkson.

Netty Fierstal had been pretty in her youth and had aged gracefully in a gnarled sort of way alongside her deceased husband who, in the most recent photographs, resembled a retired Fuller Brush salesman.

A digital telephone with an LCD window was the only visible concession to modern times. It had an extension in the bedroom—a pink unimaginative affair that reeked of age.

Nabil took stock of the telephones, checking for signs of active surveillance, and found none. Nabil retraced his footsteps to Tammy's apartment, closing but not locking Fierstal's garbage chute door. He returned the keys to the top of the refrigerator where he'd found them.

He was glad the dowager had gone to Raleigh for the week. He would have had to kill her otherwise to enact the plan he had in mind.

He was watching a rerun of *Hogan's Heroes* when the key grated in the lock. He dove for his gun and the sanctuary of the bedroom. From the front door came two quick raps and longer third one—the prearranged signal. Tammy came in fumbling with her groceries.

"Sorry. I forgot about our signal until after I had the key in the lock."

Our signal. He noted her subliminal acceptance of her situation. Good sign.

"Try and remember next time. You could get shot."

Sandy ran to Nabil and he lifted her up into the obligatory hug. Tom mooned at nothing in particular from his perch on Tammy's shoulder.

Tammy thought despairingly, *Why do my children like him?*

The rest of the day loomed drab and unwieldy. After lunch, Tammy put in a DVD she had rented titled *The Last Remake of Beau Geste*. She fell asleep on the couch during the film's latter half.

By the time she awoke, the movie was over and Nabil was watching a wildlife documentary. She didn't feel like watching the portion of the movie she'd missed. She brought out a chessboard and asked Nabil if he knew how to play.

He smiled. "Not very well."

It was an understatement. He was good at strategy—plotting, executing, and sacrificing pawns for the greater good of the queen. He beat her soundly, three times in less than two hours.

"Not very good, huh?" Her voice was thick with sarcasm.

"I try."

She swept aside the chess pieces and rose. "I've got some work to do on my laptop."

"You're always working. Don't you have any male callers?"

"Not really." She turned to look at him. "You'd be surprised how quickly men run away when they find out you're a nursing mother."

"I don't believe it. It's a turn-on for men."

"Tell me again."

"Tom is ten months."

"Even so."

"You are a very beautiful woman."

"Thank you. If I want men to come, they will come." She ran an impatient hand through her hair. "I'm really not interested. Men constitute part of a problem I couldn't deal with right now." She stalked off.

Later, she placed a call to the new nursing home harboring her mother and inquired after her condition. No changes, she was told, everything was fine. She hung up, and spent the time until near bedtime with her laptop. She put Sandy to bed, hooked up Tom's apnea monitor, and made preparations to retire.

Meanwhile, Nabil fought sleep. He had to talk to Boris tonight. At ten thirty-five, Tammy appeared from her bedroom wearing a pink, see-through nightgown and went about switching off lights, leaving only the small tableside lamp by the couch for Nabil. The TV gave off its own subdued light as Nabil, reclining on the couch, faked total absorption in the ABC Saturday Night Movie. He heard her pull the bedroom door to within a few inches of closing so as not to rouse his suspicion.

He switched off the table lamp. After ten minutes, he rose silently, grabbed a flashlight he had seen earlier in the kitchen and retraced his way to Mrs. Fierstal's apartment. No need for the flashlight after all. Lights were blazing from the interior of the dowager's age-encrusted fixtures, the offshoot of some type of security system that switched on the lights at dusk and off again at midnight to fool burglars.

Nabil dialed Boris's number from the telephone by the leather divan. After four rings, the receiver was picked up.

"Yes?"

"Infidel."

A pause. Then a more careful, "Who?"

"This is the Contractor." Nabil was getting irritated.

A pause. "Perhaps you have the wrong number."

"It's me, Boris. Nabil."

"I see. What were the names of your sales partners in Illinois?"

"What the hell is this—?"

"Answer me."

"Are we secure?"

"Don't worry. This room is soundproof, bugproof, and incoming and outgoing calls on this are scrambled."

"Alright. Beria and Grimsky."

Boris sighed. "You had me puzzled for a while. I thought something had gone wrong. I saw you calling from the Seven Oaks apartment, but from a different number. I didn't know she had two telephones."

It was Nabil's turn to be confounded. "You know where I am calling from?"

Boris chuckled. "I have GPS-enabled caller ID. What happened? You switched apartments?"

Nabil explained about Mrs. Fierstal going to Raleigh. He still smarted from the nonchalant way Boris had identified from which address and telephone he was calling. If it were this easy for Boris, how much faster would it be for the American authorities using the vast technology at their disposal?

Boris was saying, ". . . news from Moscow is bad. America is pointing the finger at Moscow. Moscow is denying it, and to show they are sincere, they are throwing in their own security units to help unmask the culprits. They've given the FBI the address of the safe house in Washington where you are supposed to be, along with Beria and Grimsky. It was supposed to be a major victory for Moscow. Deny everything, sacrifice assets. I was able to warn Grimsky and Beria. They escaped only minutes before the FBI raided the place. They are now in a safe place, I assure you. Good thing you never went near any of the supposedly safe houses from the start."

"They betrayed us." Nabil's voice was grim.

"There's more. Moscow has discreetly put their assassins onto you. You are to be terminated. Along with Grimsky and Beria. At this moment, SVR assassins are looking for you. So is the FBI and the Secret Service."

"I saw on the news that General Zamyatin and four others were arrested in Moscow. They really think this mission has failed."

"They do."

"I've never failed on a mission before. I don't intend to fail now."

"Good. Moscow will revise their opinions and make reparations if the mission succeeds." A pause. "By the way, your message to the Imam got through. I have sources too. The Engineer is on his way. He should be in the area Monday evening."

"Then everything is set. By Tuesday or Wednesday, the earth will heave again in the DC area."

"The sonuvabitches won't be expecting that one."

"There's one little snag."

"What's that?"

Nabil explained about the polygraph Tammy had to take Monday morning. She would flunk the polygraph. They would be onto him that same day. He had to move fast.

Boris pondered this development. "There's a chance. I know of a heart drug—I take it myself—that might be useful. Propranolol. A forty-milligram dose should be adequate. She should take one in the morning, one at night starting the minute she gets it. I'll call my physician and have him call it in to a pharmacy near you that makes home deliveries. It'll be in her name. Perhaps she should take an extra tablet one hour before the polygraph."

"What does the drug do?"

"I don't know exactly how it works. It's a beta-blocker. I believe it suppresses the autonomous nervous system. If her heart is pounding before the polygraph, she'll quiet down. It's worth a try."

"I agree."

"Brief her beforehand. Make sure she's there to receive it tomorrow morning. You shouldn't show yourself to the person delivering the medication."

"I know that."

"And I wouldn't—if I were you—use Mrs. Weasel's phone again. It may already be compromised."

"You're telling me. That's why I'm calling from this line."

"Well, good luck."

Nabil hung up and crept back to Tammy's apartment. He was preoccupied with his thoughts. So Moscow had marked him for death. He peeled off his socks and lay down on the couch fully clothed, his gun on the floor within reach.

He was drifting off to sleep when he heard a salacious sound from Tammy's bedroom. He listened. The sound was repeated. Nabil got to his feet and crept silently to the door, listening. He could hear the faint rustle of the bed, an occasional slurping sound, the muted gloat of self-induced pleasure. He pushed open the door soundlessly.

Through the chintzy curtains, a shaft of moonlight illuminated the queen-sized bed and the mermaid on it. Tammy lay on the bed, her legs spread, and the fingers of her right hand moving rapidly between her thighs. She was oblivious to her surroundings, her low moaning audible. Even from this distance, her keen odor drenched the room, and despite himself, despite everything, Nabil felt his member stiffen ramrod-straight.

Tammy, his Tammy, doing this to herself? How well he remembered that musk, that vaginal statement, the residue he had become acquainted with from handling her panties. Why would she descend to this?

Ah, *masturbari!* She pollutes nations!

Nabil felt faint, dizzy. All the blood had deserted his head for his loins. He pushed open the door, stepped in. Tammy froze. He shut and locked the door. In three quick strides was at the bedside. Nabil stared at her. She stared back, first at his face, then—because it was sticking out with lively independence and determination at a ferocious angle—at the huge flagpole of his erection.

"I feel insulted." Nabil's voice was thick with lust. "You could have called me."

"Get out!" she hissed. "Get out of my bedroom!"

He slapped her hard across the left cheek. A red welt appeared instantly near her left eye. She picked up the bedside AM/FM radio alarm clock to throw at him, and just so she wouldn't have any further doubt, he stepped in and backhanded her across the face.

She collapsed on the gray linen coverlet like a rag doll, her legs apart, disclosing her ripe aperture, a vicious gash ensconced on a fiery mound. She watched his face through her pain; saw the naked face of lust, intense need.

"Don't even think about it." Her eyes never left the crazy bulge behind his fly.

He really didn't remember jumping on her. She pummeled him, her fists beating feebly and futilely against his broad shoulders, his hairy chest. His fingers dug into her, explored her damp, juicy membranes that pulsed and seemed to speak to him in her own passionate heat.

"No, no," she sobbed. "You can't do that. It's not right. Stop, right now."

Yet her movements were the antithesis of her words. Did she not moan softly and hold his probing hand and help dig his fingers deeper into her, moving it to caress the spot she liked?

When they were both jabbering at each other in words neither could decipher, was it not her quick fingers that brushed against his pants, testing his turgidity, and then tug at his zipper, pulling down his pants, helping him free himself?

When he finally spilled out and he was free, did she not adjust her body then arch upward her waist so that he slid smoothly inside her well-oiled vulva, a snug fit that gripped its tumescent prey in the steamy ardor of possession, the intertwined bodies heaving and jerking. Nabil had never been so fiercely possessed by any woman.

"Fuck me, Nabil," she urged him, *sotto voce*. "Fuck me hard. Harder!" He plunged into her again with increasing ferocity, her fingernails digging into his buttocks.

"Fuck me!" she screamed. "Harder, harder, you piece of shit!"

The bed gyrated to their exertions. *There are children in the house, he thought.*

"Fuck me, Nabil!"

"I am," he pleaded.

"Scumbag! Fuck me!"

And he sensed at the tip of his penis, where it pounded and rubbed against her G-spot, the precursor to the sensation that would mother all sensations.

He was now possessed, the unbridled fury of his attack threatening to disembowel her through her natural orifice, the bedsprings protesting his onslaught, he whimpering in Arabic, she in her new-Babel, the two bodies slapping each other, slurping, the fusion of carnal intent and bacterial-exchange rising, rising until it peaked, and he knew it, he knew it, it was coming, coming . . . and he was transported, an unconscious, willing patient, deposited on this pleasant realm, this primordial plateau of two locked pelvises. Just as too much pain could induce loss of consciousness, enhanced sensation, too, obliterated the senses.

When he came to, he was on top her, for how long he did not know. He allowed his senses to creep back, hard-breathing against her fragile chest, their loins joined, his mad spasms spent, his entire being spent.

CHAPTER 26

Reston.

Breakfast was Eggs Benedict, bacon and toast with raspberry preserves, orange juice, and coffee. Nabil heaped the bacon from his plate onto Sandy's, explaining that his religion forbade him to eat pork. Sandy beamed at him from across the table. She had been beaming all morning at him.

"Did you sleep well, Uncle Ted?"

"Yes, I did. And you?"

She brushed an imaginary cowlick from her forehead. "I had a nice time."

How ominous those words!

Even little Tom from his tip-proof high chair giggled and chuckled at him, shaking his rattlers.

Somehow they know! Nabil thought despairingly.

Tammy avoided meeting his eyes all morning. A spot of color glowed on her right cheek; a healthy glow suffused her skin. Her freckles seemed to have receded beneath the complex of broken blood vessels. Her hands as they moved on the table, grabbing a saltshaker here, pushing the milk carton over to Sandy there, possessed an otherworldly milk-white transparence. Nabil thought her the most erotic woman he had ever met.

He felt a pang of regret. A pity he was fighting to destroy the values her country stood for, its satanic institutions. A country that could whelp a perfect form such as Tammy couldn't really be that bad.

After breakfast, he briefed her out of earshot of the children about what Boris had said. How propranolol was a long shot—her only chance to beat the lie detector test.

She nodded and looked at him directly. "Wouldn't it be better if I went to the drugstore myself and picked it up?"

"The arrangement has been made by my partners. The medicine will be delivered here. There's a chance you might be followed to the pharmacy. You may already be under observation—that includes all four women in that office—since the homing transmitter was found."

"How am I sure," she said, turning down the corner of one lip, "that those tablets aren't lethal? Perhaps you and your partners want me dead."

He laughed. "Ridiculous. That would draw more attention to you. I shall take one of the tablets, if you wish, before you do. Besides, I wouldn't want you dead. I like you."

Their eyes met. She started to say something but thought better of it.

He smiled. "Any objections?"

She said instead, "I suppose going to church is out of the question?"

"I didn't know you were religious."

"Episcopalian. And I don't miss Holy Communion often."

"You will today, and I hope you understand why."

"I was hoping you'd let me take the children to the park this afternoon. River View Park. I don't know about you, but if they're watching, I think it's important that I live as normal a life as possible."

He pondered this. "Fine." Then added, "I trust you." *As though he hadn't trusted her all this time she had been going to work and taking the kids with her.* He cautioned her on the risks, to be wary of the seemingly innocuous stranger who might sidle up to her and the kids on a park bench, engage Sandy in child talk, hoping for a giveaway phrase. The need to avoid discussing anything relating to the foiled terrorist attack with anyone. Anyone. The need to keep Sandy away from the FBI posters of Uncle Ted.

The doorbell rang just after eleven o'clock.

"Prescription for T. Weasel."

Tammy opened the door. "That's me."

"That'll be eleven dollars and eighty cents," said the delivery boy. "We don't deliver for less than ten dollars and the prescription was only for a few dollars. Your husband said it was okay to include a digital child thermometer to make up the rest."

Tammy started to say, "My husband?" but checked herself. She paid, tipping the boy a dollar.

Nabil, as usual, watched from the cracked door of her bedroom. After the delivery boy had gone, he first examined the child thermometer. No bugs. Still, he took it to the bathroom, lifted the cistern lid on the toilet and placed it inside the water. If this were a sophisticated bug, the only things they would hear would be flushing noises. Next, they examined the pink tablets together.

"Looks authentic," Tammy said, and took one.

That afternoon, when she and the kids got ready to leave for the park, Sandy asked, "Mom, can Uncle Ted come with us to the park?"

"*Could* Uncle Ted," Tammy corrected.

"Well, could he, Mom? I don't see why not."

Tammy stroked her head. "Of course he could, dear. But his ex-wife—the one I told you about—has spies and lawyers all over the place."

Sandy walked over to Nabil. She had dressed up in a prim white cotton dress with a crescent bow tie, her hair in pigtails tied with pink ribbon. With white socks encasing her tiny feet in ash-colored oxfords, she was no different from the Barbie dolls she often played with. "You promise you won't be too lonely, Uncle Ted?"

"I promise. I'll count the minutes until you return, sweetheart." He gave her a peck on the forehead.

"Booboo!" cooed little Tom from his mother's arms, shaking his fist at Nabil.

"I wonder what that means," Nabil said.

"He's saying goodbye," Tammy explained.

After they had gone, Nabil propped the sofa against the door just in case the FBI tried crashing through. Tammy had Netflix, but Nabil wasn't interested..Football games seemed to be showing on all channels and —the usual Sunday afternoon fare of televangelists Pat Robertson and Oral Roberts..

He turned the volume way down low on a church programme and reclined on the couch. The lethargy of a Sunday afternoon in autumn when nothing moved stole in on him. He could hear the Mormon Tabernacle Choir singing in the background, the dirge-like cantatas rising and falling in muted waves. He slept.

In the absolute remove of REM sleep, Nabil dreamed he was in a foreign land, a rocky escarpment in a hot, arid land where the sun blazed mercilessly and the waft of frankincense hung stagnant in the air. Earlier, he had left the crowded city behind, the dirty Ganges snaking its obscene course through shantytowns, urban decay, and feces-muddled swamp beaches. Scores of bathers slung muddied water over their naked bodies. He had passed full-geared Sikhs—bearded, head-banded, side-daggered, with regimental mustaches pomaded and nearly as sharp as the daggers they carried—going about their business in this quaint land of oddities. He himself was dressed in a gray flowing robe, and he deduced that he was in India. India because the rocky outcropping where he stood was part of the Marabar Hills, and only in India could the Marabar be found. He seemed to remember reading about the Marabar caves in Forster's *A Passage to India*.

Only now he was no longer Nabil but Dr. Azeez and the beautiful woman by his side with the red pouting lips that curiously resembled Tammy Weasel's was none other than Miss Adela Quested. And he was about to go spelunking with the beautiful Miss Quested. Just the two of them. Just him and this British woman with full red lips and red hair on a ravishingly pretty face crowned by a wide felt hat, this woman who looked at him with a mixture of contempt and a come-hither invitation.

He recognized those sensuous lips even in his sleep as the Sign of the Pussy. And he was alone with her in those damned hills and caves, miles and miles of utter desolation, a hillscape roasted by the sun. She was saying something to him and he strove to hear and moved closer.

"And I just wanted to see the real India," he heard her say. Abruptly she turned away and marched down the hard, rocky path.

"Miss Quested! Wait!" He took after her. "Let me show you."

She turned and faced him, waiting. The pouting lips moved. "I just want to see the real India."

"I could show you the real India," he said. And her eyes dropped to his waist level, to the gap between two buttons on his long flowing robe. "This is the real India, Miss Quested. The REAL INDIA!" And he was pointing out to her the wonderful point of this fascinating subcontinent, its real jut, its hard, characteristic meat, the lively throb of this sculpted promontory, this rigid snake, naked in the intense lethargic heat. He was pointing to his stiffened penis, telling her, "This is the real India, Miss Quested. The real India! Here, you can touch it."

She reached out her thin, white hand, venous, untamed by the merciless sun, and grasped his throbbing phallus. The sensation was unbelievable. East meets West and all hell breaks loose. He knew it, he knew it, it was coming . . . he would come in her hands. But no, Miss Quested wanted more than a digital fuck. And it was no longer Adela Quested but Tammy Weasel, and she was guiding him into her own wet, compliant orifice.

It was better than even he knew it would be. Succulent Adela Quested. No, Tammy. He would pound himself out inside her, release his pleasurable seed . . . Nabil awoke.

FUCK!

He would have killed for the opportunity to release inside her. He would kill whoever had interrupted him. He dallied in confusion for a few frightened seconds, trying to figure out who he was, what he was doing, where the hell he was.

It all came back quickly. He rose from the couch, his member still bone-stiff and cursed his luck at the dream's terminating just seconds before he penetrated Miss Quested. No, Tammy. In the movie, the actress who played the part of Adela Quested was the exact replica of Tammy. It would have been an almighty wet dream.

He yawned, walked over to the window, and parted the curtains. Against the backdrop of the parking lot, the colors of autumn were spectacular, more so even than in Illinois. The entire landscape seemed to be on fire, a spectral fire. The rhododendron hedges, trimmed and immaculate, blazed an unearthly cerise; the cherry blossom and weeping willows adjoining the Seven Oaks condominium estate sat opulent on a sea of shed yellow leaves. A treescape readying for the onslaught of winter, and Thanksgiving less than two weeks away.

And he was in love with Tammy Weasel.

Bullshit!

How could he be? He hadn't known her more than three days. He sighed, let the curtains fall into place, and found his way back to her bedroom. He found one of her used panties in the laundry basket. He picked it up like valuable treasure that might disintegrate and cradled it to his nose.

She came back to him instantly, a base assault, a mephitic statement of ownership. Yes, he had made love to the underwear's owner, and he felt a certain kinship. He stood there, aroused and getting more aroused by the minute, and considered right then and there using his own hands on himself. It took Herculean effort, but he willed himself to stop. *Why not wait for the real thing, turkey? Then you'd still have enough to deposit inside her.*

Nabil returned to the couch and slept for two hours. He woke up refreshed. He spread one of her small duvets on the living room floor as a prayer mat, He was praying when Tammy knocked on the door, using their secret signal. He didn't answer. She tried again. After the third try, she opened the door tremulously, then relaxed when she saw why he had not answered.

"We're back," she announced, in the same way Doc Severinsen used to introduce Johnny Carson on the *Tonight Show.*

Sandy rushed over to Nabil, holding out a takeout fudge sundae. "We brought you ice cream, Uncle Ted."

Nabil did not stir. He sat staring straight ahead, the prayer beads moving through his fingers. He knelt down and touched his forehead to the ground several times.

"Uncle Ted, did you see what I brought you?" Still no answer. Hot tears clouded Sandy's eyes. She ran to her mother. "Mom, Uncle Ted's not talking to me."

"Sshh! He's praying, sweetheart. He'll talk to you when he's through."" Tammy patted her on the head.

"I didn't . . . know."

"Of course you didn't, sweetie. Here, help me put away the things."

Nabil finished some minutes later. Sandy watched him from a distance. He folded the duvet and stuffed it along with the beads in a corner. He approached Sandy, who now held out the sundae uncertainly. "Uncle Ted—for you."

He took the sundae from her with one hand and with the other scooped her up and kissed away the tears on her face.

"I'm sorry, sweetheart," he said. "So sorry. I didn't mean to ignore you like that. When we are saying our prayers, we are not supposed to interrupt them for any reason."

What a blatant lie! Had it been the FBI barging in, damn right you would be diving for that Glock 9mm under the sofa.

"I'm sorry, too," Sandy said. "I didn't know you were praying."

"It's an honest mistake, Sandy." He continued to kiss her salty face. "I love you very much."

She liked that. She smiled at him. "I love you, too, Uncle Ted."

"Are you sure?"

"Yes, I'm sure."

"Then you do forgive me?"

"I forgive you, Uncle Ted. Will you stay and take care of me and Tom and my mommy?"

Tammy froze from where she was installing Tom on his high chair. Time itself seemed to pause.

"Will you?" Sandy prodded.

"I . . . I'd love to. I love you and Tom and your Mommy. But . . . conditions are not right as of now. I have to go away in a few days. I'll be able to write to you from where I am. We shall see again in future, of course."

You're sunk. In this business, when you start getting emotionally involved, you're finished. You'll be dead meat in a matter of months.

She threw her arms around him. He held her tight. After a while she said, "Uncle Ted, is that how you say your prayers? Which church do you go to?"

"A different church. We worship in a different way."

Tammy pulled Sandy away. "Come on. Go and play with Tom. He needs hug time, too."

"Yes, Mommy." Sandy walked over to Tom and began jingling his rattlers.

Tammy wrinkled her nose and addressed Nabil, "Don't you feel like taking a shower?"

"In good time."

Actually, Nabil had been reluctant to wash away reminders of last night's episode. It still seemed incredible, the range of pleasures she had given him. Her internal effluvium was now encrusted on his own body; whiffs of her dark pleasurable side came to him at odd moments during the day when his fingers passed his nose, or during those opportune moments when he breathed his own personal space. In his perverse attachment to her vulval reek, he preferred to stay away from the shower until it became unbearable; better her scent than the fresh smell of Irish Spring.

"You'll skunk out my apartment," Tammy complained. "You smell like a goat."

"Those are strong words, madam."

"That is a strong scent."

"It came from you," he said lewdly.

She gave him a strange look. "No, I don't think so. It's an exchange of germs, I agree, but the extra ingredient from you isn't exactly kosher for the senses. I don't know what I mean by that, but something's rotten in Denmark and I do not for one moment think I played more than a miniscule part in it. You are ripe, sir. Now, Nabil, you are going to have a bath or I'll call in the fire department."

Yes, you do that. And have them hose out your pussy.

She ran a bath and whistled for him. "I'll watch the door while you're naked and helpless in the tub. Keep your gun on top of the sink in case FBI the charge in."

She had said the word FBI loudly enough. Both she and Nabil looked hastily in Sandy's direction to see if she had heard. Apparently not. Sandy was busy making a face at Tom.

"Alright."

He stepped out of his white tank top and boxer shorts into the hot, perfumed bath, the water aquamarine blue with white suds. Tammy immediately scooped up the clothes, including his trousers and dress shirt, removed coins, bills, and personal items, and threw the clothes inside the washer. She spun the dial and snapped the lid shut. The washer began to fill with water. Nabil was horrified at how rapidly the water dirtied. He had to confess she was right.

Afterward, he wrapped one of her giant bath towels around himself. He felt clean and sanitized. When he had dried thoroughly, he slipped into one of three bathrobes hanging on a hook peg by the door. He could hear the jerk of the Kelvinator as the agitator kicked his clothes around.

That night, she swallowed the second tablet of Inderal. She tucked in Sandy and Tom and retired to her bedroom around nine thirty, leaving the door open just a fraction. Nabil was uncertain what this gesture meant. She flicked on the bedroom TV suspended on the wall facing the foot of the bed in the manner of private hospital rooms.

He sat forlornly in the sitting room, watching a movie channel and later a National Geographic.documentary. Tammy came out twice; first to put his clothes in the dryer, and later, long after the dryer had stopped, to remove the clothes and separate the lint and strips of fabric softner from it. She folded the clothes neatly and laid them on the ironing board.

She didn't say goodnight as she reentered the bedroom. He took this as an unspoken invitation and after ten minutes he rose, switched off the lights and the TV, and gingerly entered her bedroom. Tammy's eyes were riveted on an HBO movie. She edged sideways to make space for him on the bed. She said nothing when he crept under the covers, leaving only his shoulders and head exposed.

The tension stood between them like a bad gender wall. It diminished as he, too, became engrossed in the old movie *Visiting Hours*, where a psychopathic Michael Ironside stalks Lee Grant. Interesting movie.

After it ended, she checked on Sandy and Tom one more time, then snuggled under the covers and closed her eyes. She did not object when Nabil's hand rested on her thigh. He caressed the soft, cool skin. His hand moved upward toward an even softer delineation where the coolness interposed with warmth. Her knees jerked. His fingers rubbed the coarse foliage, the sloppy cleft mons buried beneath the mound.

She opened one eye. The green iris stared at him, reminding him incongruously of aquarium fish that swim past, fixing a baleful glare on the observer. He pushed his fingers inside her. She was already wet, and he felt her respond.

"You have to use a condom," she said. "I forgot last night."

"Don't tempt me," he snarled.

She closed her eyes. After a while her body began to jerk. She moaned. His own erection ascended like a humongous belch, and he struggled up, turned her on her back, and propped her up on her knees. He liked the way she looked now, her ochre-red mane cascading over the pillow, the long arch of her back, the brave statement of her white ass-cheeks splayed out on his face, kneadable cellulite lumped delicately at the sides, at the places he liked it.

He buried his face in her anal region, his tongue flicking in and out, tasting her base stink, his senses energized by this proximity to all her body plumbing and their sacred, primitive messages.

She moaned like some Olympian nymph, pushing up her rear, demanding penetration. He tried pushing his prick inside. She objected after the third hurtful thrust, and he desisted.

Later, he thought, much later. She was not used to this. And he would need K-Y Jelly. She reached back with her left hand and guided him into the correct orifice, and he almost yelped with the pleasure of it, sinking deep and succulently inside.

He began the instinctive movements, and she joined his rhythm. He drank in her familiar signature, conjoined to a fecal whiff, a potent ambrosia. It was a sight disturbing to all males: a well-shaped female in rutty abandon.

As he pumped her from behind with new vigor, his thighs slapping the splayed ass-mounds, Nabil reflected how impossible it was to make love in a dignified manner. The postures themselves were incongruous. He didn't care either way, because he was enamored of Tammy, and her gyrations were increasing to match his, their cries merging, and there was nothing to be done about it. He wouldn't want to anyway and he sank, sank, rushing in headlong, bursting in, and the revelation was too much . . . and he knew no more.

He collapsed on her for Allah knows how long, panting. Presently they disengaged like contestants calling it quits after a mutual fight, and each picked up their own end of the quilt bedcover and snuggled under.

After a while, he spoke. "Your husband was mad to have let you go."

"He was a scumbag," she said simply.

"Tell me about him."

"What is there to tell? All Brian cared about was his work, the meetings with his law partners, the endless dinner jacket receptions with one lawmaker or another. And his guns."

"Guns?"

"Don't you know? He's a lobbyist for the National Rifle Association. Very powerful lobby indeed. He owns two hunting rifles and one revolver. He's big on the Second Amendment. Right to bear arms. We went hunting in Maine, Wyoming, Idaho, Michigan. I wasn't particularly interested in hauling shot deer back to the four-wheel drive. He had three stuffed moose heads in our apartment then. After I left and until you came along, I never saw a gun again."

"So. You exchanged one gun user for another."

"You?"

"Yes."

She said nothing.

"Perhaps it is your destiny," he offered.

She was silent.

"Tammy," he said, and afterward he would wonder at the power of infatuation and the entire worlds, real and imagined, it spawned. "After the mission, when this is all over and I am out of the country, I want you to . . . what I mean is, will you marry me?"

———

She sat up on the bed and stared at him. *I made no mistake. She is truly a goddess.*

"Well?"

She started on her hair, pushing back the massive ochre curls with one upraised hand. "I-I don't know, Nabil. Could I think about it? It's all too sudden. Could I, like, take a rain check on that?"

He seemed strangely elated. "I'll be perfect for you. I'll take care of you and the children. I have some money, a couple of million or so—American dollars—stashed away. This will be my last mission. I'll give up my way of life so the kids can have a real father."

She laughed and ran her index finger across his hirsute chest, up and down and back to the breastbone. Nabil's hot brown eyes bored into hers, willing her to say yes. *Gee, this is complicated. Here I am sleeping with the most wanted man in America, most wanted in the world perhaps, and he's asking me to marry him.*

"Why would you want to marry me?"

"I don't understand."

"I wouldn't fit into your scheme of things. What I mean is, you're a man of . . . different beliefs." She had almost said "of terror." "We couldn't possibly have anything in common."

She watched him closely. His smile faded as she talked. The face became hard, the focus distant. A hint of moisture in the brown eyes? She added hastily, "Besides, where would we live?"

He didn't answer.

"Nabil?"

"There are islands in the South Pacific where nobody has heard of me," he said. "There's the Caymans, Eleuthera, chains of islands in the Caribbean, if you insist on staying close to the American mainland. We could live in Tehran, Afghanistan, Yemen, or Sudan otherwise. I would never be extradited from any of those places."

She bent over and kissed him on the lips. "I'll think about it, okay? Give me some time. Please?"

"One week."

"Will you be here in one week?"

"I'll call you from Europe. I'll get in contact somehow, even if the FBI is monitoring you."

"Sounds great."

Really great. I'll get him to send me a marriage proposal by mail. I'll hand it over to the FBI. They'll trace it and bring him to justice.

She flicked off the TV with the remote, then switched off the lights.

"One other thing," he said in the post-coital darkness. "I need your car tomorrow. How much fuel do you have?"

"About half a tank. How do I take Sandy to school and Tom to the daycare?"

"Call a taxi. Or use a rental. It's only for one day. You give me the car keys before you go to work."

"It'll be an inconvenience," she grumbled.

"Yes it will. Goodnight."

" 'Night."

CHAPTER 27

Washington, DC.

The offices of Klinefeld, Gadau & Associates resided on the second floor of an office complex on K Street downtown. The receptionist waved Tammy to a waiting room in which two men in gray suits and crew cuts sat nonchalantly leafing through magazines.

They're obviously FBI. Waiting to arrest me if I flunk the polygraph.

She had taken another tablet of propranolol that morning and found that though her panic remained, it was at least subdued. The time was one minute past ten o'clock in the morning.

She sat down on a leather couch across from the two suits. She crossed her legs, picked up a copy of the *Ladies Home Journal*, and leafed through it. She couldn't make out a word. One of the men coughed bogusly.

A door—one of three leading off the waiting room—opened. A man's head poked out.

"Tammy Weasel?"

"Yes."

She cast the magazine aside and stood up. The man met her at the door.

"Mrs. Weasel, I'm Mike Gadau. How do you do?" They shook hands, and he led the way inside.

Gadau was of medium height, his hair was neatly parted on the left side, and he wore round, brown horn rims. He had a benign, academic air and looked like a college professor. He consulted a list.

"Let's see. You're on the first lady's private staff, is that correct?"

"Right."

"Call you Tammy?"

"Yes." Why was she monosyllabic?

"Well, Tammy, let's get you hooked up. It's quite simple really."

He sat her down on a normal-looking wooden chair with armrests then quickly and efficiently attached electrodes to her thumb, her third finger, and several other places on her body. The wires led to a machine that had needle-sharp styluses poised over a large graph plotter. Other wires disappeared behind ominous grooves and perhaps other recording devices. He wrapped what looked like a massive blood pressure cuff around Tammy's midsection, held in place by Velcro. Machinery hummed in the background. Gadau moved to a console and flipped some switches, his face utterly blank. *It looks like the electric chair.* For one horrid moment, the thought crossed Tammy's mind that she was about to be put to death.

Mike Gadau seemed to read her thoughts; their eyes met and he smiled warmly at her. He had an avuncular bedside manner that would have put a Mayo Clinic physician to shame. She was grateful and smiled back. He was going to be easy on her.

"Tell me something."

"Yes, Tammy?" The smile hovered.

"What if I'm naturally nervous? Won't it affect my results? I mean, you might hit a nerve and the machine might say I'm lying when I'm telling the truth."

Gadau pondered. "We make allowances for that by asking you routine questions that establish your threshold for normal responses. But let me make something clear: no machine or device can convict you in a court of law. No court will accept the results of a polygraph as evidence in a criminal case. In fact, neither side can even mention in court that a polygraph was administered. But we believe strongly in it, and indeed the police and other arms of law enforcement will use the polygraph as a guide, at least in pointing a finger in the right direction. Do you understand?" He looked quite concerned.

"Y-yes."

"Now then, just a few exercises to test the machine. Relax, Tammy. Try to relax. There. All I require of you when we begin is to answer each question with one word: 'yes' or 'no.' Is that understood? Yes or no only."

She nodded.

"Fine. Let's move on, shall we."

He spoke a few words rapidly into a recording instrument, stating that for the record he was talking to Tamara Ann Weasel of her own free will on this date this month in the year of our Lord blah blah blah in the downtown annex of Klinefeld, Gadau. Then he made some notations on the graph sheet and told her he would begin the examination and from then on she should answer only with a "Yes" or a "No."

"Your full name is Tamara Ann Weasel?"

"Yes."

"And you are thirty-three years old?"

"Yes."

"Do you work in the White House?"

"Yes."

"1600 Pennsylvania?"

"Yes."

"Do you work in the office of the first lady's staff?"

"That's correct."

"Yes or no, please."

"Sorry. Yes."

"Have you ever been married?"

"Yes."

"Are you still married?"

"No."

"You are divorced or separated, I take it?"

"Yes."

"Have you ever had an extramarital affair?"

She wanted to scream, *It's none of your business.* She bit her lip. "No."

"I understand you have two children. Is that correct?"

"Yes."

"A boy and a girl?"

"Yes."

"Do you love your children?"

"Yes."

"Have you ever spanked any of your children for misbehaving?"

Silence.

"Answer the question, please."

"Yes."

"Have you ever looked at a man who was not your ex-husband and thought, 'Gee, he's gorgeous. I'd like to seduce him.'"

"I don't see how it's any of your business."

"Yes or no, please."

"No. Yes."

"Let me ask again. Have you ever looked at a man—?"

"Yes!"

Gadau didn't pause. He made notations on the plotter as the styluses rattled, his concentration absolute.

"Have you ever stolen money from a previous employer?"

"No."

"Have you written a bad check within the past five years?"

"Yes. It was a mistake and I was going to—"

"Yes or no."

"Yes."

"Have you ever lied on an income tax form?"

"Yes."

"Have you ever padded an expense account sheet?"

"You have to be specific. I—"

"Yes or no, please."

"Well, yes."

"Are you telling the truth? The absolute truth?"

"Yes."

"Have you ever had sex with a white male adult?"

"Yes."

"Have you ever had sex with a non-white male adult?"

This was getting ridiculous. What did it have to do with—

"Answer the question, please."

"No."

Gadau paused to make some adjustments on the machine.

"Have you ever had sex with an adult male who is not of the same race as yourself?"

"No."

"Have you ever lied on a job application form?"

"Yes."

"Do you intend to lie on a job application form in the future?"

"No."

Out of the corner of her eye, Tammy could see the styluses moving busily, the plotter clattering and feeding more paper. From nowhere, Gadau held up a calculator-shaped transmitter—or one that looked like it. She recognized it immediately. In the background, the styluses chattered noisily. Gadau didn't seem to notice.

"What I'm holding up is a small, battery-powered radio transmitter. Take a good look at it." He turned it over and around so she could see every angle. His face was expressionless. "Have you ever seen this device before?"

"No."

Too hasty. Her heart hammered against her ribs.

"You have never seen this transmitter before?"

"No."

"Have you had a speeding ticket in the last three years?"

"No."

"Have you ever driven your car above the legal highway speed limit?"

"Yes."

"But you never received a ticket in the last three years, is that correct?"

"Yes."

"Have you had a parking ticket in the last three years?"

"Yes. Many."

"Just yes or no."

"Yes."

Gadau made further adjustments on the machine.

"Are you a Communist? Sorry, let me rephrase that. Have you ever, or do you presently belong to the Communist Party or a similar organization?"

"No."

"Have you met any foreign dignitaries in your official capacity? In the normal course of your work?"

"Yes."

"Have you been introduced to any foreign person—Russian, Eastern European, or Middle Eastern—in the past year?"

She mulled this over.

"Please answer the question."

"Yes."

"Was that in your capacity as a staffer in the office of the first lady of the United States?"

"Yes."

"Have you met any foreign person or persons—Russian, Middle Eastern, or Eastern European—outside of your official capacity?"

"No."

"You have not conversed with or had a mutual association with any foreign person from the places I just mentioned?"

"No."

"Do you know anybody from Russia outside your official capacity?"

"No."

"In your official capacity?"

"Er . . . yes."

"Do you know anybody from the Middle East? Let us say, Lebanon, Saudi Arabia, Kuwait, Syria, Jordan, Sultanate of Oman, Qatar, Libya?"

"No."

"Are you sure of this, Tammy?"

"Positive."

"Yes or no, please."

"No. Yes. Wait. Does that include Israel? It's in the Middle East, isn't it?"

Gadau frowned at his charts and made further adjustments. He threw back the ball. "Do you know anybody from Israel outside your official capacity?"

"No."

"I take it then that outside your official capacity you don't know anybody from the rest of the Middle East, either?"

"No."

"Have you ever conspired with a person or group of persons to attack any facility within the United States using a missile or bomb?"

"No. That's ridiculous."

"Yes or no."

"No!"

"Have you ever seen a gun before?"

"Yes."

"Have you ever seen a bomb before?"

"No."

"Missile?"

"No. Sorry. At the National Air and Space Museum. At least I think it was a missile. An ICBM, I think."

Gadau bit his lip and stared at his charts. A voluminous pile had gathered at his feet. He charged again from left field.

"Tammy, you have never seen this transmitter in your White House office?"

"No."

"You are absolutely truthful in your statements?"

"Yes."

The styluses were going crazy. She could see it in her peripheral vision.

"Tammy, do you swear that you did not plant this transmitter—or one that looks like it—in your office in the White House? Yes or no?"

"Yes! I swear."

"Have you ever heard of Dr. Said Kokubani?"

"The one in the papers? About the terrorist-bombing attempt?"

"Yes or no, please."

"Yes."

"Do you know him personally?"

"No."

"Did you hear of him before the terrorist plot was foiled?"

"No."

"Do you love the First Lady?"

"I adore her."

Gadau groaned.

"Yes."

"Do you love the president of the United States?"

"Yes."

"Do you love your country?"

"Yes."

"Have you ever wished harm to any elected official of the legislature, judicial, executive, or otherwise?"

"No."

"Have you ever wished harm on the president of the United States, Donald W. Deakin?"

"No."

"Do you want President Deakin to come to grievous bodily harm?"

"No."

"Do you like strawberry cheesecake?"

"Yes."

"Chocolate ice cream sundaes?"

"Yes."

"You didn't plant the transmitter?"

"No."

"You didn't see the transmitter being planted?"

"No."

"You weren't given the transmitter to plant in the White House by a white Russian?"

"What's a white Russian? For God's sake—"

"It was a Middle Eastern guy then that gave it to you to plant in the White House?"

"No! No! No!"

"Who gave it to you to plant?"

"Nobody. Nobody!"

"It got there in your handbag, did it not?"

"No."

"And you don't know anybody named Nabil Hamdoon?"

"No."

"Have you met anyone known as the Contractor?"

"No."

"You have never met the Contractor?"

"No."

"But you have heard about him?"

"Yes. Everybody in Washington has."

"Have you ever talked to the Contractor?"

"No."

"Have you ever met or talked to anybody known as Nabil?"

"No."

"Nabil and the Contractor are one and the same man. Do you know that?"

"Yes."

"Has Nabil ever approached you?"

"No."

"Talked to you?"

"No."

"You are sure of your statements?"

"Yes."

"You are certain you did not plant the transmitter?"

"Yes."

"You did—yes or no?"

"No."

Mike Gadau smiled disarmingly and became his old avuncular self. He touched her arm reassuringly. "My dear, are you sure you are telling the truth, the whole truth, and nothing but the truth?"

"Yes."

"That'll be all then. Congratulations."

He bent down and began to remove the wires and the velcro. Tammy heaved a sigh. It had been quite unnerving, even scary at times. It was over. She got up and stretched.

"Did I pass?" she asked.

A cloud passed over Gadau's handsome face. "Well, were you telling the truth?"

"Yes."

"In that case—it's rather inconclusive. Offhand, I'd say you passed, but you know, I have to collate the results and send them to the FBI."

"Quit playing on my intelligence, Mr. Gadau. I'm sure you know by now whether I passed or not."

"It's not a question of passing or failing, Tammy. You may have answered some questions truthfully and been deceptive in others." He shrugged. "If you were telling the truth, you should have nothing to worry about. If you were not . . ." He let the sentence hang.

After she had left, Mike Gadau stared thoughtfully at the piles of paper generated by the polygraph. Then he opened the door and called in the two FBI agents.

"Well?" asked the senior agent.

Gadau said flatly, "Guilty as hell."

———

The senior agent picked up his walkie-talkie and said something to a third FBI man somewhere in the building. As Tammy stepped off the elevator downstairs, Mrs. Neal was just arriving for her own appointment. She looked surprised to see Tammy.

"Well, how'd it go?" Her smile was conspiratorial.

"Tough. I certainly don't envy you," Tammy said.

"Great," Mrs. Neal mumbled. "Just great. Just what I need to spoil my lunch. See you back at the office." And she stepped inside the elevator.

Tammy swung through the revolving doors into the busy K Street and looked around for a cab. In the lobby behind her, a third FBI agent folded his newspaper and rose unhurriedly to his feet. When she hailed a taxi and gave a 1600 Penn address, he too got into a taxi and settled back in the rear seat.

Meanwhile, upstairs, Gadau spoke to the two FBI agents for about ten minutes, pointing at times to certain parts of the chart and the questions that had elicited certain responses. The agents listened and nodded. In the end, one of them moved to a telephone and dialed a number.

"Get me the Director."

———

The Director digested the news of Tammy Weasel's deception. He nodded and gave orders into the phone.

"Continue with the rest of the polygraphs. She may have accomplices. There could be more suspects."

"Right, sir."

———

The ride back to 1600 Penn in a rickety cab was just as depressing as the polygraph. The Nigerian-born cabby drove like a madman and tried to emulate the "cool" lingo of local African-Americans; he ended up sounding like a crazed Uncle Tom. He glanced in the rearview mirror several times, trying to catch her eye. Tammy gazed at a point somewhere above or below the mirror, though she could see her face framed in it. The cabbie chatted her up, but she wasn't in the mood.

Back in the office, Peggy Swisher and Julie Berg were waiting.

"How'd it go?" Julie asked.

Tammy threw her handbag on the table and covered her face with both hands. "Somebody please hand me a steaming cup of coffee. I need it."

Peggy brought over a Styrofoam cup of joe.. Tammy took it.

"Well?"

"I'm all deflated. Couldn't really tell. I don't know. I think I failed."

"How come? You didn't put it there, did you?"

Tammy looked her in the eye. "I didn't," she said and tried not to blink.

Julie laughed. "I was examined by one creep who looked like he was a sound engineer for the Pet Shop Boys."

"Mike Gadau?"

"No. Patmore, I think. Anyway he said mine was inconclusive. I asked him how come, that I didn't plant it, and he said, well, that if I told the truth then I had nothing to worry about."

"Me, too," Peggy said. "Klinefeld examined me. He said he couldn't really tell if I passed. Was I telling the truth? I said, yes, of course. Then he shrugged and said it was difficult to say whether I'd passed or not. He asked if I had anything else to tell him. I said no, nothing. God, he made me feel like I flunked."

"I did flunk," Tammy said. "I'm sure of it. I was so nervous." She drank the coffee.

"Did he tell you specifically you flunked?" Peggy asked.

"Not quite. He said it was inconclusive. That word again. It could mean anything. I wonder how Mrs. Neal is dealing with hers right now."

"She'll be alright."

"Well, fancy that," Julie said, *soto voce*. "One of us is a traitor. So it seems."

Tammy said dully, "Someone from another office could have planted it in here."

"That's one possibility," Julie said.

The door opened and Ken Dwight walked in. Tammy's heart pounded against her ribs. His eyes rested on Tammy. She searched his face. *He knows!*

"Well, ladies, how did it go?"

"We should ask you," Peggy piped up.

Dwight laughed and ran a hand through his tousled, gray-flecked hair. The endless meetings, strategy sessions, task force briefings were telling on him. He looked as though he had slept in his clothes. "Oh yes, the reports are in. I'll soon get Mrs. Neal's. Peggy, yours is inconclusive. You might or might not have planted the device. Julie, you didn't pass either."

"Oh?"

"Yep. You were being deceptive when you were asked if you've ever used a sex toy." Dwight smiled disarmingly.

"News for you, Ken."

"Shoot, Julie."

"It's such a long shot, you missed by a mile."

"I'll be darned. Thought I hit the mark."

"What about me? Did I pass?" Tammy's voice sounded quiet even to her own ears.

"I was coming to that." Dwight came over and patted her on the arm. He was smiling, and for the first time since she had known him, Tammy noticed the amethyst coldness of his eyes. His lips were smiling, but the eyes contradicted everything. "Congratulations, Tammy. You were the only one who passed. With flying colors."

He was still smiling when he closed the door behind him.

———

"She failed," Dwight said bitterly to Larry Bodine back in his office. His face had undergone a remarkable change. "She failed woefully. I talked to Mike Gadau and there's no question. Tammy knows something about that transmitter, and we're going to find out just how much she knows—how much she's involved in it. She also flunked the part about knowing the Contractor. Hell, she practically flew off the chart on that one. And planting the transmitter, too."

Bodine shook his head. "Never would have thought it of her. Such a nice girl."

"I want all points surveillance on her. Twenty-four seven. Her apartment, her car, her telephone. Everything. Arrange the warrants. Three shifts. Three men a shift. Mix it up. Inter-agency. Strooker's been briefed, as have Creed and Kohlbus. We haven't told the First Lady yet. She'll have a fit. And Smurf One isn't to know about it. Until we get all our evidence. That clear?"

"Sounds good."

"The NSA guys will screen everything coming from the First Lady or the president before it gets to Tammy and the other girls in that office. I'll talk to Bogan about that. Make sure sensitive information isn't passed on to Tammy. Make it look innocuous."

"Got it."

"Report to me or Hy Strooker only. This is our chance to nail whoever did in poor Gus Means. Let's not screw up on this one. That's why I picked you for this, Larry."

"Hell, Ken, you made the right decision."

"Then let's get to it."

CHAPTER 28

Champaign-Urbana.

A long, oblong, rosewood-top table dominated the conference room in the east wing of the Humana Hospital in Urbana, Illinois. On one side sat Jim Delbecki and his wife Norma, the son-in-law and daughter of Vice President Walsh; Carson Walsh, the veep's older brother who, at seventy, looked ten years younger than Richard; Dick Walsh Jr. and his wife Sue, who had come all the way from Crawford, Texas. Sitting next to Walsh Jr. was Joe Silberstein, the Walsh's family lawyer, who had flown in from Washington, DC.

On the other side of the table sat four men: Vic Pollini, the hospital administrator; Jason E. Block, the hospital's lawyer; and two men in immaculate white coats who, from their name tags, were Dr. Nogarth and Dr. Wall.

"I'm sorry, Mrs. Delbecki," Pollini said to the vice president's daughter, who dabbed a handkerchief to her face. Jim Delbecki had a supporting arm around his wife. "All the documents are in order. Mr. Silberstein is quite right. Your mother made it clear that were she to be . . . ah . . . in this condition, under no circumstances is she to be kept alive by artificial means. Your father witnessed and signed the statement."

Fresh tears appeared and ran down Norma Delbecki's face. "Are you saying we shouldn't try and keep her alive?"

"Of course we should—if she were alive. But, you see, brain death has occurred. Most doctors today agree on brain death as the clinical definition of death. Your mother is no longer alive, Mrs. Delbecki. A respirator is breathing for her. She is essentially a vegetable. She could go on like this for months, years—you remember Karen Quinlan? That isn't her wish.

"We've already violated her specific request for more than a week now, as Mr. Silberstein was kind enough to remind us. The hospital's ethics committee and the Mortality Board have both looked into it and see no way to get around Mrs. Walsh's wishes. The local state's attorney's office has been consulted, as was the attorney general's office in DC, to determine whether we were committing a crime by removing Mrs. Walsh from life support. But everything is in order. We must allow your mother to die gracefully and with dignity so that her Last Will and Testament can be executed and her estate probated."

"Norma," Silberstein said, "I've been your family attorney for two generations. I knew you when you were a little tot, when your father first came politicking in Washington from your native Texas. Believe me, Norma, this hurts every one of us who know and love your mother. We wish she could live, still live . . . in some way. We wish there were some way, no matter how remote, to keep her alive as a functioning human being." Silberstein spoke with deep emotion. His Brooks Brothers two-piece gray suit and dark tie made him seem a multinational company's CEO exhorting recalcitrant employees.

"Unfortunately," he went on, "her quality of life—if we call it life—is at such a low level, it would be cruel, even criminal, to suspend her indefinitely in limbo. It is not a question of money—the Walsh family is well off financially and also well insured, not to mention that she's the nation's second lady, insured by Uncle Sam. She could be kept on that machine for years at public expense. Evelyn Walsh touched something beautiful and noble in all of us, and she enjoys the goodwill of the American people. But—" Silberstein spread out his hands, "Evelyn—your mother, Junior's mother—specifically instructed me, in my office, with your father present, not to allow this to happen to her. She would want you and your brother to get on with your lives, and for her husband, the vice president of the United States, to get on with his own recovery. It's the best thing you could do for her." He turned to Dick Walsh Jr. "You do understand, don't you, son?"

Dick Jr. shrugged. "We've got to do as Mom wishes. If Mom's gone, she's gone. It's what she wants, okay? Let's get on with it." Beside him, his young wife Sue held and squeezed his arm.

Norma raised her tear-stricken face to the doctors. "Isn't there something you can do? A medical precedent, something?"

Dr. Nogarth coughed politely and shook his head. "Nothing, Mrs. Delbecki."

Dr. Wall added, "Absolutely nothing. Brain death is irreversible. I'm sorry."

"What does Father say to all this?" Norma inquired.

"He agrees," Pollini said shortly.

"But he can't speak."

"That's true. It's too early to tell if his deafness will be permanent. He was able to write on a piece of paper that we should go ahead with the disconnection. No problem from that quarter."

"What about Mom's own family? She has a brother, two sisters. My aunts. What do they say to all this?"

Silberstein said, "They're all in England. And frankly, my dear, their opinion wouldn't matter. Evelyn—your mother—when she was a legally responsive adult, with her full faculties, wanted it this way."

The room fell silent. Everyone waited for Norma. She had voiced the strongest objections, and they had answered each one. They waited for more.

"Alright." Norma buried her face against her husband's massive chest, sobbing. Jim Delbecki held her, squeezing her body to his.

"Be brave, honey," he whispered to her.

"Oh, Jim. They're taking away mother's life!"

"It's not quite that way," he whispered back. "This is what she wanted. We're doing the right thing, don't you worry."

Norma quieted and looked up bravely. "Go ahead. Do what you have to do."

The tension in the room dissolved visibly. Jason Block, the hospital lawyer, spoke first.

"A good decision, Mrs. Delbecki. Let me commend you and the entire family. We have the utmost sympathy for your mother's condition." He paused, wondering whether to go on. "I would . . . it would be remiss of me . . . of us . . . not to tell you at this point that your Mom also signed an organ donor card. It's on her medical information bracelet. This means—"

"No!" Norma screamed.

The room fell silent. "I know what it means. Don't you dare touch my mother's organs!"

"That can wait for later."

"Jason, why did you bring it up now?"

Dr. Nogarth coughed. "Those organs have a very short life span."

"We had to let the family know before we harvest," Dr. Wall said smoothly.

"Two patients are waiting for those corneas," Vic Pollini added.

"Stop! Stop!"

Everybody was speaking at once. Pollini banged on the table for silence, as did Silberstein. The room quieted.

"Gentlemen. Norma." Silberstein's voice was sober. "I'm sure that issue is not our priority. Our priority is to respect Evelyn Walsh's wishes and get her off that damned machine. Is that agreed?"

"Agreed," Block said. "And we notify the press beforehand."

Silberstein considered. "The president and the first lady will be informed, of course. And the bicameral Congress."

Everyone except Norma nodded agreement.

"If the family wishes," Pollini added, "the disconnection from life support could be filmed by all three major networks."

Dr. Nogarth coughed again. "One other thing. In these matters, it is customary to allow a family member, perhaps the one closest in life to the patient on life support, to remove the support systems." He turned to Norma and smiled benignly. "I suspect, Mrs. Delbecki, that you are very close to your mother. I would think her wishes would be for you to disconnect her from the respirator."

"Me! Kill my mother? You're out of your mind!"

"You're not killing her," Dr. Wall interjected patiently. "She's already—you're looking at what you think is Evelyn. Everything is there, physically. But she's gone. I'm sorry. She's gone. A machine is breathing for her, tubes are feeding her, removing her waste. Disconnect her and, in minutes, perhaps hours, maybe a couple of days, and she'll float away peacefully. With dignity. About the harvesting, we—"

"No more of that," Silberstein snapped. "Evelyn Walsh will be buried intact. No missing parts. The organ donor card will be made invalid, by God, and I'll go to court. I'll get a cease and desist. What are we talking here? Evelyn Walsh is a national monument, in the same league with Eleanor Roosevelt or Harriet Truman or Betty Ford. Would you harvest the organs of those women?"

"Are we talking about my mother?" Norma wailed.

Silberstein raged on. "You guys remove any part of Evelyn Walsh, and I'll sue you to the Heavenly Cleaners. We're talking about the nation's second lady, for Chrissakes. Even if she'll be buried in Crawford, I want her body intact. She ought to be buried in Arlington, enshrined as a monument to American womanhood. Damn right. Right next to other big personalities buried there. Would you harvest JFK's organs before deep-sixing him in Arlington? No! And her eyes are old—the woman's over sixty for crying out loud—who'd want to see with those eyes anyway? Why do you want Evelyn Walsh's plundered corpse in a casket draped by Old Glory? Why?"

No one answered him.

"The issue is moot," Silberstein thundered, "and that's that."

———

Washington, DC.

Admiral Hornsby was saying, "We identified conclusively the transmitter picked up from the White House. It is part of the GLONASS system—Global Navigation Satellite System—the Russian equivalent of our own Global Positioning System, GPS. Instead of being used to pinpoint locations, we have here a homing transmitter whose signal can be acquired by an independent source and used as a waypoint or end destination. The accuracy is startling, the best even we can get, down to less than a meter—three feet—and ideal for a fire-and-forget missile."

"Kokubani say anything yet?"

"Since the preliminary appearance? Not that I know of."

Creed, like everyone else, had watched Dr. Kokubani appear briefly in court that morning where he was charged with multiple counts of criminal conspiracy, terrorism, violations of the Gun Act, and a host of federal charges. He had pleaded not guilty to all the charges and a trial date was set for five months hence. Bail was denied. Kokubani, shackled in arm and leg irons, accompanied by his lawyers and surrounded by jailhouse guards, was jeered at by sections of the packed courtroom. After the hearing, he was quickly escorted back to the federal jail through a side door.

"His lawyers filed all kinds of motions," Creed went on. "If and when their client does talk, you can be sure he'll cut a plea. The only person who would have talked if she had the chance died this morning."

"Who the hell's that?"

"Esther May Crawford. The Kokubani's housekeeper. She passed away at Montgomery General. She'd been under close observation for two weeks now. Some kind of rare food poisoning."

"That's a damn shame."

"Sure is."

"Think it was a hit job?"

"Bet your wallet. Here's the kicker. Two days ago, another woman, same symptoms of very rare food poisoning shows up at Holy Cross Hospital in Silver Springs. Maybe she and Esther May Crawford ate at the same restaurant. Could be oysters from the same pot. We're trying to pin that down."

"Where's the difficulty?"

"The hospital isn't releasing names. Lots of secrecy. Patient checked in under a false name, we assume. CDC Atlanta confirms it's a highly toxic rare bacteria cultivated almost exclusively from human feces with the right know-how."

"You get two or three of those and it's considered an epidemic. It'll kill seven times out of ten."

"Damn."

"So Dr. Kokubani cultivates a rare kind of bacteria from his dung—feeds the stuff to his housekeeper so she can be conveniently out of the way while his house and airstrip are used by terrorists. He now faces a murder charge in addition to his other problems. Farfetched? I don't think so. Who's this other lady with the same symptoms? We'll need to find out the connection."

Creed looked thoughtful. "She's no housekeeper, that's for sure. Drove in to Emergency in a limousine. Met by her personal physician. Checked in under an alias. Celebrities do that all the time. Anyway, we'll find out who this woman is before the day is out."

"And now I hear this young woman on the First Lady's staff flunked a polygraph. What's the angle?"

Hy Strooker nodded at Dwight. "That's why I sent for Ken Dwight. Ken?"

Dwight shuffled papers and cleared his throat. "I've gone over the polygraph results with Mike Gadau. Subject, a white female by the name Tammy Weasel, never met or heard of Dr. Kokubani until the news flash on the aborted terrorist plot. Subject definitely knows Nabil, aka the Contractor. She knows something about the homing transmitter found in her office. In fact, we believe she placed it there. The three other ladies sharing that office with her all passed their polygraphs—none of them knew anything whatsoever of the affair. Mrs. Weasel's statements practically took the styluses off the chart. No question she's our perp."

Creed grunted. "We're getting somewhere. Go on, Ken."

Dwight looked apologetic. "Well, on Friday, the day after we found the transmitter in the office of the First Lady's staff, before even the polygraphs, I requested and received from Verizon a record of all calls made from the home telephones of all four ladies in that office in the past month. My immediate hunch was that one of them planted the transmitter. I wanted to see if any calls to or from the Kokubani estate had been made by any of those ladies. I figured that would tell us who planted the device." He paused.

"Anything?" Creed's impatience showed.

"It was slow, tedious work, and I was still going through them when I learned of Tammy Weasel flunking the polygraph. Thereafter, I immediately concentrated on her phone transcripts. A few calls to her mother in a nursing home near Baltimore; one to her sister in California; her dentist, that sort of thing. I came across a curious fact: in the past ten days, four calls have been made to two numbers in Silver Springs. Both numbers belong to the same person, although one number is unlisted. Those numbers, gentlemen, belong to House Speaker Mario Stepzinski."

Kohlbus was the first to break the silence. He chuckled. "Who would have thought the old goat was having it on the side."

Admiral Hornsby smiled. "I am happy to see that sex does cross bipartisan lines."

Strooker was thoughtful. He asked Creed directly, "What do we know of Speaker Stepzinski?"

The FBI director shrugged. "Started out as city alderman in Chicago. Worked under the Dailey machine that swept Chicago for decades. Later won a congressional seat for the northeastern district of Illinois. Six-term congressman. Chaired several committees. Fiery orator. Considered something of a radical by some. Far left. Elected Speaker two years ago."

"Nothing unusual. Any more facts?"

Creed looked embarrassed. "Bounced two checks already this year in the House Bank. Bounced one last year. House Ethics Committee investigated him for some campaign fund mismanagement. Slush funds, sticky fingers, that sort of thing. Allegations. No charges. His book, *Capitol Blues: The Wit and Wisdom of Mario Stepzinski* was on *The New York Times* bestseller lists for four months, *Washington Post* for five. Married to Sophia Stepzinski, former sitcom actress. Three children, all grown and fled the nest. Not your ideal Jonathan Edward type, but downright patriotic."

"Disgraceful," Hornsby said. "Kiting checks, and him the country's chief lawmaker."

"About the bad checks," Creed added hastily, "all cleared when they were presented a second time. Restitution was prompt in one other instance of apparent theft of service." He shrugged. "The Speaker's not alone. Bouncing checks appears to be a favorite congressional pastime."

"Gary, do you keep these facts in your head all the time?" Kohlbus asked.

Hornsby said, "Ivan is pretending to know nothing of the bombing in Illinois or this attempt right here in our backyard. They're claiming that if there is Russian involvement, it's by a renegade bunch of army generals out to discredit the Kremlin. The SVR even went as far as tipping us off about a safe house on M Street where the Contractor was supposed to be staying. You guys drew a dud there, didn't you?"

"We sure did. And believe me, we acted within an hour of receiving the tip. Bogan says the tip came right from the top, too. From President Grachev. We arrested one useless asset—a double agent for China and the Russians. Ivan must have known he was double dealing and sacrificed him."

"The Contractor was never found?"

"Nope.

"This young woman who flunked the polygraph—she may be the key to his whereabouts. Maybe he's shacking up with her. Makes strategic sense."

"We were gonna start working that angle. We know where she lives. We'll talk to the manager of her apartment complex. Pose as utility repairmen or plumbers. Get the manager to open up her apartment, check for gas leaks, that sort of thing. Alternatively, we could set up audio listening posts. If he's there, we'll hear him."

After the meeting, Strooker pulled Dwight aside in the hallway. He was furious.

"Ken, in the future, check with me before you divulge information to the multi-agency task force. Is that clear?"

Dwight was puzzled. "Where'd I goof?"

"I sent for you to bring us up to date on the polygraph results and on the general investigation. That stuff about the telephone transcripts and the connection with the House Speaker—it wasn't wise divulging it. You don't know who's who."

"I think I understand what you're getting at."

"Damn right you do. If there's a high-powered conspiracy to assassinate President Deakin and squash MDS, it's possible even Creed, Kohlbus, or Hornsby could be involved. Remember what Hornsby suggested earlier: there's a mole right up there in the State Department, possibly in the White House or among the Service Chiefs. Someone named Boris. We've got to be careful. They anticipate our every move. Remember, even today, we still haven't heard the last word on JFK's assassination. Some of the Warren Commission's findings will still be classified long after you and I have been shoved beneath the goddamned soil. Let's be careful, shall we."

"Sorry, Chief."

———

Larry Bodine was waiting for Strooker and Dwight when the duo arrived at the White House.

"Look what just came in." He held out a computer-generated printout of names and addresses with the makes and serial numbers of a certain product. He had circled one name in red marker: Tammy Weasel. He waited while the two men examined it.

Strooker winced. "She purchased a piece?"

"That's right. A Glock 17 9mm. Just kicked off the FBI background check computer."

"Glock 9mm," Strooker repeated as if in a trance.

"Not a lady's gun at all," Dwight agreed. "She means business."

"Any follow-up on that?"

"She purchased them at a gun shop downtown on Saturday. Three packets of ammunition. Charged it to her MasterCard. She sure intends to get in some target practice."

"I always did say," Strooker said, "there ought to be a one-week waiting period for background checks before guns are sold. The present method of doing the check *after* the gun has already been sold makes no sense." He looked up at Bodine. "How'd you get on to her so quickly?"

Bodine bristled. "Gimme credit, Chief. I spent two years in Letter Threats before presidential detail. I can dig things up."

"Good work, Larry. Now let's get down to business. Is she in the building right now?"

"She's upstairs."

"Damn!"

"I don't think she's packing," Bodine said quickly. "She couldn't have gotten them past the metal detectors." He frowned. "Then again, she did get that damned transmitter inside the White House."

"Because it looked like a pocket calculator."

"Heck, if she's packing heat and she's up there in that office undetected, I shall voluntarily demote myself to ASAC."

"Where's Smurf One?" Strooker asked.

"In the Oval."

"Smurf Two?"

"At her hairdresser's. Downtown."

Strooker said urgently, "Call Didi Watts now. Tammy Weasel should be denied access to the president and Mrs. Deakin effective this minute. Not even for personal messages," he muttered under his breath. "As I recall, she's Mrs. Deakin's favorite gofer."

"We've got to find out if she has either of the guns on her."

The three men pondered this. Presently, Dwight brightened. "I got it." He pressed the intercom mike on his desk and spoke into it. "Send Agent Ferraro to my office. Now."

Within minutes, Special Agent Janet Ferraro knocked and came in. She was about five foot eight, prim, no-nonsense, and with her efficient bob and hard, gray eyes looked every inch a Secret Service agent.

"Come in, Janet. You're just what we need."

Dwight quickly explained the situation to her. She listened attentively, nodding now and then. When Dwight had finished, she said, "I'll need Doreen Stout."

Mrs. Stout was a uniformed officer of the White House security staff.

"You got her," Strooker said.

CHAPTER 29

Washington, DC.

"Tammy, are you alright?" Mrs. Neal asked, staring at Tammy from her desk. "You looked stressed. What's the matter, hon? Man trouble?"

Tammy managed a smile. "I think it's the flu."

"You mean you haven't had your shot?"

"Should I?"

"Honey, I never skip the flu shot. Me and my husband."

"And it's required," Julie Berg offered. "Dr. Mallard said something last year about every staffer coming in for their shot before the flu season. Mandatory." William Mallard, MD was the White House physician.

"But you can get the flu shot and still get the flu," Tammy said.

"You can. It'd be mild though and quickly over," said Julie.

"Yeah. I guess I should see about getting one."

"I don't think they can give you the shot after it's already begun. Can they?" asked Mrs. Neal.

"Of course they can," said Julie

"Says who?"

"Well, I read—" Julie broke off as the telephone rang on Tammy's desk.

Tammy picked up the phone. "First lady's office, Tammy speaking."

"Tammy. Dwight. Shakespeare just did a number two in the East Room carpet. Don't ask me how he got there. Mrs. Deakin has gone to her beautician's downtown. I wonder if you could come and walk

Shakespeare outside for fifteen minutes or so. He looks ready to do a big one. Would you, please?"

"Sure thing, Mr. Dwight."

Shakespeare was the First Family's Pekingese Poodle. Apart from the First Couple themselves, Tammy was the only other person the pooch had taken to. This had arisen simply because, as the newest staffer in the first lady's office four years ago, Tammy was the office gofer—the one most often called upon to take Shakespeare on one of his two daily thirty-minute walks on the vast lawns behind the White House. Mrs. Deakin herself took Shakespeare on his second walk.

She remembered with amusement the time eight months earlier when she had gone to her doctor's office and had spent an unusually lengthy time in the waiting room. By the time she'd gotten back to 1600 Penn, Shakespeare's afternoon walk had been overdue by two hours. She had run into Chief of Staff Don Panella in the East Wing, and he had looked at her accusingly. "Where have you been? Shakespeare just did a job on the Blue Room carpet. Better take care of it before Didi Watts has a fit."

"I was at the doctor's. How did he get in there?"

"Beats me. Somebody must have left a door open."

Poor mutt. Holding it in for two hours and finally letting go. She'd found the puddle on the herringbone parquet floor of fine oak, thank God, and not on the oval Peking blue rug, as she had feared. Shakespeare himself was sleeping on one of Pierre-Antoine Bellangé's priceless Empire armchairs. She'd lifted Shakespeare's shit from the carpet using a clutch of tissues. She'd felt a recent dampness at the base of one of the blue satin drapes with gold satin valances and ribbed fringes. The cleaners wouldn't come until after hours. Many more tissues and much spraying of air freshener had taken care of it. Tammy had picked up Shakespeare by the scruff of his neck and left the Blue Room.

Dwight's call today was yet another reminder that she was Shakespeare's unofficial handler. When she got to the East Wing entrance, Hy Strooker, Ken Dwight, and Larry Bodine stood in one corner engaged in earnest conversation. They all knew she would have to pass through the metal screening portal to take Shakespeare out for his walk. The east entrance was deserted, since public tours of the White House had been temporarily suspended following the terrorist scare. Bodine had earlier tested the screening walkway by walking past it with and without his gun. The device pinged on the first attempt and remained silent on the second.

The device did not go off when Tammy walked past the detector. The uniformed officer guarding the detector nodded at Tammy. Bodine had purposefully left Shakespeare's leather leash with its steel clip on a wall hook beyond the metal detector so it wouldn't sound the alarm.

"Good afternoon, gentlemen," she said to the three men as she walked by.

"Hello, Tammy."

"Dog day, ain't it?"

"What's it gonna be this time—the Jacqueline Kennedy Garden?"

She searched for the mutt.

Woof!

Tammy collared the First Mutt on a Lincoln chair in the hallway. She snapped on the leash and Shakespeare impatiently led the way outside, where he immediately commenced to irrigate all tree trunks within reach. He waited until they reached his usual place—the Children's Garden, planted by Lyndon Baines Johnson surrounding the lawn tennis court—before moving his bowels. She unleashed him and watched him scamper into the brush.

Something was wrong. Her instinct told her so. She had sensed a forced buoyancy in the three men's attitudes. Her already growing sense of unease intensified.

———

While Tammy was stepping out of the east entrance with Shakespeare, Janet Ferraro and Doreen Stout burst unannounced into the office of the first lady.

"Ta la-ah! Routine check. Everybody get up, please. Step away from your desks. Now! Move it!"

Peggy Swisher was mortified. "What on earth for?"

"How about a transmitter?" Ferraro asked icily. She was already opening desk drawers, emptying trash baskets, and sifting through the contents of handbags. Doreen Stout was doing the same thing.

"We don't have any privacy in here at all," whined Julie Berg as she left her desk.

"Things certainly have changed quite a bit," Mrs. Neal observed.

Ferraro made a cursory effort at checking the filing cabinets and Peggy's desk, letting Doreen Stout do Mrs. Neal's and Julie's desks. But it was Tammy's desk and handbag she was after, and she found and went over it with a fine-tooth comb. No gun.

Doreen drew the same conclusion. She shrugged when her eyes met Ferraro's.

"Alright, girls," Ferraro said. "Would you please squat for me?"

"I beg your pardon?"

"You heard me. I want a squat. Everyone. No bashful femininity here. Come on, let's go."

"It's not in our terms of employment," Julie wailed.

"What is—a mint julep cocktail party?" Ferraro shot back.

"What are you, anyway—" demanded Mrs. Neal, "the Gestapo?"

"Worse," Ferraro snapped. "Presidential detail."

It was Doreen Stout who defused the whole situation. "Look, y'all don't have to pull anything. Keep your clothes on, but please do a squat for us."

"What for?"

"We're looking for contraband. Like a pocket calculator."

It was easy after that. Peggy Swisher injected some unintended humor into the situation when she fell backward trying to squat on her high heeled shoes. She wore a blue, knit dress skirt and beneath it a tiny, blue thong. As she fell and sought for balance by splaying her legs and landing on her right elbow, her panties pushed to one side and for a split-second revealed a brown, curly bush gutted by a vicious pink slash.

Everyone except Ferraro laughed, Peggy included, and the tension eased. Peggy got back to her feet.

"Alright, everybody. Thanks for your cooperation." Ferraro sat down on a chair and lit a cigarette. "You may resume your work. Sorry if I sounded a bit harsh. I've got a job to do, just like the rest of you."

"Hey!" Mrs. Neal said. "We have a no-smoking policy in here."

"Sorry. Forgot." Ferraro took a drag and stubbed out the cigarette. Peggy Swisher opened the window overlooking the forsythia bush.

Doreen Stout sat down.

"Apology accepted," Julie Berg said.

"The Gestapo never apologizes," Mrs. Neal said.

"Quit that, please," Doreen protested.

"Tammy just stepped outside," Peggy said. "She'll be back any moment. Then you can do her, too, I guess."

"I know." Ferraro said. "We're waiting for Tammy. Back to work everyone, please. Just forget Doreen and me."

Five minutes later, the door burst open and Tammy entered, taking off her coat. "It's nippy out there—" she began, and broke off when she saw Doreen Stout and Janet Ferraro. The color drained from her face.

"Come in, Tammy. We've been waiting for you." Ferraro smiled. "Would you be kind enough to squat for me?"

———

"No gun, no bullets," Ferraro reported to Strooker and Dwight. "Not on her person. Not in the office."

"That leaves her apartment and her car."

"She could have purchased the piece for someone else," Dwight observed.

———

Reston.

He had no doubt the plan would work. The late Nasser Kokubani's words reverberated in his ear. *There's a doc over at Manassas owns a Tucano. Now that's as close as you can get to a jet and still fly behind props.*

It certainly would work.

If the Engineer kept the rendezvous.

If the sixty-second timing fuse worked. If the ejection seat worked. If, if, if. He hated ifs. From experience, when he worked with a preponderance of ifs, one cog in the wheel was bound to come unstuck, even with careful planning.

He entered Mrs. Fierstal's apartment through Tammy's kitchen. He found Dr. Polk under Physicians and Surgeons in the Yellow Pages. Plastic Surgery Associates. Three doctors were listed in the practice. He dialed the number.

"Associates."

"I'd like to speak to Dr. Polk."

"I'm sorry. Dr. Polk is in surgery right now. Is there something I could help you with?"

"Well," Nabil floundered, trying to sound like an undecided patient. "I sort of wanted to find out about a facelift with a nose job. How much would that cost?"

He could almost hear the chuckle at the other end. "That depends on the condition of your face, the amount of lifting that has to be done, what type of nose you want. Have you been to our offices yet?"

"Not yet."

"We can give you any type of nose you want: Romanesque profile, a ski-slide Nixon type, or a massive doorknob Tip O'Neal type. We do Robert Redford noses, too. Why don't you come in and we'll take a look at you."

"That's fine. But I want Dr. Polk to do the surgery."

The girl hesitated. "Dr. Polk is booked full until February of next year. Most of our work is elective and people wait months in advance. I could take your name down against Dr. Polk for next February. If you want it sooner, perhaps Dr. Simvali can be of use to you. As early as next week?"

"Can I just ask you a question, lady?"

"Go ahead."

"Is Dr. Polk in the office right now or not?"

"He is, but he's in surgery and I simply can't disturb him. Perhaps I could have him call you back?"

"I'll think about it," Nabil said, and hung up.

He stood for some minutes beside the telephone in Mrs. Fierstal's bedroom, staring at the rows of hairpieces in the closet. If he shaved off his mustache (it had grown again since New York) and dressed up as an elderly lady, he might be able to leave the building without being recognized. . . .

He dismissed the thought immediately: even if he succeeded in hiding his legs in pantaloons and his arms in long-sleeved blouses, his hirsute wrists and stubbly chin wouldn't fool anyone.

The kitchen window overlooked the rear lot. He could see Tammy's Chevy Cavalier. He had the keys in his pocket. She had taken a taxi to a Hertz office where she could rent a car.

He could slide down the baggage chute and emerge close to the car and avoid having to walk all the way around. One thought deterred him: what if the chute led to one of those mechanical compactors activated by motion sensors? He could imagine the steel pincers digging into his body, eviscerating, shredding, and compacting.

He reentered Tammy's apartment, stripped down to his boxer shorts and tank top and walked into the bathroom. He used Tammy's Lady Remington to shave off most of his mustache and sideburns. He lathered his face with the Gillette Sensitive Skin Foam that he found on her bathroom shelf and shaved with her Schick Twin Blade. He removed all those signs of masculinity he had so carefully cultivated. Regrets? None. The less he resembled those FBI Wanted posters, the better.

He thought about the mission as he shaved. Tomorrow, if all went well, the entire world would wake up to a lot of noise. Inexplicably, thinking about the mission gave him a strong erection. He shrugged and lathered again, trying to get the smoothest shave possible. When he had finished, the erection was still there, turgid, demanding. It would be a shame to waste it. He dried his face on Tammy's towel. He searched in the bin and found one of Tammy's soiled underwear, heavy with her female scent.

Tammy.

Her name alone could tee him off—clammy, viscous, clinging. He beat meat vigorously, staring grimly at the stranger in the mirror, a renegade he recognized remotely as himself. The set of his mouth tightened even further, his rigid face intensely engaged in the mirror. He whimpered and sucked in his breath, recalling to his mind the precise moment last night when she had surrendered to him, groping for his phallus to guide it inside her; recalling her steamy feral ardor, her taut beautiful face joined in the effort and intent of getting her own carnal needs fulfilled. That did the trick. This would mother all meat-beats. Still clutching in his mind's eye the look and texture of her soft, transparent fingers closing over his erect manhood, he whacked his seed into the white porcelain sink.

He showered afterward, aware that this might well be his last shower for some time. He dried himself, changed into fresh clothes, and tidied up Tammy's apartment, removing all traces of himself he could find. He checked the breech on the Glock—the 9mm Parabellums were in place—and tucked it in his waistband. He retrieved Tammy's soiled underwear, folded it like a triangular handkerchief and tucked it inside his left trouser pocket as a good-luck talisman. The mission needed all the help it could get.

The door to the apartment, once closed, could only be opened from the inside unless one had the keys. Tammy had the apartment's door key. The cardinal sin would be for him to forget the car keys inside the apartment, and once outside discover he couldn't get back in. He made sure the car keys were in his hand before he edged open the door, took one peek down the hallway—nobody—then another wistful look at the apartment that had harbored him for four nights.

He emerged fully into the hallway. The door clicked shut behind him. Regretfully. He was out of her life until long after the mission—if she kept her end of the bargain. He started down the hallway, his footsteps echoing like gunshots in his ear. Reaching the door marked Exit, he opened it and took the stairs two at a time down to a mini-lobby. One wall was stacked entirely of mailboxes and a security door opened to the front parking lot. No one challenged him. A cleaning lady pushed a cloth broom down the spotless hallway; another followed at the far end with a mop bucket. He stepped outside. Experienced eyes scanned the parking lot. A woman accompanied by two kids trying to open the door of a Buick Estate, a man in blue overalls working on his Dodge van.

Good so far. The comforting presence of the Glock pressed against his waistband. If he had to, he would use it, fast. He didn't believe in negotiation. He walked casually to the car and opened the driver's side door with the key fob. Again no one challenged him. Tom's car seat was affixed to the backseat behind the driver. A whiff of Nina Ricci's L'Air du Temps lingered. The car started smoothly. The gas tank was half full, just as she had said, and he drove out of the Seven Oaks condominiums and headed for Baron Cameron Avenue.

In the Seven Oaks parking lot, the man in blue overalls straightened. He wiped his hands on a grease rag and shut the hood of the dull-red Dodge van. He got behind the wheel, the engine whirred, and the van eased out. He kicked out in the general direction of the Chevy Cavalier.

———

Manassas, Nabil knew, lay south of Reston. So he was mildly irritated he had to head in the opposite direction to make the rendezvous with the Engineer. From the car radio came the news that doctors in Illinois had just declared Vice President Walsh an invalid and unable to perform his official duties as a result of his injuries from the bombing. The president and both the House and Senate had been informed The president and the Republican Party were now engaging in the onerous task of selecting a new vice president. Meanwhile, since the US Constitution did not allow the office of Vice President to be vacant, House Speaker Mario Stepzinski's daily NSA briefings had been upgraded to reflect the fact that until a new vice president was chosen, he was next in line to the presidency.

Even if this second operation fails, we have done considerable damage. We came through in Illinois; we inflicted shock and disbelief in the armor of American smugness. The MDS purpose-built computer was destroyed, setting that program back at least two years. Now if we can assassinate her principal proponent, the entire program will come crashing down.

Nabil's eyes, flitting between the rearview mirror and the road, saw the dull-red van appear from a side intersection one block behind. The same van he had seen outside the Seven Oaks. It was no coincidence.

It could mean anything.

He turned at three different intersections, and when the sloping hood of the Dodge appeared faithfully at the corner of the fourth, he knew he was being followed. Whoever was doing the following wanted Nabil to know he was being tailed, too. He drove on, a new theory forming in his mind. He soon found the shopping center off the main boulevard. Considering that it was a Monday, the plaza lot had a substantial number of cars. He located the pharmacy; predictably not too many cars were parked before it. He found a space farthest away from the pharmacy entrance and stopped.

He didn't wait long. The dull-red van with its tinted windows drove slowly past at a tangent. Nabil drew his gun and thumbed back the safety. As the van went by, he caught sight of yellow off-state license plates bearing the inscription Garden State. New Jersey plates. Simultaneously, he recognized the bearded man in blue overalls he had seen in the Seven Oaks parking lot. The van made a wide detour before pulling up alongside the Cavalier, engine idling. Nabil had also kept the Cavalier's engine idling. Both cars stayed like this for a full minute, neither driver doing or saying anything. But the lot held nothing more sinister than an elderly lady in a flowered hat driving by in a Cadillac

Seville. Another woman accompanied by three small children made her way toward the pharmacy.

The van driver killed his engine first. The driver's window rolled down soundlessly. He was bearded and his features looked more tortured, but there was no mistaking the angular, almost perfect hook nose, the intense, fretful eyes of the mad bomber, the grim sweat and inexplicably dirty clothes of a man who dealt exclusively in perpetrating death. There was no mistaking the dark olive skin that the sun in Libya and Somalia had tamed. Hamad Ghantous. The Engineer.

"*Salaam aleikum*, brother."

Nabil sheathed his gun. "*Aleikum salaam.* We meet again, my brother."

Nabil left the Cavalier and opened the passenger door of the van. He climbed in and embraced the Engineer in the traditional Arab greeting, three quick cheek-by-jowl rubbings, noting as he did so the man's dour-sweat ripeness.

"Thank you very much for coming."

"My pleasure, brother. Anything we can do for our cause. For our people."

"*Inshallah.*" Nabil noticed the huge pile of equipment in the van's interior. The rear was stuffed with boxed cartons.

"Everything is there for the bomb," the Engineer said, reading his thoughts. "The rocket pods also."

"How did you know where I was staying?"

"Your contact Boris told me to wait in front of a certain apartment building one hour before the rendezvous. To see if anyone else was watching or waiting for you. If so, I was to warn you somehow. If you didn't come out at all ten minutes before the rendezvous, I was to make the rendezvous anyway in case you had gotten out earlier."

Damn Boris. Nabil could have read the situation differently and endangered the mission.

"It could have been dangerous," Nabil said.

The Engineer shrugged. "Yes. I was careful not to have you shoot me."

Nabil brought out the road map and spread it between them on the center console. "I've located Manassas on the map. The doctor's airplane is in one of the hangars at the airport. I'll find out which one when we get there. He's in surgery all day—I verified that by a phone call—so we have a free hand. Also, I'm gambling—"

The Engineer waited. "Gambling on what?"

Nabil was on the verge of saying he was gambling on the probability that Dr. Polk kept his packed parachute inside the hangar or airplane. What the Engineer didn't know and wasn't about to be told yet, nor Boris either, was that Nabil intended to save his life by ejecting a few seconds before the Tucano plowed into the White House. To the Engineer, Nabil's martyrdom was a foregone conclusion. He was going to crash the airplane into the White House, wasn't he?

"Nothing at all," he told the Engineer. "Forget it."

CHAPTER 30

Champaign-Urbana.

Evelyn Walsh, wife of the vice president, looked pale and diminutive beneath the assault of the high-tech life-preserving gadgets. Video monitors, tubes and wires, a defibrillator unit, a traction bed, and—dominating one corner of the room—the giant washing machine-like respirator and its chilling music of life: an intake of its mechanical breath, followed by a giant pneumatic hiss. The machines breathed for her, though she was brain-dead.

They stood in a semicircle facing the bed and the big television screen. Norma and Jim Delbecki; Dick Walsh Jr. and his wife Sue; Carson Walsh; Vic Pollini, hospital administrator; Dr. Nogarth, who made last-minute adjustments helped by an ICU nurse; Joe Silberstein, the Walsh's family lawyer who was there to make sure Evelyn Walsh's rights were being protected, her wishes respected Silberstein had gotten over his earlier rant, and had met the Walsh family privately, along with his associates. He had impressed upon them the need to respect Evelyn Walsh's wishes to donate her viable organs. They had agreed after some persuasion.

Vice President Walsh was there, wheeled in on a reclining bed, attached to his IV bottles and bags, a nasogastric tube running from a clear bottle into his nose. He couldn't speak, although awake and aware of what was happening. Secretary of State Dick Thornburgh and his wife Colleen, close family friends, were present. Also present was the

Reverend Gilbert Sloane, an Episcopalian priest, there to prepare Evelyn's soul for eternity.

The Walsh family had requested that it be a private affair. To a large extent, that request was being honored. Yet at least thirty print and TV journalists, curious doctors and nurses, family and political friends, thronged the doorway, checked by the combined determination of Secret Service and FBI agents aided by a contingent of local police officers.

A hush fell on the room, save for the mechanical hiss of the respirator. The network TV man said, "Stand by for live feed from the White House . . . 5 . . . 4 . . . 3 . . . 2 . . . 1—cue him!"

On the screen, Old Glory fluttered stiffly in a brisk wind. The strains of "The Star-Spangled Banner" filled the room. Those not already standing rose to their feet, solemnly placing their right hand over their hearts. The hiss of the respirator was subjugated by the immemorial, patriotic, hypnotic singing of the American anthem. It was being played by the Marine Corps band, considered by many to give the best rendition of the song by any branch of the Armed Forces. The melody shimmered in the air recalling Evelyn Walsh's course through the perilous fight down to her twilight's last gleaming, to the symbols of the adopted land she now called her home. As the song wound down, Old Glory fluttering o'er the land of the free and the home of the brave, the solemn, lined faces of President Deakin, Doris Deakin, and Shakespeare, the First Dog hove into view They stood in the Oval Office, as though assembled for a family photograph: Deakin, tall and distinguished, his full head of black hair at nearly seventy years of age glistening with Brylcreem.

Then the camera zoomed in on President Deakin as he began speaking, somberly and with feeling. "Evelyn, we have all come to wish you goodbye. Doris and I, your husband Richard, your children Norma and Dick Jr., your family, and each and every citizen of this great country of ours. Yours was a life well lived, an example to all. I don't have the words to express how distressed Doris and I and the American people are about what happened to you. I can only tell you that we stand by our promise to catch and punish the perpetrators of this heinous crime."

The president paused and moisture glistened in his eyes. Yet he spoke with such precision and clarity, it was difficult to believe he was not reading a prepared speech. Doris Deakin dabbed at her eyes with a pink handkerchief. Even Shakespeare seemed to understand the gravity of the situation. He flopped down, crossed his paws, and rested his head on them in a curiously sad gesture.

"As the Bible says, 'There is a time to be born, and a time to die.' Evelyn, much as we love you and want to keep you on that respirator, even with only a minimal to non-existent quality of life—anything, Evelyn, dear Evelyn, to keep you with us—we must in the end contend with and respect your own wishes to be allowed to pass on gracefully and with dignity. Now, you and Richard—"

Here the president broke off. His voice faltered, tears broke out openly in his eyes. "Now—you and Richard, and Doris and me, we . . . go back a long way. I still remember that cold night back in 2005, during the New Hampshire primaries, when we were snowed in at a colonial bed and breakfast. Traffic advisories were out, people were trapped in their cars because of snowdrifts, and the salt trucks couldn't keep up. All the airports were closed. Yet we stayed up most of the night with a real log fire blazing on the hearth, and Dick and I and campaign aides plotted strategy and making last minute phone solicitations, while you and Doris provided coffee and donuts and cookies and made sure we lacked nothing. We couldn't get to Manchester until one-and-a-half days later. I remember those days as the best time we ever had together. We won that primary, I might add, thanks to you and Doris and Richard and our campaign team, plus the goodwill of a lot of decent, hardworking American folks.

"As you begin your journey into eternity, Evelyn, a journey that every one of us ultimately must make alone, I want you to know that you go with the spirit of America behind you and with you every inch of the way. Your family wishes you *bon voyage*. Doris and I wish you Godspeed.

The American people wish you well on that journey. Goodbye, Evelyn. God bless you. God bless America."

The president and Mrs. Deakin faded. Evelyn Walsh's face appeared, bespectacled, filling the screen. A photograph taken in her late forties. In the backdrop, strains of music from her favorite composer, Mozart. Coincidentally or otherwise, it was the maestro's last piece, *Requiem—Lacrimosa.*

The Reverend Gilbert Sloane stepped forward. "Make your peace with God, Evelyn," he intoned. "For the Lord giveth and the Lord taketh away."

Nobody spoke during Reverend Sloane's administration of the Last Rites. They knew that in the White House, President and Mrs. Deakin watched by video hookup. When he finally put aside the Episcopal Church's Book of Common Prayer, he moved to one side of the bed and said softly, "You may say your goodbyes to Evelyn."

They stepped forward, one by one, braving the mechanical hiss of the respirator, to kiss Evelyn Walsh on the cheek, the forehead, wherever was appropriate. Norma, expectedly, lingered. Dick Jr. was businesslike but deeply moved. He fought back tears. His wife Sue cried openly. Vice President Walsh could not move, being in traction. His bed was pulled close enough for the ICU nurse to take Evelyn's withered hand and place it in his. A brief squeeze that took in more than forty years of marriage. Tears flowed from the vice president's eyes.

It was time to disconnect the respirator.

Dr. Nogarth moved to the console to guide Norma Delbecki. Her husband supported her physically. Tears streamed freely down her cheeks. She leaned against her husband, hesitating. "I can't do this, Jim. Help me. I can't murder Mom!"

Jim Delbecki was firm. "We discussed this issue, pet. You're not murdering anyone. Take a deep breath."

"Jim, please—"

Her husband said gently, "You don't have to do it, pet. It's symbolic. You were always her favorite, and wherever she is, I'm sure Evelyn would prefer you do it. You are setting her free, giving her permission to quit all this misery. Think of it that way."

Norma quieted, though she looked as though her legs would give out under her. Dr. Nogarth, like some official, white-coated harbinger of death, pointed out which buttons to push, which switches to turn. Norma went through the sequence. A high-pitched alarm went off, startling everyone. The hissing monster ground to a halt.

"That one's for us," Dr. Nogarth said, quickly pushing buttons that silenced the alarm. The room became deathly quiet. The monitors hooked up to Evelyn Walsh each sounded their individual, urgent alarms and were silenced or switched off. The nurse gently removed the breathing tube and all the IVs and the colostomy bag.

Evelyn Walsh was off life-support.

She defied them all.

She did not die at once. She lingered on for two hours, thirteen minutes, and forty-two seconds, before translating into the endless mists of time.

———

Manassas.
Manassas Municipal/Davis Airport resembled a thousand other general aviation airports around the country. A large parking lot behind the low-shingle Fixed Base Operator (FBO) building, a Phillips-66 aviation billboard on the roof next to the cavernous hangar through the open portals of which could be seen three or four single-engine recips and one Baron B-55 in various stages of maintenance. Davis Municipal was served by one regional airline using Bombardier CRJs. Apart from the ubiquitous Cessna and Piper singles, the ramp also held a King Air B-200, a Rockwell Commander 1000, a Cessna 310, and an A-36 Bonanza.

The Engineer stayed in the van while Nabil went inside the FBO. There was no avoiding it; he had to get the charts. Inside was mainstream FBO: the attractive woman behind the polished linoleum counter; a lounge area to one side with two men watching television, another idly flipping through magazines on the low glass table; a fourth man in sport coat and colorful tie returning from a trip to the coffee pot beside the microwave and vending machine. These men were probably the crews for the King Air and Commander twins. Two hungry-looking flight instructors—you couldn't miss the type—were in evidence: one stood, hands in pockets, gazing wistfully at the flight line through the glass enclosure; another talked earnestly with a student in a corner.

The counter girl smiled at Nabil. "Can I help you?"

"I need local IFR charts."

"Sure." She pointed to a glass display case with stacks of blue Jeppesen area charts arranged neatly. "Which ones would you be wanting, sir?"

"Just the local area charts."

"That'd be Section 1 and 2."

She took the charts from the display case and handed them to Nabil. *United States Northeast Corridor Area Chart.* He opened it to Section 2, the New York–Washington area. He found Washington–National (DCA) easily, and southwest of that, Manassas Harry Davis Municipal. Just northeast of DCA (and the White House!) was College Park Airport, Maryland. This was the correct chart.

"I'll take this."

While she rang him up, he wondered about approach plates for the area. He wouldn't be making any landings so he didn't really need them. He would file his destination as College Park, but that was a ruse. He would get off the airway and crash the airplane into the White House. Yes, still he needed the approach charts for tower, departure, en route, and terminal frequencies.

"I'd like to make copies of local approach charts," he said.

"Oh, sure. NOS or Jeppesen?"

"Jeppesen."

"Hang on. I'll get you the manuals."

While she went over to the Chief Pilot's office—he could tell from the inscription on the door—the daydreaming flight instructor sauntered over, hands buried in his pockets.

"Fly, do you?"

What a stupid question. Not only do I fly, you heard me ask for IFR charts, which suggests I'm probably instrument-rated, therefore a tick above your average private pilot. Nabil wished the man would just . . . disappear.

"Yes." Maybe reticence would do the trick.

Instead, the man stuck out a hand. "Jerry Stockman. Chief flight instructor."

Nabil took the hand reluctantly. "Chuck Bermoghuli." The name just jumped to his lips.

"Base here?"

"No." Nabil waved vaguely. "College Park area."

"Ha. That's Dan Daggert's turf. Flies a Seneca. Good pilot. Friend of mine."

"He's probably alright," Nabil said carefully.

"Mean son of a gun, that's what."

"I wouldn't know. I . . . don't fraternize much with other fliers there."

The girl returned carrying the Jeppesens, saving Nabil from further banter with the hungry flight instructor. "You can make copies over there in the corner. Ten cents a copy." She smiled at him. "Donation for the coffee pot."

"No problem."

He made copies of both College Park and Manassas Municipal approach plates and airport diagrams. As he returned the original charts to the desk, he caught sight of a thin blue file folder labeled *Hangar List.* He resisted the impulse to reach out and open its pages. That might not raise eyebrows, but the last thing he wanted was to draw attention to his quest. He collected a couple of flight-plan forms from the counter, thanked the receptionist and nodded to the hungry flight instructor, who was staring wanly out the glass doors. He went outside to the back where the Engineer was waiting in the van.

The T-hangars were on the same side of the field as the FBO, farther down, opposite the last third of the runway. He guided the Engineer down the access road to where the line of zinc-roofed hangars began. The van drove slowly down each hangar lane. A few hangar doors were open, their owners tinkering around inside. A couple of airplanes had been pulled outside of the hangars and were being preflighted.

Nabil and the Engineer peered through each open door as they passed, hoping for a glimpse of Dr. Polk's Tucano warbird. No luck. The white fuel bowser bearing the Phillips-66 decal was refueling a two-tone Cessna Centurion in front of a hangar door. The Tucano was probably inside one of the closed hangars. Another possibility—one that held stark terror for Nabil—was that Polk's warbird might be inside the FBO maintenance hangar or out of the airport entirely for a periodic check. If that were the case, he had a contingency plan. He also had another plan to obtain the number of Dr. Polk's hangar.

He directed the Engineer back to the blacktop shoulder facing the hangars where several cars were parked, their owners away on business or pleasure trips with their airborne toys. The lineboy had finished refueling the Centurion and was winding back the long, thick, black hose. Nabil motioned for the Engineer to kill the engine.

"Wait here," Nabil told him.

Nabil got out of the car and walked toward the bowser. The lineboy had entered the open hangar and brought out a red towbar. He fitted the ends to the two lugholes in the Centurion's nosegear strut, and looked up as Nabil approached.

"Hi."

Nabil grabbed the Centurion's right wing leading edge. "You definitely need help here."

"Thanks." The boy was about eighteen years old, shortish, with an unruly blond mop crowning his head. "I can usually manage if it's not uphill. Just about anything but the twins. The owners help anyway. Some of them have power winches."

He didn't seem to mind the extra muscle. The Cessna rolled onto her berth—two depressed ruts in the hard soil. Nabil watched the lineboy operate the electric winch that lowered the huge split door from the hangar roof and completely enclosed the hangar. When it stopped moving, the lineboy stepped out neatly through a smaller side door, which he locked with his master key.

"Thanks for the help."

"Anytime."

"You must be new around here."

"Yes. Chuck Bermoghuli." Nabil stuck out a hand. *I must be running out of names.*

The boy took it. "Todd."

A Mercury Marquis, driven by an aristocratic-looking man with his equally patrician wife beside him, cruised around the corner of the hangar lane and pulled up beside the bowser.

"Morning, Todd."

"Morning, Mr. Siskel."

"I need to get her topped up. Just came in from Richmond. The door's open."

"Sure thing."

"Be seeing ya." The powered window rolled up soundlessly and the big sedan glided off.

Nabil smiled at Todd. "Sounds like fun. Mind if I ride with you on this one?"

The youth looked uncertain for only a second. "Sure. Hop in."

Nabil hoisted himself inside the driver's cab. While Todd checked off figures on his clipboard and left the cab to take meter readings from the last fueling, Nabil quickly ran his eyes down the typed hangar list clipped to the dashboard. He flipped to the next page and the next. *Voila! Polk, Maxwell, Dr. Hangar 43.* Every hangar tenant's home address and telephone number was listed beneath the name.

"Fly around here, do you?" Todd's voice jolted him. He was climbing back into the cab.

"Up north."

"Oh, yeah?" Todd wrestled the gear into place and the truck lurched forward.

"A friend and I bought an old Comanche. We're thinking of basing it here. What kind of people do you have here?"

"Um, well, they're okay. Judges, lawyers, doctors, self-made businessmen, engineers, accountants. We've got all types. Decent folks. A few shysters, but then you get them anywhere."

The Siskels' hangar was number sixteen, as far as one could wish from Hangar 43. The door was open, as the man had promised. The big Piper single—a Saratoga—had already been pushed inside the hangar. Todd parked the bowser outside Hangar 16. The portable VHF transceiver on his belt clip, which had been crackling static all along, came alive.

"Todd, where are you?" Nabil recognized the voice of the counter girl.

Todd unclipped the transceiver and spoke into it. "Busy."

"Galloway just called. Hangar twenty-nine. He wants his Duchess topped off—fourteen gallons each side. He'll be along in one hour. Got that?"

"Fourteen per side?"

"Affirmative."

"Got it."

"What's your location?"

"I'm doing Siskel. Sixteen."

"Well, I got two transients here, and one of them needs Jet A. Conrad's up here, and I guess he's checked out to handle the Jet A truck, isn't he?"

"He sure is. I checked him out myself."

"I hear you. The other customer is an Arrow parked in front here. Needs one hundred, low lead. How soon can you get here?"

"Ten minutes too long?"

"Five, Todd. Please. Five minutes. He's in a hurry. Got that, Todd?"

"Gotcha."

"Over and out."

Todd sulked as he re-holstered the radio. He zeroed the meter counter and pulled out the fueling hose in a huff, tugging it toward the Saratoga.

"I thought there were regulations against fueling an airplane inside a hangar," Nabil said.

Todd looked up in surprise. "Where did you get that from? Anyways, the door is wide open. The fumes don't have a chance to accumulate."

Fueling the Saratoga took almost five minutes. Nabil helped Todd close the huge corrugated zinc doors. As he took meter readings, Todd said without looking up, "They want me back on the ramp. Want a ride down there?"

"Thanks, but no. My car's up here. Thanks for me letting me observe."

Todd accepted his proffered hand. "Anytime, Chuck."

The bowser lurched off. Nabil walked back to the van. Inside, the Engineer slouched back in his seat with the window only half open, oblivious to the sickly, plastic smell of the explosives that suffused the cabin. Nabil had forgotten the sharp, ether-like signature of certain explosives and wondered what cocktail the Engineer had prepared. Whatever it was, it had to be powerful enough to level the White House while the pod rockets took out the adjoining East and West Wings. Nabil was pleased to note that, as instructed, the Engineer had brought along two walkie-talkies. He took one and told the Engineer to listen on the other. And alert Nabil if anyone happened by.

Hangar 43 was in the fourth tier of corrugated zinc structures. As soon as the fuel bowser disappeared around the corner toward the FBO ramp, the Engineer nudged the van forward. He pulled up in front of Hangar 43, and once Nabil jumped down, he moved off back to the access road to keep watch.

Nabil inserted one of his three master keys into the lock, but the door was already open. Why on earth, he wondered, would someone spend hundreds of thousands of dollars—perhaps millions—to acquire an airplane, and yet couldn't be bothered to buy a simple lock to protect that investment? Something to do, perhaps, with the American male's bloated sense of invulnerability.

He groped for the light switch. Even before the light came on, he could feel the presence of the Tucano: sleek, sexy, menacing. The harsh white light of two filament bulbs as he flicked the switch confirmed that impression. It was a new and expensive machine. An EMB-312 Tucano turbo-prop with tandem seats. On the nose cowling up to the spinner there was painted a great white shark with knifelike, multi-pronged teeth jutting from an open jaw. The shark's bulbous red eye, the serrated sharp teeth, and the snarling rictus of rage gave the impression of ferocious attack. He could see the plate scars in the wings where the Browning or Gatling machine guns had been removed, probably for cosmetic reasons and for the drag penalty they exacted. The four hardpoint mounts were still there.. Had they not been, in. less than one hour, the Engineer's silent burr drill and a few attachment bolts would have added a seven-rocket pod to each wing and turn a general aviation turboprop into a fighter airplane. Third World banana republics did that all the time. The bubble canopy enclosed the two tandem seats. Still, the Engineer had some work to do

Nabil climbed onto the left wing. Everything was there.

A pilot's dream. Full cockpit instrumentation, businesslike, hightech. Dominating both cockpits were two Martin-Baker Mk8L zero-zero ejection seats. Nabil could see the firing handle in front of each seat pan. The safety rods were in place, duly flagged to prevent accidental firing. He could see the canopy breakers on the seat shoulders which was good in case the top latch failed to release.

Nasser had been wrong: the good doctor hadn't deactivated any of the ejection seats. The parachute was the GQ Type 1000 Mk 2, drogue assisted..

It was all there and all quite deadly. Just removing the red-flagged safety rod would arm the seat for ejection. Nabil remembered an incident he'd read about some years ago at an airshow. It had occurred during a static display when a spectator leaned too far inside the cockpit of—was it an F-4 Phantom?—and inadvertently pulled the firing handle while trying to straighten up. When the thunder and the smoke cleared, the man's abbreviated torso thumped back to earth only feet away from where the hot seat landed after its rocket-velocity ride to four hundred feet.

Nabil breathed easier. He got down from the wing. In a corner of the hangar a wooden recliner sat beside a desktop refrigerator. Heaped on the floor were several cans of Mobil turbine oil and some old magazines. A second recliner, folded up, was propped against the wall. Mrs. Polk's sun recliner. On the wall beside the recliner hung a gray flight suit with helmet.

He pried open the pressurized fuel caps and peered inside. The fuel was below the gauze filter cup. He couldn't tell how much fuel was in the airplane. It certainly wasn't full. He replaced the caps.

Reaching into the rear cockpit, he looked for the battery master switch and flicked it on. The panel came alive, an alert pinged, and the fuel capacitor gauges rose. The tank was about a quarter full. He flicked off the master and permitted himself a smile. The more he found out about Dr. Polk, the more he wanted to meet the man. No doubt the man was as meticulous in his flying as in his medical practice. Many general aviation pilots routinely filled up their tanks after every flight, when in reality it was more prudent to wait until one was sure of the destination and payload. Less fuel allowed more payload. Full tanks never did allow full payload in most airplanes.

Nabil had been worried about the amount of fuel in the Tucano, because he knew the Engineer's cocktail of explosives could weigh anywhere from six hundred to one thousand kilograms or more. He wanted the Tucano to be able to lift off the ground.

He thumbed the transmit button on the walkie-talkie and spoke in Arabic. "Are you there, brother?"

After about five seconds, the Engineer answered, "I'm here, my brother. The coast is clear."

"Check again. When you are sure nobody will come in the next three minutes, bring the van and let's unload the stuff."

"Okay."

In less than a minute, the van pulled up outside the small entrance to Dr. Polk's hangar. The Engineer spilled out, the van's sliding door rolled back, and the Engineer lifted the first box so Nabil could see how he handled the delicate high explosive. Then the two men quietly and quickly began hauling boxes inside. Three minutes later, the boxes and the cords, wires and fuses, were inside the hangar.

"The rear cockpit only," Nabil said, indicating where the Engineer should place the explosives. "And any baggage lockers you see."

Ordinarily, the Tucano was flown from the front seat with the instructor sitting in the rear. But no instructor, even with full military gear, would weigh as much as the thousand pounds or more of explosives the Engineer intended to put there. And Nabil wanted the center of gravity to be within or not too far off limits. If all that weight went in the front, clearly there would be a forward c.g. problem.

"And I need a two-minute fuse," Nabil went on. "Can you give me a two-minute fuse?" After ejection, he wanted to be clear of the White House and on solid ground before the explosion.

The Engineer looked up. "Two-minute fuse? What for? This is a martyrdom operation, is it not, my brother?"

Then he saw the ejection seat and the parachute, and everything became clear. He looked steadily at Nabil, who stared back.

Nabil shrugged. "The means to eject is there. Why not use it?"

"I do not have fuses. It was not among the things you requested." The Engineer gave a half-smile. "But I am a professional, and I anticipate everything. I have a small fuse. You will have only one minute."

He went back to work.

"Thank you, brother. One minute will be enough."

"I cannot guarantee it. The impact against the white satanic house can set everything off, and you will not have had even one second."

"With you, I am willing to take that chance."

"Thanks. I try." And softly, "Now go and keep watch and let me work, please, brother."

Already his eyes were abstracted, maniacal, the decadent, sweaty effluvium rising from his overalls in a vile, unseen mist. Death comes in an unsavory whiff. His fingers, fondling the deadly fulminate, had a delicate, lover's touch, and the tip of his tongue lolled absently, so absolute was his concentration.

It occurred to Nabil that the Engineer liked his work, liked creating explosions and bringing down structures. The bigger the blast the better, and his job was to mold the blast and adjust the cocktail to suit the occasion, and leave a resounding fireball in his wake. The human cost, the dismemberments, maiming, ruined lives, devastated families—these were collateral, unfortunate, and one didn't think too much about them.

The Engineer himself was taking a big risk, one he knew he could handle well: he knew at least two different bombers who had died while assembling bombs or blown up in the aftermath of their own concoctions.

"How many kilos can you take?" asked the Engineer.

Nabil considered. He hadn't looked at the pilot's manual of the Tucano to gauge the payload, but given the low fuel state, the powerful turboprop engine, and the reality that the Tucano was designed for military applications, he had no doubt that the Tucano could lift two thousand pounds of explosives.

"One tonne," he told the Engineer. "Everything you have. Maybe one and a half tonnes." One thousand kilograms of high explosive would destroy most of the White House. Two thousand kilos would level it.

The Engineer nodded. "The rear cockpit will not be large enough. Unless you want me to stuff it in all the nooks and corners?"

"Baggage compartment, if any. No nooks. You think you can install the rocket pods?"

"No problem."

"Please, brother, try not to drill into the fuel tank and spark a fire."

"No chance of that. Trust me."

Nabil left the Engineer to his work and drove the van to a vantage point near the exit from where he could monitor all movements to and from the hangar area.

He was reaching for the keys to kill the engine when the digital pager on his belt-clip beeped. The late Jim Freidman had given one each to Nabil, Beria, and Grimsky with orders to carry it on their person at all times so that Boris could reach them in an emergency without compromising telephone security.

Nabil's first impulse had been to throw it away on the suspicion that it was yet another tracking device, but he was glad now he had kept it. The pager had a small LCD face and could display a message of up to thirty words by scrolling laterally. Nabil depressed the "Receive" switch and watched a short message scroll. *Cancel Today's Flight. Repeat, Cancel. Will Explain. Plan For Tomorrow (Tue) 3 p.m.. Boris.*

He scrolled the message twice to make sure he had missed nothing. Why the further delay?

Damn Boris. Damn all of them.

A tall man in faded jeans and blue denim jacket came around the corner carrying a red toolbox. The man walked purposefully to a green Ford pickup three cars down from Nabil's van. The toolkit was thrown into the pickup's flatbed; the man cast a cursory glance at Nabil and heaved himself into the cab. The starter groaned and the pickup jerked slowly down the blacktop.

Was it Nabil's imagination or did the Ford's brake lights flare briefly at the door of Hangar 43? The pickup turned left at the south verge road and headed toward the FBO building. Nabil felt a prickle of apprehension.

Twenty minutes passed.

Thirty.

Nabil fought the instinct to talk to the Engineer on the talkie. He knew the risks. Wave propagation could send rogue transmissions to nearby AM/FM radios or other handheld VHF radios.

Forty minutes.

One hour, fifteen minutes.

He couldn't resist any longer. He keyed the mike. "How goes it, brother?"

A long pause, then, "Just fine. Give me twenty minutes more."

Nabil clicked the mike button twice to acknowledge.

Normal activity at the airport. Todd's fuel truck crisscrossed the hangar area twice. Nabil pretended to be absorbed in a book whenever the bowser went by

His walkie-talkie crackled. One hour, forty-four minutes. "I'm ready, brother."

Nabil reached to answer the walkie-talkie just as a brown Chrysler Estate wagon cruised slowly by. The woman behind the wheel turned into the third hangar lane.

"Hold it," Nabil whispered into the walkie-talkie.

After about two minutes, he heard the creaking and rattling of a door opening in the third tier of hangars. Was the woman in the Estate bringing out her airplane for preflight? After a further sixty seconds with no change in the situation, Nabil spoke into the walkie-talkie. "Okay, brother. Road's clear. Come out now."

The Engineer stepped out smartly from Hangar 43, shut the zinc-covered entry door, and walked casually up the blacktop toward the van, his brown satchel swinging. He climbed in beside Nabil and dropped the satchel on the cab floor. If police stopped them for even a minor traffic violation, Nabil mused, and the contents of the satchel were discovered, both men would be arrested instantly on suspicion of burglary and possession of burglary tools.

The Engineer sighed. "All done." He reached inside the dashboard console and lifted a McDonald's takeout bag. He unwrapped a double-decker quarter pounder cheeseburger and sank his teeth into it. Nabil's elbow nudged his arm. He looked up and froze.

A GMC four-wheel drive with a snowplow bucket attached to the front end had pulled up in front of Hangar 43. A man in blue windbreaker and baseball cap got out. A half-smoked stogie was clamped between his teeth. The man pulled out a bunch of keys and let himself into the hangar.

CHAPTER 31

Manassas.

Ron Trasco had an outstanding fuel bill and, after locking up his hangar, he drove over to the FBO office to take care of it. As he paid with his Visa card, he said to the receptionist, "By the way, you might want to send someone to check on old Max Polk's hangar. Forty-three, I think it is. My hangar is back of his, and I thought I heard radio static and transmissions coming from inside. I drove past it and didn't see anyone. Must have left the master on or something."

"I'll have it checked out." The girl handed him his receipt. "Thanks, Mr. Trasco."

"And there's this dark-red Dodge van with New Jersey plates sitting by the hangars. Been there a while. You got a new customer just moved in?"

"Not that I'm aware of."

"Probably nothing."

"We'll check it out."

"Good idea. Don't do anything I wouldn't do, Sherry."

"Bet on that."

"Good girl. Take care"

As soon as Trasco left, the receptionist moved to the Unicom radio atop a low metal filing cabinet. She picked up the mike. "Jerry?"

Three seconds later, a crackle and a muffled, "Yeah?"

"Check out Hangar 43. Someone must have left the master switch on. Got that?"

"Got it."

"While you're at it, you might want to check out a dark-red Dodge van with New Jersey plates parked on the hangar lot. See if the owner's anywhere around and just generally check it out. Okay?"

"On my way."

Jerry DeFelitta was the security guard and resident handyman at the regional airport. In winter, he drove the snowplow that cleared the runways and taxiways and access roads. In spring and summer, he trimmed the hedges and the grass that flourished from the ramp to the runup pad and between the runway and taxiway. In autumn, he raked leaves. He was doing that when he got the call to investigate the radio static from Hangar 43. He climbed into his GMC pickup, which he'd already fixed up with a front-end scoop bucket in anticipation of the season's first serious white stuff, and drove toward the hangars.

He entered number 43 using his official keys and flicked on the lights.

He noticed at once the dark green tarp covering a length of each wing. *Wouldn't put it past ol' Doc Polk to install real-looking machine guns,* he mused. *The good doc liked that authentic fighter pilot feel. What an ego! Crazy dude.* He lifted the tarp.

Wrong. A circular seven-pod rocket launcher. Ditto for the other wing. No kidding. Even had authentic-looking live rockets. Well, Polk had really outdone himself this time. DeFelitta knew that Polk showed off his airplane and performed at select air shows around the country. Didn't surprise him none, the doctor's attempts at verisimilitude. He closed the tarp.

He climbed onto the short cockpit ladder propped up against the fuselage and inspected the front cockpit. He had performed this task numerous times in the past. Sometimes pilots returning from short trips pushed their steeds into the hangar with the master switch still on and gyros spinning away. By the next morning, they would have a flat battery. Sometimes the owner himself would call and ask Jerry to check that they hadn't inadvertently left the master switch on. Other times, if the radios were left on and somebody heard the static, Jerry would be alerted.

DeFelitta was a weekend pilot with a PPL and the pilots trusted him not to touch the wrong switches on their airplanes. The Tucano was strangely silent. No whirring of gyros, no muted hum of the avionics fan. The rear cockpit was loaded with a bunch of stuff covered by a gray tarp that obscured the instrument panel. The hangar had a sickly sweet smell DeFelitta usually associated with hospital operating rooms. What the hell was Doc Polk up to?

No red lights; the gyros had tumbled long ago. The cockpit was more silent than a tomb. He found the battery switch and enabled it. Instantly the panel lit up, the gyros whirled crazily, and the annunciators blinked. He checked the radios; they were already turned off. He flicked off the master, rechecked the radios to make sure they were not hot-wired to the battery. Negative on that. Next he checked the portable standby VHF transceiver clipped to the side panel. A lot of pilots who flew single engine had that. One of those gizmos you could buy from Sporty's or Amazon. Came in useful if total electrical failure occurred. That, too, was turned off.

Definitely the radio static had not been coming from this airplane. Maybe from the adjacent hangar. He listened for a few minutes. Nothing. He climbed down. Maybe someone had gotten here before him and switched off the master. He looked again at the big, empty boxes that littered one side of the hangar. Dr. Polk was a queer one. Fancied himself a top gun or something. DeFelitta shook his head. Just another rich dude who couldn't find enough ways to spend his money.

He left the hangar, closing the door behind him. He drove the GMC pickup to where the maroon Dodge van was parked. He pulled up alongside the driver's door and found himself at eye level with two men. The one behind the wheel was hawk faced and had vaguely familiar features. The other had a ferocious beard and the disheveled appearance of a buccaneer. The two men ate silently from a McDonald's takeout bag on the center console. Both men had close-knit watchful eyes. Beady eyes. DeFelitta knew those eyes.

DeFelitta decided on his best friendly cop voice. "Morning. You guys need any help with something?"

The hawk-faced one shook his head. "Just looking." He ate with his left hand. His right remained out of sight.

"You been here a while. Any problem?"

The hawk stopped chewing. He looked DeFelitta straight in the eye. DeFelitta looked straight into the embers of a fire shot straight from hell. A chill coursed down his spine. These men were dangerous.

"We're citizens. Got any law against parking here?"

"I got a right to ask," DeFelitta shot back. "I'm the security man around here." He tapped the ID tag clipped to his shirt pocket.

The hawk looked impressed. "That explains it. We saw you enter a hangar just now. We thought maybe you owned an airplane."

"I don't own one. I was just checking out a report on some radio chatter. Thought someone had left the master on. No dice."

The hawk seemed to relax. He gave DeFelitta a bored look. "Okay. Maybe we are trespassing." He held up a wallet with an FBI shield on it and lowered it. "Or perhaps it's the other way round, buddy. We got a job to do, just like you."

DeFelitta deflated like a balloon. "Feds, huh? You guys should have said so."

"You didn't ask."

"Got a stakeout hereabouts?"

The hawk wolfed down his cheeseburger before replying. "Not at liberty to discuss. Sorry."

"Oh, I understand."

"But if we're in your way, just say the word and we'll move to another spot. But we rather like where we're at."

"No, no. You stay right there. Wouldn't get in the Feds' way for any reason." DeFelitta ran a spotty hand through his hair, front to back. "I'll be darned. I applied to the MPD twice. No dice. Best I could get was auxiliary in some crummy sheriff's backwater. Here I am, part-time guard, part-time handyman. A stakeout, huh? Shipment of forbidden merchandise, I bet?"

Nabil gave him a look that was both pitying and scathing. DeFelitta said hurriedly, kicking his 4WD into drive, "Well, if you guys need backup, just holler."

"Thanks. We have our own backup."

DeFelitta drove off. He had a .38 Special in the glove compartment but had never used it in violent action. A few things puzzled him. FBI agents with foreign accents were one thing. He had always thought of Hoover's boys as clean-cut and in dark-gray suits. These two men looked like thugs. Or maybe they were genuinely undercover and had to act that way. Still, there was the genuine FBI badge and the New Jersey license plates. The Feds had no state boundary restrictions to speak of. As for the accent, he blamed Affirmative Action. Probably the reason he got shoved aside twice by the Metropolitan Police Force—to make room for culturally disadvantaged minorities. Heck, he was beginning to think white was the wrong color.

It did cross DeFelitta's mind that perhaps the two men were not exactly what they said they were. But the FBI shield decided him. As a former sheriff's auxiliary, he knew a genuine Department of Justice badge when he saw one—not the dollar-and-a-quarter imitation sold on the internet. He had read somewhere in the past few days about two Fibbies being killed inside a restroom in the Capitol. Perhaps these two men were pursuing a lead and were in disguise.

Unfortunately for DeFelitta, law enforcement agencies investigating a serious crime often withhold one or two crucial pieces of information from public knowledge, information that would be known only to the perpetrator. In this instance, the FBI had chosen to withhold the fact that the murderer, or murderers, of their two agents in the Capitol restroom had also made away with an FBI badge. If he had known that a shield had been stolen from a fallen agent, DeFelitta might have acted differently.

Instead, he picked up the truck radio and called the front desk, "Sherry?"

"Yes, Jerry?"

"All taken care of. I'm gonna take off for a couple of minutes, get me a cup of coffee and something to eat."

"Gotcha."

DeFelitta drove straight for the maintenance hangar office wedged behind the FBO lounge.

"Dumbass," Nabil said after DeFelitta had gone. "No wonder he couldn't make the MPD."

The Engineer wasn't so sure. He was going over the security man's possible thought processes. Radio chatter inside a closed hangar, suspicious equipment in the rear cockpit of a Tucano, rocket launchers, two men in a van. DeFelitta could put two and two together and summon help. But this didn't bother Nabil. There was Plan B.

DeFelitta never did know how close he came to dying. Nabil's gun was on the console beneath the food tray, the Engineer's inside the right pocket of his overalls. If events had taken a wrong turn, either man would have shot DeFelitta. Plan B would have commenced right then. Polk's airplane would be pulled out of the hangar; Nabil would take off and crash the airplane into the White House. President Deakin may or may not be there—he probably wasn't, considering the beeper message from Boris—but the White House would be destroyed, and that was a major portion of the mission accomplished. That was what Boris was waiting for: for the president and most of his cabinet to be in the White House when the bomb hit. The target destroyed, the president and his policy makers killed.

"Good thing about the tarpaulin," the Engineer said. "I covered everything."

"You think he saw the explosives?"

"If he lifted the tarpaulin, yes. But I disguised everything. Trust me. Unless he's a trained ordnance expert, he wouldn't know what he was looking at. No wires or anything. Well, one arming wire, but hard to find."

"Where did you get the tarpaulin? From the hangar?"

"No. I brought it along in the van."

"Good."

Nabil shoved the badge back into his coat pocket.

"Where to?" asked the Engineer.

"Town. Supermarket. I need supplies."

As Nabil drove to a nearby supermarket—both men looking out for surveillance cues in case they had underestimated DeFelitta—Nabil briefed the Engineer.

He brought out the flight plan forms he had taken from the FBO counter. He had already filled in details of the Tucano's proposed flight, listing College Park, Maryland as destination. He showed the Engineer how to call the Flight Service Station (FSS) to file the flight plan. He was to do it tomorrow, about 1 p.m., listing the estimated time of departure as 3 p.m. The flight plan would be activated automatically once Nabil took off and contacted Approach. He went over the details again and again and the Engineer said no problem, it was easy. Nabil could have filed an electronic flightplan himself if he had a smartphone. But a smartphone would have just led the FBI to their location.

At the supermarket near the airport access road, Nabil went in and bought two gallons of spring water, assorted snacks and cookies, and a six-pack of Coke.

Back at the Harry P. Davis Municipal, at the T-hangars, they scooted into Hangar 43 again. The Engineer quickly showed Nabil the arming switch for the two thousand-pound improvised explosive device. Once armed, the IED would detonate after one minute. But it likely would detonate on impact, regardless of the position of the switch, since it was not an encased bomb; he had designed it to detonate rather than disseminate after impact. That was the best he could do for the Contractor. His ejection scheme might not work.

The Engineer got into the van and started the engine. A brief wave and he was gone.

Nabil locked himself inside Dr. Polk's hangar. From now on, he was committed. If for any reason Dr. Polk decided to check on his airplane, Nabil would kill him along with whoever was accompanying him, push out the Tucano, and activate Plan B. If he came accompanied by an FBI posse, Nabil would fight to the death. He deposited the food, snacks, water, and Coca-Cola cans on the floor beside the recliner. Then he took off his shoes and sank into the seat.

He sighed. This would be his home for the next twenty-four hours.

———

Moscow.

They had been flown in from Novosibirsk the night before in an Aeroflot A-320. They were now inside Lefortovo prison, the stockade just outside Moscow. Five prisoners—pale, haggard, in summer shirts and cheap linen coats—were accompanied by guards in long winter coats and furry astrakhans. November in Moscow is like winter in the rest of Europe, and on this day—the second day of snowfall—the condemned men shuffled out to face a firing squad. Among them were a former KGB double-agent betrayed by a high-ranking American named Aldrich Ames; two serial rapists, of whom one had already been chemically castrated through a massive infusion of testosterone; a dissident poet and activist who had murdered a prison guard during an escape attempt; and a bank robber who had killed three men. But, of course, none of the selected spectators knew any of this.

From a louvered enclosure, select newsmen watched. They represented the major television and news agencies: BBC, CNN, Sky News, AP, ITN, Reuters, ABC, NBC, and CBS. One German, one French, one Swiss, and one Dutch reporter had also been selected.

The men straggled single file into the courtyard execution ground. Several news correspondents wondered why all the condemned men looked so sickly—one was positively limping, seemingly in great pain. Could this ragtag team possibly have plotted a coup to overthrow Russian

President Mikhail Grachev? Could they have executed the bombing of the University of Illinois supercomputer building in America? Perhaps they had been beaten and tortured terribly, as per Russian tradition, to extract information prior to their execution.

The newsmen watched as, one by one, the men were lined up against the courtyard wall—a wall stained brown by previous executions. Afterward, the cleaners would move in with buckets and brushes and soapy water to sanitize the wall and the ground around it for the next use. The men were tied to retaining posts against the wall, and black hoods were placed over their faces. An Orthodox priest hovered in the corridor of the east wing; he had been denied access to the condemned men. He lowered his head and administered the last rites across a hundred-yard gulf.

Six riflemen marched into the courtyard and took up their positions. A Soviet officer from a Hussar regiment read the official sentence of death—it was brief—and then gave the order.

The crash of the Kalashnikovs split the morning air.

Afterward, the reporters watched as a doctor examined the bodies and certified that they were dead. The laborers moved in and carted away the bodies for mass cremation.

———

The Reuters correspondent spoke to his editor over the telephone. "Yes, I can confirm that. Positively. Grigory Artemyev, Pyotr Gulev, Oleg Kalushkin, Yuri Zamyatin, and Mrislav Danilov. Those charged with the plot. They have all been shot dead."

"Are you sure of this, Jim?"

"As much as one can be. AP, Interfax, BBC, and the three American networks were there."

"These people were charged, tried, and executed in one week? That's preposterous."

"I'm with you on that one. It was too quick to be anything less than a charade. The Russian system defies logic sometimes."

"They can't shoot people like they did in the old Soviet Union. They're a democracy now. They'll never make it into the EU."

"My thoughts exactly. My sources say they were tried and convicted by a military tribunal. Tribunals are fast, and the death penalty still applies in the military."

The editor sighed across the line. Jim Curry was one of his best foreign correspondents. "Alright. We'll run it. Good show."

———

Manassas.

Nabil slept on the recliner for two hours. He awoke at 5:20 p.m. It was dark. He didn't dare switch on the hangar light; someone might see it from outside. He stretched, groping around in the dark toward an area of piled-up junk he had glimpsed earlier. Odds and ends, a Tanis heater that Dr. Polk probably used in the days when he'd had a recip airplane, before the Tucano, and a single hundred-watt light bulb with extension cord, also for preheating the recip on those below-zero nights when the oil would freeze solid and no amount of cranking would get the engine to turn over. The hundred-watt bulb would normally be inserted into the engine cowling, a broadcloth or thermal blanket placed over it to lock in the warmth and prevent the oil from congealing.

Nabil found the blanket in the darkness, folded it into a conical shape, and inserted the light bulb. He followed the extension cord to a small wall socket and flicked on the light.

Even inside the blanket, the bright glow blinded him momentarily. He made adjustments until he had what he wanted: just enough light to see by in the shadows, but not enough to show under the hangar door or roof beams. Later in the night, if it got much colder, he would use the warmth of the bulb or even the Tanis as needed. He found another socket and plugged in his walkie-talkie with the built-in adapter. In a couple of hours, it would be fully charged.

He ate two of the Twinkies and oatmeal cakes from the supermarket and washed it down with canned Coca-Cola. He unwrapped the egg salad also from the supermarket deli and worked on it with the plastic spoon and fork provided. Old editions of the *Post*, *New Yorker*, *Harpers*, and *Redbook* were piled on a mini shelf in the corner. Mrs. Polk's reading material while her husband slipped the surly bonds of earth in advanced aerobatics over the Virginia fields.

Nabil flipped through them idly in the dim light. Three times headlights swept down the hangar lane and receded. Around 9 p.m., he heard the heavy puttering breath of a big-six Continental approaching the hangar. Probably a Turbo Centurion or a Bonanza. The engine died. Male voices. The tortured creak of rusty hinges as the hangar was winched open. A car started inside the hangar and was driven out to make space for the airplane. Grunts and straining as the airplane was pushed inside, then more screeching of metal as the doors began their downward journey. Keys jangled, the door locked noisily. Car doors slammed, the car moved off. Silence.

Nabil loosened his grip on the Glock. The stillness of the night descended once again, its blackness broken now and again by the green-and-white flash of a civil airport beacon. The landlocked equivalent of a maritime buoy, the beacon was activated between sunset and sunrise, or at any other time when the visibility was less than the criteria for visual flight rules. A slithering sound, punctuated by episodes of nail scratching on rough surface, was audible from the adjoining hangars on each side. Rats? Raccoons? Nabil was bewildered. What could live out here among these aluminum berths? The sounds ceased, as if reading his thoughts. Just as he started to relax, the scratching sounds resumed with a vengeance.

By 10:30 p.m. Nabil had had enough of Mrs. Polk's magazines. He was also fighting an insistent call of nature—one he knew he would lose. His bowels would go any minute. The egg salad was to blame. Now that presented a problem. Or did it? He moved the covered bulb around and found a snow shovel in the corner. It was difficult with the flat spatula blade and he bent the blunt edge somewhat, but he dug a shallow hole in the firm soil. He removed his pants, squatted down over the hole and passed a long, solid, winding turd. He belted out a cathartic fart and watched his beer-colored urine streaming onto Dr. Polk's earthen floor. He waited for the second movement. It came rapidly, a belchy orgiastic evacuation, angry and frothy and mephitic. Ah, relief. He wiped his ass with an old copy of the *Post* and an old handkerchief and pasted it on top of his deposit.

The hangar stank.

What the hell. What can a man do? He felt several pounds lighter and much, much better. He rose, buttoned up, and used the shovel again to scoop back earth until the deposit was covered.

He switched off the hundred-watt bulb and removed the thermal blanket. He lay back on the recliner and, still fully clothed except for his shoes, draped the blanket over himself. Now he felt really warm. By 11 p.m., he was fast asleep.

Bright sunlight filtered in through cracks in the roof beam when he awoke. It had gotten really cold during the night, and he had thought of switching on the Tanis. But merely pulling the thermal blanket over his head warmed him enough, and he now woke up refreshed. He yawned, stretched, and did sixteen pushups on the floor before collapsing. Allah, he was out of shape. American food and the soft American life. He could have used some strong coffee. Instead, more oatmeal cakes and Twinkies and a pecan pie for breakfast, washed down with bottled spring water.

Three airplanes took off before 8 a.m. from the hangar area. Nabil sat in the front cockpit of the Tucano, familiarizing himself with the instruments and controls. He dug out the airplane's pilot's operating handbook, and with it on his lap and the Glock nearby on the glare shield, spent the next two-and-a-half hours digesting the manual. He studied the limitations and crammed vital specs in his head until he was sure he could fly the Tucano without in-flight reference to the manual. By 11 a.m., he had checked and rechecked his beeper; still no word from Boris. He climbed down from the Tucano, eased himself in a corner, and slept again.

At 1:10 p.m., he awoke for the second or third time. He sat, contemplating his fate. He willed himself up and did twelve pushups before running out of steam. He rested five minutes, then did more calisthenics to keep the circulation going.

Afterward, he looked at his watch. 2:03 p.m. The Engineer would have filed the flight plan by now. His intended flight would be in the ARTCC computers—a section of airspace within a specific time blocked off for him in the busy Washington, DC, corridor. They would not know of the deadly cargo he was carrying. Cargo that would rock the Capitol and destroy once again the bloated American sense of invulnerability. He almost smiled at the thought, but didn't. Pros didn't gloat.

He waited.

CHAPTER 32

Reston.

At Floss Mar School, headmistress Mrs. Agnes Pettijohn stepped inside one of her classrooms accompanied by a trim, dark-haired woman. Mrs. Pettijohn beamed at her wards.

"Good morning, boys and girls." Her singsong voice carried to every corner of the room.

"Good morning, Mrs. Pettijohn," came the refrain.

The hubbub dwindled.

"And now children, I want your attention. All of you." When she had complete silence, she said, "Mrs. Mulgrew is feeling a bit under the weather. She won't be coming until the afternoon. Miss Ferraro here beside me is your substitute teacher. She will take Mrs. Mulgrew's place for this morning only. Okay? Now I want all you boys and girls to give your utmost cooperation to Miss Ferraro." She paused, frowning. "Are you listening over there? Jennie? Rick?"

The two kids came to order slowly.

"Yes, Mrs. Pettijohn," said the one named Rick.

"Good. Now let's all welcome Miss Ferraro, boys and girls. And how do we do that?"

The children started clapping, and Agnes Pettijohn joined in. Janet Ferraro beamed throughout the ovation, though her trained eye quickly ran over the motley group of five- and six-year-olds and easily picked out Sandy Weasel from the Bureau's secret snapshots. The clapping subsided. Agnes Pettijohn looked at her expectantly.

Ferraro stepped forward. "Thank you, children." Her voice sounded firm enough. "Thank you for the warm welcome. I think we in turn should extend our appreciation to Mrs. Pettijohn for the good work she's been doing in this establishment. How about that? Let's give her a rousing appreciation."

Another round of clapping. Agnes Pettijohn flushed a deep red. Moisture flecked the pale-green eyes. "Thank you, children," she said, clearly moved. She leaned over and whispered to Ferraro, "Lunch is at eleven thirty. Good luck."

She fled.

Ferraro would remember the next two hours as some of the most memorable of her life. She realized that being a teacher required a lot of training and preparation. She had no lesson plan. Despite the quick briefing given by Agnes Pettijohn that morning, she found herself struggling to contain a rowdy group intent on vandalizing everything in sight or clobbering one another on the head when they thought she wasn't looking. In the end, she fell back on her own dimly remembered elementary school days, incorporating a modicum of academics into the current confusion. It was nearly eleven o'clock by the time she thought she had everything in order. That meant only thirty minutes until recess.

Thirty minutes in which to find out!

For the fifth exercise, a competition, she divided the class into groups of four. Each group had six blowup posters of famous personalities or controversial personalities to identify; four of the personalities would be well-known figures, such as former president Bill Clinton, Martin Luther King Jr., Kermit the Frog, Michael Jackson. The other two would be bonus mystery faces, and the students would get extra points if they could identify them. A tall order, Ferraro thought, having a bunch of five-year-olds trying to identify well-known faces but they did well for their age group.

So far, not one group had been able to identify one of the two mystery personalities she had circulated. It showed a handsome, sunburned figure with prominent sideburns in a navy or air force uniform, complete with peak cap, staring straight at the camera. Two children gave interesting guesses.

"That's an army officer?" one child ventured.

"Well, yes. What's the name of the army officer?"

"He's air force!" said another child.

"Well, no. He's in the armed forces, certainly. Not necessarily our armed forces. Well, Jimmy, why don't you let Kim finish her answer. She said army officer—she's on the right track. Kim?"

Kim pursed her lips, thinking hard.

"General Eisenhower?"

"Not quite, no. Half a point. Next picture."

Another tiny hand flew up.

"Yes?"

"That is Hitler?"

Ferraro laughed. "Not that either. Sorry, no bonus points." She contained her amusement. It was actually a picture of Libya's Colonel Muammar Gaddafi.

Ferraro wound her way down to Sandy Weasel's group, which consisted of one boy and three girls. Like all the others, the children's first names were spelled out in big letters across strips of paper on their desks. She picked up the posters and smiled at the group. "Now, Drake, Maryann, Connie, Sandy, ready to go?"

"We're ready, Miss F."

"Good. Let's start." She flipped to the first poster. "And who do we have here?"

Connie giggled. "Mr. Spock, from *Star Trek*?"

"Good. Score one point." She entered the point in her large notebook. "Next one, please?"

"Michael Jackson."

"Good, Drake. Two points. Next?"

Maryann spoke up. "That's Honest Abe."

"Use the proper name, Maryann."

"Abraham Lincoln."

"Good. Three points. We're really coming along, aren't we?" She flipped to the next poster.

"Ben Ten," Drake ventured.

"Nope. Want to try again?"

"Batman," Connie said quietly.

"Sorry, hon. Come on, Sandy, Maryann—are you going to let Drake and Connie do all the talking? Let's get some participation in here, okay?"

Silence. "Okay. No one? Going, going, gone—"

"Spiderman?" Sandy threw in.

Ferraro shook her head. "Sorry. No points for that one, Sandy. Nice try. It's actually Superman. Christopher Reeve's version. I shouldn't have thrown that in—you're too young to have seen it. My fault." Ferraro pushed back her hair, which had fallen over her eyes. "Anyway, three out of four is pretty good. Now to the first mystery person." She flipped to the next poster.

Blanks all around. "Anybody?"

"President Bush?" Maryann ventured.

"No, not at all. Absolutely no resemblance. Former president George W. Bush never had a moustache. Okay, next mystery person." And she flipped to the next poster.

Once more Ferraro thought she was drawing a blank and tried not to look at Sandy.

"That's Uncle Ted!" Sandy exclaimed.

"Excuse me?"

"Uncle Ted. That's him."

"Who's Uncle Ted?"

"Him." Sandy pointed at the blown up picture of the Contractor.

Ferraro said casually, "Is he really your uncle?"

"He's just Uncle Ted," Sandy insisted. "He's my mama's friend. He stays with us."

"Well, isn't that cute," Ferraro said. "I'm afraid you must be wrong, Sandy. No bonus points." She rose to collate the results of the competition on the pastel board.

"But who is he?" Drake interrupted. "I think I've seen him before."

Of course you have. On wanted posters all over America.

"I know that's Uncle Ted," Sandy said. "You can ask my mommy."

"Well, do you know his full name, Sandy? That could earn you the bonus point."

"We just call him Uncle Ted. He's been my mom's friend for about a week now."

"If you insist. But no bonus points. Okay?"

It was unfair to the girl, Ferraro knew. Sandy had correctly identified the mystery guest picture and deserved the bonus points. *Hell, it's only a game.*

"Now, boys and girls, here are the total points for each team. The winning team with four out of four points and one mystery face correctly identified belongs to the group of Charles, Patricia, Ken, and Erica. Now let's all give them a hand!"

The children were still clapping when the lunch buzzer rang.

"Right. The follow-up team with next highest number of points—" Ferraro stopped. The children were already stowing away their notebooks and drawing and looking up expectantly. She remembered that she was supposed to lead them out to the lunch room .

She did just that. Then moved swiftly to her cell phone.

CHAPTER 33

Washington, DC.

Barely fifty minutes after Ferraro's call, G. Everston Creed had his warrants from a federal judge. He called Hy Strooker over at the White House.

"She flunked the polygraph. The transmitter came from her purse. Her daughter just confirmed that Nabil is living with her mother. She's definitely involved. My men will raid her apartment before lunchtime is over. Now, where is she?"

"Upstairs, Gary." Strooker liked calling Creed by his first name, because he knew Creed disliked it. "I don't want to be calling your shots, but why don't you raid the apartment first, see if he's there and see what we come up with. She may be acting under some form of coercion. We pick her up later in the day, as she closes from work."

"We pick her up, Hyram. Not you. When she closes shop for the day. I'll go with that."

"Do you have a problem with my people picking her up? She's right on our turf."

"She's involved in an act of terrorism and attempted terrorist attacks. Clearly we have jurisdiction."

"We started the investigation with Agent Means's death, remember? There was an apparent threat to the president's life."

"I won't argue jurisdiction with you, Hyram. We kind of like to think we're the Department of Justice itself. Now this sweet little Bonnie and

Clyde cupcake of yours apparently was operating a terrorist cell right under your nose—"

"Just a minute. You're not getting personal on this are you? What in the hell do you mean by that?"

"Hy, you got a problem with us picking up a suspect in the White House? *Your* White House?"

"That does it, Gary, goddamn it. Now you don't set foot anywhere in this place! I'll pick her up myself. This has been a multi-agency operation from the beginning. You want to eat all the goddamn glory from the print and TV media, go right ahead and eat shit. But butt off taking cheap shots at me and my men. The Secret Service has always led the Fibbies by at least eight points in every poll taken among the public asking who they trust and respect more. What in the hell are you trying to prove?"

"You got a better suggestion, then?"

"Not right now—you didn't give me a chance to think. How about you put her under all points surveillance, see who she leads you to? Her handler's got to be out there somewhere."

"No chance. If another building goes 'BOOM!' in the meantime, or the president suffers a heart attack from a two hundred-grain bullet lodged in his chest, nobody on this late, great planet Earth will forgive Gary Creed. You know that. Three hours at the most, Hyram. You pick her up in three hours or we come in. Meanwhile, we'll raid her condo right now and see if Nabil is part of the bargain. Okay from your end?"

"What do you expect me to say? You already assembled your posse. Cut 'em loose."

Strooker put down the phone none too gently. His hands shook as he reached for the coffee cup on the table. The coffee, about half full, was cold and tasted bitter. No sugar, no milk, by choice. Damn G. Everston Creed. Sonuvabitch.

Dwight, across the table, was regarding him sympathetically. "That bad, Chief?"

"'Fraid so." Strooker coughed phlegmatically and waved the cup at Dwight. "Pour me some hot coffee. I sure could use some."

"Sure." Dwight collected the cup and made for the coffee maker on top of the fridge.

Tammy Weasel, of all people. How in the hell had she beaten the hermetic security around the White House? Until today, Strooker had thought he had a couple more years before retirement. Now, however, it would seem a good time to start work on the exact wording of his resignation letter. Congress wouldn't spare him once the details came out. Even that arrogant Creed might be swept up in the vortex of congressional wrath.

Dwight returned with the coffee.

"Thanks. Get me Kevin Keik on the phone."

———

He took off his coat in the large, oak-paneled office. Looked for a moment at his expensive beech mahogany desk inlaid with black leather top; a MacBook Pro; a side bookcase that served as an entertainment center, featuring a Sony DVD player; a Bose hi-fidelity music center with compact hideaway speakers that could belch Dolby surround of unsurpassed richness and quality; one full bookcase against the wall crammed with law texts; and a teak sideboard covered with a sliding flat panel. Old Glory hung limply from a pedestal tray in the corner. If he pulled aside the heavy brocade curtains by the large glass windows, he would be able to see the rotunda of the Capitol, the Jefferson Monument, part of the Reflecting Pool, and many familiar and historic sights of the Washington, DC he had come to know. On impulse, he went to the door and locked it. He walked over to the sideboard and poured himself a full glass of sherry. He downed it in two gulps.

Ahh!

He needed that. He got behind the desk and pressed the intercom button.

"Marge. No calls."

"No calls," his secretary affirmed.

He brought out the disposable cell phone and typed out a message linked to a specific pager. *THE PRESIDENT WILL BE IN THE OVAL OFFICE 3PM–5PM. TUESDAY (TODAY). THE MISSION IS A GO. REPEAT, A GO. GOODLUCK. BORIS.*

He reread the message again and decided it was satisfactory. He typed in the destination, and rechecked. Three times. It just wouldn't do for the message to fall into wrong hands. He pressed send.

He suddenly needed another drink. Vodka this time. Straight. He fixed it and took a grateful sip and leaned back in the tall, black-leather swivel chair. Not bad at all. Everything, that is, up to now. In two hours or so all hell would break loose. It had taken a long time and meticulous planning to get to this stage. Payoff time. He sighed deeply and wondered how and where he would take the Oath of Office.

———

Reston.

A combined team of FBI and BATF agents raided Tammy's apartment at 2:10 p.m. that Tuesday. They encircled the apartment building on the ground. A team of agents in full armor, gas masks, and vests moved up to her apartment. Concussion grenades flew through a smashed front window, agents kicked open the front door and rushed in, ready to blast anything that moved.

Nobody was home.

After the smoke cleared, the agents searched the apartment and then searched again. Nothing. Nick Bauman, lead FBI agent, picked up his portable transceiver.

"Dogwood, Deputy Two."

Director Creed, in a Bureau car outside, answered. "Yes, Nick."

"Nobody's in here."

"Sure?"

"Positive."

Creed got out of his car and checked that his Glock semi-automatic was in place. "I'm coming up. Hold everything till I get up there."

"Why don't you let us handle it, sir? This place might be booby-trapped."

"See anything suspicious?"

"No."

"Damn it, Nick, I'm coming up."

Creed, trailed by Larry Bodine of the multi-agency task force, and two FBI agents, entered the apartment. The two Fibbies exchanged glances. Nothing in recent memory had prepared them for the head of the FBI leading a field operation.

"This where the woman lived?"

"Yes, sir."

"Take it apart. The lot. Prints, bloodstains, anything suspicious." He frowned, looking around. "Goddamn it, nothing at all?"

"Well . . ."

"Spit it out, Nick."

"Just a feeling. After we came and I took off my gas mask and the flashbang smell was still there, I thought I detected a male scent. If you know what I mean."

Creed came up and peered closely at the agent. "What exactly do you mean, Special Agent Bauman?"

"A man was here recently. Don't you smell it, sir? It's in the air."

"I smell it," another agent said. "Kind of strong . . . a masculine scent. He must have just left."

"And then," Bauman added, "there's black tufts of hair in the bathroom sink."

They went in to see it. This time Creed could smell the peculiar human musk. It was more pronounced in the bathroom. Difficult to quantify—testosterone, a foreign habit, an alien culture, a unique body signature.

Bauman pointed to the sink. "He must have shaved here this morning. Looks like chin stubble. Some tufts also in the wastebasket."

Creed nodded. "Good observation. He was definitely here."

"Of course, it could belong to the woman herself or any of her children."

Creed looked at him. "I read the bio on this woman. You haven't. She's a redhead and none of her children have black hair. It's not hers. Quit dealing in speculation, Nick. Let's get Hair and Fiber in here so they can lift some of this stuff."

There was some sort of commotion at the door. Creed walked over. Curious onlookers had assembled at the end of the hallway to observe the police activity. Other tenants peeked from behind cracked-open doors.

Larry Bodine was talking to a woman outside Tammy's apartment. Bodine was saying, ". . . police business, ma'am. Please get back in your apartment. We'll let you know when the area is safe for you to come out."

"I heard explosions," said the woman. "God Almighty, this place is becoming like the projects. Then I look out the window and see a SWAT team converging in here."

Bodine said smoothly, "It's not as bad as you make it. We're investigating a routine burglary. We thought the suspect was in here."

"Is that right? You don't fool me, young man. I'm old enough to be your mother—your grandmother even. This was no routine burglary." The woman spoke indignantly. She wore a pink turtleneck and gray slacks. Hair the color of ash porcelain and a turtle-like hump proclaimed that she wasn't a day under eighty. Bodine eyed the hump and fought the impulse to flatten it with a karate chop.

"Well, anyway," the woman was saying, "where are the police when you need them? Burglary, I heard you say. I've been burglarized, too. Why don't you come over and take a look?"

"Ma'am, we're FBI. You've got to call the Met police for that. This here is a special matter . . ." Bodine's eyes narrowed. Then he studied the woman. "You were broken into? By whom? Where is your apartment?"

The woman pointed. "Next door. I'm Mrs. Fierstal, Tammy's neighbor. I just came back from Raleigh, North Carolina, and someone's been in my apartment."

Creed promptly flashed his badge. "Director Creed, FBI. Could you lead us into your apartment, Mrs. Fierstal, and let's have a look?"

"Sure, sure."

"One moment," Creed said. "My men will lead the way." Unobtrusively, he drew his regulation Glock. Bodine and two of the agents did so as well.

"I've been in there already," Netty Fierstal said. "Nobody's there now. At least I don't think so."

"We just want to make sure."

Inside the apartment, Creed nodded to his agents. They quickly dispersed and conducted a thorough search, including all alcoves and roof beams. After five minutes, the agents came out, shaking their heads.

"Anything stolen, Mrs. Fierstal?"

"Not that I can tell."

"What proof do you have of burglary?"

She led them into her boudoir.

"Here. Some of my wigs have been shifted around and my wardrobe rifled through." She hesitated before the chest of drawers, then led them back out to the sitting room. "My teddy bear on the couch has been moved from where I normally keep it."

"Was the door lock broken?"

"No. I tried to figure it out. I think he came in through the door in the kitchen connecting to the garbage disposal." They filed into the kitchen, and she showed them the access door to the garbage disposal ramp, with the connecting door to Tammy's kitchen.

"Don't touch anything you think he might have touched," Creed told Mrs. Fierstal. "We'll need to look at those for prints. Your teddy, too." They filed back into the sitting room.

Creed said, "Those are all the indications of burglary that you have?"

Mrs. Fierstal blushed. "I think he went through my lingerie."

"He take any?"

"I don't think so. Just scattered them."

"Mrs. Fierstal, we'll bring the Fingerprints people here. Some of my men will have you make a statement and sign it." Creed looked at his watch.

"He did use the telephone," she said suddenly.

"How do you know that?"

"Well, I just got back, and I just wanted to call my son and my daughter-in-law in Raleigh to let them know I got back safely. Theirs was the last place I called just before I left here, to let them know I was on my way. Well, all those long numbers and area codes, I didn't want to go hunting and pecking, my arthritis bothers me now and again. So I hit the last number redial. Only instead of my son in Raleigh, it's a doctor's office. Dr. Polk, I think. Never heard of him. Never used him. Now, hon, I'm old and far gone, but I don't believe I'm that absent-minded yet."

The agents rushed to the telephone.

Creed borrowed a photograph of the Contractor from Bodine and showed it to the woman. "Have you ever seen this man with Tammy?"

She shook her head. "Can't say I have. No. Never."

"Have you noticed anything unusual about your neighbor, Tammy Weasel? Anything at all?"

The dowager considered. "Nothing at all. About Tammy and her children—I hope it's nothing serious. Does she know her apartment has been burglarized? I know where she works. I can get hold of her for you if you want."

"We know where she works."

"Nice kid, Tammy. Like my own daughter. Divorced, poor girl. Doesn't sleep around or go to bars. Church every Sunday, did you know that? I hope nothing awful has happened." The faded blue eyes probed Creed's for scraps.

"Oh, nothing's happened to her. Routine burglary alarm."

"If it's routine, why are these men wearing jackets that say ATF and FBI? Would you mind telling me what's going on?"

Creed smiled. "A matter of national security, ma'am."

———

Strooker finished talking with Kevin Keik and hung up. Tammy's involvement bothered him. She had to have co-conspirators inside the White House. Who, how many? He'd already placed plainclothesmen in each wing of the mansion, ostensibly as part of the new security measures in place, but in reality to keep an eye on Tammy and make sure she got nowhere near the First Family. Concrete stanchions had been placed around the White House perimeter to deter would-be suicide truck bombers. Marksmen were stationed on the rooftop with scope rifles and automatics and night-vision goggles that cost ten thousand dollars a unit. He had done what he considered reasonable. The Contractor was out there somewhere.

Strooker had just sent Ken Dwight to brief Mrs. Deakin and bring her down. He had also been on the phone with Don Panella, White House chief of staff. By God, he wasn't finished yet. If he was going to resign, he'd go down fighting and worry about the other matter later. He sighed, picked up his portable transceiver, and walked down the corridor to the Oval Office.

Didi Watts looked up in surprise. "Mr. Strooker, I had no idea —"

"Sorry, Didi. Can't talk now." And he strode into the Oval Office, ignoring her protests.

President Deakin also looked up in surprise. "Why, Hyram. You look disturbed. What's up?"

"I am disturbed, Mr. President. You're leaving with me. Right now. No questions."

The president's face changed color. "That's no way to talk to an elected president. I'm still president of the United States, son, and don't you forget that."

"I know, sir. I'm sorry. No time for niceties. I've briefed Panella. New developments. We'd like to take extreme precautions. We think it's called for. The situation is changing by the hour, and I can't pinpoint what exactly, but something isn't quite right. I just think you ought to be out of here for now."

Deakin studied him. "I see. Does it have something to do with the recent plot to bomb the White House? This Contractor man?"

"Yes, sir."

"And where do you propose to take me?"

"Blair. Just temporarily, sir. We'll get your personal belongings later. Mrs. Deakin is waiting."

"Posterity might forgive you, Hyram," Deakin growled, "if this turns out to be pointless. But I won't."

"I'll accept the risk, Mr. President."

Ten minutes later, President and Mrs. Deakin left in a small motorcade via the Executive Office Building exit. The convoy turned left on East Executive, joined Fifteenth Street to turn left again at K Street. Farragut Square flashed past, the Washington Circle came into view. The motorcade doubled back on Pennsylvania Avenue, stopping at a squat office building that resembled many offices in the capital. President and Mrs. Deakin got out, flanked by agents, and entered the building.

Five minutes later, the president came out alone, still flanked by Secret Service agents, and entered his limousine. The siren wailed and the motorcade took off again. A second limousine remained behind to wait for Mrs. Deakin. To the casual observer, the president had just escorted his wife to an official engagement, then left to attend to pressing state matters.

Kevin Keik leaned back in the genuine leather upholstery of the lead limousine in the false motorcade and sipped wistfully on a Glenfiddich whisky on ice, served in a real glass tumbler.

"They sure don't make 'em any better," he drawled.

―――

Ten minutes after the motorcade had left the squat office building, a nondescript Buick family sedan with tinted windows pulled up by a side door. Two Secret Service agents sat in front. President and Mrs. Deakin stepped in smartly from the side door. The Buick moved swiftly down the alley, joined Pennsylvania Avenue and merged into traffic. Two other unmarked cars followed unobtrusively, each one crammed with agents. As the Buick neared Blair House, the agent in the front seat spoke into his portable transceiver. The automatic gates swung open even the car turned the corner, and the Buick swept right in.

Excluding the participants themselves, fewer than six people in America knew of the swap.

———

Tammy could see the extra security measures in place. One Secret Service agent was stationed at the end of the hallway from her office. He sat on a padded leather chair and held a battery-operated metal detector, which he waved like a wand at all passersby. She wondered why he was really there. There were at least three other metal-frisking points at various entrances and corridors.

She had a tight feeling in the depths of her stomach telling her that something was totally wrong. They were onto her. The polygraph. The fake assurances. The body search. Then the milk incident that morning.

She had expressed milk as usual into a plastic bottle for Tom's feeding later in the day. When she went back to the refrigerator to collect her tuna fish sandwich for lunch, her milk container was empty. A note attached to the rim read: *Sorry. Knocked over your milk. I'm a klutz. I'll be more careful in future.* It was signed: *White House Staffer.*

Tammy wasn't fooled. The FBI were probably sifting through the milk. They'd probably already sent samples to the FBI lab for analysis. Did they really think she was trying to poison the president?

CHAPTER 34

Manassas.

2 p.m. Tuesday.

Nabil could feel the tension already. In one hour the chain of events that would lead to fireworks would begin. He thought about Tammy, wondered if he'd see her again, if she really would marry him. This would be his last major operation. He would retire afterward, perhaps instruct at a special weapons and tactics school, be a security consultant, or work with secret police for one of the Arab countries.

Leaning back on the recliner, he brought out Tammy's underwear from his pocket and parked it on his nose. Instantly her familiar dark musk regaled his nostrils, cartwheeling him into the nether world of the melancholy and base caprices. The possibilities with Tammy seemed endless. His erection sprouted like a monstrous fungus; irritated he plucked the underwear from his face and thrust it back in his pocket.

He had no desire to die or be wounded and be carried into a morgue or a hospital emergency room reeking of carnal self-abuse. Much as he was infatuated with her, there were limits. Consciously, he tore his mind away from her and thought about the mission as his phallus wilted.

He took a nap and awoke twenty-five minutes later. He took stock. The walkie-talkie light glowing green in its charger. Dr. Polk's genuine air force uniform and helmet in the corner. The sleek businesslike outline of the Tucano.

2:34 p.m. The flight plan would be in the system now if the Engineer had done it correctly. Even if he hadn't, the mission was not jeopardized at all. He could take off from Manassas Municipal and air-file. He would stay in visual meteorological conditions until his clearance came through. It could take up to fifteen minutes in the busy Washington–Dulles corridor.

He retrieved Polk's flight suit from the wall. A bit on the short side for him, though much broader. Nabil didn't really need the flight suit. He certainly needed the helmet and visor and the protection it would provide during the shock blast of ejection. He struggled into the flight suit, putting it on over his normal clothing. It was bulky and quite uncomfortable, but he wanted to be able, after the mission, to chuck the flight gear and hide amongst the crowd. The Browning (9mm Teflon-jacketed bullets), which the Engineer had brought him to replace the one left in the late Stan Friedman's car, went into the right pocket of the flight suit while the Glock went into the left pocket. He zippered up both. The Teflon bullets could penetrate armored vests. If he ever met Deakin face to face, that would be a fitting present.

The walkie-talkie crackled just then. He hurried over, removed it from the charging dock, and adjusted the squelch. The Engineer's voice came over clearly in Arabic. "Brother?"

"*Salaam aleikum*, brother."

"*Salaam aleikum*. I've come back."

Nabil glanced at his watch. 2:51 p.m. "Good. When the coast is clear, come and help me open the door and we can pull out the airplane."

"Not now, brother," said the Engineer. "There is a problem."

Nabil froze. "What problem?"

"Opposite the hangar you are in, brother, two doors down. The hangar is open and a man is preparing his airplane to fly."

Nabil digested the information. He hadn't heard the car pull up. At this stage, though, nothing short of a shootout with law enforcement authorities could stop the mission.

"Everything went well with the flight plan?"

"No problem."

"Where are you now?"

"At the place we park yesterday, facing the hangars."

"There is no other person in the area except the person opposite? Please confirm."

"That is correct."

"Okay, brother, here is what you do. Come up to Hangar 43 normally. Come as if you have a right to be here. Then open the door. We shall pull out the airplane. If anybody asks, we came here to pick up Dr. Polk's airplane and fly it to College Park for routine maintenance. Understood?"

"To pick up Dr. Polk's airplane for routine maintenance at College Park—understood. Plus I act normal."

"Correct."

Nabil walked over to the hangar door and slipped open the inside catch. Thirty seconds later, he heard the van pulling up, the thud of the driver's door closing. The access door creaked open, and harsh daylight flooded the hangar, momentarily blinding Nabil. The Engineer walked in, looking more unkempt than ever. After a quick, traditional Arab greeting, Nabil pressed the door button for open and the hinges creaked as the pulleys ground their way upward, pulling the zinc door with it.

Two doors away, in the opposite hangar tenement, a short, capable man worked an oil rag lovingly down the cowling of a Skyhawk. Nabil prayed that the nosey, no-good security officer, Jerry DeFelitta, wouldn't choose this moment to come around.

Nabil and the Engineer pushed out the Tucano, trying not to look at the owner of the Skyhawk. Nabil checked the parachute seal. Packed less than a year ago by a certain Kleber Goncalves, rechecked by Inspector 4, and signed. He would be putting his life in the hands of a stranger named Goncalves. He climbed into the front cockpit, noting with dismay in his peripheral vision that the Skyhawk's owner was coming over to gawk. Nabil had expected that. Most pilots would saunter over to see a sleek, thoroughbred machine.

The Skyhawk's owner stopped some fifteen feet away. "Hi, there."

"Good afternoon," Nabil said. He took in the man's look and nodded at the airplane. "Beautiful, isn't she?"

"Sure is. Never thought I'd see the day old Max Polk would let anyone else fly his beloved hot rod."

"I know what you mean. Sooner or later someone else has to."

"You an instructor in the Tucano?"

Nabil laughed. "Just a pilot like you. Actually we're taking it to College Park for routine maintenance. Dr. Polk's very busy this week and asked me to ferry it over. Don't worry, he's given me a checkout on it."

"Those rockets real?" The man was staring at the starboard pod.

"They're duds. Dr. Polk likes to imagine he's a top gun or something."

"Know what you mean."

Now if Jerry DeFelitta happened by. . . .

If Nabil couldn't start the damned machine. . . .

If the fuel bowser rolled round the corner. . . .

A lot of ifs. This man, a harmless spectator, could become their worst nightmare. No time to be wasted. The Engineer was busy closing the hangar door.

Nabil strapped himself in and brought out the checklist and started it from Before Start Initials. Halfway down, the Skyhawk's owner suddenly came toward the airplane, went round the front cowling, and lifted two red flags up. "Forget something?"

The pitot covers. Damn.

Nabil's face couldn't turn red. It turned a pasty purple. He had rushed through the walkaround because of this stranger. Damn, he was getting old—this could all have been done while the airplane was inside the hangar. He sheepishly collected the covers from the Skyhawk owner.

"Thanks."

That was close. He would have had no airspeed and wouldn't have realized that until near rotation speed. What else had he missed? Better make sure now. He waved to the Skyhawk's owner, who came over.

"Yep?"

"Can you check my rudders and elevators, please? No gust locks?" While the man sauntered back to look, Nabil waggled the rudder bars and elevators full throw. No obstructions.

The man held up a thumb. "You're okay."

"Thanks again. Much obliged."

"You're welcome."

Master on. Brakes on. Beacon. Throttle idle. He hit the start switch and the big blades up front began a spirited revolution. Condition lever to start, a satisfying *Rrumph!* as compressed Jet A1 hit the combustion chamber and was promptly ignited. Seconds later, the engine was self-sustaining, and he knocked the starter out of the loop and watched the exhaust gas temperature settle well inside the the green arc. Good, healthy engine.

The Engineer waved once, Nabil waved back, and he got in the van, ready to drive away once Nabil was airborne. Good man. This was probably the last time they would meet, but there was no chance for an elaborate goodbye—not with the Skyhawk's owner watching. He would miss the man in his own way. Genius—even evil genius—had its moments. It was imperative, too, that the Engineer not engage the Skyhawk's owner in conversation; his accent was atrocious and would likely draw suspicion. Once Nabil got airborne, the Engineer would dump the van and find his way out of the country by one of three prearranged routes.

Nabil switched on Dr. Polk's VHF portable standby transceiver clipped to the side panel. From its fully charged condition, it would now begin to run down. Henceforth, too, he would use it for all transmissions. Part of his plan depended on ATC thinking and believing the airplane had a weak radio. He had been prepared to isolate the generator bus and let the aircraft battery carry all electrical loads to quickly simulate the weak-radio or NORDO condition, but the standby handheld set would serve as well.

The Skyhawk's owner waved as Nabil released the brakes and the Tucano eagerly trundled forward. *Yahoo! What a machine!* You had to keep it on a leash even with two thousand pounds of high explosives distributed in the rear seat and in various compartments.

Once out of the hangar area, Nabil leaned over and removed the two red-tagged safety rods for the ejection seat. Three beeps sounded, the Seat Normal annunciation on the panel disappeared and a green Seat Armed/Unsafe light illuminated in the corner. Nabil doubted that Tucanos in the regular air force had this feature. Probably added by the meticulous Dr. Polk.

Now he was sitting on a rocket sled. He steered with the toe brakes, monitoring the Unicom frequency. There was little chatter on the frequency, just a Piper Warrior in the circuit. He extended flaps to the takeoff setting and verified deployment as he taxied to the end of the active runway. He set the brakes, selected Dulles Clearance Delivery on 121.65 and asked for his clearance, using the aircraft call sign of November Three Two Mike Papa. No reply. He repeated the call two more times with same result. Of course—he was on the ground and Dulles was some fourteen miles away. Line of sight. He needed to be airborne before they would hear him.

He straightened his charts one more time and glanced at a copy of the flight plan. The Dulles corridor was a very busy airspace. Once airborne, things would move quite quickly. He wanted to be ahead of events. Polk's charts included an expired National Oceanic Service chart, published by the US government, and a current Jeppesen chart. He had noticed while perusing the charts in the hangar that the NOS chart depicted Dukes intersection as five miles from Armel, versus four for the newer Jeppesen. The Jeppesen also had an intersection Peege, five miles after Bonds, whereas NOS did not depict Peege at all. He decided to stick to Jeppesen.

He completed the taxi and before-takeoff checks. Everything A-okay. He announced his intentions on the Unicom before taxiing onto the active and lining up. There was 5700 feet of runway stretching before him. Time to go. He advanced the throttle, allowed for the EGT to stabilize, then militarily slammed the throttle to full power. The Tucano leaped forward, despite the extra weight. Full torque from the engine, acceleration brisk. Nabil applied substantial right rudder to keep the airplane trucking straight. Eighty knots. One hundred knots. Unstick speed. He waited ten more knots for the extra weight, then rotated the airplane. He broke ground briskly, the long engine radome with its silver spinning disc reaching eagerly for the sky. He selected "gear up."

Seconds later, the flaps came up and he was reducing to nearly 60-percent torque to keep from breaking the two hundred-knot speed limit within an airport traffic area. This was one fast airplane. Like flying a jet. He had no doubt that on the straight and level, this airplane could do 270 knots unchained, although 240 knots was recommended for block cruise. He would stay in the pattern until he picked up his IFR clearance. He dialed Dulles Approach on 120.45.

"Dulles, Tucano November Three Two Mike Papa."

Dulles answered immediately, the volume crashing into his eardrums.

"November Three Two Mike Papa, Dulles. Go ahead." He was on helmet mike, but still using the handheld for transmissions. He lowered the volume.

"You have the clearance for Three Two Mike Papa?"

"From Davis Municipal, confirm?"

"Charlie."

"Three Two Mike Papa is cleared Davis to College Park via Brooks 006 radial, Armel 091 direct. Squawk 0543. Clearance void time 1430 Zulu." A pause. "You airborne, sir?"

"That's affirmative."

"Okay, picking you up now, I think. November Three Two Mike Papa, squawk ident."

Nabil flicked the transponder code to 0543 and pressed the ident button. "Identing."

"Tucano Three Two Mike Papa radar contact four miles north of Davis. Turn right heading zero eight zero to intercept Brooks zero zero six radial. Climb maintain three thousand and report Dukes."

Damn. Nabil read back the clearance and scrambled to set up his radios as he banked the airplane and simultaneously added power to begin his climb to three thousand feet.

"And Three Two Mike Papa, Dulles?"

"Go ahead."

"In future, sir, advise you use Clearance Delivery 121.65 before airborne."

"I tried. On ground. No answer."

"No problem. Continue as cleared. Call Dukes."

"Roger."

"Three Two Mike Papa, turn left heading zero four five."

"Left zero four five, Mike Papa."

They were taking him out of the way of the airliners on the localizer course to Dulles. He climbed at 160 knots indicated. Down below to his right, a small winding lake. Just over it, the Brooks 006 radial came alive. Nabil turned with the needle and was now flying almost due north. He set up the nav. radios—Armel 113.5 frequency, 120 radial for identifying Dukes. Next, he tuned the DCA Automatic Terminal Information Service on 132.65. The fast-paced, staccato delivery of the Reagan National controller was almost meaningless to him. He wouldn't be landing there anyway.

He leveled off at three thousand feet. Dukes came up, the DME from Armel winding down. At four miles to Armel, he reported Dukes. Dulles acknowledged and asked him to track outbound on Armel 091. He intercepted the radial smoothly and again brought the power back as his airspeed reached 230 knots indicated. He slowed to 190 knots so that he would not bust all his checkpoints before he was ready. Now six miles past Armel. That meant thirteen from Peege, his Initial Point, the predetermined point where he'd begin the bombing run. The airspeed indicator read 180 knots. Just over four minutes to the IP. He was pleased to note that the muffled static in the handheld VHF had now increased. Low-battery warning.

"Tucano Three Two Mike Papa contact DCA Approach 124.7, good day."

"Twenty Four Seven, Mike Papa."

He dialed in Washington National on 124.7. It took three calls before DCA answered.

"Aircraft calling DCA, you're very faint. Understand Three Two Mike Papa?"

"Affirm, Mike Papa."

"November Three Two Mike Papa radar contact one–two miles west of the field. Maintain present heading. Report Peege."

"Present heading, and call Peege, Mike Papa."

"Will you be wanting radar vectors to College Park, sir?"

"From Peege we'll probably go visual."

"Roger. And ah, Mike Papa, confirm type of aircraft?"

"Tucano. Embraer 312."

"Roger that. And ah, be advised . . . (static, static) readability strength two. You wanna . . . (static, static) ah, check . . . (static) radio . . ."

"Say again for Mike Papa?"

"(Garbled) . . . (static) . . . (static)."

The deception was working. Gradual radio failure. Followed by loss of all radio contact. *I'm supposed to follow the flight plan up to the clearance limit or to the last amended controller-issued limit and then begin my descent and approach at the expected approach time. Only I won't do any of that. I'll just reach out and bite them in their pink asses.*

The three-axis autopilot was working okay; he momentarily engaged it while he set up his radios to identify Peege using DCA VOR frequency 111.0 and the 360-degree radial.

"Three Two . . . talking . . . to me?"

"Three Two Mike Papa requesting descent."

He could hear other aircraft on the frequency—United, Delta, American, Cactus (the call sign for US Air). Four more tries before the controller heard him. He throttled back as Bonds intersection appeared too soon. The Delta flight relayed for the DCA controller.

"Three Two Papa . . . National . . . (static) . . . descend two thousand. (Static) . . . readable . . ."

"Mike Papa leaving three for two thousand. I'll get the radio checked once on ground."

At that point, crossing Bonds intersection, Nabil throttled back even further to begin his descent. He selected transponder code 7700 for one minute, then switched to code 7600. This was the internationally recognized squawk for total radio failure. Down there on the controller's panel an alarm would sound, triggered by the 7700 code, and the 7600 appearing next would inform ATC that the squawking aircraft had no workable radio. Peege was now five miles ahead. Nabil ran through his HAT checks (height, altitude, time)—the fighter pilot's prelude to commencing an attack. Through gaps in the broken cloud cover Georgetown lay directly beneath, her narrow cobblestone streets and ancient Georgian facades discernible even from up there. The Potomac snaked through the heart of the village like a scoliotic spine. He recognized Georgetown University and the US Naval Observatory, the two most prominent landmarks.

The Reagan National controller was saying ". . . an aircraft approaching Peege intersection. Inbound College Park. Looks like he's got no radio. Can you relay to him, ah, Delta 5274, ah, how do you read?"

"Okay, sir, we'll give it a try." The Delta jet now tried to raise the Tucano. "November Three Two Mike Papa, do you read Delta 5274? Three Two Mike Papa, how do you read?"

Nabil fought the instinct to answer. He was hearing everybody perfectly well on the aircraft's radio. Peege was coming up fast. 7 DME from the DCA VOR on his present radial would be it. He would lead his turn, start at 6.5 DME and level out on heading 180. At Peege, he would be only six miles from College Park—which he had no intention of reaching—and less than four miles from the White House. He aligned the heading indicator on the HSI one last time with the standby compass and rechecked the seat ejection test switch. He turned off his transponder entirely to present as small a target as possible. This action would further convince the controller that his battery had run down, probably due to a broken alternator belt. He was now at two thousand feet and the DME was nudging seven. The Initial Point coming up. He braced himself.

NOW!

He hit the stopwatch and racked the Tucano into a 2g sixty-degree bank. He snapped out of the turn on a heading of south, pushed the nose down, and the throttle all the way forward. He didn't need to take up an intercept to stay on the DCA 360-degree radial. The compartments of the Hill lay beneath him like an open book. City landmarks and monuments laid out as predicted. He was less than three and a half miles from the White House by the time the turn was completed and screaming down to treetop level. Two hundred and forty knots indicated, speed increasing, no more than a minute to the White House. He wasn't wearing a full pressure suit—merely a flight suit over his normal clothes—and he knew an ejection at 280 knots, while certainly survivable, might knock him out for a few minutes—precious minutes that he needed to use to get on his feet and get out of there if the blast collaterals didn't kill him. He had settled at a speed of between 260 and 280 knots for his egress. And he really hated to do it: the Tucano was one beautiful and responsive machine.

He was penetrating Prohibited Airspace P-56--B, the three-mile inner restricted area from the ground up to eighteen thousand feet above the White House where no airplane may fly. He burst out through the last straggle of cloud, 2.7 miles to the White House, and prepared for his own evacuation. He pickled the bomb and sighted the starboard pod rockets on the East Wing. The Tucano was a roaring, screaming, avenging angel, bucking low-level turbulence arising from structures on the Hill.

The firing switch was on the throttle in compliance with the favored HOTAS concept—hands on throttle and stick—which allowed fighter pilots to fly their airplanes and fire their munitions without removing either hand from the throttle or joystick. He remembered the Engineer's warning that the rockets would only be fired in salvos, not singly. He cut loose the right pod and the flame and smoke spurted as the Tucano reared and bucked from the recoil.

The East Wing of the White House disappeared under a mushroom of smoke. Bullseye!

He quickly thumbed the firing switch to the port rockets, banked slightly to align with the West Wing, pickled, and sent the second salvo into the target. He counted six puffs of smoke this time and felt the jarring hiss of a misfire on one of the rockets. No matter, the West Wing erupted and collapsed in a black smoke cloud.

Only the main mansion remained.

The target for the airplane itself.

He came in exactly between Dupont Circle and Logan Circle. Less than fifteen seconds to the target, he flicked on the Engineer's little switch, arming the explosives. In a brilliant flash of clairvoyance, he saw suddenly what the Engineer had been trying to tell him, that the delay fuse was meaningless for a non-casement bomb whose integrity would be lost upon impact. In essence he was carrying an IED. At the extreme, the delay fuse might keep the explosives from igniting, making the bomb a dud; at the other end of the spectrum, it would explode on impact regardless of delay instructions. This was not sophisticated hardware where a proximity fuse in the nose exploded the device close to the target, nor a specially rigged timing device that would survive the horrendous forces of impact and detonate the bomb at the set time. No, *he* was the bomb and detonation would be on impact.

Scott Circle flashed past on his left. He was parallel to the long stream of cars crawling up Sixteenth Street. Lafayette Square loomed ahead. He could make out the oblong acreage housing the Executive Mansion. Beyond that would be the Ellipse. The White House was rushing up inexorably.

Then it zapped him.

He couldn't believe it.

His training told him it was impossible. You did not go from flying a full panel to . . . nothing. Flags appeared on all flight instruments, even engine indicator readings went to zero. Both his altitude indicator and standby horizon tumbled crazily. Luckily he was visual now and could control the airplane and stay upright using visual cues. There was supposed to be a powerful generator in the engine, and if that failed, the dual battery pack could carry the aircraft's entire electrical load for about thirty minutes—more than enough to get to a reasonable airport. He had not pulled any circuit breaker or touched anything to induce total electrical failure.

In the same instant, the answer came to him. An EMP—electromagnetic pulse. A side effect of atomic bomb detonation, it shut down all electrical appliances, cutting off communications. It could be artificially induced using special microwave towers that beamed the electromagnetic pulse toward a target. The White House defenses had been turned on. This had not been a part of Major Brobov's briefing.

Even would-be car bombers—assuming they got through the formidable stanchions and wrought-iron fence surrounding the White House—would find their car's engine dying suddenly on the home stretch. The common spark plug in a car engine was an electrical device, and was subject to EMP. The reason the Tucano's engine hadn't died was because it was a turbine. Igniters (like spark plugs) were used during start to implode misted aviation kerosene (Jet A) in the combustion chamber; once the fire was self-sustaining, the igniters were removed from the loop and the engine ran as long as there was fuel to feed it.

Someday, Nabil thought, when they have rebuilt the new White House, some lunatic in a small piston aircraft will attempt what I am doing now. He will crash into the White House grounds and die and people will wonder why he lost control so near to the target. He felt a sense of exhilaration, that he'd survived the first attack from the White House and knew that he would make it because in eight seconds or so he would be there, and they didn't have time for any other plan of attack. He couldn't see the microwave dish beaming the electromagnetic pulse on him, but he knew it was there.

Allahu Akbar. Thank Allah he had fired the rockets before the EMP blast hit the airplane.

He could see the neat circular chrysanthemum bed of the North Lawn, still blazing yellow in near-gone autumn. He noted the Fountain, Yellowstone-like, hissing its cylindrical spout. The tall Doric columns of the North Portico rushed toward him. He descended to below treetop level. People poured out of the West and East Wing rubble—those who had survived the devastation scattering in every direction upon hearing the high-pitched scream of the Tucano's engine. DCA or Andrews had probably warned them he was headed there. He pulled the canopy release button. A sudden whoosh and the canopy vanished in the slipstream, lots of wind-noise and engine blast. The noise was barely manageable. He had a sense of cars running into one another on Pennsylvania Avenue, perhaps confused by the sudden noise, tourists scattering by the fence, and what he thought were Secret Service agents in sniper greens on the rooftop reaching for scope rifles and Stingers. He was seeing what few men see and live to tell, what the *kamikaze* pilots of Imperial Japan must have seen and felt in that last, down-the-tube, headlong rush to an explosive oblivion.

Nabil fought the Tucano as it screamed toward the White House, buffeting from local eddies and uneven airflow around buildings in the capital. The last two hundred yards to the White House happened at warp speed, yet had a retarded, slow-motion quality.

Nabil knew the recoil from the ejection seat's firing could drive the Tucano into the ground short of the target. He would have to aim the Tucano's nose toward the White House attic. The ejection seat recoil should drive the Tucano into the second floor. On the other hand, if he aimed too high. . . . No time for practice. He had to get it right the first time. In a sudden flash of insight, he trimmed the aircraft a tad nose-down. Even if the seat ejection caused a shift in phugoid, the airplane at this speed would remain on course just long enough to smash into the White House.

He drew up his knees from the rudder pedals—the yaw damper had the rudder in its firm grip. Even if he hadn't done so, once he pulled the ejection handle, mechanical straps would have forcibly tucked them in to prevent his losing his kneecaps as the seat went through the canopy. He pulled the double visor over his eyes and reminded himself to close his eyes as he pulled the firing handle on the seat pan. This way, as the canopy detonating cord shattered the Perspex and the canopy breakers on the seat itself fractured the glass, fragments—like hot shrapnel at this speed—would not penetrate his visor and eyeballs. Then he remembered he had already blown off the canopy.

Don't fire until you can see the whites of their eyes. Someone had said that. Well, he was looking down the throat of the White House with dizzying speed. One split-second's further delay, and he would be part of the rubble.

Now!

He pulled the ejection handle.

CHAPTER 35

Washington, DC.

"One DUI five years ago," Bodine said. "Fifty dollar fine, six months probation. That's all on Dr. Polk. Nothing on Dr. Simvali."

Over his shoulder, Creed and ATF chairman Kohlbus peered at the computer terminal.

"Is Simvali also Iranian?" Kohlbus asked.

"Indian."

Creed said, "Let's check the Message Unit Details from Verizon for Mrs. Fierstal. All calls to or from her telephone for the past week. Ditto Doctors Polk and Simvali. Pick out the ones we think relevant and get the MUDs on those, too."

"It'll take some time, sir." Bodine said.

"So the sooner you start—"

The telephone rang. Creed picked it up, said, "Speaking." He listened, said a few words, and hung up. "Okay, our surveillance team is in place around Plastic Surgery Associates. If they make outside calls after we call them, we'll know." He looked at his watch, scratched his chin. "Let's give 'em a call now, Larry."

Kohlbus grunted. "Too many damned doctors in this thing. Kokubani, now Polk and Simvali. Maybe the Contractor's feeling the dragnet closing in. Wants to surgically alter his face."

"Maybe," Creed said.

Larry Bodine dialed the number and put the audio on speaker.

"Plastic Surgery Associates, Maureen speaking."

Bodine asked about a caller named Samir Muvdi perhaps calling to book an appointment. No such name, Maureen said. Most of their callers were women. She did recall one particular gentleman with an accent—wait a minute, Dr. Polk just came out of surgery and would talk to them.

Bodine could hear Saint-Saëns's *The Aquarium* playing in the background, the sound of a thousand other doctors' offices. A terse, surgical voice interrupted the music. "Polk speaking."

"Dr. Polk, this is Larry Bodine, attached to the FBI multi-agency terrorism task force." Bodine explained everything once again.

"I couldn't help you, I'm afraid," Polk said when Bodine had finished. "Doctor–patient confidentiality. I doubt even a subpoena could pry my mouth open. Offhand, I can tell you I've not received a call of the nature you describe in the past week. If I recall correctly, I've only done two nose jobs, three breast augmentations, one facelift, several collagen implants and suction lipectomies, and two cleft palates during that time period. Except for two children, all the procedures were on women. Was your caller a woman, by any chance?"

"Not at all."

"No chance, then. My associate Doctor Simvali may have taken a call. He's here on Saturdays also."

"Would the caller have tried to contact you at home?"

"Not that I'm aware of. Usually I'm at the airport on weekends. Only an emergency would bring me out, and there aren't too many of those in reconstructive surgery."

Creed and Kohlbus exchanged glances. Creed tapped Bodine on the shoulder. "Ask him what he does at the airport."

Bodine repeated the question.

"How is that your business, sir?" huffed Dr. Polk.

"I need to know, Dr. Polk. This is an urgent federal matter."

"Well then, I'll tell you what I do at the airport. Like any other decent taxpaying American citizen trying to unwind after a long week of work, I take my wife out on a recreational flight or go cross-country in my airplane. You got anything against that?"

"What kind of airplane you got, Doc?"

Polk started to protest again but thought better of it. "A Brazilian-made Embraer Tucano. It's kind of like a light attack aircraft or trainer for air force pilots. I bought it in civvies. Suits me fine."

"Dr. Polk, when was the last time you flew—physically saw your airplane?"

"Why, on Saturday afternoon. Just wait a minute. I got a three-party line here. I'll get the FBO on the line . . ." He spoke to somebody in the background. "How's that done, Maureen?"

Some tweaking on the line, followed by a digital squeak. The FBO receptionist answered, and Polk said, "This is Dr. Polk. Could you send someone to Hangar 43 to check on my airplane, please?"

"Dr. Polk! I thought you just took off!" The girl's voice was rife with consternation.

"Excuse me?"

"You just took off in your airplane!"

"I'm sorry, Sherry. That's Sherry, I presume?"

"Yes, it's me."

"Well, Sherry, I'm right here in my office, in scrubs. I couldn't be in two places at the same time, could I?"

"Did you loan your airplane to someone?"

"I sure as hell didn't. You wouldn't be kidding me, are you?"

"No, I'm not, doc. I kind of was disappointed, 'cause you promised you'd come in and settle your fuel bill and the hangarage."

"Oh, that. Check's in the mail. I mean it. Wait a minute, you mean someone took off in my airplane? My Tucano?"

"I thought you gave him permission to."

"Hell no. It's stolen, that's what. Highway robbery, that's what it is. When did it take off? You sure it was my airplane?"

"Of course I'm sure. Took off not quite five minutes ago."

"Did the thief say where he was headed?"

"Nope. Wait a minute—Todd's here. You speak to the lineman."

"Doctor Polk? This is Todd. I noticed your car wasn't in the usual place, and I seen the Tucano take off. The hangar door's closed, and I remarked as how you'd taken off real heavy like, sort of in a flat attitude—not your usual sprightly takeoff. Mr. Ekberg, he owns a Skyhawk, said it wasn't you flying, was a couple of strangers said you asked them to ferry the Tucano to College Park for maintenance."

"The hell I did. Jesus! I never asked anyone to touch my airplane."

Creed took the receiver from Bodine. The three-party line was still on. "Dr. Polk," he said, "I'm Director Creed, FBI. I was listening in. You positively say you never authorized anyone to take your airplane?"

"That's correct. I don't allow anyone else fly her. Insurance reasons, plus personal."

"Todd," Creed said, "do you have a description of the two men who took the airplane?"

"Mr. Ekberg said they looked, well . . . different. One man flew the airplane. The other had a beard and drove away in a van. New Jersey plates, I think."

Creed looked at his watch. Harry P. Davis Municipal airport had a 703-area code and 361 as a prefix. That meant it was either Fairfax or Prince William County. He'd notify the sheriffs for both counties to put out a BOLO and send men out to the airport immediately. If this joker was really headed for College Park, then a surprise reception awaited him.

"Has this Ekberg fellow taken off yet?"

"I think he's still around in the airport."

"And you say he saw the two men who took Dr. Polk's airplane?"

"That's correct."

"Tell him to stay put, not to go anywhere. We need to speak with him, urgently. I'll call the sheriff over there and ask him to send a couple of deputies out to take down details of what he saw."

"I'll do that, sir." Todd the lineman went off the exchange.

Dr. Polk gave a deep sigh. "Gentlemen, I have a patient due in five minutes. Based on what you've just told me, I don't think I'm in any condition to handle patients for the rest of the day. I'll see if can get another doctor to see them. It'll take me about forty-five minutes to get out to the airport. You say you're FBI?"

"That's correct."

"Do you have a number I could call you at?"

Creed gave him the number and said, "We'll notify the FAA and relevant agencies. You'll have to report your aircraft stolen and file a police report. If your airplane does touch down at College Park, we'll arrest the pilot. What is the registration number of your aircraft?"

"November Three Two Mike Papa. It's a Tucano. Blue in color."

"We'll be on it." Creed hung up. His eyes met those of Kohlbus.

"Trouble is," Kohlbus said, "will he really land at College Park?"

"You got that right," said Creed. "He may be landing on the lawn of the White House even as we speak."

"I'll let Strooker know right away."

———

DCA Northwest sector controller Mike DeSoto was upset. His voice, though, did not show it: he still maintained the imperial staccato delivery of the experienced ATCO on the busy DCA/Dulles TCA corridor. An aircraft, N32MP, was having radio problems. DeSoto winced as he stared at the radar screen, at the tagged blip among many other blips that was N32MP. His primary job was to keep the blips apart, keep them from ever meeting, and how the hell was he supposed to do that when he couldn't even talk to one of the airplanes? He could steer others out of his way and hope the rogue airplane adhered strictly to his filed flight plan. It made his job that much harder.

He had seen it a few times in seventeen years as an air traffic controller. Single engine aircraft messing around in IFR conditions suffers alternator failure and gradual loss of electrics, which the pilot fails to recognize until it is too late. The buzzing in the radios, the static, the undecipherable transmissions, as the battery faded. The radios would peter out, then the gyros, precipitating the second real and deadlier emergency—loss of control and the aircraft spiraling into the ground because the pilot was not proficient in partial panel and could no longer tell up or down inside the clouds.

Unless . . . Desoto prayed silently . . . unless the aircraft had backup electrical system, dual alternators, dual vacuum pumps, dual everything.

This airplane puzzled DeSoto a bit: usually as the electrics faded, the radar blip would fade, too, as the transponder no longer squawked its assigned code. In that case, he would resort to the primary blip, a fuzzy, no-tags, barely visible blip that he must keep other airplanes away from. Instead, Three Two Mike Papa's blip remained full squawk while the radios fizzled out.

Was the pilot using a handheld, or was it only his microphone jack fizzling out? DeSoto shuddered involuntarily. Either way, he envisioned the outcome. The live human voice he was talking to a few minutes ago would become a metal sandwich on the Beltway or someplace. He had to steer him away from the crowded part of the city, find him a park or flat area. No, more important, descend him from the clouds. When he broke out, and he should—cloud bases stood at 1400 feet—he should be able to regain control visually, if he hadn't entered a graveyard spiral, and limp to some nearby airport. He would alert area controllers just in case.

"Ah, Three Two Mike Papa, National, say souls on board."

". . . (static) . . ."

"Mike Papa, how many souls on board?" ". . . (static)."

A male voice, distinct and professional, came on with astonishing clarity. "Okay, ah, National, Delta 5274 relaying for the Three Two Mike Papa. He says one soul, repeat one soul on board."

"Ah, thank you, Delta 5274. Confirm you have contact. Confirm from him, ah, his destination. Understand College Park?"

"Tucano Three Two Mike Papa, Delta. National, ah, wants to know your destination—"

An audio alarm on DeSoto's panel blocked out the Delta transmission. The alarm went off on the screens of at least four other controllers in the area. It was an emergency alarm triggered by the squawk code 7700 on the transponder. The blip on DeSoto's screen grew in intensity and a flashing cursor indicated the aircraft with the emergency. The pilot was indicating that Mike Papa's situation had deteriorated to an emergency level.

DeSoto reached out and silenced the warning simultaneously with his identification of the distressed airplane. The flashing cursor disappeared and the squawk code changed to 7600. Gotcha! The radio failure squawk code. *Great*, thought DeSoto, *really great. Just what I need*. Right over the capital. He keyed his mike.

"Mike Papa, understand you have a complete radio failure. Please click your mike button twice to acknowledge."

But the Delta pilot, trying to be helpful, cut in. "Three Two Mike Papa, from Delta 5274. We read you just now. Go on for relay."

No answer.

"Three Two Mike Papa, Delta 5274, do you read me? Three Two Mike Papa, Delta."

An impatient airline captain's voice cut in. "Cactus 2037 Pisca inbound."

DeSoto didn't miss a beat. "Cactus '37, five miles from Oxonn. Maintain sixteen hundred until established, cleared for the ILS Runway 36."

"Sixteen hundred until established, cleared for the ILS 36, Cactus 2037."

"Contact Tower now 119.1. Good day."

"Nineteen one."

"United 612 turn right heading 290. Descend to 2500 feet, number two behind an A319 just checked Pisca."

"Right 290, down to two point five, number two, United 612."

"Ah, that's correct. I'll get back to you. All aircraft expect slight delay. I have an aircraft, ah, squawking lost comm. We're trying to get him a fix, ah, get him out of your way. Okay, Delta 5274, you able to reach that guy? He's lost his radios, I believe, and ah, just lost him on radar. . . . Okay, I got his primary, ah, just barely showing. I show him just a mile west of Peege . . . you able to make contact, Delta, uh, 5915?"

"Delta 5915, we'll try. He doesn't seem to be hearing anybody."

To DeSoto's horror, the faint primary began a right turn to the south. Rolled out on a heading that would take it directly to P56, the prohibited airspace of the White House. Damn. From ground level to 18,000 feet, no airplane was permitted to fly into, through, or over Prohibited Airspace 56. The area was depicted clearly in en route and terminal approach charts. This target was clearly going to penetrate. DeSoto keyed his mike to transmit a vector in the blind, but the landline telephone blinked urgently.

It was the Andrews Air Force base controller. He had been monitoring events, and he sounded angry. "There's traffic just turned off Peege. He's headed directly for Papa Five Six."

"Yeah, I got him," DeSoto said, thinking of the paperwork blitz in weeks to come. "He's NORDO. We were trying to get him away from populated areas. . . . Hold on—" DeSoto spoke into his live mike. "Okay, Delta 5274, if able, try contact Three Two Mike Papa now. Advise him turn left NOW, heading 070. Left 070. On that heading, he'll be visual at 1300 feet. Advise him when visual to proceed direct College Park."

"Copied, Delta 5274. We're getting a bit out of range here, but we'll give him a shout."

"Yeah. Appreciate any help you can render."

"Uh, sure thing. Three Two Mike Papa, Delta, do you read? Turn left right now heading 070. Left 070 . . ."

Shit. DeSoto watched the Mode Charlie readout on the Tucano's altimeter race down . . . 1200 feet . . . 1000 feet . . . 800 feet. What in Orville Wright's good name was happening? The pilot should have broken out of the clouds at about 1400 feet, and proceeded visually to a safe landing.

Maintain 1300 feet, DeSoto prayed. 1300 feet was below the minimum vectoring altitude for that sector, but DeSoto was an experienced

controller who had dealt with many emergencies and knew he was authorized to deviate from standard procedures to the extent required to
contain the emergency. There were at least four marked obstructions of
1049 feet in the area Three Two Mike Papa was in. Higher than 1400
feet and he would be in the soup; any lower than 1200 feet and he risked
hooking a guy wire or running into a building. Had the pilot already lost
it and was at that moment spiraling to his violent death? Unlikely. The
movements of the Tucano were perfectly orchestrated and deliberate.

From the corner of his screen, two blips appeared suddenly from
beside Andrews, glued to each other, rising fast. Andrews had scrambled
F-16s.

Then all hell broke loose. The terrain proximity warning sounded. Another bell sounded to warn of a prohibited airspace breach.
The Andrews controller was yelling like mad. The shift supervisor
on DeSoto's floor suddenly was at his shoulder, peering at the screen,
fingers curled over his own "transmit override" button, ready to issue
counter orders that would save the day if it turned out that DeSoto had
just freaked out.

The supervisor stared at the Tucano blip barreling toward the White
House. DeSoto swore. His supervisor did the same and reached out to
trigger the silent alarm that would alert Secret Service over at the White
House. "Whoever you are," he said under his breath, "you just got yourself a one-year license suspension, minimum. Maybe a revocation."

"I think he's a crasher. Look's deliberate to me," DeSoto said.

"Looks that way," the supervisor affirmed. Can we get him—?"

November Three Two Mike Papa disappeared from the screen.

Last altitude readout 500 feet. Too low for the radar to pick him up
now. Unless they had a look-down radar over at 1600 Penn.

The telephones began ringing as irate capital residents called
in with reports of a low-flying airplane. Bolling Air Force Base was
closed, but still maintained a skeletal stealth operation, and was also on
the landline, warning about a confirmed threat to Papa Five Six Bravo.
The Executive Mansion's own classified anti-terror security network

had also picked up the threat and was on the landline trying to ascertain if DCA had an explanation. The target's transponder was a Made in the USA model and certainly responded to passive IFF (identification friend or foe) interrogation. Two marines at that moment were rising from the roof of the mansion, two Stingers swiveling on trained shoulders to meet the threat.

Mike DeSoto and his supervisor were still there controlling traffic, issuing vectors, when the steel and concrete gloom of the DCA approach room rocked to the force of the explosion.

———

President Deakin took the news of Tammy's involvement philosophically. "I wouldn't have believed it," he told Strooker on the telephone.

"The evidence is incontrovertible, sir."

"Well, you're going to have a hard time convincing Doris. She thinks a lot of Tammy."

"I'll lay her the facts."

"By the way, Hy?"

"Yes, Mr. President?"

"I left my jar of jelly beans on the Oval desk. Have someone get it and bring it down here before that clown Kevin Keik flushes them down his gullet."

"I'll do that."

"Doris wants to talk to you. Here she is."

Strooker's conversation with the first lady was spirited. "Tammy involved with terrorists? My own secretary? Absolute nonsense! I hand-picked her!"

"I'm afraid everything points to her involvement, Mrs. Deakin. The failed polygraph. The Glonass receiver. The fugitive male terrorist recently in her apartment."

"You're making a serious mistake, Hyram."

"I don't think so, ma'am. I'm picking her up this afternoon."

"Trust me. Call it woman's intuition or whatever. I handpick my girls and not a single one of them has subversive instincts."

"This one does."

"Alright. Give me a chance to wring the truth from her. She'll tell me everything, you'll see. Bring her down to Blair-Lee immediately."

"Can't do that, ma'am. All due respect. Couldn't allow anyone suspected of felony association with terrorists anywhere near the First Family. I'd be negligent in my duty."

"Send her, Hyram. That's an order! Okay, I'm asking."

"Ask something else, Mrs. Deakin. Please."

"Okay, you frisk Tammy for hidden weapons and then send her over with a couple of Secret Service agents. I'll do the rest. She'll talk to me. If there's anything to tell, she'll tell me. The regular police and FBI—they're too ham-handed and tough. They wear welders' mitts when velvet gloves will do. She's a woman. I'm a woman. I employed her. She'll talk to me."

"Mrs. Deakin, I don't want more than a handful of people knowing that you and the president are in Blair-Lee. If Tammy comes over there and she's as involved as we think, she'll get the message over to her friends somehow, and we have reason to believe that her friends are after the president."

"On the contrary. When she finds out we're in Blair, you watch her very closely afterward. If she tries to contact her so-called terrorist friends, she'll lead you right to them. Have you thought of that?"

Silence. The First Lady had a point.

"Good. Listen, I'm going to call her now, Hyram. We forgot Shakespeare in the family quarters. He doesn't like to be left alone, you know. I'll have her bring him over. Leave the rest to me."

CHAPTER 36

Washington, D.C.

The telephone call from the First Lady came at 3:14 p.m.

"Tammy, dear, Donald and I are over at Blair. Do you know where that is? New security measures, you know. I left Shakespeare in the living room upstairs. See if you can find him and bring him over, will you, dear? You've always had a way with him."

"Of course, Mrs. Deakin. Right away."

"And while you're up there, go inside my bedroom. On the dressing table, you'll see my foundation. Bring it with you. I don't have any with me."

"Which? The Esteé Lauder or the Max Factor?"

"Esteé Lauder. Oh, and I probably need a couple of other things as well. I just can't remember what they are right now. I'll send Susan for them when I do." Susan was one of the cleaners for the First Family quarters. .

Tammy pulled on her ash sweater and blue windbreaker and pinned her official White House pass to her coat lapel. She felt cold in the moderate autumn weather and couldn't figure out why. Perhaps a result of the vague unease she'd been feeling all morning. She shuddered, wondering what it must have been like during the Carter years when thermostats had been set at fifty-five degrees Fahrenheit and staffers wore coats *inside* the White House. Carter's famed Moral Equivalent of War gambit. Oh well, a chance to stretch her legs, get away from the heavy volume of mail to the First Lady. Most of the mail was patriotic, pro-American, and seething with rage against the terrorist responsible for the death of Evelyn Walsh and the mayhem in Illinois.

Mrs. Neal looked up reproachfully at Tammy. "Shakespeare in distress again? You should open a puppy kennel."

"I guess I should. I don't even own a dog. But, yes, I love the critters."

"So get one."

"Not so simple. It's *verboten* in my condominium rental agreement."

"Awful shame." Mrs. Neal bent over her work.

"Cheer up," Peggy said as Tammy walked to the door. "The next stray that shows up at my door, I'll bring over to Mother Teresa Tammy."

"Great. And I'll send it right back to the Mother Teresa Dog Pound," Tammy shot back.

She climbed the carpeted stairs to the First Family's living quarters. She knew a hidden bank of surveillance cameras watched her every move. A Secret Service agent waited for her at the door. He had been briefed. He opened the door to let her in. She didn't have to look for Shakespeare. The mutt was barking its head off behind the safety of the heavy oak door. The venom was directed at the Secret Service agent, but Shakespeare hunkered down when he saw Tammy, his tail thumping furiously on the ground.

"Come here, boy. Come here, Shakespeare." Shakespeare sidled over to Tammy, allowing himself to be patted and lifted by the scruff, though still keeping a wary eye on the Secret Service agent.

"What did I do to deserve this?" the agent moaned.

"He sees through your Tom Cruise good looks."

"Cute dog." The agent reached out to stroke Shakespeare's head.

Shakespeare snapped at the stroking hand, growling low and mean, one crazed eye glaring at the agent.

"He bites," Tammy warned.

"Not so cute, after all."

She found his leash beside Mrs. Deakin's adjustable couch and entered the boudoir, still carrying Shakespeare. Gifford, the First Cat, sat sublimely on the burgundy bedroom sofa beside a couch pillow with the letters DD monogrammed on it. He watched the visitors disinterestedly. Gifford had white fur, like Shakespeare, and was a Persian. The Secret Service agent followed Tammy discreetly into the bedroom.

Tammy nodded at the cat. "Want to try catching that one?"

"Thanks, but no. My wife will never believe the claw marks came from a cat."

"Here, Gifford. Come here."

The Persian blinked long and insolently, ignoring her.

"He's not on the list. We only came for the dog."

"Are you going to leave Gifford here?."

"Well, whatever. Mrs. Deakin said to only bring Shakespeare. This cool cat doesn't look like it's going anywhere."

Tammy shrugged. The agent watched as she collected the cosmetics. They went out again, closing the door. The agent followed her downstairs. "I'll escort you to Blair-Lee," he said. Then in response to her searching look, "New security measures."

That catchall phrase. Tammy sighed. She was almost certain everyone knew by now about her and Nabil. Sure, they acted as though nothing was wrong and greeted her and bantered with her. The pleasantness seemed forced. And she felt the layer of insincerity beneath the *bonhomie*. The sudden painful silences when she entered a room, even though from outside she had been able to hear spirited conversation. The silence upon her entry meant she had been the object of the conversation—a veiled, accusatory finger. She would tell her side of the story soon enough.

She and the Secret Service man took West Executive Avenue, using the zebra crossing to walk over to Blair. She was recognized at the Blair-Lee gate and the uniformed agents there told her Mrs. Deakin was expecting her. Nonetheless, she was searched thoroughly and even Shakespeare's fur got a thorough comb-down to make sure there were no hidden gadgets. Then she was waved in. The scanty security did not fool her. When the president used Blair House as an alternate mansion, the last thing the Secret Service wanted to do was advertise that fact by deploying extra guards around the grounds. On the front side of 1600 Pennsylvania, she had seen the usual group of tourists and on-lookers loitering at the fence, before the concrete stanchions, looking toward the fountain of the front portico at the great house itself, symbol of everything American, and at what they imagined must be the man inside, the man who ruled this great nation, the most powerful man in the world. They were looking in the wrong direction, Tammy thought, not without a tug of pity.

Kevin Keik was inside the White House. Donald D. Deakin was at Blair-Lee.

She had never been inside Blair House before. It was closed to the public. Two Secret Service agents sat at a table in the small hallway. They nodded to their colleague and said to Tammy, "Upstairs. Last room facing the corridor."

The electronic eyes of two video cameras mounted above the door followed their movements on the red carpet to the upstairs chamber. A corridor of cream-colored ambiance displayed Impressionist paintings on its walls. The corridor ended at the heavy mahogany door also in a cream shade. The agent knocked on the door, a voice said, "Come in!" and they went inside.

It was an informal drawing room, large and rectangular with furniture predominantly from the Federal period. A Baltimore Sheraton-style breakfront bookcase displaying vermeil china stood beside the beige, carved-wood mantle, where a pair of unlit candelabra stood on either side. Two wing chairs in rococo style, a mahogany tambour desk on the other side of the mantle from the Sheraton bookcase, and a gilded chandelier swinging from the middle ceiling—all in the pervasive beige ambiance.

Tammy could tell that Mrs. Deakin didn't like her new surroundings at Blair. Red was her favorite color. Spotted red, checked red, bold solid red—anything but this beige. Wherever she ended up, the First Lady tended to immediately redecorate to her own cheery red taste.

Mrs. Deakin had once said, admiring Tammy's new beige, kick-pleated skirt, "How utterly charming, Tammy. You must tell me who your tailor is. (She had bought the outfit at JCPenney.) It should look really super in burgundy twill. What's your favorite color to wear?"

"Oh, I haven't given it much thought. Charcoal, I think."

The First Lady had snorted. "How silly. Green would be perfect on you. You *are* a redhead, Tammy. Every woman should know her favorite color. Just look in your wardrobe." Tammy had looked. Lo and behold, the preponderance of green fabrics revealed her subconscious preference.

Doris Deakin rose from a lilac brocade couch as Shakespeare—ears flattened, body quivering, tail thumping twenty times to the dozen—bounded from Tammy's arms into the First Lady's. Mrs. Deakin held him and shut her eyes briefly while Shakespeare slobbered over her face.

"Shakespeare," she cooed, "you lovable pooch." She kissed his muzzle then freed her face to say to the Secret Service agent, "You may go now, Terence. Tammy, you stay behind."

The agent hesitated, shrugged, and left.

"Now, Tammy, come sit beside me." Mrs. Deakin pushed aside some couch pillows and sat down. Tammy parked herself beside the First Lady, who reached for the serving tray gleaming with valuable china and silverware, and excised a small piece of raisin cake. She offered the morsel to Shakespeare. "There. Off you go." She set him on the ground and he scampered off.

"Now then, Tammy—tea or coffee?"

"Coffee, please."

"Cream? Sugar?"

"Both. Mrs. Deakin, let me do it myself."

"I won't hear of it, Tammy. You are my guest."

The conversation was unreal to Tammy. It reinforced her conviction that things were not quite right. Why had the First Lady called her in here? To fire her? She felt the blood pounding in her temples. Surely this could not be happening to her.

Mrs. Deakin crossed her legs and adjusted the hem of her skirt. "Now, Tammy—"

Feet pounded down the hallway outside. The door flew open and President Deakin burst in, closely followed by two Secret Service agents. Two more agents bounded in combative mode.

Here it comes, Tammy thought.

The president didn't even acknowledge her presence.

"Doris, come over here." His voice was urgent, and he had moved to the wide Georgian windows and pushed aside the beige brocade curtains.

"What is it, Donald?" The First Lady had caught the strident note in her husband's voice.

"Take a look. They're evacuating the White House." He pointed across Pennsylvania Avenue to the White House Lawn and its golden autumnal colors, to the stream of people—White House staffers, policemen, Secret Service agents—running helter-skelter for cover, forgetting the orderly evacuation drills they had practiced many times before.

"Why are they running? Is it a bomb scare?" The First Lady's breath came out hard.

Even as she spoke, the East Wing seemed to be enveloped in a cloud of smoke and what seemed like five or six loud explosions ripped into one shattered the afternoon's peace.

The building shook, the shock of the explosion rattling the windows.

"Mr. President," the lead agent who'd accompanied the president into the room said, "my orders are to take you and Mrs. Deakin to the cellar. Right now! There's an airplane with a radio problem heading this way, and we think it's a deliberate ploy. Mr. President—"

"I'm not running again, dammit. What in the hell is happening to the country I'm supposed to be running? I refuse—"

Loud crackling explosions. The West Wing disintegrated. Smoke rose from the mansion itself.

Deakin paused as a deep rumbling sound, growing in pitch each passing second, seemed to emanate from the very rooftop.

"What the hell is that?" demanded the president of no one in particular.

The noise reached a crescendo and became more of a high-pitched whistling sound, the sound of air disturbed by a fast-moving surface. The sound was headed their way, and they could now identify it as some sort of buzz-saw airplane traveling at great speed. The president felt himself and Doris being shoved to the ground by the Secret Service agents, and he could see from his peripheral vision the woman Tammy hurling herself to the floor. There was a crackling firecracker sound, then a sudden earth-shattering *BOOM!* Even lying down, he felt the hard slap from the invisible pressure wave and felt Blair-Lee rock on its foundation.

Deafening silence.

A Secret Service agent was the first on his feet. He peered cautiously out the window. "Oh, my God. The White House. It's . . . gone!"

CHAPTER 37

Washington, DC.

Ken Dwight and FBI Tasker Al Daniels were in the former Treasury building poring over the Message Unit Details for Mrs. Fierstal's telephone over the past two weeks. The MUDs had been obtained from Verizon. The MUDs for Tammy Weasel for the past two months lay nearby on the table. For now, he concentrated on Mrs. Fierstal's MUDs, thinking it odd that while she was verifiably out of town for one week, three calls had been placed from the telephone inside her apartment—and not from a cleaning lady either, because she didn't have one.

Two of the calls were to a suburban Maryland number, the third to Dr. Polk's office in Manassas, Virginia. The calls to Maryland had been made after 10:30 p.m. and he wondered about the significance. The intruder had suspected that Tammy's telephone would be tapped. A trained man most likely: subversion protocol moved against using a residential phone for important calls. Protocol had been breached, because the intruder in question was a wanted man on posters dotting bus stations, subway lines, and post offices across the country. His mistake—he hadn't counted on the last number redial feature on Mrs. Fierstal's telephone.

A quick check revealed the Maryland numbers belonged to the Center for Democratic Alliance.

"What the hell's that?" Daniels asked.

"We'll soon find out," Dwight said. "Gotta brief the chief first." He dialed Strooker's office down the hall. Strooker listened to the briefing but couldn't offer much help on the CDA.

"Can't remember offhand. Seem to have heard of it someplace. Keep digging. Call me when you come up with something. Run it by Creed over in Justice—right up his alley. I'm going over to the mansion now. I want to move Smurf One to Blair. Priority, you understand."

"Sure. Something come up?"

"Just a hunch. Too many loose balls in the air. Things not quite right. The old grouch won't like it. Can't be helped. If you try me at the mansion and I'm not there, try Blair. Got it?"

By mid-afternoon, a clearer picture of the CDA evolved. It had been formed in the early seventies by some young congressmen as a think tank of sorts, concerned with this or that agenda, this bill or that, and landmark mostly liberal issues. CDA recruits tended to be far-left do-gooders—lobbying congressmen, writing petitions, and distributing pamphlets. The movement waned in the early eighties with Reagan's landslide election and the country's swing to the far right. Most of the members lost interest, and the CDA struggled for years with one phone line and a single secretary who took calls, then mailed the necessary pamphlets or briefs on pending legislation to those interested, urging them to contact their congressmen and let their feelings on that issue be known.

In the last two years, it hadn't functioned at all, although still a registered think tank. Repeated telephone calls went unanswered. Initially, the CDA had resided in a downtown DC office. Now the only number registered to it was in a Maryland suburb. Eight calls in the last six months—there could have been a lot more to that number, but the MUDs only recorded when the receiver was picked up—and those eight were all after 10:30 p.m.

Why would a known terrorist be making a series of phone calls to a defunct political lobby?

Two first-term congressmen had founded the Center for Democratic Alliance. Something clicked simultaneously in Dwight and Daniels's minds.

"See what I see?" Daniels pointed to the first name.

"Sure do. His name's shown up now two or three times in the past two weeks. I don't think its coincidence."

"Neither do I. The other congressman we can eliminate. I happen to know he lost his seat four or five years back and has retired to his Iowa farm ever since."

"If you say so. We'll just confirm a few facts before we brief Creed and Strooker on this significant development."

"Sounds great."

Dwight reached for the telephone and stopped his hand in mid-air. There was a faint sound, growing in pitch every second. Then he knew what it was—a racing engine, an airplane, props at full bore. A whistling sort of terminal sound accompanied the screaming engine.

He locked eyes with Daniels simultaneously as understanding flooded his mind. He had just time to think "An airplane's going down!" when he felt the blast wave, and the Treasury building, next-door neighbor to the White House, rocked on its foundation. The *boom!* of the explosion filled the micro-space between the pressure wave and the abrupt silence of the screaming engine.

———

Nabil didn't remember much about the actual ejection. He dimly heard a firecracker sound as the detonating cord ignited. A sudden roaring, the feeling beneath him of uncontained, brute energy as a concrete fist slammed him senseless. In the split-second before he blacked out, he had a sensation of his head being squeezed by a too-solid vice, the exhilarating sense of levitation, so spirited he had a split-second thought that this was the world's best roller-coaster ride.

Because he was unconscious, he neither knew nor felt his features being pulled into a ghastly rictus by seven times the force of gravity—his body, which previously weighed 170 pounds, shot up in a split second to 1190 pounds. His gums instantly bled, his skull and body inflating and deflating like a life-sized balloon. He was still unconscious when the seat, dragging its drogue stabilizer, reached its four hundred-foot trajectory.

Barometric sensors on the parachute detected a sea level ejection and commanded instant deployment of the pilot's parachute. The jerk of the opening parachute separated him automatically from the seat, simultaneously with the sound of another minor thunderclap as the parachute filled.

Had he been conscious, he would have noted that at approximately the four hundred-foot apogee of the ejection seat ride, the whole earth shook and a massive blast wave vaulted the seat even beyond its designed trajectory. A major portion of what had been the White House—residence of every United States president since John and Abigail Adams became the first occupants in November 1800—became a pile of rubble. Dust and smoke rose in a ghastly black pall over the Executive Lawn. Had he been conscious, he would have seen two Stinger-equipped marines on the rooftop who, even as they raised the weapon to their shoulders to blow him out of the sky, were themselves launched inside the disintegrating cauldron of the mansion.

The Engineer's cocktail of destruction had done devastating work.

It seemed he was on the ground barely five seconds after chute deployment. His blackout had lasted all of twelve seconds. Incredibly, he landed in the thick shrubbery of JFK's *magnolia soulangeana*, overflowing the southwest quadrant of the crumbled South Portico. Debris rained down on his flight helmet. His parachute had snagged in some high branches of the magnolia.

He knew the ejection would not have been as traumatic had he been inside a full pressure suit. He vaguely remembered seeing the seat fall into Gerald Ford's American elm. He himself was in probably the thickest part of the President's Park, next in foliage possibly only to LBJ's Children's Garden and the Jefferson Mounds. He remembered everything vividly, abstractedly, once again giving silent thanks to the perfectionist—and the late—Major Brobov.

The West Wing had sustained substantial damage. Through the dust and ascending column of thick black smoke to his right, he could make out the East Wing, standing on a few columns of rubble. These were additions to the main structure. The White House itself—incalculably historic, symbol of America—was now total rubble.

He ducked as two F-16s screamed overhead, and peeled off to secure a 15-mile perimeter around ground zero.

He heard cries and shouts and screams everywhere. People staggered out from the debris, dazed, cut, bleeding. They had not been quick enough when the evacuation order had been given. They still were not sure what had happened.

A woman's leg jutted out from beneath collapsed masonry, white and stark, not even a stretch mark on her pantyhose. He couldn't tell if she was alive or dead and didn't dare investigate.

Acrid smoke filtered through his helmet, and he began to cough. He tried to move and found that his harness had also snagged on the magnolia branches. He pulled out his Swiss army knife and cut the shroud lines before freeing himself. He had to get out of there. Witnesses would have seen the parachute settling behind the South Portico. Nabil stepped over fallen masonry and collapsed beams to reach a gap through the magnolia where he could see daylight.

He stumbled toward the smoking White House rubble. He tied a handkerchief around his nose and mouth, entered the dim confines of the devastated building.

He heard someone groan beneath a broken chandelier from a dangling ceiling. One partially shattered hall incongruously displayed a portrait of John James Audubon. From the jumbled red furniture and torn red carpet merging with another jumble of predominantly yellow furnishings, Nabil guessed he was in the area between the Red Room and the State Dining Room, both now history. The groan came from a uniformed officer of the Secret Service.

The man lay on his side, moaning. The chandelier—a heavy piece of furnishing if ever there was one—rested on the man's shoulder and face. Nabil lifted the chandelier off the inert figure. A nasty gash had been opened on the man's left temple and it bled freely down his hair and ear to the ground. Nabil dragged the partially conscious man behind a red couch hidden by a half-standing wall.

Without warning, there was a sudden brilliant flash of light. Nabil flattened himself against an English rug a split second before an ear-shattering explosion rocked the entire foundation. More debris rained down. When Nabil raised his head, a scorching flame rose from the east side of the rubble, the tentacle of flame fanning out in all directions. The gas mains had ruptured.

Confusion, smoke. It was difficult to see. Nabil lifted the uniformed officer—he was about Nabil's height, thinner in build—and set him up at a forty-five degree angle against a slab. It was a fine Caucasian face, stubble-free, straight, chiseled nose, thin lips that stopped short of receding beneath the full mop of hair and blue eyes. A stern, boyish face. It had to be quick, it was not at all personal, and if he thought about it or looked at the man a fraction longer, he would never be able to do it and the man would live to testify he had been disrobed by the Contractor.

Nabil got behind the man, pinioned the head and twisted, pulling up sharply. It was never a pleasant sound, no matter how many times one heard it, the horrible snapping of neck vertebrae and spinal column. The man's eyes opened suddenly, incredible fright and despair rolled into them, the realization that he couldn't—wouldn't ever—breathe again. Still, he slalomed for air, for life-giving breath, and then he gurgled into silence.

It took Nabil less than five minutes to remove the man's uniform and change into it, careful not to get blood on it. A damp, discolored spot on the shoulder lapel, hardly noticeable. He left the dead man in his white vest and boxer shorts and appropriated his official holster with its .38 Smith and Wesson. He tucked the Glock inside his waistband, beneath his shirt. The pager and the Swiss army knife and Tammy's soiled underwear (his good luck talisman) he stuffed into various pockets. Then his escape fund—$6400, in hundred dollar bills with the four hundred in various denominations—he divided between his vest pockets and right trouser pocket. He bundled Polk's flight suit and his own clothing together and hid them inside the recesses of a white marble fireplace incredibly still standing with its smashed, bronze doré clock. From the clock's innards rose a preternatural chime from a miniature music box. Fascinated, Nabil looked at the clock: 3:45 p.m.

He could hear screaming and desperate shouts from inside and outside the rubble. Rescuers. In the distance, ambulance and police sirens wailed, and it seemed like all MPD cruisers were headed for the scene of carnage. Nabil retrieved the dead officer's peak cap from where it had fallen, then dashed inside the shambles of what had been the State Dining Room to consider his options.

Should he fake an injury and allow himself be ferried out of there? Medical triage teams would be out there and would quickly discover his ruse. He saw another uniformed White House officer trying to drag an injured male staffer from under a collapsed beam. The officer knelt, got the injured man in a fireman's hoist, and staggered toward safety. He saw Nabil, who was pretending to be shell-shocked and said, "Get out of here, buddy. There may be another bomb."

Nabil moved toward the rubble of the West Wing, now in flames from the gas main explosion. He saw a woman dragging herself away from the mess, her face blackened by smoke.

"Help me, please . . . help me."

That would be a good way to get out. Rescue someone. He started toward her and stumbled over something that moved. He pushed aside the tangle of broken furniture, crushed beams and powdered masonry and beheld a man, probably a mid-level staffer, in a Van Heusen shirt with polka dot tie and Haggar slacks.

Nabil knelt down and freed the man's upper torso. He could see how he had been able to breathe until then; an air pocket existed where a wood panel rested on a twisted beam. The man took a deep breath. When he exhaled, dust flew from his mouth and nose. But his eyes did not show gratitude or relief, only pain.

"My leg hurts," the man said, shutting his eyes again. "Jesus . . . I think it's broken. My back, too."

"Easy now," Nabil said. "Easy. You're almost free now."

"Sumbitch leg hurts," the man groaned.

Nabil started pulling and tugging at more masonry. Some of the brick slabs were damnably heavy, but he could just manage. And through it all, the emphysema-like difficulty of breathing the smoke-begrimed air. Just then a bullhorn cut through the noise.

"Attention! Attention, everyone. Please evacuate the premises now. EVACUATE NOW! Everybody. That includes rescue personnel. Leave now. There is a possibility of a delayed-fuse bomb going off. Stop now and get out so we can find and defuse the bomb. Attention, please . . ."

The announcer's voice was drowned out by the whistling roar of two F-16s thundering by the White House in a low pass. This time Nabil didn't duck. He scrabbled away at the debris and suddenly the man was free. You didn't have to have seen a broken leg before to know this was one. Midway between the knee and ankle, jagged white bone protruded through the fabric dampened by blood; the ankle was rag-doll twisted in the other direction. The man had opened his eyes again and tried to stand. Nabil hurriedly blocked his vision with the palm of his hand so he wouldn't see his terrible wound. Too late.

"Jee-sus," he wailed. "I won't be able to ski again."

"You'll live," Nabil said gruffly. He tried to lift the man, ignoring his cries of pain. It was easier from beneath, one arm under the knee, the other under the shoulders. The way one would carry a child. This one weighed 160 pounds. Nabil bent almost double with the weight.

"Attention please!" The bullhorn again. "Evacuate now. This instant! Leave the injured. We'll get to them very soon. We need to sweep the place for another bomb."

Ignoring the bullhorn, firemen in yellow hard hats and high boots ran across the North Lawn, wielding fire axes. Others charged into the inferno as their colleagues unrolled the massive hoses. A rapid intervention vehicle (RIV) bucking wildly on independent, four-wheel transmission raced through the north entrance to pull up sharply by the boxwood hedge. Twin turrets from the RIV belched white extinguishing foam at the licking flames.

The West Wing had suffered more damage than the East Wing as a consequence of the sixth rocket misfiring. Nabil noted with satisfaction that the Oval Office was completely destroyed.

He headed for the front gate entrance where he had seen paramedics running helter-skelter. A stretcher team suddenly appeared and took the injured man from him, carefully placing him on a stretcher. A fireman bearing a first-aid kit clapped Nabil on the shoulder. "You hurt?"

"No. No. I'm fine."

"Better get on over there and have 'em look at you."

"I'll be fine," Nabil muttered in his best American accent. Gotta call my wife, let her know I'm okay."

He staggered through the triage teams busy with the wounded and dying laid out on the Lawn and spilling out onto Pennsylvania Avenue. Cops and medics were everywhere. He bumped into one cop. "What's going on there?"

"Lots of bodies," Nabil muttered, not looking the cop in the eye, trying to appear as though suffering from post-traumatic shock. "Bodies everywhere. They'll need lots of body bags."

"What happened?"

"A bomb went off. Lots of bodies."

The cop glared at him contemptuously. "Then get in there and help out. What are you wearing that uniform for anyway?"

"Gotta call my wife," Nabil mumbled. "I'll be right back."

The cop left him and headed toward the chaos. Nabil moved on. The entire section of Penn Ave between East and West Executive was being cordoned off. More police and emergency vehicles were pulling up by the minute.

Away from the emergency personnel, he looked back. Thick black smoke rolled into the sky from where the White House had been. The sky darkened as the pall moved over the city. The red-and-blue revolving beacons of emergency vehicles threw jagged, disorienting light beams on the smoke pall, creating a stroboscopic effect. Firemen reeled hoses, and thousands of gallons of water arced into the flames. The cries of the wounded rose above all the noise as medics scurried about administering first aid. It was a scene straight out of hell.

Nabil reached Lafayette Park unmolested.

He breathed easier.

CHAPTER 38

Washington, DC.

The banshee siren wailed and the roof lights flashed, as the ambulance raced up Connecticut Avenue on its way to Walter Reed Army Hospital. This was no ordinary ambulance. Two MPD cruisers and two carloads of Secret Service agents cleared the way with full sirens. Behind the ambulance, yet another carload of Secret Service agents and an MPD cruiser kept in step.

Inside the ambulance, sitting beside the driver, was a Naval officer with a black briefcase handcuffed to his left wrist. Known as the Football, the briefcase contained the nuclear codes to launch a first strike or retaliatory second strike at an enemy of America . By official protocol, the Football must never be more than a few yards away from the president of the United States whenever he left the White House. The man holding the Football kept glancing back through the glass window at the two doctors and two paramedics working feverishly over the inert form of the president. There was no space inside the ambulance for Secret Service agents or they would have been there, too.

The doctors were in radio contact with a specialist emergency physician at Walter Reed, who monitored a screen showing vital signs from electrodes placed on various parts of the president's body. These vital signs were relayed by datalink to the hospital and they were not good.

"I still can't get a pulse," one doctor said into his clip microphone. His colleague was applying CPR to the unresponsive patient in the gurney. Both doctors were in blue surgical scrubs and had been pulled away from a nearby area hospital to assist the triage teams converging on the White House lawn.

When a barely breathing body identified as that of President Deakin was pulled from the rubble, the two doctors nearest the body had been conscripted by Secret Service agents to administer first aid and immediately accompany the ambulance to Walter Reed. The two paramedics who came with the ambulance were ejected.

"You got a faint one a while ago," the ER doctor's voice crackled over the radio.

"I sure did."

"You just continue CPR, partner. I got you covered."

Over at Walter Reed, the CPR physician watched the ECG readout on the monitor. Suddenly the squiggles bottomed out, flatlined. A continuous audio tone sounded.

"You've got an arrest!" the doctor yelled. "Defibrillate."

Inside the ambulance, the paddles were instantly placed on the patient's chest. "Stand clear!" warned the recorded voice from the defibrillator's auto pack. Two seconds later, the president's body leaped against the gurney restraints as the current swatted him.

"Shock administered," said the electronic voice.

A faint titter appeared on the monitor at Walter Reed.

"Once more," the ER physician ordered.

"Stand clear!" piped the electronic voice two seconds before a second jolt of electricity whacked the patient. Again, the president's body jumped.

A squiggle. Two squiggles. Then a continuous, flat line.

"Shit! We lost him."

The doctor resumed manual CPR.

"Stick him. Stat."

"Yeah. Okay."

The second doctor loaded a long-needle syringe with epinephrine. His hand shook noticeably, because this was the president of the United States and he was only an intern. History would judge him harshly if he missed on the stick. He now regretted not having visited the morgue more often to practice. But then he never seemed to have time for anything this past year. His colleague was a third-year surgery resident and would probably do a better stick. "How good is yours?" His voice frogged.

"Fifty-fifty. Same as yours."

"Want to try?"

"Go for it."

The intern felt along the ribs until he found the fourth rib. He got his bearings and located the groove known as the angle of Louis. He held his index finger on the right spot, took a deep breath. "Here goes." He plunged the needle in. For one moment he thought he had missed. Dark red blood cascaded into the syringe. He injected the adrenaline straight into the heart.

Ten seconds later, a faint pulse appeared.

"Great!" said the ER doctor from Walter Reed. "Really great. Stabilize with IV and we're waiting for you guys over here. The pulse looks kind of weak. Be on guard for another arrest."

"Yeah. He's holding up."

He spoke too soon. As the ambulance rounded the final curve before the emergency entrance to Walter Reed, the president's heart stopped beating again. The surgical resident pounded on his heart desperately. "Come on, Mr. President. Don't die on me! The country needs you."

"Paddles!"

"IV lines clear."

"Stand back."

"Stand clear!"

The body jumped. They both looked at the monitor desperately. Nothing.

"Oh, oh. We lost him!"

"Shit. What a royal fuckup," said the resident.

"No, no, no, no!"

"Paddles!"

"Stand clear!"

By this time, they were pulling up to the emergency entrance where Colonel Jerry Gashe, chief emergency room physician—the voice on the radio—and his team were waiting. The president was lifted into a gurney and quickly wheeled to the OR. They had lost the patient on and off for the past ten minutes, and there was grim determination and cold efficiency in the brisk way they set about resuscitation. Right there in the hallway, rushing toward the OR, Dr. Gashe read the vital signs strip, simultaneously auscultating the patient's chest and abdomen.

"Knife!" he called out suddenly.

They were entering the OR now. Someone handed him a scalpel and, without missing a beat, Dr. Gashe made a hefty incision across the president's chest. A nurse inserted retractors expertly and unwound them. Just possibly, the president was drowning in his own blood, unable to breathe, because the pericardial sac was filled with blood.

Dr. Gashe grabbed a hollow needle with obturator and inserted it deep inside the president's chest. He sucked on the open end with his mouth. Blood surged out the tube, splattered his surgical blues, splashed on the floor. A nurse quickly placed a stainless steel pan beneath the tube. Dr. Gashe dug inside the president's chest with his fingers and began to palpate the heart. A faint blip appeared on the monitor.

A cheer went up in the OR.

"Type and cross-match his blood for transfusion," said Dr. Gashe.

"Blood type?"

"Check for organ donor card. Probably quicker to ask the Secret Service."

"O-Negative," yelled a Secret Service agent.

"How about that. A universal donor."

"It'll be touch-and-go," Dr. Gashe said, his hands busy, watching the monitor. "There's lots of damage here. We'll get him stabilized, I'll widen my incision, and we'll do an exploratory."

A Secret Service agent stepped up. "We've notified Dr. Mallard, the president's personal physician. He's on his way over."

Gashe didn't look up. "Good. I know Bill Mallard. This doesn't look too good. Let's get some X-rays here."

———

Thirty minutes later, Dr. William Mallard, White House physician, rushed in. He had been over at Georgetown University Medical School to see a rare corneal carcinoma removed from a patient, and so was not at the White House when the rockets and bomb hit. He'd been summoned by pager. He fought his way through the mad crush of reporters and TV cameramen held back by hospital security and MPD officials, and made it to the OR.

The first thing he noticed was how deathly quiet the OR was. The room was filled with doctors, nurses, even three or four Secret Service agents in scrubs, lounging around. Nobody seemed to be in a hurry. Nobody seemed to know what to do. Worse still, everyone wore long, mournful looks. Dr. Mallard screeched to a halt. He recognized Dr. Gashe.

"Jerry, what's going on here?"

Dr. Gashe turned toward the speaker. His surgical face mask was untied and hanging down on his chest. His face looked stricken, dark pouches beneath his eyes gave him a weary, distressed appearance. When he spoke his voice was steady enough.

"We lost him. I'm sorry, Bill."

"You lost him," Dr. Mallard repeated.

"He was gone even before they pulled him from the rubble. We managed to bring him back a few times. In the end, far too much damage had been done. Multiple blunt force traumas from flying debris, his spleen and liver crushed, torn aorta. Come over here and look at these X-rays."

On the far wall, under fluorescent lights, were eight pictures of President Deakin's skull taken from several angles, two of which were MRI scans. In all but one, in sharp relief, two metal splinters were embedded deep inside the brain. Mallard winced. Either one of those alone would have been mortal.

"The ambulance team did a great job even getting him here," Dr. Gashe continued. "We could only raise a heartbeat for a short period. We didn't fully appreciate the head injury until the MRI. We were beating a dead horse, Bill. Nothing we could do."

Mallard shut both eyes as though unwilling to accept reality. "Oh, Jesus Lord, no."

Dr. Gashe nodded. "Sad. Dallas '63 all over again. Parkland General. Except they had something to work with. We didn't have a shortstop. Couldn't even get to first base. Go ahead. Take a look."

They walked over to the covered gurney. Dr. Mallard lifted the sheet and gazed thoughtfully at his former patient. He addressed his next words to a Secret Service agent in scrubs. "Where's Mrs. Deakin? Has she been told?"

"Not yet. She wasn't in the White House when the bomb hit," the agent said. "She was downtown. Lucky woman."

"Surely," said another agent, "she's heard the explosion and seen the ambulances heading toward 1600 Penn. You got to figure she knows something's happened."

"I'll hold on to the news yet," Dr. Mallard said. "I'll break it to her, if you don't mind, before the press and the whole nation know about it."

Mechanically, as he spoke, he pressed his stethoscope against the President's chest and listened attentively. He moved the stethoscope to the side beneath the armpit and listened again. Nothing. The silence of the tomb. No bruit, nothing from the ventricles, not even body fluids settling down.

He put away the stethoscope, reached inside the pocket of his white coat, and brought out an ammonia vial. He opened it under the dead president's nose. Not a stir. Yes, he had to admit defeat. *Once again*, he thought, regretfully, *we have another dead president*. He pulled back the sheet fully to examine the extent of the injuries.

And gasped.

"What the hell is this? This isn't the president!"

His voice cut through the room like a knife. The doctors rushed to the gurney.

Dr. Gashe dashed over. "What is it, Bill? What do you see?"

"I'm his doctor, that's what. And this isn't my patient. This man is circumcised. The president of the United States is not."

CHAPTER 38

Washington, DC.

He heard the explosion, as did most of Washington, DC. And saw thick, black smoke gushing skyward. Heard what sounded like all the police cars and ambulances in the city racing to the White House. He chuckled. Time to break out the Chardonnay and light a genuine Havana.

Again, he made sure the door was locked. Then he brought out the portable tracking device and hooked it up. Just out of curiosity. The liquid crystal display screen lit up, and he selected city map mode. To his shock, a blip appeared on the gridwork city map display.

What the fuck was this?

He peered closely at the dimly lit LCD screen and selected a higher resolution on the monitor. The blip was not at the White House, as he had thought. The blip was taking a walk! Incredulously, he watched it traverse Lafayette Square onto Sixteenth Street. Watched it turn right on I Street, left on Vermont Avenue, past the Washington Convention and Visitor's Association building.

So he was still alive. He somehow survived the bomb blast. How? It was supposed to be a suicide attack. The face watching the LCD screen puckered in deep thought.

He knew of two ex-KGB contract assassins right there in DC; he could get hold of them. They could eliminate the Contractor before nightfall. But on reflection, why should he die? The job had been done; the White House was rubble, the president of the United States was probably dead. Nabil was a professional. Money collected, job done, no further contact. No residual bad-faith maneuvering, blackmail, requests for further money. It was bad for a contract assassin's reputation. Boris didn't like loose ends, but this was one loose end he could live with.

He decided to let Nabil live.

———

President Deakin was apoplectic with rage. For one thing, the Blair House drawing room was swarmed by Secret Service agents, two of the agents brandishing sinister-looking MP5 submachine guns.

"I'm alright, gentlemen," protested Deakin, dusting off his coat sleeves. "Can't you see I'm alright? I don't need all of you here. Get on over there—" He pointed to the thick smoke pall rising over what had been the White House, "—and help. All hands will be needed. People are hurt and dying."

The agents exchanged glances—one even moved closer to the door—but no one left the room. Deakin wiped the sweat from his forehead, using the white handkerchief from his lapel pocket. Fury, determination, darkened his face. He was in let's-get-down-to brass-tacks mode.

"They will pay," he said, almost to himself. "Those responsible for this will be brought to justice. All of them! They will be hanged by the neck until they are very dead."

Doris sat in stunned silence.

Deakin grit his teeth, the faded-blue eyes icy, marble hard. "If it's Ramalan Sidi, by God, this is really it. We'll erase him and his mud huts from the desert. We'll find him in Tora Bora in his mountain caves, wherever he is." He turned to Doris. "You stay right here, hon, with—" His eyes rested on Tammy. "Tammy, is it?"

"Y-yes, Mr. President."

"I would appreciate that, Tammy. I imagine Carol and Donald Jr. will be calling in shortly from California to see if we're alright. Phone lines will be jammed, Doris will need you around here for a while." He kissed Doris on the forehead. "Honey, I'm going down to take charge of the Crisis Response Center."

A Secret Service agent stepped forward. "Sir, we can't let you leave the room."

"Why the hell not?"

"Sir, an attempt has been made on your life. The attempt may still be in progress. For now, this room is secure. We'll have to re-clear all the rooms in Blair-Lee over again."

"Well, doggone it, I'm not used to this place. I need a phone. Telephones. The Hotline. Even a goddamned cell phone. I've got to reach Scott Bogan and Creed. Moscow's got to know at once that I'm in good health and in charge before it enters their head to launch a pre-emptive first strike. I need communications, goddamn it."

"There are desk telephones and cell phones here, Mr. President. Secure."

"Yeah? Hand me one, then. And get the speed dial chart ready." He was taking off his coat as he spoke, loosening his tie. He walked over to the rococo wing chair, pulled it next to the tambour table harboring a bank of telephones, and picked up the receiver. "Get me the National Security Adviser," he barked.

Doris Deakin, several shades paler in color, turned to Tammy. She managed a wan smile. "Thank you, Tammy. For agreeing to stay." Her eyes were moist. Tammy extended a hand. Mrs. Deakin took it. Suddenly they were in each other's arms, the First Lady heaving silently on Tammy's shoulder, to the astonishment of President Deakin and the Secret Service agents. Two agents made a move toward Tammy but stopped when President Deakin raised a hand. The agents exchanged glances but held back.

"Thank you, Tammy," Doris Deakin said with forced gaiety. "Oh, thank you. It's been such a bad day for us. For America."

My acting days are long over. She knows my act is a sham. Does she really?

"It's alright, Mrs. Deakin. It's going to be alright. You wait and see."

I'll have to call the day care about Tom. Sandy will take care of herself. She knows to stay with Mrs. Fierstal until I get back.

As though reading her thoughts Mrs. Deakin pulled away. She held Tammy at arm's length and looked her straight in the eye. "You'd better call your people and let them know you're alright and that you'll be a little late coming home." She looked around the room. "There should a cell phone somewhere."

The lead agent stepped in. "I'm afraid, Mrs. Deakin, we cannot allow that."

"I beg your pardon, young man." Her frown was not an act.

"I'm sorry, ma'am. Orders are to secure this room. No phone patches, leave all lines clear for the president. We're in crisis mode. Blair-Lee and the Capitol are under lockdown right now."

"I'm sure you'll be able to make that call in a short while," the other agent added, keeping a straight face. "As soon as we get the all-clear."

——————

The House Speaker's secretary Margaret spoke on the interphone. "The attorney general holding on Line Three. Do you wish to speak to her?"

"Put her on," said the Speaker.

Seconds later, Janice Margolin's deep voice came on. "Mr. Speaker?"

"Yes, Janice. What's going on up there? We heard noises, explosions. They seemed to come from the White House—somewhere in the area. What's happened?"

House Speaker Mario Stepzinski had never liked the attorney general. Taller even than most men he knew, her gaunt Lincoln-esque profile, replete with angular spine and obsidian eyes which she hid behind thick Varilux spectacles, was an oddity even in cosmopolitan Washington, DC. Stepzinski had never seen a woman with Marfan's syndrome. He kept his voice neutral, because he sensed rather than guessed what she was about to say.

"Quite a bit has happened, Mario. Quite a bit." Her deep sigh came down the line. "Details sketchy, still coming in. I just got off the phone with Bogan and Chief Justice Malcolm Eagleton. Bogan called me from Walter Reed, where the president's been taken. He died there at four thirty-five this afternoon."

"Deakin dead? Oh, my God!" The Speaker's shock and disbelief came out a muffled sob. "Oh, God, no!"

"I know. We all are sorry. And sad. An airplane loaded with explosives crashed into the White House. President Deakin was one of the casualties."

"Oh, Jesus God. What is this country coming to? You mean, he's actually dead?"

"I'm afraid so, Mario. He wasn't breathing at all when they lifted him from the rubble. They managed to get a heartbeat en route to the hospital, but he died after arrival. Fought like a Deakin. Poor soul didn't make it."

"That's an almighty shame. Wha—Jesus. Ah, gimme a minute, Janice." Sounds of sniffling down the line. "I—I'm not myself right now. Mighty big news, all of it bad, to be imbibing this late in the day."

"I understand." After thirty seconds, "You alright, Mario?"

"Sure. Sure. I was just mourning poor Donald. I mean, we're on opposite sides of the fence, but darn it, we're all the same outside of politics. I sure will miss him. The entire country will miss him. What about Mrs. Deakin, the others?"

"We haven't found Mrs. Deakin yet. We understand she went to her hairdresser. We've gone there and been told she left for the White House a while ago. We don't know exactly where she is. She may be under the rubble, too, and we just haven't found her yet."

"God bless America," the Speaker intoned.

"The reason I called," Margolin went on, "is to acquaint you with a few facts. The ship of state is floundering. A power vacuum exists. The president is dead. The vice president is semi-comatose in Illinois. No one's at the helm. I'm sure you're aware of the Twenty-fifth Amendment to our Constitution, which deals with the incapacitation of the president. I've conferred with Justice Eagleton and FBI Director Creed and NSA chief Bogan. Under the constitution of the United States, Mario, you are third in line to the presidency. The gentlemen I just mentioned have asked me to tell you to present yourself at once to the Supreme Court building to be sworn in by Chief Justice Eagleton as the forty-fourth president of the United States."

"You are sure of this?"

"There is no precedence for this in our history—the president and his veep being dead or incapacitated at once. The Tyler Precedent doesn't address the issue confronting us. President Deakin, before his death, was about to send the name of his veep nominee to the Hill for confirmation. Then this. The logical next step would be for both Houses to declare you acting president of the United States."

She allowed the words sink in. Then softly, "Although you haven't been sworn in yet, Mario, let me be the first to offer my congratulations, *Mr. President*."

Stunned silence at the other end.

"Are you there, sir?"

"Y-yes. Yes, Janice. I am speechless," was all the Speaker could muster.

"So am I. So is the entire nation. We have to move on. I happen to know you've been receiving daily NSA briefings since Vice President Walsh's incapacitation—so you weren't entirely out of the loop."

"No, I wasn't."

"You'll just serve out the president's term. You might decide to run for the next election—that's up to you. Right now, for the past ten minutes, America does not have either a president or vice president. That is unprecedented. Constitutionally, you have just become the leader of our nation. Chief Justice Eagleton has been briefed and will be prepared to swear you in shortly as the forty-fourth president of the United States. Congratulations, Mr. President."

She hung up.

He replaced the receiver thoughtfully.

How many long years had it taken to get here? Twenty, thirty-odd years? The first Polish-American president of the Unites States, even if by default. Why not? There had been a Polish pope, a Polish chairman of the Joint Chiefs of Staff. He had been the first Speaker of the House of Polish descent. LBJ had been sworn in aboard Air Force One on the flight back from Dallas with JFK's casket in the airplane.

At least mine will be on terra firma.

He brought out a handkerchief and dabbed at a tear that had formed in his left eye.

He got up, strode to the door quickly and confidently and unlocked it. His secretary hastened back from the glass window. For the past ten minutes, every worker at the Capitol building had been glued to the window or the television set, following the events in Washington, DC.

She looked up. "A sad day for America," she said, echoing exactly the First Lady's words—though she had no way of knowing it. "It appears the president has been hit. No one is sure right now."

I am sure now. He said gravely, "It's quite bad, Margaret. I expect we'll be hearing details shortly. Any communiqué from the Senate Majority Leader?"

"Not yet." Her lips came together. "Were you expecting a call?"

"Yes, rather."

"It hasn't come yet." She rose from her chair. "More coffee?"

Mr. President? he finished for her silently. Had she been listening? Fourteen years. Good woman. He'd make her his appointments secretary. Double the salary she was making now. She didn't know it, but the next office she'd be receiving calls from would be adjacent to the Oval Office.

"No time for coffee," he said. "I've got less than ten minutes to present myself at the Supreme Court building."

"Oh." The pale blue eyes widened, the prim mouth pursed again. She looked ready to pose the big question, but seemed to think better of it.

He walked back into the office and went to the tiny wardrobe beside the hat rack where he kept two shirts and extra dress slacks for emergencies. He changed from the light blue button-down shirt he was wearing into a white Van Heusen and a conservative, gray tie. It would match better with the dark gray pinstripe and black wingtips he wore. He adjusted the white handkerchief in his left breast pocket into a neat triangle. His swearing-in costume was complete.

The intercom buzzed. "The attorney general is on the line again."

They were waiting for him. Impatient brats! Not that he could blame them. Every second he delayed, the United States did not have a sitting president. Well, let them wait just a little while longer.

He picked up the telephone and said in his best presidential voice, "Yes?"

"Me again, Mario."

"Yes, Janice." *The last time you call me Mario, you beanpole. From now on, it'll be Mr. President.*

"Thank God I caught you before you left." She couldn't hide the excitement in her voice. "There's been an absolute mix-up. The president is not dead. I repeat, President Deakin is not dead. He's alive and well and over at Blair House. You read me, Mario?"

He couldn't believe it.

He just couldn't believe it. The room did a cartwheel in front of his immobile eyes, the blood chilling inside his veins. *Just great. What do I tell my grandchildren—that I was president of the United States for just five minutes?*

Janice Margolin's voice seemed to come to him from an entirely different acoustic medium. It was as if she were speaking underwater or from inside a metal barrel. "You there, Mario?"

"Y-yes, I'm here." His voice, even to himself, was a hoarse croak. "That's great. He made it. Really great." He coughed phlegmatically. "You sure this time, Janice?"

"Positive. The mix-up—thank God there was one—was a deliberate ploy by Hy Strooker. He suspected some kind of attack on the president was imminent and substituted a double in the Oval Office. Kevin Keik, that's the one who died. He looks more Deakin than Deakin himself, if you know what I mean. Anyway, I just spoke to President Deakin and Mrs. Deakin. They're unhurt. Apparently, a handful of Secret Service agents knew of the switch. Strooker himself is dead. They found his body in the rubble. He was involved in the process of evacuating the White House when the blast occurred. White House Chief of Staff Don Panella was also killed, as were five Secret Service agents, uniformed or otherwise. Ken Dwight, chief of detail, survived. He confirmed for me that the First Family were moved to Blair just twenty minutes—get this, twenty minutes—before the airplane crashed into the White House. Close, I would say."

"I'm happy to hear that, Janet. Smart move by Strooker. Pity he had to die in that fashion. I sure am glad our president made it. Long live America."

"Amen. Sorry about . . . my premature call to you. Bogan and Creed were on my neck and Justice Eagleton said it was unconstitutional for the country not to have a sitting president."

"I understand, Janice. An honest mistake under the circumstances." He had regained himself; his voice was fully back. "I suppose I better get on over to Blair myself to offer my condolences and pledge bi-partisan support for any bill or measure he wishes to invoke to get the perpetrators of this heinous act."

"That'll be a nice gesture on your part. I'm sure he'll appreciate it. All America will be behind him on this one. I have to go, Mario. It's absolute hell around here, phones ringing off the hook, press conferences scheduled, whatnot. Regards to Sophia."

"Sure. Mine to ol' Peter." Her husband.

As he hung up, his face underwent a total transformation. His forced neutrality changed into dark, furious, aorta-bursting rage. *Just great! President of the United States for five fucking minutes. Not even that, Mario Stepzinski. Just president-designate.*

Who was it who said, "It ain't over till it's over?" George Steinbrenner? Yogi Berra? He couldn't remember. But the words tugged at his brain.

———

The black Cadillac DeVille limousine trailed the walking figure for one and a half blocks. It accelerated when the lone figure stopped for a red light. The limousine pulled up to the curb, the passenger side window rolled down soundlessly.

"Good evening, Nabil," said a voice accustomed to rich leather.

The man at the pedestrian crossing turned around very slowly. His hands were inside his coat pockets, his eyes narrowed into two hard slits. For one nasty moment, the limousine driver thought the man would draw. He said quickly, "Come inside, Nabil. It's cold out there. Good job you did this afternoon. Come on in."

The walk sign changed to green, as did the traffic lights. The man hesitated. Then he opened the front door and got in beside the driver. The window rolled up noiselessly, and the DeVille moved swiftly and just as silently into traffic. The car's interior was ill lit by the green glow of the dashboard instruments. The air conditioning, despite the invitation, chilled the interior to arctic levels.

Nabil was thinking: *So they can still find me this easily. It must be the pager.*

"Cigar?" The limousine driver held out a wrapped Slim Panatela. Henri Wintermans.

"No."

The driver tore off the cigar wrapping, using his incisors. He was two-and-a-half inches over six feet tall, his girth disproportionate to his height. He was beefy, with red skin and a prizefighter's nose. The rest of his features were in shadow under the black Homburg balanced perfectly on his round head. He stuck the cigar into his mouth and lit it with the dashboard lighter. Pungent smoke wafted.

"Like I said, good job. My congratulations. You are every bit as good as they say you are." The big car took the notorious Washington potholes as though it had been made precisely for them. Each independent suspension rode up and down; the movement traveled along the suspension beam and shock absorber strut and was not transmitted to the occupants inside. The cigar moved. "Except, it was all for naught. President Deakin is still alive. You killed the wrong man."

For the first time, the Nabil showed interest. *Why is he so quiet?* the limousine driver asked himself. Post-traumatic stress syndrome? Strangely enough, he was in the uniform of the White House Secret Service detail. *I wouldn't have recognized him if not for the passive tracker feature in the electronic pager. Wait a minute!* A new thought began to evolve inside his head. Who said luck didn't belong to the enterprising? Just maybe . . .

"Is that my fault?" Nabil was saying, trying to make out the red face and the pudgy features beneath the black hat. "Your people told me when he would be in the Oval Office for sure. I delivered the bomb. I am still alive, but that is of no concern to you. The contract is fulfilled. If the president is not dead, the fault lies with you. If he was anywhere inside the White House, surely he would be dead, or at the very least incapacitated."

The driver sighed. "They made a switch, the bastards. They put a double in the Oval Office and didn't tell anyone. The real President Deakin is at Blair right now. You killed the look-alike president."

"What a pity. All that planning and risk."

"A further quarter-million US dollars will be credited to your Nicosia account by our people if you finish the job tonight. You have never failed on a mission, Nabil."

Nabil fixed his gaze on the driver and said fiercely, "Who the hell are you? Who gave you the authority to negotiate? And where the hell are you going?"

The driver took his eyes off the road and met Nabil's gaze. His eyes were slate blue and radiated self-control and immense lust for power.

"Let me introduce myself. My name is Boris.

CHAPTER 39

Washington, DC.

The White House Lawn and the cordoned-off area of Penn Ave resembled a battlefield. Stretchers littered the sidewalk and meadow, medics circulated, ambulances were everywhere. It was a scene straight from *Guernica*, the driver thought as he maneuvered the big, black car toward the security gate of Blair House and stopped.

Two MP5-toting agents loitered near the guard shack. A uniformed Secret Service agent approached the car as the driver's window slid down.

"Havoc Two Detail," said the Secret Service man behind the wheel. "House Speaker Stepzinski to see Wolfman."

The rear window slid down on powered hinges. The guard took a good look at the driver.

"Name?"

"Meissner. Andy."

"I thought you were on the Whiskey Hotel beat?"

"I am. I was asked to bring the Speaker here. The president is expecting him. Technically, he's number two in the country now."

"I don't need lectures." He took in the backseat and its occupant. "Good evening, Mr. Speaker. I bet your day has been full."

"That's putting it mildly. Twenty-plus years on the Hill. Never seen it like this."

"Could be raining," said the guard. He looked at Meissner again. "You're bleeding. What'd they do—pull you from the rubble?"

"Actually, yes."

The guard nodded, walked back to the gate, and spoke into a telephone for about a minute. He gave a signal to the man inside the guard shack. The electronic gate slid open silently.

The guard pointed to a spot between two cars. "Park over there."

The big car entered the driveway, crunching gravel, and parked. More armed agents appeared. The door was opened for the House Speaker.

"Mr. Speaker? The president is expecting you."

"Yes, I expect so." The Speaker adjusted his tie and straightened his coat. They started toward the front lobby door. "He wasn't hurt in any way, was he?"

"Not a scratch. Wasn't even there."

"Good. Quick thinking on your part, boys."

The metal detector pinged as they went inside the lobby door. The Speaker was searched. A key ring, a bunch of coins, wallet with credit cards and twenty-dollar bills. No lethal hardware. He was waved through. "Second-floor drawing room. He's with Mrs. Deakin. Agent Ballasemo will accompany you."

"Thank you."

Meissner said to the guard who had accompanied him from the gate, "Tell you what—if you can get a relief for me, I wouldn't mind going to the hospital to have my injuries looked at."

"What injury?" sneered the guard. "I lose more blood shaving than that little nick you have there."

"I do feel beat up," Meissner whined. "All that rubble falling around me, I got knocked around a lot. I need a break."

"Not a chance. Take a breather while your charge is with Wolfman. Maybe take an aspirin. Duty first."

One of the agents at the guard table pointed to the leather settees in the lobby. "Have a seat, buddy."

"You want my piece?" Meissner unbuckled his holster with the .38 Smith and Wesson.

The agent shrugged. "We'll keep it for you." He collected the holstered gun and ammunition clip and shoved the lot under the counter.

Meissner sat down on a white leather divan. One of the agents walked toward a white door and went inside. In the brief moment the door was open, Meissner saw it was a restroom.

"Got a head around here?"

"It just got occupied. If you're desperate, there's one right up the stairs, first door to the left."

"Thanks."

Inside the restroom upstairs, he unbuttoned his pants and passed a long stream of urine out of genuine need. He brought out Tammy's wrinkled pink cotton underwear from his pocket and sniffed it. It reeked of her energizing scent—dark, mephitic, suggesting powerful unexplored sexuality. Good. This was what he needed. He was ready for the final act.

When it was all over, he would call her from Ibiza, Spain. The amount in his Swiss account should be close to three million USD now; the one in Cyprus had one and a half million. Two other accounts in Liechtenstein and Monaco held various amounts totaling nearly another million USD. If he couldn't live on that with Tammy and Sandy and little Tom—then he couldn't live on one hundred million dollars either. Of course, Tammy would have to convert to Islam. He couldn't marry an infidel just like that. In time, she would come around—they always did—and embrace the true religion. Look at Queen Noor of Jordan.

He retrieved the Glock from the inner waistband of his trousers. He placed the gun inside his right pocket. The Glock was standard agency issue, and since he had already handed in Meissner's .38 Smith and Wesson, they wouldn't be expecting another piece on his person. On ascending the stairs en route the restroom, he had seen a lone Secret Service agent seated at a small desk guarding the entrance to the drawing room. The agent's presence tacitly confirmed where the president was. There could be, and probably were, hidden surveillance cameras. The only ones he had seen were outside, by the gate, and at the entrance door. It didn't rule out one for the hallway. Unfortunately, Brobov's thorough debriefing had not included Blair House.

He flushed the toilet, ran water over his hands from the faucet, and dried them. He was ready.

He stepped out the restroom and walked purposefully toward the lone agent at the desk. With each step, he felt tension laced by a ridiculous sense of the sublime. The agent was dressed in a black suit and trousers with a narrow, black silk tie. He was in his late forties, his receding hair white-fringed, his clean-shaven face, aquiline nose, and studious air made him look dignified and thoroughly dependable. He resembled more a college professor than a Secret Service agent. He looked up quizzically as the uniformed agent approached.

"Hi there."

His hands rested on the table beside a metal screening wand—it looked like an oversized magnifying glass. He was staring at a patch on the agent uniform, on which the words *Meissner* were embroidered in black capital letters. He seemed to be trying to remember something, or figure out something, and it wasn't quite there.

"Don't touch anything," Meissner said quietly and with such deadly seriousness the agent actually started. His Blair House ID tag proclaimed him to be Sid Nappy, US Secret Service. He looked at Meissner, at the hand in the right pocket, which undoubtedly held a gun—he could see the blunt, hard outline pointing directly at his heart. To the surveillance cameras, to anyone watching, this was a routine interaction between colleagues, one uniformed, the other not. "Just move back from the seat. Stand up. No, don't raise your hands. Don't try anything either or you'll be dead before you can blink. Your vest won't help you a bit."

Sid Nappy—a hurt, puzzled expression on his face—did as he was ordered. "Can I ask what this is all about?"

Nabil ignored his question. "Where's Agent Ballasemo? He escorted someone up here."

"He's gone back down," Nappy said.

"Good. Lead me inside," Nabil said.

"No can do. You know that."

"Are you being stupid or what?"

"Negative. You know our rules. We are sworn to defend POTUS—with our lives, if need be. If you try to go in there, gun or no, I will stop you by all means possible. Even with my life."

Nabil had a brainwave. "Sid, for God's sake, trust me. I am trying to *save* the life of the president." The gun in the pocket moved menacingly. "And I will shoot you and explain later. Now open the door."

———

President Deakin was on the telephone when Speaker Stepzinski entered. Deakin waved a hand to indicate the Speaker should take a seat. Doris Deakin rose and embraced the Speaker.

"Oh, Mario. I'm so glad you could come. It's dreadful what's going on out there. Thank you for coming. Donald will be with you in a minute. Isn't it awful, an airplane falling on the White House?"

"Absolutely terrible, Doris. I rushed over here immediately when I heard. Glad to see you and our president are in good health."

"They moved us out in the nick of time. Have a seat, Mario. I'll ring the butler to bring you some coffee. Or is it tea?"

Stepzinski sat on a Franklin-style sofa. "Black coffee, if you have it."

Tammy bounded to her feet as Mrs. Deakin, unfamiliar with Blair House, hunted for the right button to push. "I'll get it. Coffee for everybody, I guess?"

"That's right, dear. You know where the pantry is? Just through the glass door."

Tammy disappeared. The Speaker crossed one leg over the other and steepled his fingers. "Doris, I can't say how terribly sorry I am—"

"Mario—how good of you to come." President Deakin had finished on the telephone and now advanced toward Stepzinski. The Speaker rose to shake hands with the president.

"Mr. President, I am at a loss for words." Genuine emotion tinged the Speaker's voice.

"Aren't we all, Mario? Aren't we all? The White House reduced to rubble. Scores of people injured or dead." He shook his head dazedly. "Never thought I'd live to see the day."

The Speaker was sympathetic. "Whatever you decide to do, Mr. President, to find and punish the people responsible for this . . . this terrible act, let me assure you of the full support of the bicameral congress and the support of the majority of the American people. Any act of terror on our soil always unites us. That much I know. Have they forgotten 9/11 so soon? We'll sock it to those bastards, when we find out who they are."

Very Nixon, the Speaker thought even as he said the words.

Doris Deakin nodded. She felt wetness against her ankle and knew it was Shakespeare's nose. She picked him up from the rug and placed him on her lap. Shakespeare's tough, leathery tongue lapped her face. She reached down and stroked his white, sheep-like fleece.

"Sit down, Mario," Deakin said, and he himself sat down opposite the Speaker. He looked tired and stressed. A grim determination had set into the thin, hard mouth, pulling his cowboy features into a tight knot.

"I was just talking to my speechwriters," the president went on. "I've got to be on the air in half an hour. Live. All three networks and CNN will carry it. The American people expect that. I bet they're confused right now, wondering what the hell is happening in Washington. They've got to be reassured that their president is alive and on top of the situation."

"Mr. President, let me say on behalf of Sophia and myself, and indeed for all Americans, that we're happy to see you escaped this attack unscathed. For one awful moment there—" The Speaker's hand moved vaguely, "the entire country actually believed you had been killed in the explosion. It even went out on two of the networks. They quickly retracted when they learned it was a mix-up."

"A terrible mix-up," the president agreed. "Janice Margolin called me just before you came in. Apparently this fellow Keik acting as my double was killed when the building collapsed. Bless his departed soul. Terrible business." Deakin shook his head and reflected for a long minute. Then, "Mario, you've been in the loop since—when?"

"How do you mean in the loop, Mr. President?"

"I mean NSA briefings, the nuclear codes, that sort of thing."

"That. Oh, right after the vice president was incapacitated. Bogan kept me in."

"You should remain in the loop, Mario. If anything had happened to me this evening, the entire future of the country would have been in your and Dick Thornburgh's hands. I believe—"

The door opened just then. Sid Nappy entered, followed by a uniformed Andy Meissner.

The president frowned. "I don't recall asking a detail to come in. We're having a private conversation here."

Nabil withdrew the Glock semi-automatic and pressed it into Sid Nappy's back.

"Raise your hands! Everybody!" With the other hand, Meissner turned the key in the lock. "Up against the wall. Don't look back."

Tammy was bent over the tambour table, her back to the door. She had just finished pouring the coffee and was about to bring it over to the Speaker. The cup crashed to the floor, and she spun around.

It's him.

A White House guard's uniform complete with formal peaked cap made him almost unrecognizable. He had also shaved the mustache. Yet there was no mistaking that razor voice, despite the disguised American accent.

"Nabil!"

He was surprised to see her there. But he was too much the professional to be distracted. He knew Sid Nappy would spring if he had half a chance. He ignored her.

"What's going on here?" demanded the president.

Nabil ignored him, too. His eyes never left Sid Nappy, and he covered the others with his peripheral vision. "Bring out your gun slowly," he told Nappy. "By the barrel. One hand only. If you blink, I shoot you."

He had seen that the agent was right-handed from their encounter outside the door. Nappy, face to the wall, complied. Agent Nappy said, "You won't get away, you know. This building is surrounded."

"Let me worry about that."

"You can surrender to me quietly," Nappy went on. "No fuss. I guarantee you will receive the best pre-trial treatment—"

"Shut the fuck up! Drop the gun to the ground. Kick it to one side."

Nappy kicked the gun, a service revolver, near to the smashed cup.

"Hands back up," Nabil ordered. He reached forward, suddenly swung the gun by the stock, and hit Nappy squarely on the back of the neck. As the agent slithered down, Nabil dealt another brutal blow at the base of his skull. Nappy grunted and collapsed hopelessly on the rug. He didn't move.

The president and Mrs. Deakin were ashen in color. Speaker Stepzinski had a look about him of the utmost terror. Tammy Weasel looked ready to faint.

The president was the first to speak. He was breathing hard, trying to stay calm. "Young man, you are misguided. Please put down the gun. We'll get you help and good counseling—"

"Keep quiet!" The Glock pointed straight at President Deakin's forehead. An icy chill of realization coursed down Deakin's spine. *He knows I might be wearing a Kevlar vest. He's taking no chances. I'm a dead president.*"

Doris Deakin found her voice. "Don't shoot my husband, please. We'll give you whatever you want."

"Don't be naive, Mrs. Deakin. You have nothing to offer me. I wouldn't accept anyway. This is something I must do."

"Must you?" pleaded the First Lady. "Can't an old lady appeal to you—to your sense of mercy? We need Donald. Myself. The American people. The whole world. Do you know what I mean?" Her plea was pathetic; tears rolled freely down her cheeks.

"Nabil, please . . ." Tammy added.

"You, too, shut up!"

"You know this man, Tammy?" The president faked astonishment. He wished now he had paid closer attention to Strooker's suspicions regarding Tammy.

"Nabil, please. Don't. I'll marry you. Now. Anytime. Anything you say. Please don't shoot the president."

A wan smile touched Nabil's lips. "Of course you'll marry me." Then he spoke to the president as if reading from a prepared script. "Mr. President, my name is Nabil Hamdoon. Also known as the Contractor. I am here to kill you. Compliments of Ramalan Sidi. Have a nice trip to hell."

He began shooting immediately.

CHAPTER 40

Washington, DC.

In all his years of killing people, Nabil had, without exception, come to find the process of death fascinating. He had once seen a woman giving birth without anesthetic in a refugee camp in Lebanon and had been struck by the parallel between the drama of entering life and the manner of leaving it. Both involved struggle—the struggle to begin life, and the reluctance to leave it when the time came. Dying was a sad, grotesque *danse macabre.*

With revolvers especially, at less than very close range, death was not always immediate. He had shot people through the head or heart and seen them run away on rubbery legs, trying to convince themselves that they weren't feeling the vital juices of life ebbing away.

There was the man he'd shot at fifty feet with a Browning 9mm, who performed a unique St. Vitus dance for thirty more feet, collapsed, got up again and staggered another twenty before quitting. When Nabil reached him, he was still alive; seizures ran through the body three times before the body became absolutely still.

Another man he had shot with a Winchester .303 deer rifle fell pole-axed. The man sat up again three minutes later, staring at his would-be killer, his eyes unseeing. Nabil pumped two more bullets into him before the body was stilled.

Dying gracefully, neatly, from a gunshot wound was the stuff of Hollywood and more often than not the exception. Only a trained sniper or professional killer such as himself beat the odds with the single

well-placed bullet that dispatched the victim without the victim knowing it, becoming aware only of darkness and an icy chill descending
upon him.

By the second shot, the Contractor knew something was terribly
wrong. President Deakin exhibited none of the well-known signs—the
snapping back of the head (he had seen the Zapruder tapes of Dallas,
'63), the absolute mortification on the victim's face as he realized the
bells tolled finally for him. The president had shut his eyes and raised
his hands in front of his face in the defensive pose. With the third deafening crash of the heavy Glock and no trauma to his person, Deakin
was now raising his head in surprise, perhaps at the thought that death,
if this were death, wasn't unpleasant at all.

"You fool," hissed the Speaker. "You fouled everything up! I'll finish
it myself."

Everyone, except Nabil, missed the import of his words. The Speaker
started toward the prostrate Sid Nappy's gun.

"Shut up, Boris," snapped Nabil. His surprise, nonetheless, was evident. In seemingly one swift move, that was actually two separate and
distinct moves, he opened the chamber, checked the contents, snapped
back the magazine and—since the Glock had no safety—raised the gun
to fire again. Tammy grabbed up Sid Nappy's gun, beating the Speaker
to it, and was raising it in what seemed like an eternal slow-motion dis-
cus throw, snapping back the safety with her left hand.

Nabil turned and fired point-blank at her gun hand. Realization
dawned on him too late. He saw the muzzle flashes, bunched, from
Tamnmy's gun . A bee stung him in the throat, another on the left side
of the chest, a gnat lit hotly on his cheek. He knew there were no insects
in the room, and vaguely understood he had been shot multiple times.
He felt the Glock drop from his nerveless fingers onto the rug. He must
have fallen, for he was looking up at the chandelier and the rich textured
ceiling. His knife. The Swiss Army knife. With superhuman effort, he
willed his fingers to move. Just one more time.

"Lookout, he's got a knife!" the Speaker yelled.

Tammy stood in a near-stupor, hands down by her side, the gun dangling from her fingers. She was staring in horror at what she had done, when the Speaker's shout startled her. She started to raise the gun again, and then realized it was not necessary. The knife slithered out of the dying man's fingers; a terminal croak came from his throat. The body kicked once.

The Speaker bent down and picked up the Glock from beside the dead man. "That was close." He was breathing hard. He looked at the president and Mrs. Deakin in turn. They stood rooted to the same spot like mannequins. Both looked as though the events of the past minute had shocked them beyond speech.

"I think he's dead now," said the Speaker, looking down at Nabil's still form. He pulled open the Glock magazine and checked it. Five bullets. One in the breech ready for firing. He snapped it shut again. He turned to Tammy and said gently, "Very well done, my dear. You saved the president's life, no doubt about it. You'll be a hero in the capital tonight." He paused. "Perhaps you'd better let me have the gun."

Tammy nodded. She held out Sid Nappy's gun. Her hands shook miserably.

———

"No!"

The shout came from the president.

Everyone froze. Tammy's gun clattered to the floor.

"Don't give him the gun!" Deakin's voice sliced through the room.

Speaker Stepzinski, who had been leaning forward to collect the gun, swiveled around, and the barrel of the Glock 9mm he had taken from Nabil's corpse now pointed directly at the president. The fear had fled the president's face. In its place, stark comprehension. His eyes bored into the Speaker's.

"He called you Boris, didn't he?" the president went on, fascinated. "Before he died. I heard it."

The Speaker, too, had a strange, almost beatific snarl to his features. "He sure did, Mr. President. Didn't you know?" His voice was that of a stranger.

"We knew there was a mole inside the capital named Boris. We've been trying to locate him for over two years. I must say, Mario, I never dreamed . . . even in my wildest thoughts . . ."

"What did you think, Donald?" the Speaker snarled. "We couldn't afford to let you live much longer. You've done far too much damage. Your so-called Missile Defense Shield. Too expensive. Who's gonna fund it? My grandchildren and your great-grandchildren. You were mortgaging their future to finance a post-Cold War Rube Goldberg device." The Speaker's voice was icy with contempt. "There's no money to meet Social Security obligations as of now. Yet we have the biggest peacetime military buildup in history. Two wars fought this last decade. Iraq and Afghanistan. What did you think the world stage is—the O.K. Corral? I could go on and on, Donald, but you get the picture. Time's up. I'm next in line for the Oval Office. Only it isn't there anymore. There's Blair-Lee, but that'll do. I'll be president this evening, Donald, while you settle your accounts with St. Peter."

"I don't believe this," Mrs. Deakin whispered. "Mario . . . but you and Sophia and us are . . . good friends."

"That's irrelevant, Doris, and you know it," Stepzinski snapped. The gun in his hand never wavered, even though he covered all three of them and kept an eye on Sid Nappy's gun at Tammy's feet.

Tammy was thinking, *This can't be happening.*

"You won't get away with this, Mario," Deakin said. "Secret Service agents will be swarming the place in minutes."

"Is that right? Then why aren't they here yet? Look out the windows, Donald. Over there." His free hand waved at the window. Beyond it, amidst the klieg lights, flashing beacons of ambulances and police vehicles and fire trucks, the earsplitting chatter of jackhammers and pneumatic drills filled the night as the rescue effort proceeded at full blast. "Nobody's gonna hear the gunshots, Donald. I'm going to kill everyone in this room, then wipe off my prints and plant the gun on Nabil over there. It'll be his handiwork. No witnesses. I'll say I managed to overpower him and kill him with the three slugs dear Tammy just pumped into him. And if they want me to, I'll take polygraphs to prove my innocence. But you'll all be dead and the first Polish-American president will be in office. Goodbye Donald and Doris."

He fired point-blank at President Deakin. Then another. The third shot he aimed at Mrs. Deakin.

Impossible! I must be dreaming!

For the second time in less than five minutes, Tammy was diving to retrieve Sid Nappy's dropped gun. The Speaker twisted himself to confront Tammy, a look of utter bewilderment on his face. Not one of the three shots he'd fired had any apparent effect.

Tammy picked up Nappy's .38, still warm, and palmed it, shooting hand straight out in front of her, support hand clasped around gun hand but bent straight down at the elbow, feet apart with the non-shooting foot forward and the shooting foot behind and at forty-five degree angle, both knees slightly bent, the upper body leaning forward, the classic Weaver stance. The way Brian had taught her, the way she had seen him do hundreds of times at the shooting range, snapping back the safety and squeezing the trigger again and again and again until the hammer clicked on successive empty chambers.

The Glock dislodged from the Speaker's hand. A disbelieving expression lingered on his face as he slowly pirouetted on unstable legs and pitched face downward on the beige rug.

Tammy threw the smoking .38 across the room as though she couldn't get far enough away from it. Her mouth dropped. She looked up helplessly, first at the president, then Mrs. Deakin. Like previously rehearsed choreography from a stage play, she staggered forward, as did Mrs. Deakin. The two women collapsed into each other's arms, hugging convulsively. They fell as one onto the three-seater couch, sobbing.

On the floor a few feet away, Sid Nappy moaned, his body twitching. He was coming around.

The door burst open, splintering wood and paint chips into the room. The room was suddenly full of Secret Service agents, all with drawn guns, two of which were Heckler and Kock MP5A submachine guns. Ken Dwight led the group and he took in the situation at once. He walked over to President Deakin.

"You alright, Mr. President?"

Deakin straightened his tie. "I'm fine."

"Case the adjoining rooms," Dwight ordered his men. "Secure all exits and entrances. On the double."

The agents scattered, leaving only Dwight and three other agents in the room. He turned to the president. "Sorry, sir, we couldn't get here in time. We heard what sounded like several cars backfiring. With all the noise across the street, it was a reasonable assumption. When the last volley was fired, there was no mistaking the source. Thank God you're alright." He waved his revolver menacingly. "More of them around?"

"Who?"

"The attackers."

Deakin indicated the two inert forms on the ground and said dryly, "I guess this little bunch here is all there is."

Dwight pocketed his gun. He removed a pair of handcuffs from his side belt and advanced toward the couch. "Tammy Weasel. You're under arrest. Turn around, place your hands behind your back. I warn you, anything you say can and will be held against you in a court of law—"

"What are you talking about?" the president broke in. He looked weary, tired. "This woman here saved our lives."

CHAPTER 41

"So now we know why she bought two boxes of blanks when she purchased the gun," Kohlbus said.

Across the table sat Director Creed, Special Agent Daniels, and Secret Service Chief *pro tempore* Ken Dwight, and NSA Chief Bogan. Deputy CIA Director (Counter-terrorism) Ignacio Corsetti sat on same side of the table as Kohlbus.

"Glock 17 nine-millimeter," Creed said. "We found it in the trunk of her car where the Contractor abandoned it. Inside the spare tire rim. If he'd had to change a tire, he would have found it. Not very imaginative, is she?"

"She's accounted for herself very well," Dwight said.

"All she had to do was give us a call. We'd have taken it from there."

"Nabil threatened her, remember?" Dwight pointed out. "Usual. Repercussions to her children, her mother, by his people if she turned him in. Purchasing the gun was her first attempt at fighting back. She substituted blanks for the real bullets, with the Glock we now know belonged to the slain FBI agent. She hid the blanks inside an old cereal box in the kitchen and made the substitution at different times when the opportunity arose."

"She should have put them inside her drawer. They'd be safer there."

"Not a bit. She suspected Nabil was raiding her drawers. We know that for a fact. We found one of her pink lace panties among his personal effects before the autopsy."

"How about that. A terrorist with a fetish," Creed sniffed. "Did she have to sleep with the enemy, too?"

Dwight shrugged. "The Patty Hearst syndrome. I would think she was confused. Who wouldn't be in her position? The man was strong, domineering, a Svengali. They lived together for a few days. The juices were bound to flow."

Scott Bogan said, "We know her former husband Brian is a National Rifle Association lobbyist and quite fond of guns. He taught her all about guns. Why didn't she just put real bullets in that gun she purchased and blow him away when she had the chance?"

"Right," Corsetti agreed. "What was she hoping to accomplish by buying blanks?"

Both men had addressed the question to Dwight. Dwight had become the source of explanation, perhaps because Tammy had worked at the White House—his turf—and they had known one another on a personal basis.

Dwight sighed. "She knew he was trying to kill the president. She just didn't know how. She had seen on television that the missile attempt from Kokubani's estate had failed. She suspected a lone-assassin attempt might be made. She switched blanks into his gun in an effort to save the president. Also, she hoped that if he got into a gunfight with Secret Service agents during the attempt, his bullets wouldn't do any damage while theirs would take him out permanently. In effect, that's exactly what happened. She could retrieve Sid Nappy's gun with confidence, knowing that Nabil's Glock held only blanks. She was lucky he didn't have occasion to fire that weapon before confronting the president. He would have discovered the ruse, and the results could have been disastrously different."

Kohlbus suppressed a smile. "It obviously made sense to her. That was her way of getting out of it."

"That doesn't answer my question," Corsetti persisted. "Why not fit real bullets in the gun and plug him when he wasn't looking? A 9mm Parabellum in the head would bring him down just like anybody else."

Dwight fixed his eyes on Ignacio Corsetti with a look just short of distaste. "I don't think she trusted herself fully. Nabil was a professional. She was not. What if she missed? Or bungled it? Under the circumstances, I can see her reasoning."

"In the end, she killed two men and didn't miss. One of them was a world-class assassin. The other a top Russian mole who got as far as Speaker of the House of Representatives and damn near sat in the Oval Office. That's pretty good, if you ask me."

"Some woman."

Creed said, "I still want to nail her ass to the bathroom door on all accessories to terrorism charges we can think of."

"Fat chance, Gary," snorted Kohlbus. "The White House—I should say, Blair House—is letting it be known that if a grand jury is convened to hear evidence against Tammy Weasel regarding this whole affair, the president would sign an order granting Tammy an executive pardon."

"Presidential pardon, my ass! What message is he sending to others who have collaborated with terrorists, fringe militia, even with their own kidnappers, and been tried and convicted? What do you say to those people, huh?"

"Don't ask me. Ask the president."

"What does Janice Margolin have to say to all that?"

"She's climbing Mount Rushmore in frustration. She can't do a thing except convene a federal grand jury and indict. What's the use of going to trial when you know the outcome? That's by the way, anyhow. Tammy Weasel resigned her position on the First Lady's staff effective this morning."

"Whoa! What do the president and the First Lady have to say to that?"

"Dead against. Both of them. Asked her to stay on. Tammy is adamant. Wants out. Wants to leave DC, move as far away as possible. Her children, her mother included. First choice is California. Start over."

"It's expensive out there. What's wrong with Idaho, Wyoming, perhaps the other Washington—Seattle maybe?"

Dwight looked at Creed meditatively. "I don't think money's going to be her problem from now on. I hear she's got book offers and a movie deal. Guess who brokered it—Marvin Flatsch. Same joker who represented Kevin Keik. Tammy has indicated she would donate a percentage of the book's proceeds to Mr. Keik's estate. Keik, by the way, is to receive the highest honor Congress can award to a civilian. Posthumously. Even Tammy's husband Brian, I hear, is making conciliatory moves."

"She should let him. He taught her about guns. She wouldn't have been able to do what she did if she hadn't known him."

"I believe she's made it clear to him that the divorce will be finalized, as planned. They remain friends, nonetheless, I gather."

"Hey, Ken. Do you think she would have married Nabil if he'd made it?"

Dwight shrugged. "Who knows? A confused woman might do anything. I think in her own way she mourns him. She's never killed anybody in her life before. In five minutes, she kills her kidnapper and the third-most-important man in Washington, DC."

Daniels shook his head pensively. "Unbelievable. About the Speaker, I mean. Who would have thought?"

"You got it figured out toward the end, didn't you, Ken?" Creed said.

"Yeah. Those MUDs. The calls to the Center for Democratic Alliance. Mario Stepzinski was the founding congressman and a key figure. His wife Sophia never knew the double life he led. Imagine that. Always thought her husband retreated to his private study upstairs to continue his ardent work for the needy and disadvantaged masses of America. She's clean, by the way, Scott, I take it?"

"She checks out," Bogan said shortly. "He tried to kill her for Chrissakes. Put her in the hospital with the same stuff Dr. Kokubani fed his housekeeper. Stepzinski wanted her out of the house 'cause he guessed he would have to harbor those two Russian technicians, Grimsky and Beria, prior to their exfiltration. Which he did. No other safe house for them in DC."

"They stayed at his house a couple of days before fleeing the country via Mexico and Santiago, Chile. They ended up in Austria, where our boys picked them up."

Creed nodded. "Corsetti's people get much of the credit for that. Good work, Ignacio."

The CIA deputy director nodded. Taciturn, expressionless, his round face bland, totally forgettable, the ageless spook. He gave nothing away and never would. "Our men spotted them in Vienna and tipped off the local police. Both men were apprehended."

"I bet the State Department is seeking formal extradition," Daniels said. "Pronto."

"I doubt we'll get them. European courts generally don't extradite to countries where the suspect will likely face the death penalty."

"We were going to seek extradition," Corsetti said sadly. "Both men died in their cells this morning. Cardiac arrest."

"That's a load of bullshit! Cardiac arrest?"

"That's what I said. Same way your man Throck in Dublin got iced. Pacemaker induced."

"That's a crying shame. Now how in the hell did they do that? We must have had those men under twenty-four seven suicide watch."

"We did. Suicide watch, maximum lockdown, twenty-four seven observation—the lot. The surveillance videos are awful to watch. Each man clutches his chest one after the other, looks like he's gasping for breath, falls to the floor. They spasm, and it's all over."

"And the guards?"

"They were still fumbling for the keys to the cell when the men expired. Prison doctors could not revive them."

The men sipped their coffees thoughtfully.

"The nuclear codes," Daniels said. "I hope Stepzinski didn't give out too much."

"Everything's been changed from the ground up," Bogan said. "If he did, those codes are all useless to them now. New codes, different templates—no chance they'll figure out anything."

Creed said, "We found a maroon Dodge van abandoned in Fairfax. Definitely the van used to load the explosives into Dr. Polk's airplane. Residue on the van floor was consistent with material found in charred fragments from the White House rubble. FBI lab positive on all counts. No sign of van occupants. Descriptions from several witnesses match one of the van occupants to a suspected superbomber with links to Al-Qassam, a man known as 'Ghantous the Engineer.' No sign of him."

"The Contractor named Ramalan Sidi," Daniels said. "So we know who to go after. I know the President will authorize unlimited drone strikes and worse. Far as I'm concerned, Al Qassam is finished as an organization."

"The Russians teleguided all this. Bet on it," Creed said.

Bogan nodded. "We all know that. We're not likely to pursue it. Who wants to risk a thermonuclear Armageddon?"

"Grachev is denying everything, of course. Those executions were a fraud. Everyone knows that. You mean we're just going to sit here and take it?" Daniels's face was uncommonly hot.

Bogan coughed. "Well, we've recalled our Moscow ambassador for consultation. That's a start."

"Congress has approved 144 million dollars for rebuilding the White House. A conservative estimate."

"Think of what we lost. All those priceless paintings, the tradition, the history. The White House belonged to us. To the American people."

"History begins where it leaves off."

"Can't get over Hy Strooker's death," Dwight said, shaking his head. "Shrapnel right in the heart."

After a long pause, Bogan said, "Damn pity. The Secret Service lost one of her best."

"I'd say."

The telephone rang. Ken Dwight picked it up and nudged the switch to speaker.

"Larry Bodine, from the Damage Assessment Center. We've got the final tally."

Dwight's face tightened. He pulled a blank pad toward him and reached for his pen. "Go ahead, Larry."

The room fell silent.

"Twenty-nine dead, sixty-two wounded, one missing, presumed dead," Bodine intoned.

Dwight scribbled fast. "That all?"

"Yes, sir." Bodine hesitated. "The First Pooch was killed. We found a bundle of white fur, mangled. I don't know how we're going to break the news to Mrs. Deakin. She was fond of that mutt."

"That won't be necessary," Dwight said. "Shakespeare is alive and well. I saw him at Blair myself. That must be Gifford, the First Cat. He's got white fur, and he's missing."

"Well, then, Gifford is dead."

"That's the final figure? The one we'll give to the media and the nation?"

"Yes. We've dug through all the rubble. Sniffer dogs, geologic equipment, thermal imaging—the whole lot. There can't be an ant left in there."

EPILOGUE

Tammy did not go to Nabil's funeral. They asked her if she wanted to. She declined. Nobody came forward to claim the body. A local Islamic cleric administered last rites. The man known as The Contractor was buried in a potter's field.

Tammy stared at her face in the bathroom mirror. She angled her face to the left, the right. Examined every pore, every mark, the straight ridge of her nose. She noticed nearly transparent tufts of hair jutting out her ears. She had to do something about those hairs. She pursed her lips, and then changed to a pout, trying hard to make her lips as seductive as Angelina Jolie's.

I have killed people.

She would do it again if she had to. Never hurt a fly in her life, but when it came down to it, she hadn't failed herself or her country.

I slept with him.

Under duress. Now he's dead. But you enjoyed it, didn't you, Tammy slut you. Hey, girl, that was inconclusive. That word again. From the polygraphs. Okay, so I was wet when he penetrated. Conclusive? Hell no. Every woman's naughty bits lubricates by default when a foreign object enters or prepares to enter. Defensive mechanism to prevent injury. Yeah right, Dr. Tammy.

Countless FBI, DHS, Secret Service interviews, depositions. Two more polygraphs, even though her lawyer advised against it. She wanted to prove she had no prior agenda before the assassin known as the Contractor entered her life. He thought they believed her in the end.

She was never arrested nor charged with any crime. It came down to the fact that she acted to save the president's life and shot two people in the process.

The questions were endless, came from all angles. How had she switched the bullets? Women's Room secret, she told them. What's that, they asked? Simple really. She had worn him out during the rape/lovemaking. She knew from experience that he would conk out immediately after he climaxed—most men did—and she seized the day. The time also she had forced him to take a bath and made sure the tap was at full deluge while she carried his holster and his trousers to the washing machine. That gave her the cover to switch clips. Opening and closing the hamper door while hacking a coarse cough all served to camouflage the sound of the gun being racked. She hid the live clip inside a place she knew he would never look: a female sanitary product. The next day she had smuggled it out in her handbag and later put it in the car trunk inside the tire jack receptacle.

Sandy and little Tom seemed not to be traumatized by the entire affair, although Child Services and the FBI provided free counseling for both Sandy and Tammy. Tammy said she didn't need it, but the FBI insisted. Even their own elite agents underwent mandatory counseling and evaluation after an agent-involved shooting resulting in death or injury. Her daughter Sandy kept asking when Uncle Ted would be back. Tammy rubbed her hair, kissed her on the forehead and told her Uncle Ted would come back if he decided to come back. Sandy had to prepare herself that he might not come back.

"But I've seen him on TV," Sandy said. "They said you shot him when he tried to kill the president."

Tammy stared at her.

"Is he dead, Mommy?" Sandy asked.

"Yes, he is. He did some very bad things, honey. He was a bad man. And he was going to shoot Mommy, so Mommy shot him first."

The media blitz was inescapable even though Tammy tried not putting on any news network on TV when Sandy was home. Tammy's face was on newspaper front pages, and the news media camped 24/7 outside her Seven Oaks apartment made it impossible for Sandy not to know her mother was a heroine.

"Uncle Ted is not my uncle," Sandy said. "He was a very bad man."

"That's right."

"I love you, Mommy."

"Love you too, sweetie."

"Moo-moo," gurgled little Tom.

"You too, Tom." She kissed him on the forehead. "You won't even remember Uncle Ted by the time you lose your milk teeth."

———

The hardest thing was leaving Washington, DC. and her many friends to move to Southern California. Temecula, population approximately 109,097. Away from anything remotely D.C. In constant touch with her new agent Marvin Flatsch. The seven-figure book deal with movie tie-in Flatsch had negotiated for her, solved most of her financial problems overnight. Her mother was in an assisted-living facility much better than the one in Halethorpe and just a fifteen minute car drive away. After the IRS took its cut, after Flatsch's agency fees, and paying the ghostwriter assisting with her book, and the two-percent of her advance she was donating to the Kevin Keik estate, she'd still bought a nice Spanish style bungalow outright, and a new car, a Lexus ES four-door sedan. Sandy and Tom had new schools, and as she had promised tearfully when parting with Mrs. Fierstal, they chatted weekly on the phone.

The hedge-fund manager she was dating, a blueblood from Los Angeles County and a millionaire several times over was on the verge of proposing. She just knew! And the Mexican maid who came in four times a week made it easy for Tammy to concentrate on her tell-all book. She had a deadline. After delivering the book, and revisions with her ghost, she would take a long holiday to Europe with Sandy and Tom, and only begin to think of the future after the holiday.

She watched the ochre sun set in the Mediterranean climate of this Spanish-themed city of wine valleys and circumspect countryside. She might buy a vineyard yet. It was beyond surreal that a climate so dry and free of the cloying humidity of the northeast existed on the Lower 48. But it did. And she intended to enjoy it. She sighed and exhaled deeply. Glanced at her wristwatch. Time to get back in.

The ghostwriter was waiting.

The End

ACKNOWLEDGEMENTS

To my editors Constance Renfrow and Tracey Seybold who worked hard to correct my errors. I am especially indebted to Constance who opened my eyes to a whole range of things in the writing industry and helped me grow immensely. Both of you are awesome and I'm deeply grateful.

To the close-knit team of Slobodan Cedic and Jelena Gajic for their unique cover design for this book. Also to Andrej Semnic who has now designed two fantastic covers for two of my books. I say thank you all for a job well done.